AF215561

THE
SILVER
KINGDOM

Praise for
THE SILVER KINGDOM

'This swoony, sparkling romantasy stole my heart.' Mia Kuzniar, author of *Forest of Hearts*

'A stunning, sweeping romantasy filled with electric chemistry, intrigue and witty banter that had me kicking my feet. I thoroughly enjoyed this book.' Sara Jafari, author of *Heavensent & Hellbent*

'An utterly gripping fantasy that we need more of; this is the kind of story you don't want to leave ... Devastating and addictive. This is fantasy at its finest!' Sarah Mughal Rana, *Sunday Times* and *USA Today* bestselling author of *Dawn of the Firebird*

'A beautifully-woven tapestry of elemental magic, post-colonial politics and forbidden love.' Morgan Owen, author of *Gladiator, Goddess*

'The immersive world building, captivating characters, and an intoxicating romance with *chef's kiss* banter between the MCs meant I couldn't put this gorgeous YA romantasy down!' Ellis Hunter, author of *Blood Bound*

'Suffused with rich worldbuilding, *The Silver Kingdom* had me entranced from the first page. It glitters with political intrigue, a thrilling romance and spellbinding characters. This is a must-read for romantasy readers!' Niyla Farook, author of Indie Book Award-shortlisted *Murder for Two*

'I haven't been this obsessed by a book in a long time! Everything is executed to sheer perfection. I absolutely loved both the protagonists; they're fierce, the banter is electric, and their chemistry will send shivers down your spine. I couldn't put it down.' Tasneem Abdur-Rashid, author of *Odd Girl Out*

'Utterly brilliant and hits on all levels.' Ayesha Ansari, Bookseller

THE
SILVER
KINGDOM

RADIYA
HAFIZA

SIMON & SCHUSTER

London New York Amsterdam/Antwerp Sydney/Melbourne Toronto New Delhi

First published in Great Britain in 2026 by Simon & Schuster UK Ltd

Text copyright © 2026 Radiya Hafiza
Illustration copyright © 2026 Naina Lamba

This book is copyright under the Berne Convention.
No reproduction without permission. All rights reserved

The right of Radiya Hafiza and Naina Lamba to be identified as the author
and illustrator of this work has been asserted by her in accordance with
sections 77 and 78 of the Copyright, Designs and Patents Act, 1988.

1 3 5 7 9 10 8 6 4 2

Simon & Schuster UK Ltd, 1st Floor
222 Gray's Inn Road, London WC1X 8HB

For more than 100 years, Simon & Schuster has championed authors and
the stories they create. By respecting the copyright of an author's intellectual
property, you enable Simon & Schuster and the author to continue publishing
exceptional books for years to come. We thank you for supporting the author's
copyright by purchasing an authorized edition of this book. No amount of this
book may be reproduced or stored in any format, nor may it be uploaded to
any website, database, language-learning model, or other repository,
retrieval, or artificial intelligence system without express permission. All rights
reserved. Inquiries may be directed to Simon & Schuster, 222 Gray's Inn Road,
London WC1X 8HB or RightsMailbox@simonandschuster.co.ukk

www.simonandschuster.co.uk
www.simonandschuster.com.au
www.simonandschuster.co.in

The authorised representative in the EEA is Simon & Schuster Netherlands BV,
Herculesplein 96, 3584 AA Utrecht, Netherlands. info@simonandschuster.nl

Simon & Schuster Australia, Sydney
Simon & Schuster India, New Delhi

A CIP catalogue record for this book is available from the British Library

HB ISBN 978-1-3985-4625-7
eBook ISBN 978-1-3985-4626-4
eAudio ISBN 978-1-3985-4627-1

This book is a work of fiction. Names, characters, places and incidents are either
a product of the author's imagination or are used fictitiously. Any resemblance
to actual people living or dead, events or locales is entirely coincidental.

Typeset in Begum by M Rules
Printed and Bound in the UK using 100% Renewable
Electricity at CPI Group (UK) Ltd

MIX
Paper | Supporting
responsible forestry
FSC® C013604

In loving memory of Bushra
The girl I grew up with, the sister of my heart

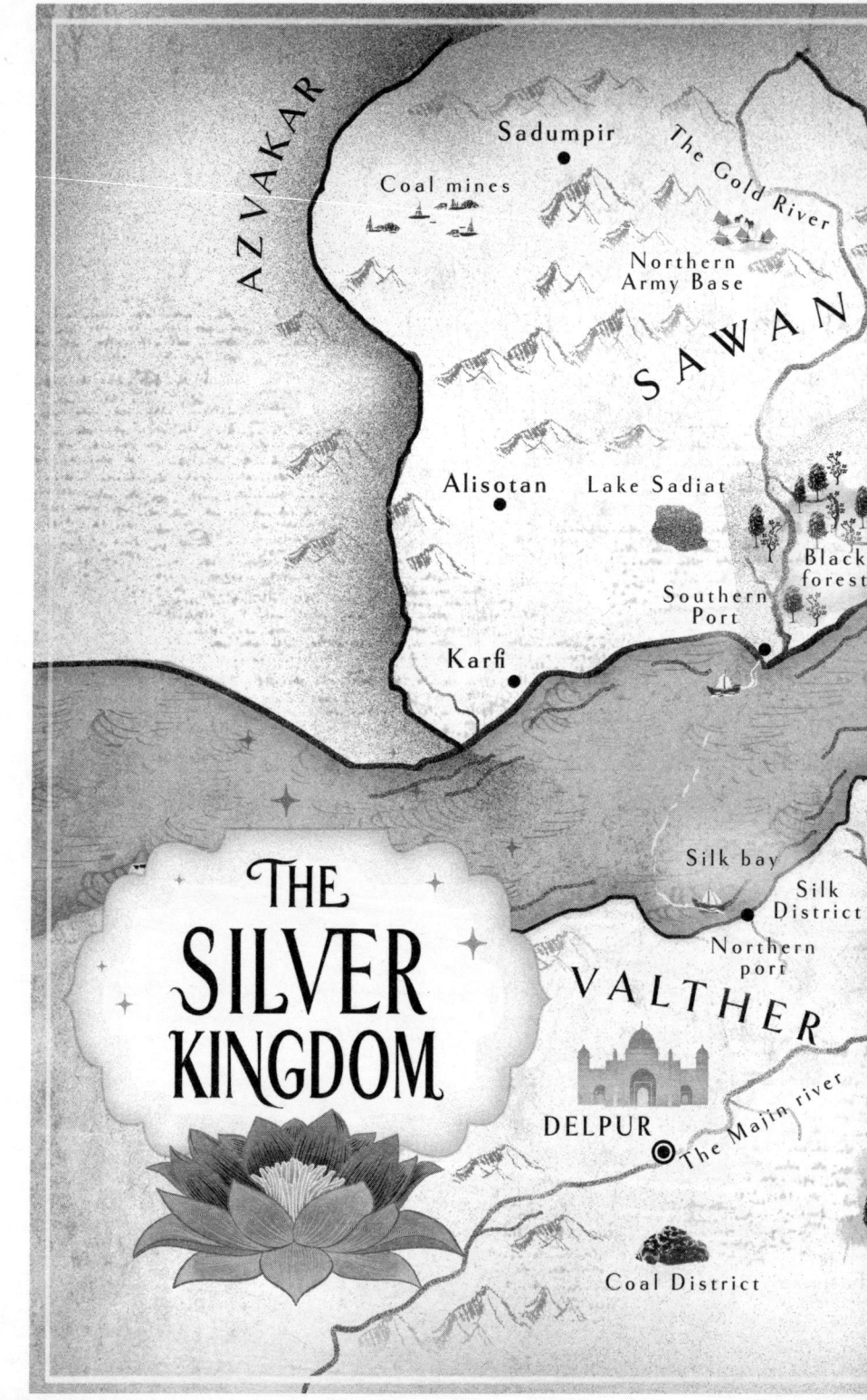

NEVARIM

The
Nuswa River

ALRAND

Ayasembad

Mountains
of Nidar

Mountain
pass

Wastelands

DAKARIA

Sylfal

Sanji
forest

DUKHHA

The Ujad River

Raibur

Chittabagh

The Bay
of Dukhha

The
Silver
Mines

Silver
Port

Khalutta

Zaibur
forest

Fatimsar

OCEAN

'Though parted our two loving souls combine,
For mine is all your own and yours is mine.'

—'Layla and Majnun', Nizami Ganjavi

PART I

Prologue

It was almost time.

I looked up to the stormy sky: dark purples and greys swirling above. Eighteen years ago, there had been a cosmic shift. Many had written it off as chance, or a misstep of fate.

But no more. I could feel it. Such power had a presence in the atmosphere. Change was coming.

For decades, my people had lurked in the shadows, relegated to the outskirts of society. Finally, the time was coming for us to be free. For our saviour to lead us in the darkness.

'Captain, where do you want the silver?' one of my men asked, carrying a large sack and sporting a bloody wound on his arm.

I looked away from the sky, across the wet deck of my ship.

'Put it in the pit. We'll take it back to the base for melting.'

He nodded and took the silver and dragged it down the dank steps towards the inner cabin.

I leant over the railings, watching the rabid waves crash towards the mainland, where the royal army stood aboard their ship. Soon I would have my vengeance. I was only just getting started.

1

Zayd

Even in the dark, my arrows never missed their marks. I nocked another to my bow and prepared to strike until every last pirate fell.

It was taxing, protecting the Silver Port. At night, there were raids aplenty. The last few months had been a blur as we'd held off attempts to slaughter us. Everybody wanted our silver.

The weak moon only afforded a sliver of light amidst the dark ocean, but it was better to have an element of cover than risk being seen. I ducked down as an arrow came whistling towards me and clattered onto the deck. I jumped up and fired off another arrow, focusing on the figures lining the invading ship some fifty yards away.

I let out a ragged breath and wiped the sweat off my brow.

'Second line of attack, now!' I shouted.

The soldiers around me ducked as the second flank, who had been hiding along the middle deck, rose up and set off a rain of burning arrows.

Terrified cries rang out from the enemy ship as bodies splashed into the ocean. I looked through the gap in my ship's railing and heard frenzied shouting as the pirates took cover.

Their ship began to turn away. We continued our attack; I had to make sure they didn't come back. I waited until the pirates' ship was beyond our reach before commanding my troops to stop their onslaught.

The air was heavy with laboured breathing as the soldiers around me slowly relaxed. One came carrying a torch, the flame billowing in the wind, casting a golden glow about the ship alongside the burning arrows some of the troops still held. Three bodies lay slumped on the wooden deck. We murmured prayers for the dead as a number of us carefully took them below deck to the resident healer to shroud them for burial.

'Anas, write to their families immediately,' I said to my second-in-command.

'Right away, Your Highness,' he said with a nod, heading for the captain's cabin.

I exhaled another hard breath. A throbbing pain in my shoulder pulsed beneath the fabric of my clothes. I removed my armour and found a bleeding cut. I'd been sliced in the gap between my shoulder pads. Sighing, I found a clean cloth and stemmed the flow.

Another day, another wound. Some soldiers were given medals; I was gifted scars.

'If you give me a moment, Your Highness, I can tend to that,' Alom, the healer, said from the other side of the room. 'It looks terrible.'

'Perhaps it will scare off any potential brides,' I muttered.

Alom snorted.

After Alom had patched me up, I returned to my post. I looked out to the dark sky, the smoky clouds parting to give way to the moon. White light rippled amongst the black waves, the horizon clear of enemies. For now. The cold ocean air bit at my face, sending a chill down my spine.

I cast a glance back towards land, the shoreline just visible in the dark. Something flickered in the distance.

I squinted, trying to make out the strange orange light. The sound of hooves thundering our way filled the air. I locked and loaded an arrow before I could take another breath.

A familiar trumpet sounded. The green-and-red flags of Dakaria flapped in the wind as the royal guard neared.

'Stand down,' I shouted at the soldiers who had raised their weapons, lowering my own bow.

The guards approached the shoreline and dismounted. I made my way down the ship's ladder and into a small boat where Anas was waiting. He rowed us back to land. I jumped out once we reached the shore, wading out of the cool water to meet Noor, the head of my palace guards.

He jogged forward, bowing hastily as he stopped in front of me. 'Your Highness, I have urgent news from Her Majesty.'

'Time to go home, is it, Noor?' I asked, taking the scroll. I tore it open and read over the brief updates about trade and building progress. And then at the bottom:

His Royal Highness Zayd Anwar Hussayn is discharged from the Silver Port and will return post-haste due to the Sultan's ailing health.

I looked up at Noor. '*Ailing health*?' My insides flooded with dread.

'I am afraid Sultan Anwar is quite unwell, Your Highness,'

Noor said, worry lining his face. 'Perhaps we may talk more discreetly in the carriage?'

'Let's go,' I barked. 'Anas, send a messenger every twelve hours to update me,' I instructed, striding away.

Noor pulled open the black carriage doors and I sank against the dark leather seat. I closed my eyes. It had been weeks since I had slept a full night. Every time I tried to shut my eyes, the alarm would sound, signalling a new attack. My soldiers were drained. We had lost two hundred and seventeen men over the past three months. With more forces needed around Dakaria's borders, as well as by the sea, we were thin on the ground – despite having lowered the age of recruits to sixteen.

'What happened to Father?' I asked Noor as the carriage trundled away.

'He has not recovered from the influenza, Your Highness,' Noor said. 'The healers say the infection has spread to his lungs.'

'Can they not do anything?' I demanded.

'They are trying, Your Highness, but ...'

'But what?'

'The Sultan and Sultana want to hold your coronation within a matter of months. They are not sure how long the Sultan has left.'

Each word was a blow to my gut. 'What do you mean *how long he has left*? How many healers have been consulted?'

'A dozen or so, Your Highness.'

'I want another dozen at the palace by morning,' I commanded. 'The Sultan will be cured.' I ignored the grave look in Noor's eyes. 'And make sure Sayyidah Shafiya is amongst them. I believe she will be able to assist with some other matters as well.'

He looked at me quizzically before nodding.

I stared out at the darkness, grinding my teeth. *Coronation? Within months?* Dakaria was in no position to lose my father. We were only just beginning to become an equal player amongst our neighbouring states. The Sultan was respected by our neighbours' rulers, loved by our people. I would need to build these alliances all over again.

Ours was a small nation, bordered to the west by Valthar, a large country whose fabrics were sought all over the world and which boasted an abundance of natural minerals and resources for mining. Sawan was our northwestern neighbour, similar in size to Valthar, with impressive infrastructures that rivalled those of more powerful nations. They had struck gold decades ago, after the Great Revolt, and climbed out of the hole the colonialists had left us in. By comparison, Dakaria was still catching up - our tea and rice fields and vast fishing waters the main sources of export. And now our silver.

We rode through old towns by the sea - clay huts and wooden houses, aged buildings in dire need of renovation. As we travelled farther into the cities we began to see foundations were being laid for new homes. We finally had the wealth to start developing our country. The muddied lanes would be replaced by paved roads, improving transport around the kingdom so that rainfall couldn't hinder travel in the monsoon months. There was much work to do, many areas to improve, but we were on the right path thanks to the Sultan's unwavering commitment to our people. Though even he couldn't protect us from the leeches attempting to take our silver.

My eyes drooped as we neared the large moonstone palace in the centre of Dakaria, shining against the dark night. The flags of Dakaria rustled in the wind, sitting atop the palace's high-domed turrets and minarets. I longed for my bed, instead of the thin wood-and-cotton excuses I'd been beholden to on the ship.

Our horses trundled the path alongside a trailing fountain of water that stretched from the palace gates to the central courtyard. Fond memories of trying to wrestle my younger brother into the spray flickered across my mind.

The carriage finally slowed to a stop, and I dismounted, desperate to stretch my legs. But first I needed to see my father. I headed towards his quarters.

Noor intercepted me. 'The Sultan is asleep, Your Highness. It is three in the morning.'

I sighed and changed direction, marching off towards my wing of the palace.

'Good morning, big brother!' a loud voice boomed as the door to my chambers was thrown open.

The bane of my existence – also known as my younger brother, Yunus – sauntered in, hopping over an armchair to sit down. He grabbed a paratha from the table of breakfast laid out for me in my parlour.

'Haven't you eaten already?' I griped. I was too exhausted to deal with his foolishness right now.

'You're much leaner than I am; you don't need all this food,' he said, smirking. 'My muscles, on the other hand, do.'

I snorted. 'What muscles? You've barely turned seventeen and you think you have the body of a soldier.'

Something flashed across Yunus's expression. 'Beauty, brains – some of us are just born with it all, Brother,' he said, devouring the paratha in a large bite.

'Animal,' I muttered, leaning back in my chair.

'Your Highness, you look terrible,' he said, feigning care. 'Do they not feed you on the ship?'

'If you had an ounce of military experience, you might understand why five course meals are scarce,' I retorted.

Yunus's face fell. 'Not all of us can go and risk our lives, even if we want to.'

'Such a difficult life you lead, Brother,' I said dismissively. 'Why didn't you write to me and tell me Father was this ill?'

'Mother made me swear I wouldn't. She didn't want you to leave any sooner than you had to.'

'Still, you should have told me,' I said. 'How can I be Sultan if I am the last to know everything?'

'Yes, poor you: it must be so tough to be heir to the throne,' Yunus snapped. He swiped a bowl of vermicelli steeped in sugar and milk and downed it in one gulp. 'Delicious. Farewell.'

I grunted in response. Yunus's loud boots carried him away, the door slamming shut behind him.

After I had finished eating, I glanced briefly at the clock beside the window. It was almost eight. The morning sun was slowly rising, turning the skies from their dark hues into strokes of violets and blues. Father should be awake by now.

I changed out of my nightwear and put on a pair of navy trousers and khamis, strapped on my leather boots and grabbed my cloak.

Outside my door, Noor stood guard. He bowed as I strode out. 'Good morning, Your Highness,' he said. 'Your mother is waiting for you—'

'Tell her I am going to see Father first.'

'Yes, Your Highness,' he said, muttering something to a guard beside him, and fell into step behind me.

I headed down the corridor, basking in the comfort of being home again. I had missed being on solid ground these past few months; trading the cold, creaky ship for the palace was a welcome relief. I walked through white hallways lined with arches, their ceilings carved with silver geometric patterns that resembled a million small suns, past the endless portraits of ancient ancestors who had ruled the region before us, and made my way down the spiral staircase.

The air was mildly cold outside, a silvery sheen of moisture from the early morning rain coating the green lawns and towering oak trees that encircled the palace grounds. It was the last of the winter chill as spring encroached. I longed for blistering Dakarian summers; the sea's cold felt like it had settled into my bones. I walked past more guards into the east wing, making my way up another winding staircase to the room I sought.

A couple of servants were in the room, taking away Father's breakfast. Hakim, a grey-haired man who had grown up with Father on the palace grounds, came in carrying his medicine.

I watched them flit in and out of his room, feeding him this and that, until we were alone. When I had left for the Silver Port, Father was able to do everything by himself. It was disorienting to see him so weak now.

'Beta, do not be angry with me. Come,' my father wheezed from his bed.

He was propped up against a number of pillows, his plush bed so large that it made him seem even smaller beneath the rich velvet sheets. He had once been a mighty man – when I was a child, he had towered over me – but in a matter of weeks he had shrunk to this weakened figure.

To the people of Dakaria, he was their strong Sultan, but I had never seen my father so frail. His dark hair was streaked with more white than before, the usually neat beard around his lined, round face haggard. His brown eyes were clouded, filmy.

'You should have called me home earlier,' I said, attempting not to sound irate. 'I would have come, Father.'

'Our soldiers needed you more,' Father said wearily. 'No sign of any let up?'

'None. It seems everybody wants our silver.'

'We must do something soon: an alliance with someone to give us more soldiers.'

'I'm working on it,' I said, trying to be reassuring. 'You don't worry, Father. Just concentrate on getting better.'

Father nodded, his eyes beginning to droop again. 'Have you had your breakfast yet, beta?'

'Yes, abbu, I have. You can rest now. I will go to see Mother.'

'I used to feed you when you were small,' Father continued with a sigh. His eyes roamed over my face, as though he were seeing me through the haze of another time. 'You were dreadfully picky. We were worried the future Sultan would never eat his vegetables.'

I grimaced. I couldn't say much had improved on that score.

Father put his cold, wrinkled hand on top of mine. 'I want to die knowing our kingdom is secured – that you will reign on, and your children after you.'

I bristled. 'We *will* find a cure for whatever is ailing you. I am sending for more healers today. Clearly the ones here already are not doing their jobs.'

'Death is calling me, beta,' Father said, his eyes fluttering.

'Sometimes I can see the angel of death, waiting for me. I do not have long.'

The hairs on my body stood up. 'You are not dying,' I said angrily, squeezing his hand back. 'You still have many years in you yet.'

Father looked at me with a weak smile. 'You can fool everyone else, but you can't lie to me. You wear the truth on your face. A noble Sultan you will make.'

I was unable to meet his eyes.

Father began to snore. I looked back at him – his eyes were finally shut, and his head sagged to one side.

I gently patted his hand before withdrawing, casting a quick look around for supernatural beings, but his room was empty. Perhaps he was hallucinating in his weakened state, imagining angels and shadows.

Hakim stood outside the door with Father's guards.

'Look after the Sultan. I will return in the evening.'

I headed back into the main wing of the palace towards my mother's study. The doors were opened for me, revealing a rich oak room bathed in morning light. Mother's desk was overflowing with maps and books as she pored over papers. She looked up through her silver-rimmed reading spectacles.

'Zayd, finally come to see your mother?' she said, a playful smile on her oval face.

'Good morning, Mother. Looking as radiant as ever,' I said, dropping into the chair opposite her.

'Charm will get you far in life, beta,' Mother said. 'Did you see your father?'

Something in my chest stung. I'd barely returned home but already sorrow had settled over my family.

'You should have told me sooner.'

A shadow fell across her features. 'I know, dear, but I didn't want to worry you. You were needed at the Silver Port.'

'Noor is arranging for more healers to arrive this afternoon. There will be someone out there who can do something,' I said.

Mother looked at me sadly, folding her hands together. 'We must begin preparations, Zayd. Your father hasn't got long left. You will be Sultan soon, and you will need to produce heirs to keep the line secure.'

I balked. 'What?'

Mother took a deep breath, her olive eyes firm. 'I have found you a wife.'

2

Layla

My dagger hit the dartboard with a loud thud. I threw several more, creating a perfect pattern around the centre. I was picturing my mother's face as I threw every blade.

'Close one eye and go again,' Junayd instructed.

I sighed through my teeth and did as he asked. One of the servants, a young boy called Kareem, sprang from the shadows and removed my blades, handing them back to me with a hasty bow.

The daggers were heavy – black leather wrapped around a length of sharpened steel. I steadied my feet and threw another, just missing the centre.

'Again,' Junayd barked.

I gritted my teeth and went again and again, Kareem returning my blades four times before I finally hit the centre with one eye closed. After two rounds of my hitting the centre mark, alternating which eye I kept closed, Junayd finally grunted in approval.

'Come summertime, I believe you'll be able to do it with both your eyes closed, Princess,' he said – his version of a compliment.

'Only if you promise to stand as target practice, Junayd,' I replied sweetly.

He laughed, the lines around his dark eyes crinkling before he bowed and walked off towards the soldiers training behind us.

Mira, my maid, rushed forward from the side brandishing a towel. I wiped at my sweaty face, my breath ragged. 'Is the bath ready?' I asked.

'Yes, Your Highness, everything is prepared,' she said, falling into step beside me as I headed back towards my room. 'I'll have Cook send your breakfast in when you are finished.'

'Thank you, Mira,' I murmured.

We made our way through the sandstone corridors, warm sunlight streaming in through the arched windows carved with ornate gold-laced frames. The hallways were lined with pillars that held up the high-domed ceilings, decorated with geometric patterns carved into the stone.

I retreated into my room, which was markedly different from the rest of the bright, golden palace. The walls had been painted dark blue at the request of my nine-year-old self, with silver wisps swirling across them. I headed straight for the bath, stripped off my training clothes and plunged into its delicious warmth.

After I had bathed and dressed in the day's clothes – a deep purple shalwar kameez threaded with pearls and beads – Mira braided my hair and laced it with white flowers and silver jewels. Ready to have breakfast, I went into my parlour.

'Where is the food?' I asked.

Mira's warm brown eyes were apologetic. 'Her Majesty has requested you join her for breakfast.'

I sighed. 'Have I not been tortured enough?' I muttered, stalking out of my chambers.

My mother was posed gracefully in the dining hall, the early spring light pouring in through the windows behind her. My shoes clacked against the marble floor as I headed towards the large oak table, which had been decorated lavishly with pastel flowers and was laden with food. The aroma of warm spices greeted me as I took my seat beside her.

'Daughter, how are you?' she asked. Mother was a ridiculously beautiful woman – dark hair that fell in perfect waves down her back, bright brown eyes that looked like firelight in the sun, a face that was both sharp angles and high cheekbones. Her ice-blue lehenga flowed perfectly down her body, sparkling with diamonds that complemented the ones she wore around her neck. A matching dupatta sat atop her head, elegantly framing her face.

'Fine. How are you, Mother?' I asked, barely looking at her. I focused instead on the servants weaving in and out of the chairs to place a steaming vegetable paratha on my plate alongside cut fruit.

It was as boring a breakfast as any, and purposely light.

As if reading my thoughts, Mother tutted. 'Do you think a small waist is achieved through eating heavily?'

I sighed through my nose. *Here we go.*

'You can sigh all you like, but perhaps if you were a bit leaner you would have had more suitors by now.' Mother took a delicate mouthful of fruit.

I ripped off a small piece of paratha, worrying it between my fingers. I didn't feel so hungry any more.

There wasn't a day that went by during which my mother

didn't list at least a few of my flaws. Either I was not light-skinned enough, or I was too short, or my hips weren't wide enough for childbearing. Right now, she was fixated on finding me a husband, and it was my failure that I hadn't secured a match.

Mother tutted again. 'You must take this matter seriously, Layla, if you want to attract good suitors.'

'The suitors you find for me look questionable anyway,' I said.

'Don't mutter,' she snapped. 'The suitors were perfectly reasonable. It's just a shame you couldn't entice at least one.'

I wanted to disappear. There was nobody else in the world who made me feel as small and hideous as my mother did.

'Well? Do you have anything to say for yourself?' she demanded.

I stayed silent, hoping she would move on to another topic.

Mother sighed dramatically. 'Very well. As usual, it is left to me to fix everything. You should ready yourself for travels; we are heading to Dakaria in a few days.'

I stared back at her in surprise. 'Dakaria?'

'Oh, not to find a husband – don't be silly!' she said with a tinkling laugh. 'I would never marry you to one of their princes – they're too dark.'

I grimaced. Despite having heard iterations of them for years, her hateful words never got easier to hear.

'We are going there for business purposes.'

'*Business,*' I repeated. 'You mean for their silver?'

Mother smiled coyly. 'Amongst other things. It's always good to see how the enemy is doing – what their capabilities are.'

'What enemy? They're our neighbours,' I said in

frustration. Mother had been angling with the court for months to find a reason to invade Dakaria. With the new stores of silver they had struck recently, they had become of prime interest to many. 'Can't I just stay at home?'

'No. The court thinks it's time you start learning my trade. You have much to learn, child,' she said with a flash of irritation. 'One day you will be Sultana, after all.' Her tone suggested she was wishing for anything but that.

Coming of age was starting to feel like a curse. Ever since I had turned seventeen, a new pressure had been mounting to secure me a powerful husband and ready me for the day I would rule. As the only heir to the throne, and with my eighteenth year fast approaching, the stakes were high.

'That's why I need to find you the right husband,' Mother continued. 'If only you had more of my looks and less of your father's. Have you seen yourself in the mirror recently? With those dark circles and that sour expression, one might wonder how you could ever be *my* daughter.' She eyed me pityingly, but I could see her underlying glee.

One of my mother's favourite sports was pretending she was the most beautiful woman in all of Sawan. If only our people knew her pale skin was due to the bleaching creams she kept in her bedchamber. But she wasn't done insulting me just yet.

'If you are to rule one day, I need to make sure your husband has a brain to make up for the lack of yours.'

Her spiteful words felt like a slap across the face. I abandoned my plate and stood. 'I am done eating; I have some studies to attend to. Goodbye, Mother.'

She looked annoyed. 'Very well. It's probably better you don't finish your meal.'

Hurt spread through my body like knives being drawn

down my flesh. I raced back to my room as fast as I could, my sandals slapping against the marble floor, and slammed the door shut behind me. I went to the bathroom, and splashed cool water over my face.

I hated her. I hated her with every fibre of my being.

A current began to pulse through my body, my hands trembling with energy.

'*Do not lose control. Conquer yourself.*' Father's soothing voice echoed in my mind. '*If you allow your enemies to get under your skin, you have lost.*'

I balled my hands into fists and breathed deeply, in and out, until the trembling stopped and my body ceased shaking.

Exhaling heavily, I stretched out my fingers. Mother knew how to push every button I had. Over the last several months, my nervous attacks had been growing in frequency. They had started when I was a child, the first time Mother had beaten me. It started off as shaking, then my heartbeat quickening until I thought I was sure to collapse.

When Father found out, he'd forbade Mother from ever striking me again, but she still had other ways to leave her marks - namely with that poisonous tongue of hers. But Father had always been there to get me through.

I stared at my reflection, touching the shadows beneath my eyes. *They're not that bad*, I thought. I just hadn't slept much last night.

I opened the drawer and took out some powder to cover up the dark circles. It stung a little but I persevered. My skin was the colour of warm sand through winter, turning darker as the warmer months returned. I never used to wonder about my colouring so much, not until Mother began to complain one hot summer, when I was eight years old or so.

Suddenly the parasols came out, gloves had to be worn at all times and the maids scrubbed me extra hard in the bath. The scrubbing was surely the reason my skin was sensitive to most lotions and powders. I felt like my skin had been grated for years.

I missed my father deeply. It was a feeling no words could ever express. The disbelief that he was truly gone still lingered in my mind, despite almost four years having passed. It had never become easier, bearing this pain. Every day, I felt like I lost him again.

I tried to remind myself of his words whenever I felt this way, but lately, with the weight of the court's expectations and Mother's increasing hatred, I felt like I was losing control of myself, day by day. A knock interrupted my thoughts.

'Come in,' I called.

Faisal, the guard who stood watch over my door, walked in with a note on a golden plate.

'Good morning, Your Highness. Your itinerary for the day is here.'

I took the piece of parchment, sighing as I looked over Mother's tasks for me. After my morning walk, I was to head to the city to open a new healing house, visit an orphanage and then join the court meeting later in the afternoon.

I left the sanctuary of my room for my morning walk in the gardens.

Mira joined me, walking a few feet behind me. Guards flanked us, one wielding a large parasol above my head. Even with the sky overcast, Mother demanded that I was shaded. I wished I could turn the sun on her; perhaps she would burst into flames.

The fresh air did little to make my bitter thoughts drift away. Growing older had made me angrier, frustrated, aware of how little control I had over my own life. But I strolled along anyway, picking the last of the winter flowers from the bushes that lined the walkways.

I walked down a set of stone stairs towards the family crypt. Bilal, one of the guards, pushed open the door for me.

Weak light streamed in from a small window in the roof, casting the crypt in an eerie glow. There were many graves inside, dotted along the ground, my ancestors and their families lined up. My father's grave was closest to the door.

I removed the old flowers from my last visit and laid the new bouquet I had picked.

'Peace be with you, Father,' I murmured. I touched his headstone for a moment.

No reply came; it never did.

I laid another bouquet on my late aunt's tomb. When my father's sister passed away last year, it felt like the last link I had to him had departed too. There were only my aunt's daughters left but they lived far away: Mariya was married to a Nevarim prince and Aroosa had moved back to Azvakar to live with her paternal family after my aunt died.

I sat for a while in the quiet crypt. A cough outside alerted me that it was time to leave. I bade my father and aunt farewell and headed back outside. I put the old bouquets down on the soil, the withered flowers rustling beneath my touch. As I wondered where a breeze had come from, I heard Mira calling me.

'Your Highness, the carriage is ready.'

'Coming, Mira,' I called back, hurrying away.

I sank down on the plush velvet seats in my carriage. Mira sat down opposite me, and our guards rode beside us. My eyes roamed the expansive green scenery as we moved away from the palace, past towering palm trees and old oaks that spilled onto the road that ran alongside the river. I watched life flit by – people tending to their crops or fishing in the greeny-blue waters, birds soaring in the brightening sky.

We arrived after some time at the new healing house, a large white building with black-framed windows and a wooden door patterned with geometric carvings. A crowd had gathered.

'Your Highness!'

'Princess!'

'Welcome!'

A clamour of excited greetings met me as I walked up the stone pathway to the healing house. I looked into the smiling faces of the children and adults dressed in their finest attire.

'This is for you, Princess!' a little boy declared, holding out a drawing for me.

'Thank you. It's beautiful,' I said, patting his curly hair.

The boy smiled up at me, his green eyes shining. It always gave me a lump in my throat to see how kind our people were.

I didn't deserve it. Not with the way my mother treated everyone. In Sawan, the rich stayed rich and the poor got poorer. She never came to these events with our people; she sent me instead. She had no time to 'mingle with the commoners'.

The healers escorted me inside and showed me around three storeys of newly furnished rooms before leading me out into the garden, where archways wrapped in vines and beautiful flowers adorned the grounds to give patients somewhere serene to take their walks.

I took out some of the gold coins I kept stashed in my inner pockets and slipped them to the children before I was whisked away to the orphanage to repeat this dance again.

No sooner had I finished a late lunch back at the palace than Faisal summoned me to court. The chamber was filled with my mother's twelve advisors, all seated around a large oak table. They stood and bowed as I entered, murmuring greetings that I returned. Mother looked up from her position at the head of the table, an unnerving smile breaking over her face.

'Layla, there you are!' she said eagerly. 'In you come!'

I stepped forward hesitantly. The doors shut quickly behind me and I took my seat at the opposite end.

Everybody stared at me.

Mother waved what looked like a letter. 'I have some excellent news, Layla.'

I doubted that.

'Well, do you want to know what it is?' she demanded, her smile faltering briefly.

I held back a sigh. 'What is it, Mother?'

'I have found you a husband!'

The room broke into stilted applause as the advisors shared knowing looks.

My stomach fell. 'W-what?' I stammered. 'Who?'

'A prince from the royal family of Fallowmere. Edmund,' Mother announced proudly. 'He is the fifth-born, so you need not worry about leaving your dear mother. He will move here and learn our language, and I will make sure he becomes a fine Sultan for when you are eventually ready to rule as Sultana … one day.'

Words failed me. For months – and, just this morning – my

mother had been lamenting that nobody wanted to marry me, and now she had apparently plucked a husband out of thin air? From Fallowmere? From the land of the people who had destroyed our countries? How could this be?

'Well, you could say *thank you*!' Mother said sharply. 'This will be a powerful alliance for our kingdom. With their military support, we will be unstoppable.'

Of course – this had nothing to do with me or my future. This was about her plans, as always. 'But ... how?' I spluttered.

'The letter only arrived today, but it was signed weeks ago,' she said gleefully. 'They are requesting to fix the marriage for three months' time and will be setting sail soon to travel here.'

My insides felt hollow.

'I do not want to marry a Fallowmere prince,' I blurted out.

The room fell deadly quiet. The advisors shared nervous glances as my mother narrowed her eyes at me.

'There is no choice in the matter,' she snarled.

'Your Majesty, perhaps we may pause to consider the proposal thoroughly?' suggested Hussam Rabat, an elderly man who had sat on my father's council and could be counted on for seeing reason. 'This is rather unprecedented, after all.'

'There is nothing to consider,' Mother snapped. 'We need a strong alliance.'

'There is a risk of causing civil strife, Your Majesty,' another advisor said carefully, a middle-aged man by the name of Emran Tariq. 'The Fallowmere have not been welcome in our lands since the Great Revolt.'

'Indeed, the destruction they left in the Eastern world in the name of their crusade to purge mages from the earth is still being felt,' Hussam said gravely. 'Some Eastern nations still refuse to open their borders to anyone. How will our trade fare if these countries find out our future Sultana is marrying a Fallowmere prince?'

'That was a long time ago,' Mother said impatiently. 'And this is for the good of Sawan. Fallowmere has become one of the richest nations on the Earth; they will invest in our country and help it advance beyond our neighbours. This is a good deal,' she said adamantly.

The grim expressions around the table gave me a sliver of hope.

'If I may speak, Your Majesty,' requested Fayzan, a snivelling man who loved to kiss up to Mother.

She nodded at him.

'This is a rather advantageous match, and Her Majesty has chosen most excellently, of course ...' he began in gushing tones. 'But we may need to do some publicity work around this, so that everybody else feels the same. Perhaps we start off with gifts on behalf of the Fallowmere – for example, new educational institutions, or new mills, that kind of thing.'

'Excellent idea, Fayzan,' Mother said decidedly. 'There is no reason for anyone to be aggrieved by this news. So that is how we play it.'

Hussam cleared his throat.

'Yes?' Mother said through gritted teeth.

'I would urge caution, Your Majesty. Princess Layla is the only heir to the Asad throne,' he said pointedly, invoking my father's name. 'The late Sultan Aziz's great-grandfather was part of the revolution that overthrew the Fallowmere. This marriage may be seen as an insult to the princess's lineage.'

'It's been a hundred years since the Great Revolt,' Mother

said angrily. 'That is plenty of time for people to get over what the Fallowmere did. This time, they are coming in as our partners – not our persecutors. And anyway,' she added irately, 'they did the world a favour by ridding our lands of mages. Even if they didn't finish the job.'

'The mages were not a threat until the Fallowmere made them out to be. They lived in peace alongside us,' Hussam said sharply. 'Perhaps we should change our approach.'

The room stilled.

'Are you questioning my judgement?' Mother said in a steely voice.

Hussam held firm. 'No, I am merely suggesting publicity control. You have been questioning the mages for months – they are no threat to Sawan. Perhaps it's time to stop pursuing them.'

'They are an abomination to society,' Mother snapped. 'They must be kept down. Can you imagine if they banded together and tried to use their powers on us?'

'People are growing afraid, Your Majesty,' Hussam continued severely. 'They worry they will be rounded up just for knowing the word 'mage'.'

'Good,' Mother snarled. 'Anyone caught helping a mage is a danger to us.'

My skin prickled with nerves. The hairs all over my body stood up.

'We must show reason, Your Majesty,' Emran chimed in.

'Enough,' Mother barked. 'Mages are a threat to society and I will continue my interrogations. Now, let us ready ourselves for the wedding. The proposal has been accepted. You are all dismissed.'

The room grumbled with unhappy murmurs. Hussam and Emran gave me sympathetic looks as they filed out.

'You as well, get going,' Mother growled in my direction.

I forced myself to move, though my body felt like lead. That was it. I was being married off, and to a Fallowmere prince, no less. Father would be spinning in his grave.

I didn't need to be an investigator to know that Mira and the guards outside had heard everything. I hurried past them, running back to my room, the three of them hot on my heels.

I slammed my bedroom door shut, bolting it from the inside so nobody could come in.

My heart was pounding. It was so hard to breathe. Marriage? In months? To a stranger? To rule here under her eye? I hated her. I hated her with every fibre of my being. This time I couldn't think of my father's words quick enough.

Panic swelled in my chest. I gripped an armchair for support, fear overpowering all my senses.

My hands began to heat up, like they were burning from the inside out. I gasped and let go – to see a scorch mark imprinted upon the velvet fabric.

I gaped at my palms. Faint orange light pulsed beneath my skin.

I shook out both hands, as if that might dispel the light. But they continued to glow red hot.

'Your Highness, I have some tea,' Mira called through the door.

'In a minute!' I called back.

'*Steady your breathing.*' Father's words rang in my mind.

Tears welled in my eyes at the thought of his voice. I missed him. I needed him back. He was the only one who could stand up to my mother.

I forced myself to take deep breaths and watched the light slowly fade from my hands. I grabbed a throw from the sofa and covered the burn mark on the armchair.

What had I done?

Mira came in tentatively, guiding me down into the armchair. She poured me a steaming cup of masala chai.

'I am sorry, Your Highness,' she whispered. 'It is not fair how she treats you.'

'Hush, Mira,' I whispered back, my eyes darting to the door. 'I have you, at least.'

She nodded with a sad smile. 'You'll always have me, Princess, for as long as I live.'

I looked back at her with guilt swirling inside me. 'You could do so much better than this job, Mira,' I said quietly. 'I could give you enough gold to set up somewhere else, away from my mother.'

Mira looked at me indignantly. 'And leave you with nobody to look out for you? My mother would never forgive me. I'd never forgive myself. You're like a sister to me, Your Highness. We grew up together. I won't walk away from you so easily.'

I squeezed her hand, a lump swelling in my throat.

Later that evening, a knock sounded on my door.

'What is it?' I called from my bed.

'It is time for the questioning, Your Highness,' Faisal called.

I recoiled. 'I am coming.'

I gathered myself and grabbed a wool cloak; the dungeons were always so cold. I wrapped it around my shoulders and followed the guards as we made our way down. The light faded away as we descended the stone steps into my mother's torture chambers.

Faisal opened a door for me and led me to a seat.

In the dark room, a row of four figures sat hunched on

30

the wooden floor. The smell of urine and blood soaked the room, acrid and repugnant. I closed my hands over my lap and held them together as tight as I could.

Mother came into the hall, dressed in her training clothes – dark trousers and a tunic. A belt was strapped around her waist, loaded with weapons. She held a whip in one hand and a dagger in the other.

'Ready to talk yet?' she snarled at the prisoners.

My stomach clenched.

Nobody spoke, mere whimpers escaping them.

'You are living descendants of the fire mages. Where are the ones with power?' Mother demanded.

'We already told you: we do not know!' a young woman cried out.

Mother growled and cracked her whip.

I flinched as an excruciating cry echoed through the hall. I willed myself to stay silent, to keep my emotions in check. It was nauseating watching Mother do this. But she demanded that I watch and learn what it meant to be a real leader.

'Please,' the youngest of the group sobbed. She was probably no more than eighteen, the age when mage affinities begin to manifest. Almost the same age as me. Her terrified face was marred with blood.

There was only one way to describe my mother: power hungry. And nobody was allowed to be more powerful than her. The mages, with their affinities for earth, fire, water and air, threatened her position as head of state, so she was on a quiet mission to eradicate every last one of them in Sawan, despite the court being against the idea.

I clasped my hands tighter. If what happened earlier was real – that I had somehow created fire – I was in more danger than I had ever imagined.

3

Zayd

'**W**hat do you mean *no*?' my mother demanded, all but growling at me.

'I am not ready to marry yet,' I replied steadily. 'I have an army to lead. I have not even begun my tours of our neighbouring lands to start building relationships with the incoming heirs.'

'You can do all of that whilst you are married; your marriage will complement your duties,' Mother said reassuringly. 'Princess Munira from Valthar will make a wonderful wife and Sultana.'

'How will that work? Valtharians believe in many gods; we only believe in One,' I said.

'She has agreed to convert,' Mother said.

I tried for vanity instead. 'I recall she had a rather sweaty forehead as a child.'

Mother sighed. 'You were probably ten the last time you met. She is now a most accomplished young lady: excels in her studies, knows several languages and is beautiful, I may add.'

'Good for her.' I gripped the armrests on my chair. Anger was simmering inside of me. 'You can't just decide my marriage without consulting me. I am to be the Sultan.'

'You can be Sultan of fifty kingdoms – I am still your mother,' she said sharply. 'And I am Sultana until you are coronated. Your marriage affects the kingdom; therefore, I must ensure you marry someone suitable.'

I stared back at Mother. 'Clearly there is no discussion to be had, then. Why bother telling me at all? Please just send word of my wedding day when you have decided: I shall free up my calendar.'

Mother sighed. 'Zayd, you know marrying the princess of Valthar will give us the protection and military might we need to fend off these attacks. This is a good thing.'

Perhaps my ego was bruised – my marriage being decided for me, like I was too foolish even to consult. I'd thought my parents would at least ask my opinion before they made any agreement.

'When will the wedding take place?' I asked tersely.

Mother almost smiled. 'In five months. Enough time for us all to prepare. I shall have the guest wing redecorated in time for it.'

'Very well. I shall take my leave. It seems you have a wedding to plan.' I tried to keep the bite out of my voice.

I heard my mother sigh as I left her study. I had only been home five minutes and already I had found out my father was dying and my marriage was arranged.

'Noor, are the healers here yet?' I asked my guard as we strode down the corridor.

'Yes, they are in the library, Your Highness, taking stock of the reports on the Sultan's health.'

'Let's go there now.'

We made our way through the labyrinth of the palace corridors, heading to the central wing, where the library lay behind ornate silver doors. The familiar scent of old books greeted me as I stepped inside. They lined the walls from ceiling to floor, with vines and overflowing plants trailing down the shelves and up the winding staircase to the upper floor.

A number of people sat amongst the desks, poring over books. Upon my arrival, they stood and bowed.

'Shall I ask the healers to present their reports, Your Highness?' Noor asked.

'Go ahead,' I said, taking a seat on one of the velvet armchairs.

Each healer came forward and suggested what had already been prescribed by the palace healers – rest, fluids and a tonic made of root vegetables and spices to provide some pain relief – but nobody could present a cure to stop death. I dismissed them, one by one. It seemed Mother was right – again.

The last healer left in the room was older than the others and clad in dark robes, wisps of grey wiry hair escaping the dupatta around her head.

'Sayyidah Shafiya,' I said before she was formally introduced.

She looked at me in surprise, her dark eyes widening. 'Shall I read you my report, Your Highness?'

'Is it any different to what the others have said?'

She blanched. 'No, Your Highness, I am afraid not.'

'Then you may spare me.'

'Very well. I shall bid you farewell—'

'There is something else you can help me with,' I said quietly.

'Yes, Your Highness?' she said curiously.

I had been mulling over this idea since seeing my soldiers fall day after day, attack after attack. What if there were a more surefire way to protect the Silver Port? Then perhaps I wouldn't need to marry so soon. And it just so happened that Sayyidah Shafiya could hold the key to doing so.

I motioned to Noor. He nodded and left the room.

'I want you to help me find the last living descendants of the water mages,' I said in a low voice.

Sayyidah Shafiya froze. 'I–I do not know what you mean.'

'Please, do not play the fool,' I said. 'We have much work to do. Your late husband had an interesting lineage, of which I'm sure you are aware. The mages have been in hiding since the Fallowmere drove them to near-extinction. Your husband's ancestors are the last known water mages in Dakaria.'

She flinched – another tell.

'Now, you and your husband never had children, did you, Sayyidah?'

She bristled. 'No, I was not blessed with children, Your Highness.'

'But your husband did have a sister,' I continued. 'Despite birth records, there seems to be no known location for her.'

Sayyidah Shafiya paled. 'My sister-in-law does not wish to be known.'

'I am afraid that simply will not do,' I replied, smiling.

Later that evening, after dinner had been served, I headed back to Father's quarters before I retired for the night. I yawned as I climbed the stone steps to his chambers, eager to meet my own bed.

Yunus was sitting by Father's sleeping form when I entered the room, his feet up on the small oak table. He was knitting.

'What are you doing?' I asked, confused by the sight.

'I'm making Father a hat,' Yunus said slowly, focusing intently on the blue threads he was weaving together.

'Since when do you knit?' I scoffed.

'You can mock me if you want, Brother, but if we are ever overthrown and become destitute, I will be able to make a living from knitting while you sit around flexing that one muscle of yours.' Yunus looked up at me and smiled genially.

I shoved his shoulder. 'My one muscle could drown you.'

'I'd love to see you try,' Yunus snorted and carried on knitting.

In one quick swoop, I grabbed Yunus in a headlock.

He swore and dropped his things, trying to push me off.

'Boys,' Father reprimanded sleepily.

I released my hold on Yunus, straightening my clothes as I sat down beside Father. 'Forgive us, Father; we woke you.'

'It's all right, beta,' he mumbled, and closed his eyes again.

Yunus glared at me as he grabbed his knitting things off the floor. 'Congratulations, by the way,' he said with a smirk. 'I hear wedding bells are to be tolled.'

Rage simmered in me again. 'I suppose you knew about this wedding before I did?'

He shrugged, putting his feet back up. 'You do hear things when your sole purpose is sitting around and looking handsome.'

I made a disgruntled noise. 'Why are you making Father a hat, anyway?'

'His head gets cold these days,' Yunus said quietly, peering intently at his threads.

I stopped scoffing.

'I thought Father's favourite colour was black,' I said lightly.

'No, it's blue,' Yunus said decisively.

'It is actually green.' I started, looking over to the bed. Father was opening his eyes again slowly, a weak smile on his face.

'It reminds me of the days I used to run through the palace with my brothers, playing in the gardens and fields,' Father went on. 'And your mother's green eyes looked like jewels in the sunlight.'

We were quiet for a moment.

'Show me this hat, my young prince,' he said to Yunus.

Yunus threw me a triumphant smirk before showing his progress to Father.

'Excellent. It is always good for a royal to have many talents,' Father said, smiling proudly.

'See, Brother? Why don't you make yourself useful and pour us some tea?' Yunus smiled devilishly at me.

'Yunus,' Father said warningly. 'You must not undermine your brother in front of anyone else, do you understand?' His speech was slow now, paced but breathless. 'We have to show unity before our people. He is your future Sultan, and you will be his right hand.'

It was my turn to smirk at Yunus.

'Yes, Father,' Yunus said humbly, his face serene. 'Forgive me. I was merely joking.'

'I know, beta, but I will not always be here to keep you two together,' Father said, lifting a withered hand to Yunus's arm. 'You must protect each other when I am gone. Never part from one another, no matter what comes.'

'Don't talk like that, Father,' I said, feeling a stab to my gut.

Father smiled sadly at me, his dark eyes cloudy. 'I know this must be a shock for you, Zayd. You have returned home and everything has changed. But we must face reality. I do not have long left.'

'I won't give up so easily,' I replied tersely.

There was a knock at the door and the state secretary, Usman, strode in to give his daily report, followed by Mother. She cast me a disgruntled look.

We listened as Usman listed off a number of issues: the fallout from a rainstorm; drowned crops; discontent amongst the people. The only thing keeping our nation afloat was the silver in the mines. Most of our neighbouring lands had accepted the increase to our prices on the silver, all except one.

'Sawan is proving most difficult to work with, Your Majesty,' Usman said gravely. 'We have intelligence that suggests they may cease working with us and take a more … active approach to getting what they want.'

Mother sighed. 'Their Sultana is the greediest ruler I've met in my lifetime. Her people are impoverished, but instead of fixing her own issues she will come and create problems for us. We need to recruit more personnel for our military.'

'We have already lowered the age of recruits to sixteen, Your Majesty,' Usman said hesitantly. 'Any lower and the people might revolt; nobody wants to send their child to war. I do not know where else we might find more soldiers until the wedding.'

'We need to know how soon she might start mounting attacks,' I said. 'Can you get your spies to find out any more?'

'We must be delicate, Your Highness, so as not to blow their cover,' Usman said worriedly. His dark hair had greyed at the temples long before today, at odds with his youthful face. He was only a few years older than me, but stress had aged him.

'Perhaps we need to fortify our land sooner rather than later,' Father said, looking at me warily. 'It would be one way to bring more soldiers in.'

I froze.

'It would be wise, Your Majesty, to speed up the impending nuptials,' Usman said, giving me a nervous glance.

'Yes, I believe you are right. See if your spies can discover Sawan's next steps, then we will know how soon we need to act here,' Mother ordered.

Usman nodded and left the room.

'Looks like you won't be single for much longer, Brother,' Yunus said jovially, clapping me on the back.

Dread coiled in my gut.

4

Layla

The screams of the prisoners still echoed in my ears as I was escorted back to my room. I changed into my nightgown and burrowed into bed, pressing my face into the pillow.

Crack. Crack. Crack.

The sound of Mother's whip striking flesh felt ever present. I scrunched my eyes shut, willing myself to forget it all, but I couldn't forget what she did to those prisoners, or the ones before, or the ones before.

It had started several months ago, when a young boy had been reported practising fire magic in one of the towns far south. It was the first sighting in decades.

I willed myself to breathe slower. I was still shaken from what had happened earlier. Had I really burned the chair? Was I going mad?

Candles cast my room in a golden glow. I headed to the parlour and looked at the armchair.

It was definitely burnt. I looked down at my palms – the colour of my skin was normal.

Maybe it had been a fluke, the result of stress from my

betrothal. Yes, that must be it. I was just overtired and imagining things. There was nothing to worry about.

The next morning, I sat outside on the balcony with my itinerary for the day. Thankfully, I didn't need to leave the palace. There was just a meeting with Mother in her study after breakfast, then training later with Junayd, and finally dress fittings for the wedding I was being forced into. Suddenly I wished I had duties to tend to outside the palace.

Mira brought in breakfast: sugar-frosted pastries, fruits and tea. 'How are you feeling, Your Highness?' she asked tentatively.

I gave her a smile. 'I'm all right. I can help with that,' I said, offering to take the heavily laden tray she was about to put down on the table.

'Please don't, Princess,' Mira said, her eyes darting towards the door, fear washing over her face.

'Right, sorry.' I pulled back, ashamed.

'It is my job to serve you, Princess Layla,' Mira said quickly. 'A job I take much pride and honour in.' Her voice was a little louder than usual as she projected towards the chamber doors. 'Can never be too careful,' she whispered.

I nodded, shame heating my cheeks. She carried the scars on her back from the last time I had tried to make my own bed. Faisal had seen me doing it when breakfast was brought in and reported it to my mother. She had been furious. I was to behave like a princess, not a peasant.

'Is it not to your liking, Your Highness?' Mira asked as I poked at my breakfast. 'Should I ask Cook to prepare something else?'

'Hm?' I looked up and saw Mira smiling earnestly at me.

'No, I'm fine. I just have a lot on my mind.' I picked up a pastry and swallowed it whole.

'Perhaps he will be kind,' she said quietly.

I snorted, stabbing a piece of fruit. 'Anybody my mother chooses will definitely not be kind.'

Mira grimaced. 'You'll just have to wait and see, I suppose. I did hear some of the servants talking last night,' she continued in hushed tones.

'What are they saying?' I asked nervously.

Mira looked back at the door. She hesitated.

I pulled her into my bedroom, shutting the balcony door on us. 'You can speak freely.'

Mira spoke in a whisper. 'They are saying the people might revolt; they are already unhappy after the rise in taxes. Poverty is spreading through the land. This could be the straw that breaks the camel's back.'

I wanted to believe the threat of revolt might persuade my mother to alter course, but she listened to no one - least of all our own people.

The golden doors to Mother's office opened, revealing a white room with golden panelling and lush red trees in large clay vases that hailed from ancient times. Mother sat at her mahogany desk, draped in an emerald lehenga that glittered with dark beads.

Her brown eyes fell on me, a cold smile lifting her lips. 'Sit down,' she said, taking a sip of tea from an ornate gold cup.

I took a seat opposite her, my maroon kameez fanning around me on the velvet armchair.

'Have you seen Edmund's miniature?' Mother asked over her tea, a gleeful glint in her eye. She knew I hadn't.

'No,' I said thinly.

Mother rooted around in her drawer and pulled out a small portrait, handing it to me.

'He's not too hideous,' Mother said with a smug smile.

I looked at the canvas. A weedy-looking young man with dark hair and a poor excuse for a beard looked back at me. His green eyes were wide, his lips thin and nose strikingly sharp. We would look like chalk and cheese beside each other. It was hard to imagine this was going to be my husband.

'How old is he?' I asked warily.

'Twenty-eight,' Mother said.

'He's a bit old, isn't he?' I said, frowning.

Mother snorted. 'Your father was thirty years my senior. Your betrothed is a child in comparison.'

I grimaced, placing the miniature face down on the desk. 'But he's so ...'

'Well, your prospects were slim: this was the best offer I could get,' Mother said haughtily. 'With any luck, this will be your first and only marriage.'

Here we go. I sighed.

'I was thrown into mourning at such a young age,' she lamented, looking at her reflection in an oval mirror on her desk. 'That's what happens when you marry an old man, though.'

I bristled. Mother loved to complain about my father, as though she had done some great act of charity by marrying him, when it was my father who had made *her* a Sultana.

'He was—'

'A great man, yes, yes,' Mother said dismissively, cutting me off. 'Have your maid start to pack your things. We are leaving for Dakaria in two days.'

I groaned inwardly. 'How long for?'

'A week or two. Don't worry, we'll still have plenty of

time to prepare before your betrothed arrives. They'll take at least two or so months to get here.'

'Wouldn't you prefer to go alone?' I asked. A week or two without my mother would be bliss.

'As tempting an idea as that may be, you need to see your great mother in action, learn how I deal with the enemy,' she said briskly.

I looked steadily back at my mother. There was no remorse in her face at all.

'Why do we need their silver?' I asked. 'We have our own resources.' Back when Sawan, Valthar and Dakaria had been one country, our lands were raided of most of their gold and natural resources when the Fallowmere ruled. Finding new sources of wealth was the miracle every nation needed. Luckily, Sawan had not been completely looted, and more resources were discovered after our liberation. But my mother's spending habits in favour of bolstering our military prowess were causing a strain on our people.

Mother sighed in frustration. 'Yes, and we need *more*. The rich do not stay rich by saving their money. If we conquer Dakaria, their wealth will become ours.'

'Conquer them?' I looked at her in shock. 'You want to wage war? Is that why you arranged my marriage to a Fallowmere prince?'

Mother smiled coldly. 'As I said, daughter: you have much to learn. When you are Sultana one day, you will have to make tough decisions for the good of Sawan.'

'But—'

'Silence!' she snapped. 'Now off you go. I haven't got time to listen to you witter on about things you know nothing about.'

I glared at her and stalked out of the room, cursing her under my breath. I stormed back to my bedroom.

The anger simmering beneath my skin felt like something physical – like it had yesterday. My body froze in place as I remembered the heat from my palms, the scorch mark hidden on my chair. I balled my hands into fists and forced myself to take several deep breaths, quelling the emotion.

I headed over to the grand window overlooking the palace gardens, wondering where my days had gone. My life was an endless circle. Wake. Eat. Walk. Read. Wave. Eat. Sleep. Repeat. Stuck in the same routine.

Looking out to the gardens, I saw the palace staff flitting around the grounds, walking freely. I couldn't set foot outside this room without someone shadowing me.

Would that change when the prince from Fallowmere arrived? When Father died, Mother had declared herself Sultana Regent with the entire court's support – except for Hussam and Emran. The court decided it was best Mother ruled until I came of age as I was just a child. I would be eighteen in less than three months. But it was unclear *when* I would actually take the throne. Would it be after or before I wed?

Mother kept saying 'one day' as if she had no intention of ever giving up the crown to me. But I wondered if, even once I was coronated, I would continue being a background actor on a stage that was never made for me. What would be the point in being Sultana then?

I lifted up my kameez and looked in the mirror. Faded silvery scars laced their way up my back, a gift from my mother the first and only time I had tried to run away after my father died. I'd felt trapped and alone in my grief while Mother pranced around as Sultana Regent, revelling in her new status.

The urge to leave had been overwhelming. I could feel that urge rising once again. Perhaps it was the only choice I could make for myself.

I dropped the folds of fabric and made my way over to my desk. I surveyed the pile of books stacked against the wall and pulled out a volume of maps.

Spreading it out before me, I inspected the borders of our land. We had Valthar to the southwest, Dakaria to the southeast, Azvakar to the west ... where to go?

Was I being foolish? Royals were married off all the time with little consent. I'd watched all of my cousins be married to royals from neighbouring lands. But at least their alliances had been made with countries with whom we had good relations – not the nation that had destroyed our lands only two centuries ago.

Should I just pick a country and head there? Would I be able to make a living alone? Women were shunned from society for much less.

I could speak the languages of Valthar and Dakaria fluently, since they were rooted in the same alphabet as Sawani. And I spoke the language of Nevarim, too. My cousin Mariya was married to a prince there – perhaps I could seek refuge with her. But would Mother see it as an act of aggression if Nevarim gave me sanctuary?

Or I could lose myself in the mountains and live as a nomad ... Our folklore was rife with stories of humans and mages who had lived in caves before civilization came to the land. Perhaps I could find one to disappear into before Mother caught me, especially if ...

My eyes flicked to the scorched chair covered by the throw.

I traced the map lines. Could I really do this? Did I have any other choice?

We would be travelling to Dakaria soon. Perhaps I could use that to my advantage.

5

Zayd

The afternoon sun streamed into the training room. The smell of sweat lingered in the air as thuds and smacks sounded from the soldiers around us. I punched the training dummy harder and harder, sure my knuckles would soon split. That didn't stop me from continuing.

'Angry much, Brother?' Yunus huffed from beside me, practising with his own punching bag.

I ignored him. I was not in the mood for his particular brand of humour right now.

It had been a few days, and Sayyidah Shafiya had so far been unable to find her elusive sister-in-law. My hopes of getting the water mages to work with us hung from a very thin thread, and my patience was wearing out

'You know, I could help you,' Yunus said, pausing. He wiped the sweat from his dark brow.

'Help me how?' I asked through gritted teeth. I delivered a final blow before stopping to face Yunus.

'Send me to the front lines,' Yunus panted, staring at me firmly.

'Mother won't allow it,' I huffed.

'You will marry soon, you will make heirs, thus rendering me tenth in line or something,' Yunus said dismissively. 'I can do more for Dakaria if I am on the front lines. I can help lead the army.'

I sighed. 'Yunus, you have no field experience. I can't send you out to command an army you've never even fought in.'

'So, send me out as a soldier where I can get experience,' he said, standing tall. 'I am of no use here.'

'You are of plenty use—'

'Really?' he scoffed. 'Is my advice sought on important situations? Am I told about our nation's security concerns? You think you're the last to know everything, Brother? I only find things out by accident.'

'Yunus, that's not true—'

He cut me off. 'I'm not a crucial member of this family or this royal institution. So, send me to the port to do something useful for once!'

'I have to consult with our parents.'

'Piss off, Zayd,' Yunus growled, and walked off.

'Yunus, wait!'

I watched his skulking figure leave the room. He had no idea how lucky he was to be second-born - the freedom he had to choose what he could do and who he might marry.

Fatigue began to crawl through my veins. I went to wash off the sweat plastered to my body. Despite my exhaustion, my nerves felt like live wires. It had become increasingly difficult to relax since returning home.

A mere week after the wedding, I was to be crowned Sultan. Father wanted to see me take the throne before he ... died. He spoke about it like it was a minor event.

I couldn't let that happen.

I poured steaming water over myself until I could bear the heat no longer.

Once I was dried and dressed, I headed over to Father's chambers. Mother was already there, helping him with his supper.

I stood by the door for a moment while she fed him, gently wiping spills from around his mouth. Theirs had been an arranged marriage too, but I knew my parents loved each other deeply. Was this what would become of me and Munira? I found it hard to fathom. How could I love somebody I didn't even know?

Loud boots clacking against the cobbled floors alerted me to Yunus's presence behind me. I made my way into the room and greeted my parents, quickly taking the armchair before Yunus could.

'Bastard,' he muttered only for my ears.

'You wish,' I murmured back.

'Yunus, have you seen the tailor yet?' Mother asked, narrowing her eyes at him.

Yunus sat down on a wooden chair. 'Yes. I'm thoroughly ready for my big brother's wedding. Tell me, Mother, have you managed to agree on a new date?' he asked, throwing me a pleasant smile.

I glowered back.

'Actually, yes,' Mother said carefully, looking at me.

I stilled.

'We are bringing the wedding forward – it will happen in three months. The engagement will be announced in the coming days,' Mother continued.

'I think we need to send Zayd to the hammam before his

new wife arrives, though,' Yunus said, wrinkling his nose. 'We don't want to scare her away on their first meeting.'

'Yunus,' Father chided weakly.

'My son is the most handsome boy in the land,' Mother said affectionately, trying to give me a warm smile.

'What about me?' Yunus said dryly.

'Well, of course, you are too,' Mother said quickly, her cheeks reddening.

Yunus scoffed. 'My own mother forgets me.' There was an edge to his voice.

'Perhaps when you do something other than knitting, you might become worth remembering,' I said, trying to diffuse the tension.

He glared at me. 'Why don't we speed the wedding up – bring it forward to next week?'

'Boys,' Mother said, trying not to laugh. 'Stop squabbling. It is very unbecoming for princes to fight.'

'On the contrary, Mother, I think princes *should* fight,' Yunus replied, his eyes narrowed at me.

We continued to bicker as Mother laughed and Father smiled faintly at us. A sudden loud knock on the door sounded. No sooner had Mother called 'Enter!' than Usman strode in, his face red with a sheen of sweat. He must have run the whole way here.

'Your Majesties,' he said, bowing breathlessly. 'I have news from Sawan – she is heading here now!'

'She?' Mother repeated, confused.

He waved a scroll of parchment in front of us. 'Sultana Zahra of Sawan. She is on her way with her daughter, the princess! The letter says it is a friendly visit to discuss further opportunities between our two nations.'

We all crowded around Father's bed to read the parchment.

50

It was brief, but marked with the Sultana of Sawan's emerald seal: a curly-horned markhor with a crown at the centre.

'When will she arrive?' I asked.

'By tomorrow, Your Highness,' Usman replied.

'But we have a wedding to prepare; she cannot just turn up!' Mother exclaimed. 'We are not expecting guests yet. The rooms are not ready! They are all being repainted!'

'I do not think she will care what colour the walls are, dear,' Father said slowly, looking even paler.

'We must prepare for all scenarios, Your Majesties,' Usman said. 'At best, she may be coming to negotiate better terms for our silver.'

'And at worst?'

Usman looked at me gravely. 'She may try to take the silver by force before you are wed, Your Highness.'

'Did I not say we should speed the wedding up again?' Yunus said half-heartedly.

'Not now, son,' Mother said faintly. 'Zayd, you and Princess Layla are the future rulers of your nations. You must spend this visit charming her into friendship. Take her on tours around the palace, the grounds, those sorts of things. Perhaps she can convince her mother not to invade if the two of you become good friends.'

'I don't have time to play host to some stranger,' I said irately.

Mother narrowed her eyes at me. 'Part of being Sultan is building relationships with other rulers. Diplomacy doesn't come out of thin air.'

I sighed through my teeth. 'Usman, try and draw up a new proposal. Perhaps we can hold the Sultana off with a more favourable rate,' I said.

Mother raised a scolding brow at me.

'And I will ensure the princess enjoys her time here,' I added shortly.

'We need to announce the wedding immediately,' Father said with laboured breath.

Cold dread crept through me. 'Perhaps we should wait and see what the Sultana wants first,' I countered. 'If we can secure an alliance with Sawan over the silver, it might work to our advantage.' The more military support we could get, the better.

'The Sultana doesn't want to make peace,' Usman said gravely.

'Then we must *all* play the perfect hosts,' Mother said firmly.

'If she finds out we are allying with Valthar, it may well stop her in her tracks,' Father said. 'We need to make it known now. Send word to Valthar and then to the press houses for tomorrow's papers.'

Usman nodded. 'Right away, Your Majesties.' He darted from the room.

My family all wore the same worried look.

'I wish we had an army big enough to stop these endless attacks. Heaven only knows how many invasions we will have before the wedding,' Mother lamented. 'What were the figures this week?'

'Seventeen attacks,' I replied. 'I would be happy to get back to the Silver Port, tighten up our defences?'

'You are going to be married soon,' Mother said sharply. 'You cannot be on the front lines any more. There is too much at stake.'

'Send me instead,' Yunus said quickly, straightening up.

'You are just a boy! I cannot have you out in the field!' Mother replied, aghast.

'I am only a year younger than him!' Yunus protested. 'I'm not going to be Sultan, anyway – I want to do something useful.'

'You will be your brother's second-in-command. We didn't even want to send Zayd out to the naval base, but he is crown prince. He had to go.'

'Do not get worked up, dear,' Father said, struggling to sit. 'Zayd will be wed soon, and we will have the might of Valthar behind us. Sawan would not dare.'

'Let's hope that your bride does not run away screaming when she sees your face, then,' Yunus said with a gleeful look at me. I glared back.

'Yunus!' Mother reproached him.

'Perhaps we need to find a bigger diamond for the ring,' Father said worriedly.

'I don't think the size of the rock is what matters,' Yunus snickered.

'Yunus!' Mother snapped again. 'If you want to be treated like an adult, start acting like one!'

'Open your mouth one more time,' I snarled at Yunus.

Yunus glowered back. 'I quake in my boots, Your *Majesty*,' he scoffed, getting up from his seat.

Father coughed, though the rattling noise sounded oddly like a laugh he was trying to hide.

'Where are you going now?' Mother asked.

'What do you care?' Yunus muttered, stalking out of the room.

'Yunus!' Mother called, but the doors slammed shut behind him.

Father sighed. 'You're too harsh on him sometimes, my love.'

'That's because he takes after you – troublesome since

the day he was born,' Mother said, but her voice was affectionate as she gave Father a look.

'He's not troublesome, he's high-spirited,' Father protested with a small grin.

'Hakim!' Mother called.

The door opened again. Hakim poked his head through. 'Yes, Your Majesty?'

'Get Farouk, please. We need to plan for our visitors tomorrow! We'll need to throw a welcome ball! Honestly, how inconsiderate for the Sultana to just show up ...'

'I shall leave you both to it. Get some rest, Father.' I bade them farewell.

As I walked back across the grounds, the sun set, leaving me in darkness. A few lanterns lit the pathway around the palace, fiery orbs that hung in the dark. I breathed in the cool night air, exhaling a sigh. It frustrated me that we needed a strong alliance to secure our kingdom. The match with Valthar was advantageous, I knew that, but it was all happening too soon. Father's weakened state felt surreal, but his laboured breathing, the waxy pallor that was starting to claim his once bronze skin ...

How long could I pretend my father wasn't dying in front of my eyes?

I'd been preparing to be Sultan from the moment I was born. I just never imagined it would happen like this.

Instead of heading to dinner, I made my way to Usman's office to go over the new trade deal he was drawing up. We had already offered Sawan a twenty-five per cent reduction – the highest we had offered any of our neighbouring lands. Any higher and we would end up devaluing our silver before the rest of the world.

I wanted to pull my hair out. Father's sickness was no

doubt inspiring the increased attacks on us. Changing monarchs was always a time of fragility for a nation. I couldn't let the Sultana of Sawan find any weakness here.

I knew why this marriage to Munira was important, but this impromptu visit was making the dire state of our situation all the more apparent. This marriage was for the good of my country, a country I was expected to lead in a matter of months. And if Sayyidah Shafiya could not locate the water mages, any discomfort I had needed to be squashed, even if it felt wrong to hold a wedding during my father's dying days.

The next morning, I was holed up in my office going through the healers' reports again. They all suggested pain relief. There was nothing that could stop death.

His body was shutting down, they had concluded. All they could offer was to delay the inevitable. But surely there was some unheralded cure out there, something that could help him?

The door to my study flew open, revealing my harried-looking mother.

'Where has Yunus gone?' she demanded, scanning my study as though he was going to materialize.

'I don't know,' I replied uncertainly. 'Why?'

'He left on his horse with his guards this morning. He wasn't scheduled to leave the palace – where is he?'

'He's probably just exploring somewhere; you know he likes to hunt,' I replied, looking back to my papers.

'I do not need to remind you that a roaming prince is what our attackers would love to stumble upon – or that the Sultana of Sawan is arriving today,' Mother said gravely.

'Surely he's just within the palace walls?' I said, putting down the reports.

'Zayd, he is nowhere on our grounds!' Mother said desperately. 'The stableboys said he left after breakfast. My guards cannot find him in the woods - he should have been back by now.'

I cursed and rose from my chair. 'Noor!'

The door swung open again. 'Yes, Your Highness?' Noor replied, stepping in.

'Get the horses ready. I want a full guard to search for Yunus. See if you can find out whether he has been spotted anywhere.'

'Right away, Your Highness,' Noor replied.

'This is the last thing I need,' Mother said, on the verge of tears. 'Your father can't hear about this - he needs to focus on resting.'

I grimaced. 'Don't worry, Mother. He won't be far. I promise we'll find him.' I said, putting a comforting arm on her shoulder. I knew exactly why Yunus had run off. I had to bring him home safely.

6

Zayd

I raced into the woods surrounding the palace with the guards, the pounding of hooves loud in the air. I tried to think of other places Yunus might seek solace – but they were all inside the palace walls. Yunus left home much less than I did, save for the occasional royal ceremony.

We rode deeper into the woods, bearing south as we followed fresh horse tracks.

I cursed as realization hit me. Yunus needed to prove a point, to show he was just as much a soldier and a leader as I was.

'He's heading towards the Silver Port!' I yelled at Noor, urging my horse faster.

Noor shouted something to the guards around us. Our horses thundered through city after city, racing down the sloping hills as we pushed towards the silver mines.

I hoped I was wrong. The port was no place for Yunus; he'd never been engaged in field combat. He was right. He was the spare. If I fell, he had to rise. But now was not that time. Not when endless attempts on our silver were being made night and day; not when the Sultana of Sawan was due any moment on our doorstep.

Agonizing hours passed until we reached the silver mines. There was no sign of Yunus or his guards, but a soldier stationed by the port confirmed that the prince had been seen heading towards the coast.

I looked out to the horizon as we neared our naval base. I could see a new ship in the distance sailing closer, a dark maroon flag with a black skull waving from its sails.

We dismounted, met by the commanding officer. He called for my armour. Soldiers lined the port, readying their weapons. I hurried down to shore, and just boarded the ship as it headed off to meet our new attackers.

'Your Highness, we were not expecting you, or Prince Yunus,' Anas said nervously.

'We weren't supposed to be here,' I snapped, looking for my brother. I strode along the perimeter where soldiers had lined up, weapons poised and ready.

I spotted Yunus by the centre, his bow aimed and arrows strapped to his back.

'Yunus, stand down!' I ordered, grabbing him by the shoulder.

Yunus shoved me back. 'Respectfully, Brother, piss off!'

'Your Highness, you should get below deck,' Noor said urgently.

I ignored him. 'You haven't participated in field combat; you cannot be here!'

Before Yunus could respond, a loud horn sounded.

Somebody pushed me down as arrows rained around us, sharp and precise. I heard thuds as two soldiers fell.

I pushed up and grabbed Yunus, who was struggling to reload his bow. 'I said stand down! You need to have trained to fight here! You haven't even put your armour on properly!'

'I can do it!' he growled, pulling away and nocking the arrow at last.

I heard the whistling of the arrow coming for him.

I lunged, slamming Yunus onto the deck as something struck my arm. 'Are you out of your mind?' I shouted.

'The crown prince is wounded!' someone yelled.

'Load the cannon balls!' another cried.

I stayed down, pinning Yunus to the deck as he stared at me in horror. Blood dripped down my arm, staining his steel armour.

Cursing, I grabbed the arrow stuck in my right arm and tore it out of my flesh. I stifled a scream as searing pain shot through my arm.

'Brother,' Yunus whispered, his face ashen.

'Stay down,' I growled.

The carnage continued. Arrows ricocheted around us, cannons exploded as Noor and the royal guard sheltered us from the onslaught, slowly pulling us towards the trapdoor leading below deck.

We fell into the captain's cabin. I looked down at my arm – I'd been struck in the gap between my armour again.

'What are the chances,' I muttered.

'Brother, I'm sorry,' Yunus said from across the room, his voice barely audible.

'It's better if you stay quiet,' I snapped.

The healer was summoned. I was given a cloth to bite into while he worked the wound on my arm. I did my best not to scream, but the stitching of my flesh was so excruciating that my vision blurred, stars dancing before my eyes and then fading into black.

I was vaguely aware of the pressure on my arm. I opened

my eyes slowly, fatigue weighing them down. The room unblurred before me as my eyes focused. A shape appeared; Yunus's mortified face looked back at me.

'I'm so sorry, Brother. I didn't mean for you to get hurt,' he said urgently.

'Did I not tell you to stand down?' I huffed out angrily, my breath short. 'What were you thinking coming out here?'

'I wanted to help,' he replied quietly, his dark eyes filled with shame.

'Great job you did there. You're a liability,' I spat at him, fuming.

Yunus looked away.

We sat there in silence as the fight continued above deck. My arm burned with pain. I heard another two thuds, the sounds of bodies falling. Dismay filled me. How would our country ever achieve stability like this?

Finally, I heard Anas call out that the pirates were retreating. Once it was clear, I was hauled off the ship under the cover of our guards, and into a carriage back to the palace. I slumped against the window, the cool glass a welcome relief to my feverish skin.

Some Sultan I was shaping up to be. Not only had I let Yunus disappear from the palace, I'd been wounded in the process of bringing him home. And any moment, the Sultana of Sawan would be coming to lay down her threats.

Yunus watched me solemnly from his corner of the carriage. He had not uttered a single word since we'd left the ship.

'I know you want to prove yourself,' I said slowly, meeting his gaze, 'but there is no need. There will come a time when Dakaria will require you to lead and you will rise to the occasion. But now is not your time.'

'I'm sorry, Brother,' he mumbled. 'Truly.'

'Stop apologizing. I'd rather you insult me.' My eyes began to droop closed. My head was ringing.

I did my best to fight the darkness threatening to take me under again. It was excruciating. The pain in my arm singed at my flesh, as though it were being burned from the inside. Perhaps if I just rested my eyes for a moment …

I jerked awake as we came to a stop. 'Where are we?'

Yunus looked back at me worriedly. 'We're home, Brother. Are you all right?'

'I'm fine,' I muttered, getting out of the carriage.

Noor was at my side instantly, but I shrugged past him and marched inside. My injured arm felt heavy, but I persevered, refusing to accept help from the guards who hovered around me. Yunus skulked behind us, disappearing onto his floor without another word.

I hurried past a clamour of servants sweeping up broken crockery in the hallway and was relieved to finally step foot in my room. I headed straight for my bed.

The sound of a footstep in my bedchamber made me pause. I grabbed the blade strapped to my belt and proceeded slowly.

A cloaked figure stood at the edge of my room, looking over my bookshelf.

'Who the hell are you?' I demanded.

The figure whirled around, revealing itself to be a girl. Before she could respond, I crossed the room in three strides and slammed her against the wall.

'Unhand me, you brute!' she protested angrily, shoving back against me.

I kept her pinned with my good arm, putting my blade

to her throat. 'Who are you and how did you get in here? Who sent you? Answer me!'

'What do you mean? This – is that a dagger? Put it down!' she demanded angrily, shoving against me again with surprising strength. I just about managed to hold my stance.

The girl glowered at me. Her eyes were like pools of amber on fire, her oval face the colour of golden sand, framed by dark hair that hung down in waves beneath her hood.

'Who are you?' I growled again.

Her knee connected with my groin. I stifled a shout, almost losing my grip on her.

'If you were my future Sultan, I'd be very worried you didn't know who was in your own room, let alone your palace,' the girl replied scathingly. Her Dakari was perfect, but there was an accent to it. She wasn't from here. 'Clearly you aren't used to visitors.'

'Believe me, sweetheart, plenty of visitors come and go from this bedroom,' I snapped back, irritated by her bravado. I had a blade to her throat, but she was goading me.

She balked at that, faint disgust in her eyes. 'Unhand me this instant.' I felt the sudden pressure of something cold and sharp against my left side.

My eyes flicked down to see a dagger pressed above my kidney. I held firm. 'You're in my room, and I don't take orders from strangers. Who are you and what are you doing in here?'

'Enjoying the view, what do you think?' she spat back. 'My name is Layla, you insolent troll. Now get your hands off me!'

'Layla?' I repeated slowly, realization dawning. Damn everyone to hell. I dropped my arms and stepped back immediately. '*Princess* Layla?'

She glowered back at me. 'So, you are educated,' she said, massaging her throat.

I sheathed my blade hurriedly. I fought a flinch as my arm throbbed with pain. 'I thought you were an assassin.'

'I entered the wrong room by mistake,' she said coldly, putting her dagger away. 'And if I were here to assassinate you, Prince Zayd, you wouldn't still be standing.'

I had just held a knife to the crown princess of Sawan. I might as well declare war now.

Layla began stalking away.

'Wait, Your Highness,' I said, catching her by the elbow. My injured arm stung with pain.

She snatched her arm back, turning livid eyes on me. 'Don't touch me.'

I tried for diplomacy. 'A thousand apologies, Princess. It was an honest mistake, surely you can understand. There's no need for this to sour our relationship as future leaders of our nations. Truly, I'm sorry.'

Layla looked me over with narrowed eyes. 'If you're afraid I will tell my mother, don't worry. In your position, I would have done the same.'

Relief swept through me.

'But touch me again and I will make sure my blade goes through your heart,' she said in an ice-cold voice.

The scathing look in her eyes told me she wasn't joking. Layla stormed out of my room, her cloak billowing behind her.

Shit.

I sank down on my bed, winded from the exertion, my arm throbbing. I pulled my sleeve back; the bandages were intact. I knew I had to think of how to remedy this situation with the princess, but my eyes drooped shut before I could form any more thoughts.

7

Layla

I startled awake in a strange room, soft light breaking in wisps through gaps in the heavy curtains. I looked around the magnolia walls adorned with silver panelling, at the beautiful paintings of turquoise rivers and lush fields.

It had been such a long journey to get here – riding to our southern port to sail to Dakaria, then mounting the carriages again to complete the journey to the palace. I stretched out my stiff limbs and felt a twinge of pain at my neck.

My hand went to my throat as last night came flooding back to me. That damn prince. As it turned out, my *actual* room was exactly opposite that troll of an heir. One of the servants had dropped a plate of food last night and, in all the chaos, I'd gone into the wrong one like an idiot. Still, Prince Zayd had no right to hold a dagger to my throat. The nerve of him. As if I wanted to be here in the first place.

I got up and checked my reflection in the dressing-table mirror, but thankfully there was no lingering mark on my neck.

Mira came in soon after, bringing fresh hot water. I sank into the silver bathtub gratefully, eager to scrub the travel off my body.

I made a face when Mira pulled out my morning dress: an ice-blue lehenga patterned with swirling floral threads.

'It's a bit much for breakfast, isn't it?' I muttered as she helped me into the puffy skirt.

'Sorry, Your Highness, but Her Majesty wants you in formal wear for all mealtimes,' Mira said as she fanned out yards of tulle underskirt.

I grumbled to myself as Mira swept my hair into a bun and placed a silver necklace and matching earrings on me. She brushed rose powder over my lips and cheeks before fitting the dupatta atop my head. It draped down to the floor.

The palace was much different in the daylight; it had seemed like a dark maze last night, silver accents gleaming in the moonlight. The white stone hallways felt wider in the sun, intermittently decorated with beautiful mosaics across the ceiling that mimicked the ocean waves. The aura around the palace felt lighter, more open, than it did in Sawan.

My stomach recoiled when I saw Mother walking towards the dining hall. She appraised me briefly, her lips pursing with displeasure.

'Mother,' I said curtly.

She nodded at me, her eyes roaming the palace walls, narrowed with distaste.

The gilded doors were thrown open to a large hall. Light streamed in through the grand windows, showing off the vast fields and woods that surrounded the palace. At the head of a long dining table laden with food was Sultana Aysha, who had greeted us last night, and the two princes on either side.

The Sultana rose to greet us. She kissed my cheeks and

led me to the chair on her right, beside Prince Zayd, while Mother was seated opposite us, next to a young man I took to be the other brother, Prince Yunus.

'Good morning, Princess,' Zayd said smoothly as we sat down.

I cast a sideways glance at him, unimpressed. So, he had manners today.

He cut a confident figure in the daytime. The fitted jacket he wore emphasized his broad shoulders and lean frame, the cut of his lightly bearded jaw sharp as he watched me. But I could see a touch of worry in his olive-green eyes. Good.

'How did you sleep, Your Majesty?' Sultana Aysha asked.

'Very well, thank you,' Mother replied warmly. 'I did not expect you to have such spacious rooms available at such short notice. A pleasant surprise.'

Sultana Aysha merely smiled graciously in response, the thinly veiled insult rolling off her back. 'Well, we are most happy to receive you, even if it was very unexpected.'

'How were your travels, Your Majesty?' Prince Zayd asked, turning his attention towards my mother.

'Oh, tiresome,' Mother complained. 'But here we are.'

'Next time you come, you must let us know in advance, so we can ensure you travel comfortably,' Zayd said easily.

'What charming rulers Dakaria has,' Mother simpered.

I fought the urge to roll my eyes.

'You are too kind, Sultana,' Zayd said. 'We are nothing in comparison to the beauty of Sawan.'

I didn't like the way he looked at me when he said that, or the way the corner of his mouth tugged upwards. If he thought flattery would make me forget last night, he had another thing coming.

Mother laughed, batting her eyelashes. She was so irritating.

Mercifully, the servants began to lift the lids off the dishes of breakfast food, seamlessly weaving in and out of our chairs, quelling the awkward small talk. It was an impressive spread: fresh sweet pastries drenched in honey and cinnamon, spicy omelettes, slices of meat with rolls of paratha, and all manner of fruit.

'Can I pour you some chai, Princess?' Zayd asked me.

I looked up at him in surprise. He was allowed to pour me tea? 'Fine, thank you,' I replied shortly.

I feigned boredom, looking down at my plate, watching curiously through a sideways glance as Zayd reached out to the teapot between us and poured me tea, his mother not even seeming to notice. 'Would have got slapped if that was me,' I muttered.

'Did you say something, Princess?' Zayd asked quietly.

'Me? No, just glad you aren't throwing me against a wall this morning,' I said, low enough for only him to hear. I took the cup, and the edges of our fingers brushed, his warm skin grazing against mine.

Zayd had the decency to look embarrassed. 'I am really sorry, again,' he murmured back.

'How did you sleep, Princess?' Sultana Aysha asked, turning her attention towards us. 'I hope everything was all right with your chambers.'

I felt Zayd still beside me.

'It was lovely, Your Majesty, thank you,' I replied.

'After breakfast, would you like to join us on a tour of the grounds?' Sultana Aysha asked.

'That would be most appreciated,' Mother replied. 'You have parasols, I assume?'

'Yes, of course,' Sultana Aysha replied, looking confused.

'I have delicate skin: I do not like to be out in the sun,' Mother explained with another tinkling laugh.

'*Vampire*,' I mumbled under my breath as I pushed a piece of fruit around my plate.

Zayd leant closer, the smell of warm, musky oud wafting over me. 'Is your breakfast all right, Princess?'

'My brother is quite the chef,' Prince Yunus chipped in. 'He could always make you something else.' He gave me a hesitant smile.

'Everything tastes wonderful, thank you,' I replied, breathing a little easier when Zayd leant away.

'My, my. Do you all cook and serve yourselves here?' Mother said, clutching the diamonds around her neck. 'In my palace, the servants do everything for us.'

'My servants do plenty for us, but the Sultan and I wanted to make sure our sons could do things for themselves, too,' Sultana Aysha replied pointedly.

'How sweet,' Mother said in a tone that suggested it was anything but. 'I suppose some royals have more time on their hands to busy themselves with … chores.'

Sultana Aysha smiled politely back at her. 'On the contrary. My sons have a rigorous schedule, but I prefer them to be self-sufficient rather than lazy.'

'Indeed,' Mother replied with a thin smile.

The verbal sparring was starting to wear on me. I wanted to go back to my room, away from the tiring ceremony of dining with strangers. And away from Prince Zayd, whose belated attempt to play model prince this morning was grating on my nerves.

'I should like to tell you some wonderful news, Your Majesty,' Sultana Aysha said after a while.

I heard Zayd sigh quietly beside me. I cast a quick look at him; his jaw had gone tight.

'Do tell,' Mother said with a glowing smile.

'We have arranged Zayd's betrothal to Princess Munira of Valthar.'

I saw the shock flicker across Mother's face before she plastered an even brighter smile on. 'Well, congratulations! This is wonderful news. An advantageous match, no doubt.'

'Indeed,' Sultana Aysha said happily. 'You are, of course, invited. The wedding has been set for three months' time.'

'We wouldn't miss it,' Mother said, but her voice was tight. I could almost see the thoughts running through her head. Valthar had a military that rivalled ours. If Mother was planning to invade, this certainly threw a spanner in the works, even with the Fallowmere in tow.

'That is quite soon though, is it not?' my mother continued.

Prince Zayd sat up straighter. 'I wish for my father to be at my wedding while his health permits.'

An uncomfortable silence followed. 'Of course,' Mother said sweetly. 'How is the Sultan?'

'He is well. He's a strong man,' Zayd said proudly, but I didn't miss the touch of sadness that lingered behind his words. I felt a fleeting moment of understanding.

'And what about your beautiful princess?' Sultana Aysha said tactfully. 'I imagine she must have suitors falling at her feet.'

I felt my cheeks heat up. I quickly popped a piece of melon in my mouth so I wouldn't have to respond.

'Well, not really,' Mother said, disdain evident in her voice. 'She has her father's looks, so it was a bit harder to find suitors for her.'

I held back a sigh. Anything to complain about me.

There was an awkward silence from the Dakaria royals.

'I cannot imagine you would have trouble finding such a stunning princess any number of suitors,' Yunus said, giving me a winning smile.

My heart warmed a little. At least one of the princes was kind.

'You are too sweet,' Mother replied tightly. 'I have actually managed to find her a suitor after *years* of refusal. I thought I would never see the day!'

I reached for a glass of water, my mouth suddenly dry. My hand shook.

'He is a prince from Fallowmere – very far in line to the throne, so they do not need him in the country, really,' Mother said, as though she were referring to a prize cow. 'He is not the most handsome boy, but he will do. Some princesses get frogs, or so they say.'

Shame filled my body. I looked down at my plate, unable to meet the gazes I could feel on me.

I saw Prince Zayd's hand clench beside me.

Sultana Aysha sounded taken aback. 'From Fallowmere? We have not been in contact with them since we revolted and took our countries back from them.'

'Oh, I have been mending bridges for some time,' Mother said proudly. 'They have endless wealth and resources; they are planning to invest in our infrastructure. And, of course, they have a strong military.'

And there it was, her not-so-thinly veiled threat.

'Well, I wish your daughter well in her future marriage. You will make a beautiful bride, I am sure, Princess Layla,' Sultana Aysha said kindly to me, but I didn't miss the tightness in her eyes.

I forced a smile back. 'Thank you, Your Majesty.'

My mother was radiating smugness.

'Shall we take our walk now?' Sultana Aysha said.

'Yunus and I have a meeting,' Prince Zayd said, rising from his chair. 'It was wonderful to meet you both – Your Majesty, Your Highness.' He inclined his head towards Mother and then me, a slight furrow in his brow as our eyes locked.

I looked back at him steadily, despite my quickening pulse.

The prince strode away.

I traipsed behind my mother and the Sultana of Dakaria as we headed to the gardens.

'Give the princess a parasol too,' I heard my mother say when we stepped outside.

Within moments, I was being shaded as we headed into the mild spring air.

The sun was beginning to break through the clouds above the palace. The grounds were finely manicured, full of grand hedge sculptures shaped like elephants and tigers, and majestic peacocks strutted about the lawn. Cobbled pathways wove in and out of the grounds, encircling flower beds and benches wrapped in roses. Every so often, the green spaces would be broken up by pools of water – sometimes fountains, sometimes ponds – all dotted with floating water lilies.

I trailed behind Mother and the Sultana as they made small talk about the weather and various plants. There was an edge of boasting under Mother's words, as always. It seemed like a sickness sometimes, her endless need to brag about something. If the Sultana of Dakaria noticed, her poker face and polite replies were something to aspire towards.

'Shall we head back? That is quite enough fresh air for me,' I heard Mother say, her eyes flicking up to the sky.

We were led back to the palace doors, where the Sultana bade us goodbye, and the guards guided us back to our rooms.

'Make sure you scrub extra hard when you bathe,' Mother muttered before she disappeared to her floor.

Insufferable woman. I retreated into my room and sat down in the parlour.

'Tea, Your Highness?' Mira asked.

'Yes, please,' I replied.

'Did you enjoy breakfast?' Mira asked as she tipped the silver teapot over a small cup.

'It was all right,' I said, though I failed to remember what I had eaten. 'Mother decided to announce my engagement to the table.'

Mira grimaced, her dark eyes full of understanding. 'How did they take it?'

'They were shocked, like everyone else will be when they find out. It's as though my mother *wants* people to hate us.' I groaned, sliding further down the chair.

'If she's told the royals of Dakaria, she must be announcing it soon in Sawan,' Mira said worriedly, lowering her voice.

My stomach flopped uncomfortably. 'I wish … I could stop it somehow, Mira. But she won't listen to me.'

Mira glanced nervously at the door, placing the tea on the table. 'I wish I could help you too, Princess.'

I smiled sadly at her and picked up the cup. The urge to disappear began to fill me again as panic rose in my chest.

'What have you got planned for the rest of the afternoon, Your Highness?' Mira asked, breaking me from my thoughts.

'Nothing,' I said quickly. 'Perhaps I'll visit the library. The Sultan is said to have almost every book in the world here.'

Mira's eyes widened appreciatively. 'That's amazing.'

Once I had finished my tea, I headed outside and asked Faisal to take me to the library. One of the Dakaria guards stationed down the corridor led the way.

The palace was truly something magnificent. The marble hallways were decorated with grand portraits of former rulers and beautiful landscapes. Ornate silver tables were scattered throughout the halls, displaying various ancient trinkets and pottery that spoke of a rich past that long preceded the people within the palace. I lingered at a few for a moment, reading the plaques that spoke of their provenance. Several pottery pieces hailed from historic times. There were swords crafted by mages before the dark age, and tattered uniforms held up in glass cabinets that belonged to the freedom fighters of the liberation war.

I eventually entered the library through double doors that opened onto rich oak floors and grand arched windows. Golden-lettered spines gleamed in the sunlight – endless rows of leather-bound books extended up to the ceiling. A few mahogany desks were dotted around, and plush emerald armchairs. I breathed in the musty smell of the books and smiled. Finally, somewhere I could enjoy myself.

The guards waited outside the door while I browsed my way through the shelves. A spiral staircase led to another floor. I ran up, wondering what more was upstairs. The books here seemed to be mainly poetry, with selections from around the world. I scanned through, stopping short when I saw a number of books in worn leather, the lettering faded gold.

A History of Mages
An Exploration of Mages and Their Affinities
The Dark Age and the Fate of Mages

My heart began to race. I looked around nervously, but I was entirely alone. We'd never had these kinds of books in Sawan, even when Father was alive.

Hesitating, I took the books about mages and carried them back down the stairs. I found a few more tales from around the world too, great expeditions to the northern and southern isles. These would be enough company for the rest of the trip.

As I headed towards the exit, the doors swung open, and Prince Zayd strode in.

He stopped short when he saw me. 'Oh, hello, Your Highness,' he said, inclining his head.

I threw him a contemptuous glare as I attempted to curtsey – not easy when there are ten books in your hand – and a few volumes fell from my towering pile.

Zayd moved fast, catching them before they hit the floor.

'Thanks,' I muttered, snatching them back and drawing them closer, hoping he hadn't noticed my subject of interest.

Zayd smiled back. 'No bother. Shall I help you? That's a lot of books you're carrying.'

'I'm fine, thank you,' I said stiffly. His false nice act at breakfast this morning had riled me.

'Allow me,' Zayd said, taking a few copies from my pile.

'I can carry my own books,' I insisted. 'Unless you're desperate to throw those at me?'

Zayd's smile disappeared. 'I can only apologize, Princess. Truly, I *am* sorry.' He put the books back, his olive eyes intent on mine.

'Whatever,' I snapped, stalking off. But the books wobbled ominously so I slowed my pace.

'Please allow me to help. It'll be sundown by the time you make it to the door,' the prince said dryly.

'Why are you still talking to me?' I retorted. 'Don't you have another unfortunate lady to hold at knifepoint?'

Zayd sighed heavily and walked around me. 'We got off to a bad start – which I realize is my own doing. Please allow me to make it up to you.'

'I get to put that knife through your heart now?' I asked sweetly.

Zayd raised a dark brow, a smile playing at the edge of his lips.

My stomach did an uncomfortable flip as he gazed at me, irritating me even more.

'Have you been inside the greenhouse?' he asked.

'No,' I replied shortly.

'Well, if you are free this evening, perhaps before dinner, I would be happy to take you there,' he offered.

I stared at him in surprise for a moment. 'Just you and me?'

'Yes,' he replied, a smile dancing in his eyes.

I looked at him incredulously. 'I'll have you know, Your Highness, I can't be so easily impressed.'

'Who said I was trying to impress you?' he countered. 'I am a betrothed man, after all.'

'*Man* is a bit of a stretch, Your Highness. Aren't you but seventeen?' I found myself replying sarcastically.

This only seemed to amuse the prince. 'Eighteen, actually. Seven months older than you, according to your royal biography.'

'It's a shame you didn't do your homework *before* I arrived,' I said tartly.

He looked like he wanted to laugh, his olive eyes radiant in the sunlight. How was anything I was saying amusing?

'You're right,' he said in that infuriatingly deep voice of his. 'I might have saved myself some embarrassment if I had done my research. I just didn't expect to meet you in my bedroom.'

'I got our rooms mixed up,' I said, heat blooming on my cheeks.

'And I mistook you for someone else,' he said easily. 'We all make mistakes.'

'I walked into your room by accident – that's not the same thing as you holding a dagger to my throat,' I snapped.

In one swift movement, Zayd took the pile of books from my hands and put them down on a table.

'What are you—' I started to say.

Zayd looked at me intently for a second before his hand moved to his inner jacket. He pulled out a dagger and held it out to me. 'OK, so give me a taste of my own medicine. Or do more damage, if you prefer. It's entirely up to you.'

'What?' I spluttered. 'You can't just hand me a dagger.'

'Well, you seem really offended, so I'm merely giving you the chance to have your revenge,' he countered, stepping closer with the blade still held, hilt out, towards me.

I stepped back. 'No. Stop being ridiculous.'

'Take it,' he said, as though he were holding a sugar cane and not a sharp weapon.

'And do what exactly?'

'You can do whatever you want to me,' he said, amusement playing in his eyes.

'I'll take my revenge a different way,' I said coolly. 'Consider yourself indebted to me.'

'As you wish,' he said with a smirk, putting the dagger away.

'Troll,' I muttered, grabbing my books off the table and stalking past him.

'I shall see you before dinner, Your Highness,' Zayd called after me, laughter in his voice.

8
Zayd

I rifled through the library, looking for something that might help me track down the water mages. Sayyidah Shafiya had sent a letter this morning: her sister-in-law was still nowhere to be found. And now that Sultana Zahra had announced Princess Layla's marriage, time felt even scarcer.

The Fallowmere? Of all people?

Even taking into account my marriage to Munira, if Sawan tried to invade with the backing of Fallowmere, I didn't want to think what kind of condition we would be left in. It would be a bloody war, no doubt.

I scoured the birth records with no luck. Perhaps the tax records in Father's archives might have the answer. I headed over to his wing of the palace, rubbing my aching arm as I walked. That bloody arrow had really left its mark.

Grabbing a torch, I took the stairs down into the cellar where all the tax records were kept, lighting the torches hung up on the wall as I went. Dust greeted me. Noor's footsteps echoed behind me.

If the sister-in-law had ever paid tax, there would be an address in here somewhere. The family had lived in the south, but their home had been destroyed in a flood many years ago, leading Shafiya's husband to relocate and come work at the palace.

I found a box holding scrolls of parchment relating to the husband, his parents ... nothing from the sister. Aside from the birth record, it seemed she didn't exist. Had she left Dakaria?

After searching through a few more boxes, I cursed and gave up, heading back up a couple of flights of stairs to Father's room. Mother was already in there, pacing.

'I had to endure her insults for far too long!' she was saying.

My father greeted me with a wary look. I sat down quietly on the edge of Father's bed.

'Then she goes on and on about marrying her daughter to a Fallowmere prince. As if their people didn't drive our countries into ruin for well over a century!'

'Their late Sultan's great-grandfather was one of the lead commanders who expelled the Fallowmere from our lands, along with my great-grandfather,' my father said in a hollow voice. 'They would all be turning in their graves if they could see this now.'

'She must be desperate for power to side with those barbarians. Our streets ran with blood for weeks when they took over!' Mother was raging. I didn't blame her. The histories of our countries were tied inextricably together. For the Sultana of Sawan to do this was a cold slap in the face of all our ancestors who had lost their lives to drive out the Fallowmere.

Perhaps most criminal of all was the way the Fallowmere had slaughtered those who resisted them, and anyone they deemed a threat. Our people, with all their varying languages and beliefs, used to live side by side – even with the mages. The mages had been seen as something akin to healers, a special group who were able to command an element – wind, fire, earth or water.

But the Fallowmere turned our people against one another with their propaganda papers, forcing people into land wars and claiming that mages were the cause of all strife, so they became something people feared. The Fallowmere killed anybody who resisted with their new weapons, and sliced up our countries so they could rule them more easily. Our countries used to be one, and it took decades to reach an alliance and overthrow their bloodthirsty rule, but they left us in ruin – the mages were all but exterminated, our lands bled dry of our own resources.

'And the way she speaks to her daughter! Heaven help that poor child,' Mother was saying now.

I sat up a bit straighter.

'Such a lovely girl, but the Sultana talks about her like she's no better than the dirt on her shoe. What kind of mother speaks about her daughter like she's a failure – in front of her?'

My father shook his head, unimpressed. 'Some people do not deserve their children.'

'The poor girl looks broken down – I wish I could just take her away and look after her. Heaven only knows if her mother even feeds her; she seems so afraid to eat a thing in front of her.'

I looked at Mother in confusion. 'She's afraid to eat in front of her mother?'

'Did you not notice? She hardly ate after her mother started insulting her,' Mother replied. 'I used to feel nervous as a young girl, eating in front of my mother-in-law. Dreadful woman.'

'Excuse me,' Father protested weakly.

'Yes?' Mother countered in a sharp voice, narrowing her eyes at Father.

'I know my mother treated you poorly, dear,' Father said apologetically. 'She regretted it, though.'

'Yes, on her deathbed, so she could get a "save me from hell" card,' Mother grumbled.

'Right,' I said swiftly, before Mother and Father could descend into an argument. 'We must consider this threat from Sawan and the Fallowmere. Any time the Fallowmere go somewhere for trade, they start wars under the guise of freeing the people from some concocted oppression.'

Mother snorted. 'As if we need their idea of freedom. Hypocrites.'

I grimaced. 'We need to strengthen our defences,' I said. 'If the Fallowmere are coming back, we must prepare.'

'At least we will have Valthar on our side if Sawan tries to launch an attack,' Mother said with some confidence. 'Try not to fret, dear. Everything will be all right.' She took Father's hand in her own.

Father looked back at us worriedly. 'We all know the Fallowmere have one of the largest, most advanced militaries in the world. How long will we be able to hold them off?'

I took a breath before speaking. 'We do have another option.'

My parents looked at me.

'What option?' Mother asked, eyeing me curiously.

'The mages,' I said.

'Zayd, you cannot be serious! There aren't many left, and

those who remain live in hiding – for a reason. They are dangerous beings, son.'

'They are only seen as dangerous because the Fallowmere poisoned everyone against them,' I said impatiently. 'We should overturn the old law that made magecraft illegal.' Maybe *that* would be an easier way to track down the water mages.'

'The Fallowmere drove the mages to near extinction, and the rulers of the time were unable to protect them. Those who remained refused to have anything to do with society, so the law was never really changed,' Father said.

'If the mages wanted anything to do with society, I'm sure they would have voiced it,' Mother added. 'I think it's best we leave them alone.'

'Well, perhaps we can establish mages back into society again and they can help us against the Fallowmere,' I said.

'The mages will not work with us,' Father replied gravely. 'And our people may not react well. People are afraid of what they don't understand.'

'How can you know that if we don't try?' I insisted.

Father looked at me, something like shame flickering in his eyes. 'I ... tried to make contact with the last line of water mages we have in Dakaria some years ago.'

Mother looked at him in surprise. 'You did?'

'Much like my son here, I thought we could ask them to help – we were having such a hard time with floods that year,' Father said.

'What happened?' I asked.

'The chief of the water mages refused,' Father said with a sigh. 'I failed.'

'Perhaps now that the Fallowmere are coming back, they may reconsider,' I said.

Mother looked unconvinced. 'These wounds run deep, Zayd. Anybody caught harbouring a mage back then was killed by the Fallowmere, alongside their entire family. The mages never forgave this betrayal. I can't say I blame them, either.'

'But think of the stability we could have if the water mages helped us fend off attacks from the sea!' I continued. 'We'd be able to redeploy our soldiers to the borders, keep Sawan at bay with better odds.' *And delay my marriage*, I added silently.

'Zayd, you do not understand the power of the mages,' Mother said tersely. 'My grandparents used to tell me terrifying stories. They could plunge a nation underwater or set a thousand men on fire. Such might makes for a formidable enemy. We cannot risk causing any issues with them again. And had I known your father was trying to contact them years ago, I would have warned him of the same thing.'

'I would never do anything unless it was for the good of Dakaria,' I replied firmly. 'This is what you both raised me for: to be a leader, to make difficult decisions. With the Fallowmere coming back now, we have to do something to defend ourselves.'

Father looked at me, his eyes full of sadness. 'I am sorry I could not give you more time to be a boy, Zayd.'

'You have given me more than enough,' I said, reaching over to hold his arm.

'We can continue this conversation after the Sultana leaves,' Mother said decisively. 'Your father needs to rest.'

'Very well.' I bade my parents farewell and headed back to the archives. I'd been looking in the tax records, but if Father had made contact with the chief water mage some years ago, the information I needed would be in his correspondence files somewhere. It had to be.

9

Layla

When the orange sun began to slip away from the hazy sky, Mira readied me for dinner. She pinned back my hair and let a few curls loose at the front, then placed a silk dupatta on my head. It fell down elegantly, like the lilac embroidered lehenga I wore, threaded with gold and sparkling with small crystals.

'Must I?' I grumbled as Mira slid matching gold-and lilac-bangles up my arms.

'Her Majesty wishes—'

'I know.' I sighed. 'I just hate getting dressed up only for her to declare to everyone how hideous and unmarriageable I am.'

'It's not true,' she said firmly. 'Not for one moment.'

'Try telling her that,' I muttered.

'My mother always said insecurity is loud and stupid whereas confidence is calm and quiet,' Mira said gently as she brushed kohl along my eyes.

'I miss her,' I said with a sigh. 'How is she?'

'She's frail, but doing OK,' Mira replied sadly, adding rose colouring to my cheeks and lips. 'I'm just glad my cousins live next door to keep an eye on her.'

'You will tell me if she needs anything else, yes?' I implored. 'Anything at all.'

'But you've already given so much, Your Highness,' Mira said.

A knock on the door interrupted our conversation.

'Yes?' I called.

Faisal stuck his head in. 'Your Highness, Prince Zayd is here to escort you to the greenhouse.'

My stomach flipped uncomfortably. I had hoped the insufferable prince had forgotten about that. 'I'll be along in a minute,' I replied grudgingly.

Faisal nodded and shut the door.

Mira gave me a conspiratorial smile. 'Prince Zayd wants to take you to the greenhouse? Let me add some more kohl!'

I rolled my eyes at her. 'He's just trying to be a diplomat.'

Mira had a mischievous glint in her eye. 'All I shall say, Your Highness, is you aren't married yet.'

'I'd rather gouge my eyes out with my bare hands,' I huffed. 'The prince is arrogant and rude.'

'Really? The servants say the entire family is so kind,' Mira said in surprise.

'He's a troll,' I said decisively.

'Trolls have looked worse,' Mira sniggered.

'Have you been sniffing the bath salts again?' I said, shaking my head and leaving Mira to her laughter.

I went outside and found Zayd leaning against his bedroom door. He looked up, his eyes widening as they took me in. 'Princess Layla, you are a vision,' he said, standing straight.

'His Highness is most kind,' I said flatly.

The prince wore a dark suit, fitted to his lean body. The

navy against his warm brown skin was the perfect contrast. His dark hair was swept to one side and a smile played at the edge of his lips as he continued to look at me.

'Well, *you* could have made an effort,' I said as he continued to stare.

His eyes gleamed. 'So, you made an effort for me? I'm honoured.'

'No, this is just my dinner outfit,' I said irately.

'You wound me, Princess. Shall we?' He gestured towards the end of the corridor.

I stood still, debating whether to actually go with him.

He dropped his arm, chuckling. 'You aren't going to make it easy to win you over, are you?'

'I never told you to,' I said with a shrug.

'Well, if you'd rather stare at a wall until dinner, be my guest,' he said, setting off down the hallway.

I watched his retreating back, weighing my options. What options? I had nothing else to do.

Grudgingly, I set off after the prince, our guards a few paces behind us.

Prince Zayd paused until I caught up with him, an infuriating smile on his face as he looked down at me. 'For a moment, I thought I'd lost any chance of you joining me.'

'Sorry to disappoint you,' I sniped back.

The prince smirked. 'Are you always this ... challenging?'

'Only with people I dislike severely,' I replied sweetly. 'Besides, I never told you to take up this "challenge" of winning my good opinion.'

The prince let out a dramatic sigh. 'Well, when the challenge looks as radiant as you, how can I resist?'

I felt my cheeks warm. I cast him a sideways glare. 'Your attempt at being charming falls flat, Prince.'

'And yet you're blushing,' he said with a grin.

'Cease talking; you're interrupting the silence,' I grumbled.

Zayd chuckled but didn't speak again.

We walked silently as Zayd led the way towards the greenhouse at the end of the grounds, down a number of steps that opened out to another garden. Under the setting sun, the palace was cast in a golden glow, the burnt-orange skies fading slowly away into darkness. I stopped for a moment to take in the breath-taking view.

A thousand flowers were planted around the greenhouse – marigolds, lilies, roses, chrysanthemums – I could hardly count them all. Beautiful colours from pinks and yellows to deep reds and violets dotted the field. It felt like I was walking in a dream.

Zayd bent down and plucked a pink rose from the ground. 'A flower for you, Your Highness. A small token of Dakaria.'

I took the rose from him, our hands slightly brushing again. My skin shivered – from the oncoming cold, I reasoned. 'You'll need more than one flower to convince me you're a nice person,' I said dryly.

Zayd smirked. 'Don't worry, I still have plenty up my sleeve to win your good opinion. This way,' he said.

I followed Zayd deeper into the flower fields until we reached the greenhouse, a large, magnificent glass building with a domed roof and silver fixtures, covered in vines.

'Noor, you and the rest can wait around the perimeter,' Zayd said, talking to one of the guards behind us.

The guard nodded and motioned to Faisal and the others to spread out.

We stepped inside the greenhouse, a wave of intense heat washing over us.

Zayd let out a deep breath as the glass doors closed. 'Finally, some privacy.'

'Are you going to fight me again now we're alone?' I said, raising a brow.

Zayd looked at me, his eyes sweeping over me. 'No, but if you want me to pin you up against the wall again, you only have to ask, Princess.'

My mouth fell open.

'Forgive me, I was merely joking,' he said breezily, walking past me.

A waft of his perfume washed over me, vanilla and golden oud, sweet but strong. Insufferable troll.

I turned on my heel and began walking in the opposite direction.

'Where are you going?' Zayd called from several paces behind.

'Anywhere that isn't near you,' I muttered, looking around me. He was so incredibly irritating. He clearly thought himself a charmer.

Endless greenery surrounded me - large plants that wrapped around posts, towering ferns and flower bushes that boasted a kaleidoscope of colours, and tall trees and plants that fanned across the glass dome ceiling, blocking out most of the light.

It felt surreal in here. I was in another land, my mother was not in earshot, and not a guard in sight. Was this what freedom could feel like? I took a deep breath, inhaling the fresh, earthy scent.

'This is one of my favourite places,' Zayd said, appearing beside me. 'A small reprieve from the daily duties of being a royal.'

'It is lovely,' I said grudgingly.

Zayd chuckled. 'Would you like to sit?' he asked, gesturing to a wicker bench coming up.

'Fine.'

I took a seat, my dress fanning out around me. Zayd sat down beside me, careful to avoid sitting on the material.

A thread stuck out on my dress. I picked at it, wondering how long I'd have to endure this tour with Zayd.

'Can you tell me what I can do to earn your forgiveness?' Zayd asked in a soft voice.

I looked up and found him gazing at me, his olive eyes intent upon my face. He looked almost ... sincere.

'You have no idea how sorry I am,' he said earnestly. 'Tell me, there must be something you'd like to do or see? I'll make it happen if it means you'll forgive me.'

I looked at him curiously. 'You're this desperate for my forgiveness? Why? I already told you I won't tell my mother.'

'We're future rulers. I want us to have good relations for the sake of both our peoples.'

'Do you think I'm like my mother – that I will make for a difficult ruler?' I asked, genuinely interested to hear his answer.

'No, of course not,' Zayd said quickly. 'Her Majesty is not a difficult ruler at all.'

I scoffed. 'You're far too kind. My mother is a cruel woman. You don't need to sing her praises to me. I certainly have none to offer her.'

Zayd's voice was gentle but sure when he spoke. 'I can see you are nothing like her. And I can tell you will be a strong, compassionate ruler when you are Sultana.'

I held back a snort. *If I'm still around by then.*

We sat in awkward silence for a while, the sound of a

fountain trickling somewhere within the greenhouse filling the air.

'It'll be time for dinner soon, no?' I asked.

'Almost. Come, let me show you around some more.' Zayd stood, extending a hand towards me.

I took his warm, rough hand, our fingers twining together. For a moment, I revelled in the touch, the feeling of being held. And then I was standing and Zayd slowly pulled his hand away.

'There's an olive tree over here my father planted for my mother,' Zayd said, gesturing behind us.

'Why an olive tree?'

'He said it reminds him of the colour of her eyes,' Zayd replied with a small chuckle.

'That is quite romantic,' I remarked. I started walking towards it, when I noticed a stray vine on the floor, broken in two. I had the strangest urge to put my hand near it, as though I could mend its stem, when suddenly the vine began to snake its way towards me, moving as if on its own accord on the ground.

I shrieked, stumbling backwards.

Before I could fall, a strong arm grabbed my waist.

His face was so close, soft green eyes looking back into mine. I felt the press of his warm body against mine, heard the pounding of my heart in my ears.

Zayd gently tucked away a wisp of my hair that had come loose, his fingers softly grazing my cheek and leaving a trail of fire along my skin.

Then he seemed to remember himself, breaking the spell and pulling me up. He let go of me quickly. 'Are you all right? There are quite a few stray roots around – apologies, Your Highness.'

I nodded and smoothed down my dress. 'Yes, I'm fine. Thanks.'

Zayd smiled briefly and began walking ahead. He touched his right arm absently.

'We should head to dinner,' I said as the skies grew darker overhead.

The guards joined us as we walked back towards the palace.

'I hope you enjoy the food; I hear our cook has pulled out all the stops for the meal tonight,' Zayd said as we made our way to the dining hall.

'Aren't you coming?' I asked as we stopped outside the grand doors.

'No, I have some business to attend to,' he said. 'I shall see you tomorrow, Your Highness.'

'For another thrilling walk?' I asked dryly.

Zayd's eyes gleamed. 'Is that your way of asking for my company, Princess? I'm flattered.'

I rolled my eyes. 'You are impossible.'

'You still haven't said no,' he said with a grin.

'No,' I said slowly, throwing him a glare before I escaped into the dining hall, my insides twisted with a feeling I didn't understand.

10

Zayd

I walked quickly away from the dining hall, Noor hot
on my heels. Once we were safely in the confines of
my chambers, I asked him to change my bandages
immediately. Something felt wrong with my arm.

'The wound looked like it was closing yesterday, but it
seems you've opened it again,' Noor said, inspecting it. 'I
shall see if the healers can make a salve, Your Highness. It
may speed up the healing process.'

'All right. And send for Sayyidah Shafiya,' I said.

Noor raised a brow. 'Why?'

'Because I think I've found her sister-in-law,' I said,
brandishing a letter from my pocket. I'd finally found it in
Father's correspondence files earlier, addressed to a remote
part of the coastal cities in the south.

Noor looked surprised but nodded. 'I will send for her,
Your Highness. She should arrive tomorrow.'

'Good. Bring her to me immediately – no matter the hour.'

He nodded, re-dressed my wound and left.

'Your Highness, I have your dinner,' Iris called.

'Come in!'

Iris had looked after me since Yunus and I were children.

She was a kindly woman who felt like a second mother. She laid down my dinner in the parlour.

'Care to join me?' I asked.

She smiled affectionately. 'I have already eaten, Your Highness. How are the royal visitors?'

'Interesting,' I said carefully. 'All the rumours about the Sultana are true.'

Iris grimaced. 'That's a shame. The princess seems so lovely.'

'Yes, she is very different from her mother,' I replied. 'It's a pity she isn't the Sultana.'

'Well, you never know, things change all the time,' Iris said absently. 'Do let me know if you need anything else, Your Highness.'

'Thanks, Iris. Have a good evening.' Iris closed the door behind her, leaving me with my dinner and my thoughts.

It was a looming problem that Layla was betrothed to a Fallowmere prince. Perhaps we could have forged a better relationship for our nations if she were on the throne. Though I might have scoffed at Mother's initial instructions to charm Layla, maybe she was right – again. If I could cement a good friendship with her, it might work in my favour. I wondered if the princess would be coronated soon after she married ...

I looked over the reports Noor had left for me in my room – another three pirate attacks at the Silver Port over the course of last night.

If I could just get a water mage to raise a barrier in the sea, or a sinkhole of some sort, it would deter the pirates. My soldiers needed time between attacks. We needed numbers; we needed a reprieve. Especially with Sultana Zahra trying to broker ties with Fallowmere, time was of the essence.

*

94

When I woke at dawn, my arm was still aching. It had festered as I slept, a sharp sting that kept pulsing beneath my skin. I groaned as I struggled to sit upright.

'Your Highness,' Noor called from outside, knocking on my door. 'May I come in?'

'Yes!'

Noor walked in, with Sayyidah Shafiya behind him.

'Sayyidah, how are you?' I asked, trying to keep my breathing even.

'Your Highness,' she said, inclining her head. 'I hope you are well?'

'I'm fine,' I said, blinking rapidly. My head was swimming.

She narrowed her eyes at me. 'You look a bit pale, Your Highness. What's wrong?'

'Well, as you're here,' I muttered. I pulled up my sleeve, revealing my bandaged arm.

She walked over and dropped her bag beside me. With careful hands, she unwrapped the dressing. Her eyes widened.

'What? How? How did you get this?' she demanded, looking at me in horror.

My stomach sank at her reaction. 'I was struck by an arrow at the Silver Port, a few days ago.'

'*Days*?' she repeated angrily. She dropped my arm and began rooting around in her bag.

I gritted my teeth as another wave of pain pulsed through my arm. 'What's wrong with it? The wound should be healing. It's getting worse.' Despite the palace healer having made another salve last night, the black wound on my arm looked anything but better.

'You are poisoned, Your Highness!' Sayyidah Shafiya said

tersely, as another flash of burning pain coursed through my arm.

I looked at the wound – the blood on my arm was bubbling black. I almost keeled over, bile rising in my throat.

'Your Highness, be still!' Sayyidah Shafiya said, pushing me back towards the bed.

'Mind how you handle the prince!' Noor snapped.

'Be quiet, boy!' Sayyidah Shafiya griped. 'Did your parents never teach you how to speak to your elders?'

Noor stopped, seething. 'How can His Highness be poisoned? It was a flesh wound!'

'The arrow must have been laced with poison. Was it pirates that struck you?'

'Yes,' Noor replied as I cursed.

Sayyidah Shafiya took out various herbs and mixed them together with a pestle and mortar. I waited in agony as she set to work applying a thick green salve to my arm.

A cooling sensation spread through the wound. I sighed with relief as the pain ebbed away.

'Better?' Sayyidah Shafiya asked, watching me with grave eyes.

I nodded curtly, my heart rate slowing to its usual pace. 'You have my thanks, Sayyidah,' I huffed out.

'That is a terrible wound, Your Highness,' she said.

'You said it's poison?' I asked.

Her face was lined with worry. 'It is not just any type of poison, Your Highness.'

'What do you mean?' I asked tersely. 'You may speak freely here,' I added when she continued to hesitate.

She looked back at me nervously. 'Whatever struck your arm was laced with a rare poison. It is dark magic, Your Highness. And it will take magic to undo it.'

'What do you mean? Was a mage behind this?' I demanded, fear pooling in my stomach. Mother's warning rang in my mind.

'A dark mage, no doubt.'

I took a steadying breath. 'Those damn pirates. So how do I undo this? I can't walk around with a poisoned arm when I am due to be coronated in weeks!'

Sayyidah Shafiya shifted uncomfortably on her feet. 'Antidotes to this kind of poison require a specific ingredient, Your Highness: the tears of an earth mage.'

I looked at her in confusion. 'The tears of an earth mage?'

'They have powerful healing properties, Your Highness.'

I stilled. 'Could that help cure my father?'

She shifted again. 'I'm afraid nothing can stop death, Your Highness. Not even magic.'

'We could try, couldn't we? If we get these tears for my arm – why couldn't it work for Father? It was just the influenza that overtook him. Surely—'

'Your Highness, an earth mage's gifts are all about nature's balance,' she replied carefully. 'It can be used for illnesses when mixed with other medicinal herbs, but to stop death is unheard of.'

'We will try, at least,' I said finally, refusing to give up hope.

'Might the water mages know an earth mage?' Noor suggested urgently, looking to Sayyidah Shafiya.

'I don't know where my sister-in-law is,' she replied nervously. 'I did try, Your Highness—'

'I know where she is,' I cut in. 'We will go today.'

'Your Highness, you can't travel like this,' Noor protested.

'I have no choice,' I replied. I looked into Sayyidah Shafiya's lined face. 'How long until the poison claims me?'

Sayyidah Shafiya inspected my wound again, her cool fingers turning my arm over. 'It's spreading, Your Highness. You have weeks, maybe a couple of months if we keep renewing the salve every day.'

The air in my lungs left me for a moment. The world was crashing in on me. This couldn't be happening.

Sayyidah Shafiya re-dressed my wound, tying the bandages securely.

'Neither of you are to breathe a word of this to anyone – do you understand?' I demanded.

'Yes, Your Highness,' they chorused.

'I mean it,' I said severely. 'Nobody can know, especially not our enemies.'

'You have my word, my prince,' Sayyidah Shafiya said solemnly.

'Good. I do not take treason lightly,' I warned.

She flinched.

I felt immediately like an arse, but I had a kingdom to keep secure. 'Noor, have a room made up for Sayyidah Shafiya in the servants' quarters. She will be tending to my arm from now on and living in the palace until I'm cured. And both of you get ready to leave in an hour. We need to find the water mages.'

They nodded before withdrawing from the room.

The pain had ebbed slightly from my arm, allowing my head to clear. I got up and walked slowly over to the window, pressing my warm forehead against the cool glass.

Poisoned? Weeks to live?

Everything my parents had hoped for me – the years of training, the studies, the missions – would all be for nothing.

I couldn't die, not now – not with Father ... How would Mother and Yunus cope?

Yunus.

If he hadn't left the bloody palace ... If he'd just listened instead of trying to prove himself!

I forced myself to take steady breaths. I couldn't think about that now. There was no undoing what had happened.

But how would he fare as Sultan? If Yunus had to take the throne, with me and Father both gone, our enemies would take Dakaria before he could adjust.

I couldn't let this happen.

As if I'd summoned the devil with my thoughts alone, Yunus bounded into my chambers.

'Coming to breakfast, Brother?' he called in his mocking voice.

Anger simmered inside my gut. 'Get lost, Yunus,' I replied.

'Well, good morning to you too,' he said dryly, leaning against the doorframe.

I had half a mind to hit him around the head as he lounged there, the picture of ease. 'Do you want something?'

'I see we're going with extra arsehole today, then,' he said with a snort. 'What's got you in such a foul mood?'

'My arm is still recovering after I took an arrow for you,' I said through gritted teeth.

Yunus looked abashed for a moment. 'I'm sorry, Brother. Perhaps you should rest for a few days. Your arm might heal faster.'

'I don't have the luxury of rest,' I snapped at him.

He flinched.

'Was there something else?' I snapped again as he continued to stand there, floundering.

'Um, I was going to ask if you minded whether I had Princess Layla's first dance,' he said in a quieter voice than before.

'Dance? What are you on about?'

'The ball to welcome the princess and Sultana Zahra in two nights?' Yunus said, looking at me nervously.

'I wasn't informed,' I said. 'Dance with whomever you want. Why would I object?'

'Just checking – protocol etcetera, as you're our heir apparent and she's theirs,' he said. 'I'll, um, leave you to rest, Brother.' He left quickly.

Guilt washed over me. I sighed, kicking out at an armchair.

Another knock sounded on my door.

'What now?' I fumed, storming over to my door. 'I don't have time for constant chit-chat!' If it was Yunus again—

I opened the door, and realised too late that the person stalking off was Layla.

Her door slammed shut.

Shit.

Noor grimaced at me. 'Her Highness was asking if you wanted to walk to breakfast together.'

I sighed through my teeth. My arm was poisoned, I'd pissed off our enemy's daughter – *again* – and our kingdom was insecure. Some Sultan I was going to make – *if* I made it.

'Send for Iris, please,' I said to Noor. 'I need to find some gifts.'

11

Layla

So much for friendship. I flopped down into an armchair in the parlour, my mood soured. I thought I'd been too harsh at the greenhouse last night. Perhaps extending an olive branch to a fellow future ruler was the diplomatic thing to do. Apparently not.

Prince Zayd had the manners of a gorilla. I wouldn't be bothering with him again.

'Are you okay, Your Highness?' Mira asked from my bedroom as she tidied the sheets. 'I thought you were going for breakfast?'

'I am. I just wanted to change my jewellery; it's too heavy.' I took off the golden emerald-studded choker and put it back inside its box. It felt so excessive to be dressed like I was attending a wedding for mealtimes.

I smoothed down my green lehenga and eventually left my room. The door to the prince's room was closed. Troll.

Yunus seemed quiet at breakfast as well, which just gave my mother more space to talk at Sultana Aysha as we ate. I didn't even register half the things Mother spoke about – something about how lavish my wedding would be, but how much more extravagant her own had been.

I retreated back to my room after breakfast and sank into my bed. I pulled out one of the books I'd stuffed under the bed. *A History of Mages.*

My heart began to race a little, even though I was alone. If Mother ever found out, I would be sitting at the bottom of the dungeon, or worse.

There were chapters on where mages had lived, the types of relics and weapons they had created ... but it was all social and economic information. I needed specifics.

I opened the second book I'd taken from the library. *An Exploration of Mages and Their Affinities.*

'*Mages are born with one affinity, either for earth, fire, water or wind ...*'

I skipped hurriedly through the pages. There were details about the kinds of magic mages could wield, the way they could interact with Earth and its atmosphere ...

The last chapter was titled 'Mages with more than One Affinity'.

My heart sank.

After the chapter title page, the rest of the text was missing. The remaining folds were jagged – at least six papers had been torn out. But why?

I'd taken one more book: *The Dark Age and the Fate of Mages.* I leafed through, but saw nothing of consequence, just the names and details of some mages who had lived in the land centuries ago ...

I thought the burnt chair had been a fluke. A hallucination. But in the greenhouse last night, the vine had undoubtedly come towards me, as if calling to me. Could I be a mage? And could I have two affinities? How was that even possible?

I pushed the books to the side. My eyes darted around the room before I pulled the candlestick on my bedside table towards me. Some magnetic force drew my hand closer to the unlit wick, a surge of energy coursing through my veins from a deep well within me.

Heat pulsed from my palm.

I yanked my hand back, but not before a flame flickered to life on the candle.

I quickly blew it out, watching the black smoke tendrils disappear into the air as panic swelled in my chest. The smell of the flame hung in the air before me.

Unwanted tears sprang to my eyes. I was a dead girl walking. Mother would never allow this.

The screams of the mages trapped in the dungeons at home filled my ears.

'No, no, no,' I whispered, sobs threatening to overtake me. My chest felt so tight.

Even if I could hide this from Mother, how could I hide it from my future husband? The amount of time we'd be forced to spend together ... a Fallowmere prince, no less. The same people who had gone on a bloody rampage through the Eastern world to purge mages from the earth. My marriage would be a death sentence.

I had to get away.

A sharp knock sounded on my door. I ignored it, trying to breathe through the tears and panic.

The knocking grew more persistent.

'What?' I called out.

I heard the outside door open and footsteps. 'Princess, it's me,' Zayd called.

I stopped and hastily wiped at my face. 'Just wait in the parlour. I'm coming.'

'Okay,' he replied.

Damn him, what was he doing here *now*, of all times? I checked my reflection in the mirror and dried my face on my sleeve. My eyes were rimmed red – I'd have to say I was having a sneezing fit or something.

I opened my bedroom doors, stepping into the parlour. 'Can I help you?' I asked briskly.

Zayd stood by the window, dressed in a fine black jacket and sherwani, his hair neatly combed to one side. His olive eyes looked me over, confusion growing on his face.

'I just wanted to apologize for earlier. I hadn't really woken up yet and I didn't realize it was you,' he said, gesturing to the table.

A large bouquet of pink and white roses took over most of the table.

'What's this?' I asked warily.

'A gesture, to apologize.'

'Fine,' I said, twisting my hands together. 'Is that all?'

Zayd looked at me curiously, his head tilting to the side. 'What's the matter? You look upset.'

'Nothing,' I said shortly. 'Don't you have business to attend to?'

'It can wait,' he said, still watching me. 'If there's anything wrong with your stay, I can try and make arrangements so you're more comfortable?'

'There's nothing wrong,' I said. 'Your gesture is appreciated. You can go.'

Zayd didn't leave. Instead, he crossed the small distance between us. He towered over me, his eyes intent, searching mine. 'If you ever need someone to talk to, Princess, you have my confidence,' he said quietly, putting his hands over mine, stilling them. 'I really do want us to be friends.'

I looked back up at him, frozen by the weight of sincerity in his gaze. His touch was grounding, his fingers soft against mine. I almost believed him, almost wanted to spill all of my secrets to somebody who might actually listen.

'Layla, are you sure you're all right?' Zayd asked, concern etched on his face.

My treacherous heart thumped unevenly. I pulled my hands out of his – they were cold in the absence of his warmth. 'I'm fine,' I said, my voice snappier than I intended.

A flash of disappointment crossed his features. 'Fine.'

I stalked back into my room, shutting the door. I heard Zayd leave a moment later.

What was all that about? I stretched out my fingers, as though they stung from where he'd held them.

I stepped out onto the balcony for some fresh air. The fields stretching beyond the palace were light green, bleached by the constant sun. In the distance, dark clouds encroached, promising rain. I imagined myself running into them and disappearing into the unknown, where I wouldn't have to put up with this nonsense parade of being a royal.

And leave your kingdom? Father's disappointed voice rang in my mind.

But he wasn't here any more. I had nothing but the future my mother was orchestrating. And if what I feared was happening to me was actually happening … there would be no future for me at all.

12

Zayd

We travelled underneath the rising sun towards the mountains of Chittabagh, down towards the south. Noor kept glancing at me as we sat in the carriage. The fiery pain in my arm had been coming and going, though the salve stifled it somewhat.

'Are you quite sure this is safe, Your Highness?' Noor asked cautiously, eyeing Sayyidah Shafiya warily. She sat opposite us, her eyes roaming the passing scenery.

'We don't have a choice,' I replied.

The royal carriage trundled along down to the coast, winding in and out of towns and through muddied lanes, sheets of rain having begun to fall around us.

Dakaria in the rain was a sight to behold. The towering palm trees and thick bushes came to life in vivid greens, stark against the clouded skies. But this rain was both our blessing and curse; no doubt a number of towns would flood if the rain kept up as the bruised skies seemed to suggest they would.

Our people were desperate for a solution to the flooding we suffered during the wet months; the new houses and roads were not being built fast enough. I only hoped there wouldn't be a protest at our doorstep while the Sultana of Sawan was here.

As the rain lightened some, we finally came to our destination at the foot of the mountains. My guards set up a tent for us to shelter in, lighting a fire in the centre.

I pulled a wicker chair closer to the fire, attempting to warm away the cold that had settled in my bones as we travelled here. I wondered what might be happening back at the palace as we waited. I hadn't managed to find Yunus before I left to apologize for my curtness, only Layla. Not that it had gone well.

I wondered if she was actually that angry at me, or if something else was bothering her. She'd looked like she'd been crying. There was an aura of loneliness around her, perhaps the result of having the mother she did. It bothered me more than I cared to admit. I found myself wanting to befriend her not only for the kingdom's sake or on Mother's instructions – but because she seemed to need a friend.

'Your Highness,' Noor said quietly. 'The chief of the mages is here.'

I snapped out of my reverie, looking towards the tent flap as it was pulled open to admit a woman shrouded in an onyx cloak. She lowered her hood, revealing a withered face and a shock of raven hair that was wound in a braid that scraped the floor. Her eyes were dark, almost grey. She met my gaze with a blank expression.

'Prince Zayd,' she said in a rasping voice.

'It is customary to bow before the crown prince,' Noor said pointedly.

'I do not bow to your royals,' she replied evenly.

'Please, sit,' I said, gesturing to a chair opposite me. 'Sayyidah ... ?'

'Just Roshni will do,' she replied, moving as though she were gliding to take her seat.

'Thank you for agreeing to meet.'

'Do not thank me yet,' she said, eyeing me curiously. 'I have not agreed to your demands.'

'I believe you last had contact with my father some years ago,' I began. 'I am hopeful that we can open a dialogue between our communities again.'

Roshni considered me with her dark eyes. 'You seem sincere, boy. But you will do well to remember that it was your ancestors who failed to protect us from Fallowmere. Had you royals truly been leaders for all of your people, there would be more than a handful of us alive today.'

'I cannot right the past, but I can do something about the present,' I replied. 'And I have been informed the Fallowmere are returning. The Sultana of Sawan has arranged her daughter's marriage to a Fallowmere prince. They marry in a few months.' The words tasted bitter in my mouth.

Roshni's face hardened. 'They dare to darken our shores again?'

'Sawan wants our silver mines. Sultana Zahra will use the Fallowmere to conquer us.'

'So, you want the mages to protect your silver? This is why you have been trying to contact us,' she said with a croaky laugh. 'How convenient that you seem to remember us only when you are bereft of other options.'

'Please, Roshni – it is for the good of Dakaria,' Sayyidah Shafiya said.

'Is that you, Sister-in-law?' Roshni said, eyeing Shafiya with no affection. 'Working for the royals as well now, are you? You and my foolish brother were well suited.'

Sayyidah Shafiya bristled. 'My husband was no fool.'

'No, he was a sell-out,' Roshni said hatefully.

'That didn't seem to bother you when you were accepting the money he sent you every month,' Shafiya replied coldly.

Roshni glowered back at her.

'Why don't we leave family politics aside?' I said carefully. 'I'm sure we can come to a favourable agreement for you, Roshni.'

'And what is it you want from us, *child*?' Roshni asked bitingly, turning her dark eyes back on me.

I bristled. 'You can manipulate water, yes?'

She nodded stiffly.

'I need you to raise a barrier in the sea, to stop the pirates trying to attack us night and day. My soldiers need rest – especially with Fallowmere on the way.'

'And what do we get in return?'

'This is not a simple favour,' I said. 'I would like to propose a truce: under my rule, you will have the freedom and protection to travel and settle within the land wherever you wish, with monetary support from the palace.'

'You cannot buy our magic,' Roshni snapped.

'I am not trying to. I am trying to keep our country safe. When the Fallowmere come back, it is only a matter of time before war breaks out. But with the water mages on our side, we stand a chance of surviving – *all* of us. If a truce is not enough, then what else do you require?'

'There is nothing you could offer us,' Roshni growled. 'Find more soldiers to defend your land. The mages will never forgive or forget what the leaders of yesterday damned us to. We were near-exterminated because the Fallowmere didn't understand our magic. Did you know my mother had to hide beneath my dead father's body so she wouldn't be killed by the Fallowmere? That the mages and their families were refused asylum by your ancestors?' Roshni's voice was a hiss. 'So do not speak to me of stakes and war, boy. The mages will not help the same people who turned their backs on us.' She rose from her chair with an eerie grace and turned to leave.

'Wait, Roshni,' I called, standing. 'I am not my ancestors. I wish to put things right – for mages and humans to live in harmony as they once did before.'

'We don't need you. We will walk freely again, when the time is right,' Roshni replied in a serene voice.

'What do you mean?' I asked.

'It means we have no need of you or your petty prizes. Farewell, boy. I hope you find what you are looking for – but I will never help you.'

'Wait, please. Let us discuss this,' I implored, gesturing for her to sit back down. I fought a wince as my arm spasmed with pain.

Roshni's eyes zeroed in on my arm. 'What's wrong with you?' She sniffed the air. 'There's something dark here.'

I looked at Noor. His face was set in a grim expression.

Roshni looked at me, her eyes widening in shock. 'There is great darkness around you, boy. But also … something else.' She inched closer, peering at my other hand. Her brow furrowed, as if she was seeing something that wasn't visible to the naked eye.

'This is … strange magic indeed. I can smell it on you, but it's not *from* you,' she said curiously.

'Can you help him?' Sayyidah Shafiya asked tightly. 'We need the tears of—'

'An earth mage,' Roshni finished, stepping back. 'This is no ordinary poison, is it?'

I was silent.

'Do you know of anyone?' Sayyidah Shafiya pressed.

'No. My family are the only mages I am aware of,' Roshni replied, all trace of frostiness gone from her voice. She looked at me strangely. 'Perhaps we can be of use to each other after all, boy.'

'What do you mean?'

She looked over her shoulder at Noor and Shafiya.

'Both of you wait outside, please,' I ordered. 'Now,' I said as Noor began to protest.

Shafiya and Noor left hesitantly.

'Who was last in your company?' Roshni asked in a quiet voice, her eyes searching my face.

'What's it worth to you to know?' I countered.

Roshni actually smiled. 'The Sultan speaks. There is something about you. Something ... different. The last person you touched before you came here, perhaps?'

Layla? 'What is it to you?' I asked again.

She pursed her lips. 'Let's just say I need to verify something. Bring the person to me.'

'In exchange for what?'

'Perhaps my family and I can assist at the Silver Port,' she said grudgingly.

'You were adamant you'd never help us, and now you've suddenly changed your mind?'

'I said *perhaps*.'

'Perhaps isn't good enough,' I retorted. 'I want your word you'll agree to help at the Silver Port.'

She glared at me. 'You uphold your side of the bargain, and then I'll uphold mine.'

111

I nodded. 'Meet me in the Dukhha town square in three days' time, nine o'clock.'

Roshni surveyed me distrustfully. 'If you try anything, I'll flood the entire city.'

'You will not harm my company,' I growled.

'I would never,' she said indignantly. 'We are not barbarians like you royals. I merely wish to speak with this person.'

'Speak to them? About what?' I pressed.

'It does not concern you,' she retorted. 'Do we have a deal?'

I surveyed the water mage carefully. She just wanted a meeting with Layla. I would take a full guard. No harm would come to her. And I'd get the protection for the port we desperately needed.

'Very well. We have a deal,' I said.

Roshni nodded, throwing me a glare before stalking out of the tent.

What was it she had sensed around me from Layla? Could she tell she was another royal? Was Roshni trying to forge a new alliance? Layla would certainly be more agreeable than her mother.

'What was that about?' Noor asked as he and Shafiya returned to the tent.

'I'm not sure I know myself,' I replied.

It was nightfall by the time we returned to the palace. My head was throbbing with an ache that had everything to do with my arm and the conversation with Roshni. The vitriol in her speech, the contempt in her eyes. The bargain we had struck. And no earth mage.

Three days to convince Layla to leave the palace with me.

Three days to win her over. Three days before I might finally have some protection for the Silver Port, leaving Yunus with one less problem if I didn't find a cure.

13

Layla

'Princess, can I get you anything?' Mira asked.

I had spent most of the day in bed and had no intention of making the night any different. There was too much going on in my head. All I wanted was to shut everything off.

'I'm fine. You may go, Mira. Get some rest,' I said, turning away from her onto my other side.

'See you in the morning, Princess,' she said gently, retreating from my room.

I blew out a sigh, flopping onto my back. Sleep had evaded me all day. I wasn't one to sleep during the day, and it felt like there was this current pulsing through my body I couldn't shake.

Perhaps I ought to try harder to sleep now that night was here. But it didn't matter how long I pressed my eyes shut, I was still conscious.

I kicked off the bedsheets and got out of bed, and traipsed into the parlour. The room was cast in a golden glow emanating by candles dotted around.

A small tug at my fingertips made me want to lift my hand up.

My heart began to race.

Why did the flames call to me so?

I got up quickly and blew out all the candles, but on the last one ... it was like an itch beneath my palm. I found my hand moving of its own accord.

The flame grew brighter, surging towards me. Golden flames tickled my skin.

I turned my palm over and saw no burn marks, felt no discomfort.

What if I ...

I waved my hands over an extinguished candle, heat coursing through my veins, and jumped as a flame flickered to life.

I gasped.

Slowly, I edged around the room, bringing each candle back to life. My heart hammered away in my chest as panic and wonder swirled inside me.

I blew the candles out again. I placed my hand over the flames in the hearth and twisted them up, watching with wonder as the columns of light grew. Could I ...

Driven by some primal instinct, I flicked my hands downwards and watched with amazement as the flames disappeared entirely, leaving me in darkness.

I hurried back to the bedroom to retrieve the books on mages, leafing through until I found something.

'Mages begin to manifest their abilities as they come of age. The reason why is not known, though many speculate that the affinities lie dormant until a balance according to nature's laws is enacted in the body, and this is the time when a mage has left behind childhood and is venturing into adulthood.'

My eighteenth birthday was only a few weeks away. Fear coiled around me. Perhaps I was dreaming?

Or perhaps I needed to accept the truth.

Either I had to learn how to control this, or be far, far away from my mother before the powers fully manifested. We were only here for a few more days. I had to find my opportunity to escape, and I had to do it soon.

I felt hollow when I woke up in the morning. I kept wanting to believe that this wasn't happening. All through breakfast, I avoided my mother's gaze in case she could detect a change in me.

'Would anyone like to go for a walk?' Sultana Aysha asked as the servants cleared the plates away.

'I'm not feeling too well – I think I'll go lie down,' I said, hastily excusing myself.

'Still?' Mother remarked unhappily. 'You were holed up in your room all of yesterday too. Have you caught something? Perhaps it's the food here.'

'No, it's not that,' I said quickly as I saw Sultana Aysha's nostrils flare. 'Just my monthly cycle.'

Mother's eyes widened with understanding. 'Oh. All right.'

'I'll have the servants make you a special brew. It always helped me,' Sultana Aysha said.

'Her Majesty is most kind, thank you,' I said, feeling terrible for lying.

When I returned to my chambers, another bouquet of blue hydrangeas and beautiful silver gypsophila sat on my table. I reached for it, and the flowers seemed to respond to me. The petals unfurled further, their colours deepening. I quickly pulled my hand back.

'What are these?' I asked Mira as she came from my bedchamber carrying old sheets. I hoped she couldn't hear the tremor in my voice.

'Prince Zayd delivered them earlier for you,' she replied, an excited smile on her face.

That annoying prince and his games. He was bordering on obsessive with his insistence we be friends. I didn't have time for this – not when so much was happening to me.

I snatched the flowers up, careful only to hold them by the paper they were wrapped in, and I marched out of my room and across the corridor to Prince Zayd's door. 'Is the prince inside?' I asked his guard, who looked rather alarmed when he saw my expression.

'Yes, Your Highness,' he said, pulling the door open.

He wasn't in his parlour. I threw the flowers down on his table and charged towards the doors to his bedroom, banging my fist on the wood.

'Where's the fire?' Zayd said angrily, pulling his doors open.

The angry remark I had locked and loaded died on my tongue. My hand fell to my side.

Zayd stood before me dressed in nothing but a towel slung low across his hips. His warm, brown torso glimmered with beads of water; his wet hair was slicked back. That sculpted chest had to be carved out of marble. My eyes flicked to a bandage wrapped around his right arm.

Our eyes met and, for a moment, I was sure he could hear the uneven thumping of my heart in the silence of our weighted gaze. Desire coursed like heat through my body.

'Can I help you, Princess?' Zayd asked pointedly.

'I was just ...' Words evaded me. I'd seen handsome guys before – not that I could recall any right now – but this was ...

I lost my train of thought as I realized we were standing inches away from each other, transfixed. Glistening droplets of water were dripping down his torso, the tops of his muscled arms; there were new and faded scars scattered across his taut skin.

'You were just ... ?' he prompted, that ever-present smirk threatening to reveal itself to me.

'What happened to your arm?' I asked, snapping out of whatever *that* was.

'Field injury,' he replied shortly. He pulled back, closing his bedroom doors on me.

Crap. Should I leave?

I waited for a moment, uncertain. I should leave. He'd seen me ogling him. Best to get out of here before I humiliated myself more.

I had my hand on the door handle when I heard Zayd's bedroom doors open again.

'Layla, wait,' Zayd's low voice called.

I turned slowly, my face heating up.

He was dressed now, crisp white clothes covering his body, but in his haste the khamis was damp, reminding me of how uncovered he had been moments ago.

I cleared my throat, finding myself suddenly reaching for formal language. Anything that would dispel the tension in the air. 'Forgive me, Your Highness, I didn't mean to intrude.'

'It's fine,' he said, leaning against the doorframe. 'Did you need something, Princess?'

'I was returning your flowers,' I said, remembering why I had come, gesturing to them on the table.

A smile tugged the edge of his lips. 'Most people just say thank you,' he replied.

'I didn't ask for them,' I said pointedly.

'I didn't ask for you to walk in on me half-naked, but here we are,' he replied, arching a dark brow.

'That was an accident ... I didn't know,' I said hurriedly, heat flaming my cheeks.

'Didn't you?' he replied, levelling me with a piercing gaze that made me want to retreat. A dangerous smile played on his face. 'You took no pains to stop staring at me until I shut the doors.'

Embarrassment made my cheeks flare. 'I don't want your flowers.'

'Why?' he asked, still watching me intently.

'I don't need them,' I said shortly. 'And if you're trying to change my opinion of you, you're failing.'

'Perhaps I should go topless more often; I think your opinion of me has definitely changed,' he said with another smirk.

'Wishful thinking, is that?' I countered, refusing to rise to his bait.

'Well, you haven't said no,' he replied, smug.

He was so infuriating. 'Just stay away from me.'

'You're the one who came to my room.'

This wasn't going how I intended. I let out a frustrated sigh and turned to leave.

'Wait,' Zayd said, grabbing my hand.

Heat danced along my skin. I quickly pulled my hand away. 'What?'

I could see the amusement fade from his olive eyes as he looked down at me. 'Why don't I take you for a boat ride before dinner?' I wanted to say something snarky, but the sincere look in his eyes melted my acidity. 'Unless you want me to go round telling everyone you walked in on me naked,' he added with a half smile.

'You came out in a towel. I didn't force you to!' I spluttered.

'You barged into my chambers, banging on the doors demanding to see me,' he said indifferently. 'Rumours travel fast in the palace.'

My eyes widened with horror. 'You wouldn't.'

He leant closer, smiling. 'Try me.'

The heady scent of his golden oud drifted over me, inviting me in. I stood rooted to the spot as Zayd loomed above me. 'I want us to be friends, but I keep messing it up. Let me make it up to you. One boat ride, please?'

My stomach fluttered with nerves. 'One boat ride,' I found myself agreeing. 'If you offend me again, I'm throwing you in the river.'

'Trying to see me wet again?' he asked with a cocky grin.

'Don't flatter yourself, Prince,' I said scathingly, stepping away towards the door. 'I've seen better abs than yours.'

He let out a low whistle. 'You wound me, Princess.'

'I wish,' I grumbled, hurrying out of his chambers. I should have stabbed him when he'd given me the chance.

His low chuckle echoed behind me as I hurried back to my room. My face was going to burst into flames from embarrassment.

Thankfully, Zayd wasn't at lunch, so I didn't have to see his smug face again. I wasn't sure what the point of us forging good relations was - especially when I wasn't planning to go home to Sawan. Not that he - or anyone, for that matter - knew that. A boat ride sounded nice and all but ... I needed real-world experience, without a trail of guards hovering around me, my every move watched by someone.

Perhaps if Zayd was so desperate to be friends, I could use that to my advantage.

That afternoon, Sultana Aysha took me and Mother to the palace hammam. Mercifully, Mother and I were given separate chambers. I relaxed into an afternoon of being scrubbed with turmeric and sea salts, my skin infused with rosehip and argan oil, and my hair massaged with coconut oil and washed with a soap bar made of marigold and rice grains. To finish, I had a warm bath made of milk and rose petals. I was entirely melted, my body happily relaxed for the first time in a while.

I smelled incredible as I grudgingly emerged from the bath and dried off. The servants seemed so at ease here, laughing and smiling with one another. At home, our servants walked around on tenterhooks.

'How was the hammam, Princess?' Mira asked as I returned to my room.

'So good,' I replied. 'Just what I needed, I think. You should definitely go.'

Mira smiled sheepishly. 'I went last night, actually. The other servants said we're allowed to use the hammam too. Don't tell the Sultana, though,' she added with a grimace.

'I definitely won't.'

She smiled. 'I have your dinner outfit ready, Your Highness.' She gestured towards the dress hanging from the armoire.

She helped me change and sat me down in front of the dressing table, brushing my hair back into a sleek bun and leaving a couple of strands out at the front. Just as she was brushing rouge over my lips and cheeks, someone knocked on the door.

'I'll go see who it is,' Mira murmured, hurrying away.

I heard a low voice at the door, and the hairs all over my body stood up. In my steamy euphoria from the hammam,

I'd forgotten that I had agreed to go on a boat ride with the prince.

Mira returned with a knowing smile. 'His Highness Prince Zayd is here to escort you to the boats. I told him you'd be five minutes.'

Before I could reply, Mira was attacking my face: putting kohl under my eyes, using some kind of bristled wand to lengthen my lashes, and adding diamond jewels to my neck and ears.

'Tell the prince I'm sick,' I said, swatting Mira's hand away as she forced bangles up my arms.

'I cannot tell lies, Your Highness,' Mira said innocently.

I rolled my eyes. 'Why are you enjoying this so much?'

'You deserve to have some fun, Princess,' she said quietly.

'You are ridiculous.'

'And you are leaving now,' she said decisively, hurrying over to the door.

'Mira, wait!'

Before I could stop her, Mira was already pulling on the door handles.

14

Zayd

The doors to Layla's chambers swung open.

'Your Highness.' Mira curtseyed, stepping back to reveal Layla.

It was my turn to gawk. She was the picture of elegance in a form-fitting pink dress studded with simple crystals. A matching dupatta fell down her head, her dark hair just visible beneath with a few tempting strands framing her face. Her lips had been painted a dangerous shade of red, and those fierce amber eyes were rimmed with kohl. Her golden skin was glowing, and floral notes washed over me as she approached with an unimpressed look on her face.

'Princess, radiant as ever,' I said.

'Come on then, how soon are you going to try and drown me?' she replied.

I fought a smile. 'A little faith, Princess.'

I led the way to the boathouse. A small river lay south of the palace, giving out onto an underwater forest that I hoped might interest the princess. As far as winning her good opinion went, it was clear all my ideas so far had been useless. This had to go well tonight, otherwise there was no way I was going to be able to convince her to leave the palace with me.

Noor went into the boathouse and pulled out a large wooden canoe. He looked at me disapprovingly.

'It's hardly any exertion,' I muttered to him. 'Keep a distance with the other guards.'

He nodded unhappily.

I helped Noor drag the boat onto the green waters, taking the large oars from him. My arm flared with pain, but I persisted.

'Give me one,' Layla said as she lithely stepped in.

'Sorry?'

'Give. Me. One.' She spoke slowly, holding her hand out.

'Your Highness, I can steer,' her guard said, springing forward.

'I can row a boat, for crying out loud,' she huffed, annoyed. 'Give it.'

I gave her the one my injured arm would have had to hold. 'Are you sure?'

'I'm not a child,' she replied, taking a seat on the right side.

Heaven help me. With an attitude like that, I had no chance of winning her over. I sat down beside her and placed the oar into its oarlock while our guards got their boats out.

'Let's go fast so they can't keep up with us,' Layla said gleefully, looking back at her guard.

'Your wish is my command, Princess,' I said, turning the oar.

We set off down the river, away from the looming white palace. A cool breeze brushed over us as we travelled through the waters, the sun slowly beginning to set above our heads. The sky cast a hazy orange glow as we wended further downstream, into a thicket of trees.

'Oh, wow,' she murmured.

We turned a corner and entered the underwater forest. Tall trees submerged in the green waters sprouted high, their thick boughs tangled like snakes as they curled upwards. A canopy of leaves above us blocked out almost all the light, leaving us with a dim glow. It always felt a bit like a reprieve here – another time and place, somewhere the outside world couldn't intrude upon.

We continued through the dark underwater forest, the birds overhead chirping their evening song. I chanced a glance at Princess Layla and felt relief to see her with a soft smile on her lips, her face serene. Her eyes roamed the surroundings, her bangles clinking like windchimes as she rowed.

'Are you OK, Princess?' I asked.

Layla turned to look at me, raising a brow. 'I am capable of exercising my arm muscles, you know.'

'I never questioned your capabilities, Princess,' I replied. Why was she always this argumentative?

'I'm fine,' she said. And then: 'Thanks.'

I smiled. I was counting that as a win.

The trees began to thin, giving way to open sky again. We emerged from the last circle of trees into a field of water lilies, their pink flowers dotted across the entire river. Green hills loomed alongside the riverbank, the waters turning more blue than green as the river widened out.

'We can stop for a bit,' I said, resting the oar in its hold.

Layla obliged, putting her oar down. I watched as she looked around with a peaceful smile on her face.

'Did we manage to lose the guards?' she asked.

'They're keeping a distance back there,' I said, gesturing to where Noor and the others waited several yards away, closer to the underwater forest.

'Dakaria is really beautiful,' Layla said.

'You're welcome here any time,' I said

'Well, who can say no to an offer like that?' she replied dryly.

I shook my head, smiling despite myself. 'Do you know how long you're staying for?' The ball was tomorrow, so I wouldn't expect Layla and the Sultana to leave so soon after, but who knew – especially with the princess's own marriage on the horizon.

'Why? Eager to get rid of us already?'

I opened my mouth to protest but she interrupted me.

'I'm joking, I'm joking. Sorry, I know I'm giving you a hard time.' Her smile was more of a smirk, but it was progress at least.

'It's fine. I assume you don't have a lot of friends in Sawan, so your manners are a bit unrefined,' I countered.

Layla scoffed. 'Well, you're not that wrong,' she mumbled, looking away.

'I was just joking, Princess,' I said lightly. *Shit.* I'd landed my foot in it again. 'I think Yunus is probably *my* only friend – and that's when we're not pissed off with each other.'

Although the palace was still visible in the distance and our guards were nearby, it felt like we were miles away on an ocean made of leaves and flowers, the sweet musk of the lilies perfuming the air, the golden rays of the sun casting everything in a magical light. Layla closed her eyes for a moment, the last embers of the sun casting a golden glow on her face.

I was struck by her beauty. She was a vision, a flower in bloom amongst the water lilies, sitting like the subject of a painting.

'My father was my best friend,' she said in a quiet voice, breaking me out of my thoughts.

'From what I have heard, he was a great man,' I said. 'My father always spoke highly of him.'

'He was a great man,' she echoed fondly, looking at me with sombre eyes. 'He was incredibly kind.'

A quality her mother evidently lacked. 'I'm sorry, Princess. You must miss him terribly.'

'More than I can say,' she murmured, looking away again. 'How is your father doing? It must be a difficult time for your family.'

My stomach sank. 'He's a strong man. I'm hopeful he'll beat this illness – even if everyone else thinks he won't.'

Layla cast me a knowing glance, a sad smile on her face. 'It was hard for me to accept my father was dying too. He fell suddenly ill; I was so sure he'd recover, even though the healers said to make preparations.'

Despair crept into me. 'How did you accept it?'

Layla sighed. 'Over time, you have no choice. You keep waiting for them to come back, so sure they'll just turn up out of the blue. But they never do. That's the harsh thing about death; it's so final.'

Her words made my gut feel hollow. I wasn't ready to lose my father, doubted I ever would be. But I couldn't quite give up on my plan to find an earth mage, even if it was foolish.

'Your Highness,' Noor called. 'Dinner will be served soon.'

'I guess that's our cue,' I said.

Layla nodded, and we picked up the oars again, rowing back. An air of apprehension coloured Layla's face as we dismounted.

'Not looking forward to dinner?' I asked.

Layla shrugged. 'I prefer eating in my rooms; I like the quiet.'

'So have I won your good opinion yet?' I asked hopefully.

Layla looked up at me shrewdly. 'That remains to be seen. I told you I'm not so easily impressed.'

'So, what does impress you?' I asked.

Layla shrugged. 'I'll let you work that one out, Prince.'

I took a step closer, hoping my luck would persist. 'How about a trip somewhere beyond the palace grounds?' I asked quietly. 'Somewhere without everyone watching.'

Layla looked at me in surprise. 'Really?'

'Would you come?' I asked. 'I could show you the city square, the night markets ... ?'

'When?' I saw a hopeful glimmer in her eyes.

'The night after the welcome ball.'

To my surprise, Layla considered me for a moment. 'Maybe. But how?'

'Leave that to me,' I said.

I stepped back at the sound of our guards approaching.

'Thanks for the boat ride,' Layla said, smiling.

'Wow, is that an actual smile?' I pretended to be shocked.

She rolled her eyes. 'I could still push you into the river.'

'Keen to see me wet again?' I asked, grinning as her face turned red. I hadn't forgotten the way her eyes had roamed over me earlier. I enjoyed that blush on her cheeks far more than I cared to admit.

'You seem rather desperate to be naked in front of me again,' Layla said, raising a brow.

I shrugged, a smile tugging at the edge of my lips. 'I just like giving my fans what they want.'

'If you need help carrying that big head of yours back inside, let me know,' she said dryly, shaking her own as she left the boathouse.

I watched Layla go, the end of her dupatta dancing in the wind. She was definitely warming up to me. It seemed like I might be able to secure the water mages' help after all.

15

Zayd

The following night, the banquet hall had been transformed into some type of glacial forest for the welcome ball.

Silver trees had been placed all around the space, their leaves shimmering from the glow of thousands of candles that lit up the room. White cloth-tables were topped with elaborate ice sculptures, and long white flowers hung from the arched ceiling, coating every inch. A sea of people milled about, dressed in fine sherwanis and saris of varying shades of silver, and adorned in endless jewels.

I pulled at the collar of my clothes – a fitted grey sherwani with intricately patterned silver thread-work. I stifled a yawn; I had spent the day holed up in my study working on plans for how best to utilize the water mages and was in desperate need of my bed.

Music wafted in the air from the sitar quartet in the centre of the room. More people arrived, members of the court and their families.

'I heard you took the princess for a boat ride yesterday,' Mother said, as she batted my hand away and adjusted my collar herself. 'Good work, beta.'

I nodded. If only she knew. Last night at dinner, Layla had been warmer towards me. Not friendly, but at least not outright hostile. I just needed to make sure I didn't piss her off again tonight so she would leave the palace with me tomorrow.

'Yunus.' I nodded at my brother as he came to a stop beside Mother.

He nodded back, his stance reserved. 'Oh, take cover, Noshin is coming,' Yunus said, quickly heading away.

Before I could run, a girl appeared in front of me, fluttering her eyelashes and flapping her fan. 'Your Highnesses. Your Majesty,' she said with a deep curtsey.

'Noshin, lovely to see you, dear,' Mother said graciously.

Noshin looked directly at me, her dark, striking eyes intent. 'His Highness looks most handsome tonight. Such a beautiful sherwani you have on, my prince.' She touched my sleeve.

I pulled my arm back quickly. 'Thank you. I hope your family is well,' I replied politely.

She laughed as though I had said something funny. 'His Highness is most concerned for his subjects; how lucky we are that you'll be our Sultan.'

'Come along, dear,' Noshin's father said, bowing his head towards us. 'Your Majesty, your Highnesses – an excellent ball, I must say.'

Mercifully, Noshin and her family departed as others came forward to greet us.

'Has anybody told the poor girl Zayd will be married soon?' Yunus said, reappearing by my side with a snigger.

Mother was grinning. 'I think it's sweet. She has always had a soft spot for Zayd.'

'Are you both quite done?' I grumbled.

'Ah, the ice queen is here. No wonder it's got so cold,' Yunus muttered.

I looked up and saw the Sultana of Sawan making her entrance. She wore a soft gold sari that shimmered with crystals as she walked, her eyes roaming the room as if sizing it up.

Then I forgot everything for a moment when Layla walked in.

The princess wore a white lehenga heavily embroidered with white gemstones. As she and her mother neared us, her kohl-rimmed eyes looked about the room in wonder. The dupatta draped over her head made her appear more regal - if that were even possible. Large diamonds hung from her ears and around her slender neck. She exuded royalty.

The space seemed brighter suddenly, the hanging flowers more fragrant. She commanded the entire room as everyone turned to look at her.

'Your Majesty, a beautiful ball,' Sultana Zahra said as she kissed Mother's cheek.

'How wonderful you look, Your Majesty. And Princess, you are a vision!' Mother said warmly, taking Layla's hands in her own.

I noted the way Layla's cheeks flushed red, almost matching the colour of her painted lips.

'A vision indeed,' Yunus said with a winning smile.

Layla smiled easily. 'His Highness is most kind.'

'Princess,' I said, inclining my head as she finally turned her gaze upon me. Those piercing eyes, like pools of fire in the candlelight, made my heartbeat falter for a moment.

'Your Highness,' she said in a measured voice, curtseying. I noted the slight parting of her lips, the frown between her brow as she looked at me.

Yunus leant closer to Layla. 'Come, Princess, let's leave these boring people and go dance.' He held out his arm.

I watched Layla take his arm with a warm smile, and the pair of them headed towards the centre of the room. Sultana Zahra and Mother went off together to work the room while I stood on the side. I took a drink from one of the servers, trying not to watch Layla and Yunus twirling around the floor together – the way she laughed at whatever he said, how closely they seemed to be swaying together.

I downed the drink and set it down on the next server's plate. Mother floated back towards me alone. 'Go and ask the princess for her next dance, Zayd; the song is almost over.'

'Yunus seems to be better suited to the job,' I said lightly.

'Remember what we said about building future relations?' She arched a brow.

I sighed and walked over to Yunus and Layla, who were still busy laughing away. Layla's laughter stopped abruptly when she noticed me.

'May I have your next dance, Princess?' I asked politely.

'All right,' she said as if the prospect bored her.

'See you both in a bit,' Yunus said easily, walking away.

I held my hand out to Layla and she slipped her hand into mine. I tried to ignore how smooth it felt, or how the curve of her waist seemed to be a perfect fit for the shape of my palm. I cleared my throat and looked above the princess's head as we began to move in a neat formation around the floor.

'What, no smart remarks this evening?' I said after several moments of awkward silence.

'It's called trying to be nice,' she said with a polite smile.

'You? Nice? Are you feeling unwell, Princess?' I asked teasingly.

She rolled those beautiful amber eyes. 'Don't push it. I'm still undecided on how much of an arse you are.'

'Just as I am undecided on how much of a creep you are,' I said with a smile.

Layla flushed red. 'It was an accident!' she hissed, her eyes darting around nervously.

'One you seemed to enjoy,' I said, chuckling.

'I did not,' she protested.

I spun Layla out, slowly drawing her back into the circle of my arm. 'That blush on your cheeks says otherwise,' I murmured in her ear before spinning her back out again.

Layla glared at me as we stepped back into each other's space. I looked at her for longer than I should have, lost with the soft music in the air, the feel of her in my arms.

'Why are you so bothered by it?' Layla asked coldly. 'Haven't you got a wedding to get ready for?'

'I could say the same to you,' I replied.

I shouldn't goad her. I needed her to come with me out of the palace tomorrow. But winding her up was too much fun to stop.

'Well, I'm not married yet,' she muttered, averting her gaze.

'Neither am I,' I said quietly.

Layla's eyes snapped back to me in confusion, her brow puckering. 'You should be careful with your words, Prince. Anyone might think you're trying to cause a scandal.'

'I'm merely teasing you, Princess,' I said nonchalantly. 'You fall for it too easily.'

'You're so annoying,' she griped. 'Forget this secret escapade out of the palace. I'd rather watch paint dry.'

She was bluffing. I spun Layla out and drew her in again, holding her close to me so I could murmur into her ear. 'Meet me in my bedroom tomorrow night after dinner. Listen out for a distraction.'

It shouldn't have thrilled me the way she shivered from my words, or how - for just a second - she melted back into my hold.

The music slowed to a stop. I spun the princess one last time before letting her hand slip from mine.

16

Layla

My racing heart slowed its pace as Zayd departed with a playful smile, the ghost of his warm scent lingering on me.

'He always loves and leaves, that prince,' a voice crooned in my ear.

I looked around to see a beautiful young woman dressed in a pale-blue sari, curls framing her face beneath her dupatta. 'Excuse me?'

'Forgive me, Your Highness, my name is Noshin,' she said with a deep curtsey. She batted her dark eyelashes. 'It's a shame the prince is off the market now, isn't it?'

'Were you hoping to purchase him?' I asked dryly.

She tinkled a laugh. 'How funny you are, Your Highness! There isn't a girl in this room who wouldn't have rushed forward to marry Prince Zayd, but he is betrothed now. He was always rather fussy.' She didn't sound happy about that.

'You sound like you know him well?' I couldn't help but ask.

Noshin smiled demurely. 'A lady never kisses and tells, Your Highness. But a prince always does as he pleases.' She curtseyed again and left, a waft of her sickly-sweet perfume brushing over me.

What was that about? I traipsed off towards the side and grabbed a cold strawberry drink. Zayd's words still rang in my mind: '*Meet in my bedroom tomorrow night after dinner.*'

I had half a mind to go to sleep early tomorrow. As useful as it would be to get out of the palace for an evening, I wasn't sure whether it was a wise idea after all. I was treading dangerous waters with Zayd. I didn't miss the way his eyes roamed over me like a caress, or how we always seemed to end up closer than was perhaps warranted.

He was infuriating.

He was also ridiculously handsome. He looked entirely lethal tonight. It really didn't help that I knew just how lean that body was beneath his clothes.

Tension rolled through me. I let out a few deep breaths, calming myself so I didn't set anything on fire. I had to be careful, especially with so many people around.

Was this my life now? Afraid of my own body?

I pulled the sleeves of my dress down, as if that would help. I wanted to believe it wasn't true, but I couldn't ignore the way every damn flame in this large hall felt like it was calling to me.

Think about something else, I berated myself. *Anything.*

Yunus came up to me with a few of his friends from court, introducing them as Rashid, Hadi and Shah. I tried to focus on pleasantries but found my eyes drifting of their own accord.

Zayd was to the side with one of his counsellors, discussing something that seemed more appropriate for a meeting chamber than a ball. I tried not to notice the circle of girls who lingered near him, Noshin included, though he seemed oblivious.

When the party began to wind down, I took my leave and headed back to my room. I plunged into the hot bath Mira had prepared, closing my eyes and thinking about anything other than the feel of Zayd's hands around me or how deliciously low that towel had been.

'Have you got any plans today, Princess?' Yunus asked over breakfast the next morning.

I shook my head. 'Just the usual. What about you?'

'More of the same,' he replied with a bored smile. 'Fancy doing something interesting?'

I looked at him quizzically. 'Define interesting.'

We were alone, with Zayd nowhere to be seen, as usual, and our mothers having eaten and left already.

'I hear you're a trained fighter. I'm curious to see if you live up to your reputation,' Yunus said with a dangerous smirk.

'Well, who am I to deny you the opportunity of getting your arse kicked?' I replied sweetly.

Yunus laughed. 'See you in the training room in an hour?'

'Done.'

When I returned to my rooms after a quiet stroll in the gardens, Mira helped me out of my day dress and into training attire - a simple black shalwar kameez made of cotton that stretched with the movement of my limbs. My hair was tied into a neat bun, all jewellery taken off. It felt good to walk down the palace halls in normal clothes and not the decadent outfits Mother insisted on.

I arrived at the training room with my guards in tow. Double doors opened to reveal a big stone room flooded with light from the large arched windows that lined the walls. A faint smell of sweat hung in the air as various soldiers trained, their swords clanging loudly.

'Princess!' Yunus called from the centre of the room. 'I was beginning to think you weren't coming.'

'Hoping, more like?' I called back, heading towards him.

Yunus grinned, a devilish glint in his eye. 'Your weapon, Princess?' He gestured to the wall behind him. It was lined with rows and rows of gleaming silver swords, daggers, arrows and bows.

I walked up to the wall and surveyed the swords on display. I opted for one of the larger ones, close to what I had at home, with a golden hilt.

Yunus picked out his sword and led us towards one of the rings.

I slipped beneath the ropes and felt around the floor, learning its hollow and strong parts.

'Dancing, Your Highness?' Yunus teased.

'Is this how you throw your opponents off? Talk them to death?' I replied dryly.

Yunus chuckled, all mischief. 'Nobody in my company is ever bored, I assure you.'

I rolled my eyes. 'Shall we?'

Yunus nodded at the trainer who had entered the ring between us.

'Ready yourselves!' he called.

Yunus and I straightened up.

'Draw your swords!'

We lifted our weapons.

'Go!'

Our blades met in a mirrored arc, coming together with a loud clang. Yunus smirked before spinning his sword, moving fast and lunging at me.

I met it with a deft blow, turning out of his way and bringing my sword back around to strike at his feet.

It felt like we were dancing again, only this was my kind of song. I didn't have to think about steps; my survival instincts took over completely. Our swords spun endlessly, clashing together as we moved around each other, diving low, aiming high, all the while pushing each other back and forth. All at once Yunus almost had me in a corner, but I shoved his sword and spun out of the way, bringing my sword back to knock his out of his hand.

The air in the room suddenly changed. I felt his gaze on me before I heard him.

'I think the princess wins that round,' Zayd's low voice called.

I turned around to look at the crown prince. He walked over to us. His eyes fell upon my face and travelled slowly down the rest of my body, appraising my outfit. 'Black suits you, Your Highness.'

My cheeks felt warm.

'I thought you were in meetings all day today?' Yunus asked, looking at Zayd curiously.

'They were rescheduled for later,' Zayd said dismissively, his eyes still on me.

'Right. Round two, Your Highness?' Yunus said, turning back to me.

I looked back at him with a sweet smile. 'If you're feeling up for it.'

Zayd's low chuckle sent a shiver down my spine.

The trainer had us take our positions again.

Our swords met in a clash of silver as we collided once more. But I could feel the weight of Zayd's gaze on me – and it was throwing me off.

'Distracted, Your Highness?' Yunus asked with a smirk. 'I have been known to dazzle people.'

'You wish,' I huffed, spinning out of the way as he brought his sword down.

Yunus lunged at me, forcing me off balance. I fell backwards but rolled away just as his sword came down and I managed to swipe my sword at his feet.

Yunus jumped out of the way, but it was the distraction I needed to leap up and knock his sword out of his hand.

'Twice lucky, Princess Layla,' Yunus panted, sweat beading his brow.

I smirked back. 'It isn't luck.'

'Call it a day, Yunus,' Zayd said with a laugh.

'Not a chance,' he huffed with determination.

We went again. Yunus picked up his pace, our swords clashing again and again as he came at me relentlessly. We pivoted and sidestepped, swords meeting angrily as we tried to push the other back.

Yunus lunged, knocking my sword out of my hand.

An elated sound ripped out of him.

'I'll let you have that one,' I said as Mira handed me a large glass of water to glug down.

'You put up a good fight, Princess,' Yunus replied. 'I wouldn't want to meet you on the battlefield.'

'Hopefully we never will,' I replied.

'Have you got time for one more?' Zayd asked, stepping into the ring. While Yunus and I had been sparring, he'd started to strip down, leaving him in trousers and a shirt that had a few buttons undone. I tried not to notice the dark hair that escaped from beneath his collar, hinting at that broad chest I definitely didn't remember. A sword gleamed in his hand.

'I'll go easy on you, Princess,' Zayd said, humour in his eyes.

'Spoken like a true loser,' I said sweetly.

He smirked.

I picked up my sword. I was going to wipe that smug smile off his face.

'Don't be afraid to wound him, Your Highness,' Yunus said from the side bench.

'Ready yourselves!' the trainer shouted.

We stood straight. Zayd's olive eyes bored into mine. Why did I notice those eyes so much? The shade of them was mesmerizing, like a beautiful lake under the summer sun.

Or a swamp.

'Draw your swords. Go!'

I lunged at Zayd but he stepped aside neatly. He thrust his sword forward, but I pushed it away with mine, our swords meeting with a resounding clang. I twisted out of the way and struck at his side, but Zayd was quick. His sword met mine with another loud clash. I planted my feet and swung at him again, his sword stopping mine.

We parried and spun through the ring, clash after clash. He was quicker than Yunus, but his movements were deliberate, calculated, where Yunus had been freestyling. I hit at his feet, hoping to knock him off balance, but he merely stepped out of the way and spun his sword back. I dodged the weapon, swiping at him as I faced him once more, but his sword pushed mine off.

We went again and again, our breaths heavy in the air. Zayd tried to throw me off, but I met his sword with as much force as I had. Beads of sweat ran down his warm brown face, his hair dishevelled. I ignored the inappropriate feeling burning through my body and struck again. If dancing with him had felt intimate last night, fighting with him was electrifying.

Our swords caught each other in a deadlock.

'It seems we have an impasse,' the trainer said.

'Like hell,' I growled, shoving Zayd's sword back with all my force. He stumbled back in surprise, allowing me a second to knock his feet out with a wide kick, his sword clattering away.

Zayd fell, but his arm swiped at my leg and caught my ankle, yanking me down with him. My sword fell to the side as I tumbled to the matting beside him. I rolled over fast, slamming him into the floor and pinning my arm against his throat.

'Yield,' I huffed out.

Zayd smirked from beneath me. I became acutely aware of how my body was pressed entirely against the long length of his, solid and strong.

In another breath, Zayd rolled us over, my head connecting with the floor as he pinned me down. 'Yield, Princess.' His face was unbearably close. I could see each individual dark eyelash framing those gorgeous olive eyes. The heat of his body against mine threatened to cloud all my senses.

'You wish,' I growled, bringing up my knee to slam into his groin.

Zayd let out a groan of pain that felt entirely inappropriate while he lay on top of me, but it gave me a moment of relief to roll out from under him. I quickly got to my feet while Zayd crouched on the mat.

'That,' he said, looking up at me, 'was dirty.' But he still had that irritating smirk on his face.

'That was me winning,' I replied. I picked up my sword and looked away. 'Mira, can you have my bath drawn?' I was desperate to get away from him. My blood was singing in my veins for entirely impossible reasons.

'You should train some of our soldiers,' Zayd said as he stood, wiping his face with a towel.

'Are you impressed, Your Highness?' I replied. 'High praise, indeed.'

'Credit is given where it's due,' he said indifferently, but he was smiling. 'Allow me,' he said, taking my sword from my hand.

His fingers brushed mine, sending a shiver of heat up my arm. Our eyes caught and for an instant there was a dark hunger in his gaze that stopped my breath.

I blinked and the prince was gone, returning our swords to the wall. I was imagining things. I took the towel Mira handed me and dabbed at my face.

A loud clash made me look up.

The swords had fallen out of Zayd's hands.

'Your Highness?' his guard said, striding towards him.

'Brother?' Yunus had been lounging but hurried over to Zayd.

'Just an accident,' Zayd said curtly, bending to pick the swords back up.

'Did I overexert you?' I asked, as Zayd walked back towards me.

He smirked. 'Is that an invitation?' he asked quietly, stopping before me.

My treacherous heart picked up its pace.

I felt the weight of his gaze as his eyes swept over me, his stare somehow penetrating and soft at the same time. 'See you later,' I huffed out, turning on my heel.

Zayd kept pace beside me. 'Mind if I join you? Our rooms are in the same hallway, after all.'

'Don't you have other duties to attend to?' I shot back.

'I'd much rather get on your nerves, Your Highness. Your cheeks turn so red when you're mad.'

'Is this why you have no friends?' I retorted.

Zayd chuckled. 'How long have you been wielding a sword?'

'For years now,' I replied. 'I suppose I should count myself lucky Father wanted to ensure I was able to defend myself.'

He raised a dark brow. 'Lucky?'

'Not every woman is taught to read, let alone wield a sword,' I said. 'I know I live a privileged life while many don't. Even getting to spar with you and Yunus – another privilege that would have detrimental consequences for the social standing of a normal woman.'

'I suppose royals are allowed to be exceptions to rules,' Zayd said carefully.

I snorted. 'Have you considered what your army might look like if you allowed women to train and fight? Perhaps it would solve your personnel issues.'

'Believe me, I have – but it would never be allowed,' Zayd said.

'Perhaps when you are Sultan, you can make more exceptions to the rules.'

Zayd looked back at me with something like admiration in his eyes.

'Stop that,' I snapped, looking away.

'Stop what?' I could hear the smile in his voice.

'Stop looking at me like that.'

'Like what?' He was definitely smiling.

I glared back at him.

'Your Highness, Usman requires a word,' Zayd's guard called from behind us.

Zayd sighed. 'I shall have to leave you, Princess. Thank you for a fun fight – I hope you're not in too much pain.' But before he left, he leant in for just a moment and said in a whisper, 'See you tonight. Remember, listen out for a distraction.' He smirked as he left.

'Ugh,' I muttered, walking away.

When I got back to my room, Mira, like a miracle worker, had a steaming bath ready. I sank into its fiery depths, the steam filling my head.

'I never thought I'd see you meet your match,' Mira said as she lathered soap into my hair.

My cheeks flushed.

'Or see you speechless,' she said with a little laugh.

'He is … the crown prince is …' I couldn't find my words.

'Impossibly handsome?' Mira supplied.

'Mira!' I reproached, my eyes darting involuntarily around.

'What? For a young man, he isn't unpleasant to look at. Not that he's my type,' she added with a snort. 'The two of you fighting together was amazing. You were moving in sync – like two halves of the same body.'

'Well, he can definitely fight,' I said brusquely.

'I'll bet,' she sniggered. 'His future wife will be delighted when she sees him.'

I sank lower into the water, my stomach churning. 'I bet their wedding will be nothing short of spectacular.'

'Absolutely,' Mira said, nodding. 'Do you think he will take a mistress?' she asked in hushed tones.

'That's not really becoming for us to speak of,' I hissed.

'What? Everybody knows most royals have a lover in the shadows.'

I wondered if that Noshin girl was vying for a place in Zayd's shadow. Perhaps she had a place with him already.

Mira chuckled and continued to rinse out my hair while I went under.

After I had been scrubbed and renewed, I threw on another shalwar kameez.

'Mira, send for my dinner here,' I said. 'I can't bear another meal listening to my mother's voice. If anyone asks, tell them I am feeling tired and will be resting in my room tonight.'

I wanted to eat in peace, without my mother watching my plate from the corner of her eye – calculating how much food I ate, how much bigger my waist would get.

'Yes, of course, Your Highness. I shall inform the maids,' Mira said, heading out of the door.

I sat down on the sofa and picked up Dakaria's newssheets.

SAWAN READY TO LIE IN BED WITH THE FALLOWMERE AGAIN

PRINCESS LAYLA BETROTHED TO THE NATION OF THIEVES

PROTESTS BEGIN AS THE FALLOWMERE ANNOUNCE THEIR RETURN

My insides turned cold. I read through every paper – they all lamented the same thing. My marriage to Prince Edmund had been announced yesterday and was now being declared a betrayal by the Dakaria press. I could only imagine that the newssheets from Sawan would be even worse.

I wondered if these protests would be enough to stop the wedding, but I knew my mother would never give in. The papers made me sound mindless, an empty pawn in my mother's quest for power and influence. And they weren't exactly wrong, were they? I was nothing like Zayd, who spent his days actually running his country – he was the next in line for the throne and behaved as such. My mother handled all political matters, and I still didn't have a date for my own coronation.

I hated to see turmoil in Sawan. I hated that I was powerless to do anything to stop it. I had half a mind to burn the newssheet in my hand.

I wondered if I could.

Mira wasn't here, but I looked around anyway before I waved my hand over it, feeling a current pulse through my veins as the paper caught fire.

A small shriek escaped me. I dropped the paper and promptly stamped on it before I could cause any more damage. I gathered the burnt remnants and threw them into the fireplace.

Dread and worry plagued me all evening. I didn't want this wedding any more than our people did. This was even more reason for me to disappear.

Will you leave our people to your mother's mercy? Father's voice rang in my mind.

Since he'd died, it had seemed like my conscience had taken on his voice. He had been my fountain of reason, after all.

But I was no match for my mother. So why pretend?

Sometimes you had to accept you couldn't change the world around you; sometimes all you could do was look out for yourself.

I didn't raise you to be selfish, beti. It was like he was here with me, but when I looked around the room, he was nowhere to be seen. I wondered if I'd ever stop hoping he might come back one day.

The papers were right about one thing. I was betraying the people of Sawan. They deserved better than me, a princess who couldn't even stand up to her own mother.

17

Zayd

This was a terrible idea. I was being foolish, taking risks I shouldn't. But every time I thought about my father lying in his sickbed, it added to my resolve. I had to do this for him. This alliance with the mages could help bring protection to the Silver Port. I had to do this.

I just hoped Layla would actually come. It seemed like we'd turned a corner in our strained relationship. She still tore chunks out of me, but I was starting to realize that was just her personality - witty, sharp and amusing. She was fun to be around, at least.

And beautiful to look at?

I shook that thought away. Whether I was engaged or not, Layla was betrothed too. To a Fallowmere prince. The thought made my skin crawl.

A glance at the dark skies told me it was well past the time my family and our guests would have retired to their rooms for the night. I took the tray of teas and cakes that Iris had left for me after dinner and carried it out of my chambers.

'Your Highness, allow me!' Noor insisted, hurrying after me.

'No, it's all right,' I said, noting Layla's guard outside her door.

I strode quickly down the corridor.

'Your Highness, please,' Noor pressed.

I shrugged him off. 'Noor, it's fine.'

'I must insist, Your Highness!'

He made to grab the tray and I just happened to let it slip out of my hands. Ceramic shattered on the floor as the silver tray crashed onto the marble.

'Your Highness, I must insist you go back to your room,' Noor said angrily, half-shoving me back towards my door.

'Apologies, Noor,' I said sheepishly, sloping off toward my room.

As I had expected, Layla's guard rushed over to help Noor, and her maid came hurrying out to see what the commotion was about. I saw Layla past the door, staring at me with a disapproving look on her face.

I gestured towards my chambers.

She raised a brow.

For a second, I thought she wasn't going to come, but quick as a flash, she darted from her room and into mine. I chanced a glance backwards, but everyone was too busy fussing about the damage on the floor. Quietly, I closed the door behind me.

'That was fun,' Layla said with a laugh.

I turned to face her. My breath almost stopped. She was smiling, a full-on smile that lit up the fire in her eyes and made her look more carefree than I'd seen her since she'd arrived here.

I looked away. 'There's more to come, Princess,' I said, walking past her towards my bedchamber. I stopped in the doorway and turned back. 'Coming?'

Layla eyed me uncertainly but followed.

I opened my wardrobe, pulled out one of my cloaks and handed it to her. 'So you don't get cold.'

'And here I was thinking you were getting ready to pull a sword out,' Layla said dryly. But she took the cloak, her delicate fingers carefully avoiding mine.

'Speaking of,' I said, heading towards my other armoire. I opened the doors, revealing a display of arrows, daggers and swords.

'I spoke too soon,' Layla said, sounding appreciative.

'I like to collect weapons,' I said, taking out two silver daggers with heavy hilts and sharp edges. 'Here, keep these on you.'

Layla looked warily at the daggers I held out to her before carefully taking them from me.

'There are pockets in the cloak,' I said as she turned them over in her hands.

Layla freed a hand to feel for the pockets, but after several moments of searching, she looked at me questioningly.

I stepped closer, pulling the cloak up to reveal the compartments that were hidden seamlessly inside. I revelled in the way Layla's cheeks blushed so easily as I loomed over her. I took the daggers and stowed them away on either side, drawing the cloak around her again. 'There,' I said quietly, still standing close.

Layla looked up at me, her eyes burning amber in the light. Could she hear the racing of my heart when she gazed at me like that?

I looked away reluctantly, stepping back. The sight of her in my clothing was more than I had bargained for. 'This way,' I said.

Outside my bedroom there was a wraparound balcony

with a few chairs where one could watch the sun rise and set.

'Does this go all the way around?' Layla asked, looking surprised as she surveyed the scene.

'Yes, our balconies actually meet at the ends,' I said.

I led Layla towards another door. I pulled out the key I had taken earlier from my dresser and unlocked it to reveal a spiral staircase.

I turned back to face her, lifting the hood of the cloak over her head. 'Just stay close to me, do not leave my side, and keep your head down. OK?'

She looked up at me, feverish delight on her face. 'OK. Where exactly are we going?'

'Just trust me, Princess,' I said as we walked downstairs and out onto the grounds.

Layla sighed dramatically.

We headed towards the front gates, where I motioned for Imdad, one of the guards, to bring a plain carriage forward. 'I want eight guards to accompany me,' I told him.

'Yes, Your Highness, right away,' he said, throwing a curious glance towards the hooded figure behind me.

'Just a friend. Your discretion is appreciated,' I said, handing him a bag of coins.

He smiled at me knowingly, pocketing the gold.

It was better he assumed he knew who was with me, rather than find out the truth.

Layla was good to her word, keeping her head down as she got into the carriage. I climbed in after her, sitting opposite. She lifted her hood just a little to reveal the rest of her face.

The smile she wore was worth every risk this trip carried. Something shifted in my chest.

'*Now* will you tell me where we're going?' Layla asked.

I shrugged. 'Patience, Princess. All will be revealed soon.'

Layla narrowed her eyes at me. 'Try anything and I'll dagger you.'

I snorted. 'What would I try? My head will be on a plate if I don't return you to the palace in one piece.'

She eyed me warily, but the undercurrent of glee was still there. I watched her looking out at the dark streets as the carriage trundled into the capital city. Guards rode around us, which eased my worry. Roshni had only asked to see the one whose aura she had sensed on me. And with both me and Layla armed, as well as my guards, there was little she would be able to do.

Roshni had sensed something from her just from the contact on my skin, had been desperate enough just to see Layla that she had agreed to help us at the Silver Port. What was so special about her?

'I honestly didn't think you had the guts to sneak me out of the palace,' Layla said, turning to look at me.

'You underestimate me,' I replied.

She shrugged, a smirk playing on her lips. 'Maybe.'

The carriage made its way through the capital, fiery lanterns bringing the dark streets to life as we neared the centre of the city. The houses we passed were sprawling mansions, their hulking frames large against the dark sky.

The streets began to narrow as we neared the bazaar, businesses replacing the residences – slim buildings with wooden shutters displaying signs for restaurants, healers and silk merchants. We drove past a large fountain spilling water from the mouths of several stone dolphins and splashing into a pool of silver tiles.

Finally, the horses turned down a side street.

I dismounted from the carriage, offering Layla my hand. Her smooth fingers clasped mine but quickly let go as she stepped onto the street. The cool night air welcomed us, a reprieve from the day's sweltering heat.

'Where to?' Layla asked eagerly, looking up at me with those dangerous eyes.

'I thought we could walk around first, if that suits you?' I suggested.

'Absolutely.'

'Be discreet. I don't want anyone to recognize me,' I said to the guards.

They nodded and shrugged out of their green uniforms, turning the coats inside out so they were plain brown, inconspicuous.

I took another cloak from the trunk of the carriage and drew it over my head. 'This way,' I said, holding out my arm.

Layla cocked an eyebrow. 'Really?'

I sighed. 'I'm well aware you can walk by yourself, but I'm not taking any risks tonight. You stay close to me at all times.'

She looked like she wanted to argue but she looped her arm through mine, her hand resting in the crook of my elbow. She was practically bouncing as we walked into the town square.

'Stop acting like you've escaped prison for the night,' I murmured.

Layla shot me a glare. 'Lighten up, tiny Sultan. This is the first time I've ever been free.'

I glowered back at her. 'Behave. Or I'll take you straight back.'

'I am trembling in my boots,' she grumbled. 'Look! The markets have so many stalls!'

Before I could stop her, Layla sped off towards the

various vendors, dragging me along beside her. Delicious aromas of spiced chai and sugared pastries filled the air. I grabbed myself a cup of chai, which Layla snatched from my hands and drank instead. I was starting to regret bringing her here.

'Delightful,' she said, handing me the half-empty cup back.

Before I could respond, she was off again. I trailed behind the princess as she inspected every stall – studying trinkets and jewellery, marvelling at leather notebooks and elegant feather quills, leafing through silks and scarves with the energy of a child who had been let loose in a sugar cane field.

Over by the fountain in the middle of the market, a number of street performers were displaying their tricks to the cheers of a small crowd. A woman juggled fire rings with her bare hands, a snake swayed to the flute of its charmer, and a cluster of children danced to the beat of drums played by a group of elderly men.

'It's so wonderful here,' Layla said softly, watching the performances.

I made a murmur of agreement, stepping closer to her as I scoured the market for any sign of danger. My guards had a tight perimeter around us, but I was on edge. One wrong move could destroy everything I was trying to do for Dakaria.

A vendor walked past with a tray of spicy amra on sticks.

'Ooh, that looks good!' Layla said.

I slipped the vendor some silver coins as Layla took one from him.

'Where's mine?' I asked dryly.

Layla sighed exaggeratedly. 'Fine, I'll share.' She held the amra out to me.

I took a large bite, the spicy fruit exploding in my mouth.

'Hey, you just bit half of it off!' Layla said, snatching it away and eating the rest.

I laughed, shrugging. 'You drank half of my tea, seems only fair.'

Her eyes were accusatory.

'Where do you want to go next?' I asked.

'This is your city,' Layla replied. 'Where do you recommend?'

I scanned the stalls, wondering where on earth Roshni would be. I steered Layla around the market, pretending to look at all that was on display until, finally, I spotted her.

Roshni was sitting at the last table amongst other ladies, some applying henna, others haldi masks. I came to a stop in front of her table.

Roshni looked up with curious grey eyes, her gaze falling on Layla beside me. She froze for a second.

'What's your trade, madam?' I asked her.

'Palm readings,' she said in her raspy voice.

'Care to try?' I asked Layla.

Layla smiled easily and sat down opposite Roshni, holding out her hand. I stepped forward to stand beside Layla, keeping one hand on the back of her chair.

Roshni gingerly took Layla's palm and her eyes widened at the contact. 'My, you are a special girl indeed.'

Layla looked back at me incredulously. *What a load of nonsense*, her expression seemed to say. I smiled back briefly, my other hand firmly on the dagger on my belt.

'I see a very strong future for you, young one,' Roshni said, looking at Layla with something like adoration in her eyes. It was a marked difference from the hostility she had been spitting at me three days ago.

'You do?' Layla said, unconvinced.

Roshni turned her hand over. 'You must overcome your fears and let the light within you be free. You hold yourself back. Many people depend on you to be brave.'

I saw Layla's face fall.

'I think that's enough for me,' Layla said lightly, pulling her hand away.

Roshni looked at me, awe in her eyes. 'Thank you for coming. I foresee we will meet again, my young friends.' She inclined her head.

I looked at Roshni questioningly.

She gave an imperceptible nod.

I took out a bag of gold coins and put it down on the table, using the opportunity to lean closer to Roshni. 'Come to the palace tomorrow morning,' I murmured quietly.

Roshni nodded, her eyes flicking to Layla.

'I just need a minute,' Layla said, slipping away.

'Layla, wait!' I said, but she was quicker than I had anticipated, hurrying away into the market.

I pushed through the crowd of people, searching for her figure, but she was nowhere to be seen.

Abdul, one of the guards, appeared beside me. 'Sir, is everything all right?'

'Find the girl, now,' I ordered quietly.

I tore away from my men, pacing through the bustling night market as I tried to spot the princess. Where could she have gone? What was she thinking?

Panic began to course through me. If she got lost or hurt herself, what then? If anything happened to her, Dakaria was finished. I stopped in the centre of the market, looking over the people clamouring around me.

A skulking figure in the alleyway ahead caught my eye.

I ran over, shoving through the crowds, earning a few choice words as I went. The joys of being unknown.

I could see Layla snaking her way through the alley. I pounded after her, but she began to run.

'Layla, what are you doing?'

She chanced a glance back at me, her eyes wide with worry.

'Layla, stop!'

I was gaining on her, just succeeding in catching the tail end of her cloak as she took another turn. I grabbed her by the shoulder and spun her around to face me.

'What are you playing at?' I demanded.

Layla's chest rose and fell rapidly, her mouth set in a hard line. 'It's called Hide and Seek, Your Highness. Have you never played?'

'Don't start,' I growled. 'What were you thinking? Have you no idea who you are? You're a crown princess - you can't just run off into the night!'

Layla flinched. 'I wasn't running away; I just needed a minute, after ...' She looked away, blinking rapidly.

'Are you upset?' I asked, my anger waning. 'She was just a lousy fortune teller,' I lied, hating myself for it.

Layla clenched her fists.

'She didn't even say anything bad,' I said. Roshni had just spewed some nonsense about Layla needing to be brave. It was generic enough for any mystic to come out with.

'She made out that I'm some hero waiting to bloom. I'm nobody's hero,' Layla said angrily, looking at me finally. There was a simmering rage in her face but also something that felt like despair. Roshni had struck a nerve.

'You're the future Sultana of Sawan. You don't think your

people see you as a hero?' I knew every ruler in the Eastern world would see her as one when she finally took over from her mother.

'I don't want to talk about it,' she muttered.

'Do you want to go back to the palace?' I asked, guilt tugging at me.

'No, I just wanted this evening to be different. I don't want to be a princess tonight. I don't want to be reminded of my duties.' The sadness in her voice made me feel even more guilty.

'I know somewhere quieter we can go, if you'd prefer?' I offered.

Layla shrugged, deflated. 'Okay.'

I took her hand. 'You don't let go until we're back at the palace.'

'Not the most romantic way to ask me to hold hands, but sure,' she scoffed, though with none of her usual fire.

'Don't flatter yourself, Princess; you're just a flight risk,' I said gently.

Layla's soft fingers tightened around mine as we walked back out to the market, and I tried not to care about how right it felt, as though her hand had been made just to fit mine.

18

Layla

Z ayd was as good as his word, keeping a hold of me as we wove through the throng of people milling around the various stalls. Perhaps a part of me had thought I could run away. I wasn't trying to give my mother an excuse to wage war on Dakaria, but the fortune teller's words had made me feel so pathetic, so helpless, that my hands had begun to shake. I knew I had to calm down before I set the whole market on fire.

I forced myself to take steady breaths as I walked with Zayd, his warm hold grounding me in the present. I realized that if I just focused on the soft surety of his touch, the strength of his grip, I could dull the current humming away deep beneath my skin.

Zayd grabbed another chai, draining half before handing the rest to me. I downed the warm drink, the perfect antidote to the chill that was beginning to creep through the night air.

He led the way down a quiet street where a large set of stone stairs took up one side of a building. His guards tailed us, keeping a close perimeter. I followed Zayd up to a roof terrace overlooking the bustling market and out to the wider city of Dukhha, its lights twinkling in the distance.

'Wow, this is a beautiful view,' I murmured.

'That it is,' Zayd replied, gesturing to a bench by the balcony edge.

We sat down, looking over the starlit city, the moon a sliver in the dark sky. Despite Zayd's guards lingering not far behind us, tonight was the first time I had understood what freedom might feel like. To walk around unknown, on your own schedule, just a normal person with no expectations ...

Well, until that fortune teller had come along. Her grey eyes had been so full of awe; I wasn't sure if it had been part of the act, but it had unsettled me nonetheless.

'Many people depend on you to be brave.'

There was nothing brave about me. My great big plan was to run away from my life, from my future marriage, and let my mother do as she pleased.

'You know, you aren't the first royal to have wished they could leave behind all their responsibilities,' Zayd said, his deep voice quiet in the cool night.

I turned to face him.

He looked at me steadily for a long moment. I felt the ice in my heart begin to thaw a little.

'You've wanted to run away?' I asked incredulously.

'Not from my family,' he amended. 'But, growing up, I was always made aware of the fact that I was to be the next Sultan. Sometimes I wish I'd had more time to just be a boy instead of the perfect heir.'

'Look at us with our privileged problems,' I said lightly.

He snorted, a smile on the edge of his lips.

'Things just aren't the same any more without my father,'

I told him quietly. 'The palace just feels like bricks. I have no place there.'

Zayd's brow furrowed, concern in his eyes. 'That palace is your birth-right: you have more right to it than anyone, Layla.'

The softness of how he said my name made my heart stutter. I looked away. 'It doesn't feel that way.'

Zayd touched my hand gently. 'Why do you feel like this?'

I raised a brow. 'Not all of us are put on a pedestal by our parents.'

He smiled, shaking his head. 'Do you always deflect with that sharp tongue of yours?'

'I've been told it's one of my many charms,' I replied, mirroring his smile.

His fingers played with the tips of mine, soft and tracing. 'Maybe when you're ready, you'll be able to face your fears. But it's OK if you need some time until then. And for the record, you are your people's hero. Even we in Dakaria know how much Sawanis love their princess ...'

'Not any more,' I muttered, folding my arms across my chest. 'Not since my engagement.'

Zayd grimaced. 'Ah, yes, the protests. I heard.'

'They're saying I've betrayed our country, our ancestors – everything we fought for. They aren't wrong.'

'It wasn't your decision,' Zayd said firmly. 'Besides, a lot can happen in a few months. Maybe the Fallowmere ship will sink on the way here.' He grinned.

I laughed despite myself. 'You can't say things like that.'

'I can if it gets you to smile,' he said.

I shook my head, grinning as I looked back out to the city spread before us. We sat in comfortable silence for a while, our shoulders almost touching. The heat radiating from Zayd's body felt like a warm flame against the cool night.

'We should head back soon,' Zayd murmured.

'Yes, we probably should,' I said reluctantly.

Zayd stood, holding out his hand. I slipped my fingers into his as we headed back down onto the street. The din of voices and metal clanging grew louder as we made our way into the market, the vendors beginning to pack away their stalls for the night.

'Come on, it's story time!' a young boy said excitedly, rushing past us with his friends.

'Story time?' I repeated.

'It's a weekly tradition in the market,' Zayd explained. 'Everyone gathers around to hear an ancient fable or two.'

'Can we go? Before we head back?' I asked.

Zayd hesitated, his hand tightening ever so slightly around mine. 'It's getting late, Princess.'

'Exactly, let's make the most of it.'

Zayd looked like he really wanted to say no, his eyes darting around us like they had so many times this evening. 'Fine ... but stay close.'

'Catch me if you can,' I said jokingly, letting go.

His nostrils flared. Suddenly, Zayd put his arm around me. 'Try running now.'

'What are you doing?' I grumbled, trying to shrug out of his hold.

He held firm, his hand hooked onto the curve of my hip. 'If you want to stay out, you stay close.'

'Any closer and people might think we're being scandalous, Your Highness,' I replied, arching a brow.

Zayd leant into my ear, his warm breath tickling my skin. 'I'm not afraid of a little gossip, Princess.'

I shivered involuntarily. I hated that stupid, smouldering look in his eyes. Those damn eyes.

Zayd led us over to where a crowd of people had gathered by a firepit. I noted his guards hovering nearby as we took our seats on the edge of a row of crammed benches. One of them caught my eye and nodded respectfully. If the guards thought anything about the way we were pressed into each other's side, they didn't show it.

With a sinking feeling, I wondered how often Zayd brought girls out to the city like this.

'Are you going to let go now?' I muttered to him.

'What's wrong?' Zayd asked, looking at me with amusement. Firelight danced in his eyes. 'Scared of being this close to me?'

'I'm only afraid of your breath,' I bit back.

Zayd chuckled, a low sound that made my stomach flip.

I had half a mind to make a run for it again to annoy him, but just then a woman settled on a wooden stall before everyone. A gust of cold wind blew over us as she began to speak. With a start, I realized it was the fortune teller. I hoped she couldn't see me seated a few rows from the front.

'Welcome, one and all. Tonight, we journey back to ancient times, when humans lived in peace with mages ...' She blew powder from her palm into the fire before her, and a colourful array of figures made from smoke danced above the fire.

The crowd murmured with awe.

'Is it normal here to tell stories about mages?' I whispered to Zayd.

He nodded thoughtfully, but there was a tightness in his features. 'Mages have become part of the folklore here, myths told around fires or at bedtime. Not the case in Sawan?'

If only he knew. 'Definitely not.'

The fortune teller went on. 'The mages provided healing

and good fortune for people who were often left with nothing after bad harvests, diseases that spread like wildfire in communities and ...'

What was she saying? I tried to focus on the fortune teller's words but the feel of Zayd's arm wrapped around me, keeping me pressed into his side, was making it hard to think properly. He was so comfortable, his body solid muscle. I wanted to lean closer and rest my head on his shoulder, but I kept my back straight.

A familiar hum of energy began to course through my blood as my anxiety spiked. I took a few deep breaths, clasping my hands together as they began to tremble.

'Are you cold?' Zayd whispered, his free hand covering mine. His fingers were warm.

'I'm OK,' I said, despite the pounding of my heart. I willed myself to calm down, breathing through the spike of energy trying to fizz up inside me.

Zayd's thumbs stroked the back of my hands and eventually my heartbeat slowed, the hum of power ebbed and my hands stilled.

'... But what the barbarians didn't know was that the mages would be brought out of hiding by a victor one day.' The fortune teller's voice boomed dramatically. She blew into the fire again, and a cloaked figure swirled out of the flames, standing tall and strong in a kaleidoscope of colours.

The fortune teller's eyes met mine across the crowd. I shivered involuntarily as the lady looked away.

'When this victor will come, nobody can say,' she continued. 'But one day, a great storm will come through which the balance of nature will be restored and prosperity will return to our lands!'

'We don't need mages to restore our land, we need more jobs!' someone heckled.

'Hear, hear! And better houses and roads!' another person chimed in.

'Maybe we should leave,' Zayd murmured, as the gathering began to grow more animated.

'Probably a good idea,' I said. I could only imagine what would happen if someone recognized Zayd's face beneath his hood.

We left the rowdy crowd as they began to debate the virtues of their Dakari leaders, and headed back down the side streets towards the carriage.

I felt the absence of Zayd's body when he let me go. We got into the carriage and sat quietly opposite each other, looking out of the window the whole way back to the palace. I chanced a few glances at him, but Zayd's face was unreadable. He stretched his arm a few times, as though it ached.

'Interesting story about the mages, don't you think?' Zayd asked, a playful smile on his face.

I shrugged, clasping my hands together. 'I guess it's just another tale.'

'Yes, you're probably right,' he said thoughtfully. 'We don't have many mages left in Dakaria - perhaps just one family of water mages. But they keep to themselves.'

My heart quickened its pace. 'You don't have anything to do with them?'

Zayd shook his head. 'Not really; there's no need to. Are there any mages left in Sawan?'

'Some fire mages are known of, but that's it,' I said hesitantly, my skin prickling with nerves.

'The Fallowmere did one hell of a job purging mages

from our lands,' Zayd said bitterly. 'It's no wonder people are angry at their return.'

I didn't reply, too ashamed to speak. Zayd looked out the window.

All was quiet when we returned to the palace. I kept my hood low around my face as Zayd led us to his wing, his hand hovering over the small of my back as if I would run off again.

Once we were safely inside the warmth of his room, I took his cloak off and hung it over his armchair.

'Thank you for tonight,' I said sincerely.

'Thanks for not running away,' he replied with a pointed look.

I shook my head. 'Are you still upset about that? I thought we were friends now.'

'Friends?' he repeated slowly, his eyes sweeping over my face.

I swallowed. 'Yes. Friends. That's what you've been saying to me all week.' I busied myself with the cloak, removing the daggers he had lent me. 'Here you are.'

'Keep them,' he said, pushing my hands back gently.

'What?' I looked at him in confusion as he went over to his armoire and rooted around for something. He came back with a small leather satchel and held it open. I put the silver daggers inside.

'Consider them a gift, or a memento from tonight,' Zayd said.

'No one has ever gifted me weapons before,' I said with amusement as I slung the satchel over my shoulder.

'Glad I get to be the first.'

I stepped forward hesitantly and leant up, kissing the side of his cheek. 'Thank you, truly.'

I heard the sharp intake of his breath. I felt the way he caught me by the waist, his eyes darkening as he looked into mine. For a wild moment, I felt the desperate urge to lean closer and close the gap between our bodies. Something about him called to me, a magnetic force that threatened to override my good sense.

'You should get some sleep, Princess,' Zayd said in a tight voice.

'I should,' I replied, not moving.

His fingers tightened ever so slightly on my hips. 'Layla, I ...'

My heart stuttered at the way my name fell off his tongue. I didn't stop to think too hard about it. My hands trailed up the length of his arms—

Zayd stepped back suddenly, something flickering across his face before he fixed on a strained smile. 'I'll distract the guards, just wait by the door,' he said hurriedly.

I froze with confusion as Zayd disappeared out of his chambers. I heard him trying to compel the guards to play poker with him. Forcing myself to move, I rushed to the door and poked my head out. Zayd and the guards were a way down the hall.

Quick as lightning, I bolted across the corridor and into my chambers, my heart hammering away in my chest.

I did my best not to think about anything as I tried to go to sleep, but the sting of Zayd pulling away from me when I thought we ...

We what? What was I thinking? He was betrothed. So was I.

Tonight with Zayd had been a fanciful dream and that was it. Even if my treacherous heart wanted more.

19

Zayd

The next morning, I woke with a raging headache and pain in my arm. I didn't even remember falling asleep. Memories of what happened last night came back in pieces: Layla, the market, Roshni … the moment in my room.

She was impossible. Distracting. And so damn captivating I had been on the brink of risking my alliance with Valthar.

Guilt lurched inside of me. I had already lied to Layla about why I snuck her out. Keeping her close last night had been a necessity, but a part of me had enjoyed the proximity as well. And if she hadn't touched my injured arm, I might not have snapped out of whatever was happening between us.

My arm throbbed again. Had summer come early? It felt unreasonably warm in my room.

I fumbled around for the bell and rang for Noor.

'Good morning, Your Highness,' Noor said, entering my room.

'Get Sayyidah Shafiya please,' I grunted, pushing myself up.

Noor nodded at me in alarm and rushed from the room.

My arm was burning now. Gingerly, I peeled back the bandages and nearly retched.

Black ink seeped down my veins around the wound, the affected skin grey, as though it had lost its affinity for life.

Noor returned hastily with Sayyidah Shafiya.

'Have you been applying the salve?' she asked severely, opening a large leather bag and rummaging inside.

'Yes, every day, three times a day.' Though perhaps I had forgotten last night.

'You must rest, Your Highness, I cannot stress that enough,' Sayyidah Shafiyah said, pulling out another tub of green salve. I hissed as she applied it to the wound, the stinging giving way to a cooling sensation. She rooted around in her bag again and began mixing an elixir together from vials of different coloured liquids. The result she handed me was oddly lumpy and dark.

I frowned at the vial. 'What is that?'

'Mainly herbs and marigold – hopefully it will help your body fight this from the inside too,' she said. 'Drink.'

I took the vial and drank the unpleasant liquid, almost gagging.

'I'm sorry, Your Highness,' she said, grimacing.

My gut twisted as the contents made their way down my throat. 'Have you found any earth mages?'

'There may be mages hiding in Valthar and Sawan, but I couldn't say. It could take months to find someone. And I am not sure if you have that many months, Your Highness.' Her expression was worried.

Dread filled me at her words. 'Thank you, Sayyidah, that will be all.'

She nodded, withdrawing from the room.

'Had a busy night, Your Highness?' Noor asked, raising his brows.

I looked at him in surprise. 'How did you—?'

'Well, it's funny, but there are these things in the palace called *windows* that allow you to see someone leaving the grounds with a young lady friend in tow,' Noor said dryly.

'It was just for a few hours,' I said dismissively.

'You should have taken me: I'm head of your guards for a reason,' he said irately. 'If anything happens to you, it's my fault.'

'I'm capable of looking after myself, though I appreciate the concern,' I said. 'Besides, it would have made my absence more noticeable if you'd left with me.'

'Yes, but—'

The doors to my chambers burst open. I quickly pulled on my khamis, covering my arms. Yunus sauntered through my bedroom doors a moment later. 'Brother, why was that healer here?' he asked, eyeing me suspiciously.

'Just to check on my wound. You know – the one I got protecting you.' My tone was harsher than I intended.

Yunus's face fell. 'I said I was sorry.'

'Forget it, it's fine. What do you want?' I asked.

'I'm not sitting at another breakfast with the ice queen,' he said but his tone was off. 'You have to come today.'

I sighed. 'All right. I just need to freshen up.' At least I'd get to see Layla this morning.

Yunus nodded and sloped off towards my parlour.

Guilt gnawed at me as I hastily washed my face and brushed my teeth. I would take an arrow for Yunus every day if I had to; I just couldn't help but resent that his foolishness was now costing me my life.

'Hurry up!' Yunus shouted.

There was an unhelpful feeling swirling in my stomach as we headed to the dining hall. I was only half-listening to Yunus making jibes about Sultana Zahra's many nefarious qualities. The anticipation was fraying my nerves.

The ice queen and Princess Layla were already seated in the dining hall, talking with Mother. Yunus strode over and took a seat beside Layla. I tried not to curse the day he was born and sat beside the Sultana of Sawan.

'Good morning, Your Majesties. Your Highness,' I said, looking over at Layla.

Layla merely mumbled a response, not meeting my gaze.

'Good morning, young prince,' the Sultana of Sawan said with her sneering smile.

'I was just telling the Sultana about how you both love horse riding,' Mother said with a warm smile.

'My, my! Princes in the stable? Whatever next?' the Sultana said with a derisive laugh.

I noticed Mother's disdain before she quickly smiled. 'Do tell me, what did young Layla get up to growing up? I presume she was allowed outside?'

The Sultana looked annoyed. 'Well, of course she was. For some time. She is very accomplished in all her pursuits, as any child of mine would be.'

'Naturally,' my mother replied dryly.

Breakfast was torture. Yunus kept the jokes coming, and it bothered me to see how easily Layla laughed with him. Today, she would hardly look in my direction.

One of the servants handed me a newssheet.

PROTESTS IN SAWAN GATHER
MOMENTUM ACROSS MORE CITIES

'It seems your announcement has not gone well, Your Majesty?' I said, showing the paper to the Sultana. My insides were smug, but I kept a blank expression.

She narrowed her eyes at the newssheet. 'It is all in hand. My armed forces are dealing with the dissenters.'

'Would it not be wise to pause, Your Majesty, and consider your people's concerns?' my mother asked. A strange spark of hope ignited within me. If Layla's engagement with the Fallowmere fell apart, it would reduce the threat of their return, ease tensions, and suspend whatever Sultana Zahra was planning.

'While I appreciate your kind advice, I would prefer not to discuss state matters. Certainly not at the breakfast table.' The Sultana's reply was clipped. 'Once the Fallowmere arrive and bring their wealth, the people will be satisfied.'

'What wealth are they bringing, Your Majesty? The wealth they stole from all of us?' I replied genially.

Layla dropped her pita.

The Sultana of Sawan glared at me before plastering another sweet smile on her face. 'The past is the past, young prince. There is no need to get hung up on it.'

'The past is never over, Your Majesty,' I said. 'History is always rippling into the future. We can only hope the Fallowmere have learned to behave this time.'

'I assure you they are coming with good intentions,' she said simperingly. 'In fact, they will be paying an extensive dowry to my daughter: land in Fallowmere, and estates across their other colonies, no less.'

'Will they be returning the crown jewels they stole from our ancestors for the princess to wear too?' I scoffed.

'Zayd,' Mother said sternly, her tone warning me off.

'It's quite all right, Your Majesty, I appreciate that the prince is passionate about history,' Sultana Zahra said, eyeing me distastefully.

'I'm passionate about keeping our lands free.'

'Well, it's a good thing Dakaria has such an energetic Sultan incoming,' Sultana Zahra replied pointedly.

'I'm sure the people of Sawan feel the same about their princess,' I replied with a warm smile. 'I always hear how excited your people are for Layla to become Sultana soon.'

The way Sultana Zahra's face fell was ridiculously satisfying.

'I assume the coronation won't be long after Princess Layla is married?' my mother added.

'We shall see,' the Sultana said tightly. 'Layla has much to learn still. She must be fully prepared before she takes over.'

'A challenge she will no doubt rise to perfectly,' Mother replied, throwing a kind smile in Layla's direction.

Layla smiled back fleetingly.

'Indeed,' Sultana Zahra said thinly.

Breakfast continued more quietly until we were finally relieved of the ice queen's company.

'I shall see you for our meeting later this afternoon, Your Majesty,' she said to my mother.

Mother nodded. 'Yes, we shall meet then.'

Once the Sultana had left the hall, Yunus let out a loud breath. 'It feels warmer in here already, doesn't it?'

'Yunus!' Mother reproached him, her eyes darting to Layla.

'Don't hold back on my account,' Layla said with a small smile.

'Did you have a good night's rest, Princess?' I asked, wondering why she wouldn't look at me.

Layla met my eyes briefly. 'Yes, Your Highness.'

'Shall we go horse riding after this?' Yunus asked Layla.

'I'd love to.'

Something like irritation spiked along my nerves.

'Wonderful!' Mother said, pleased. 'I'll leave you all to it. I'll just go check on the Sultan.'

I gave Yunus and Layla my goodbyes too, trying to keep myself from wondering why she was being so distant with me again. I thought we had finally reached some common ground, but then the way she'd looked at me when I basically kicked her out last night made me think that I had perhaps soured things. What else was I supposed to have done, though? I didn't want her to think my intentions – though jumbled – were anything less than honourable.

'So, this is how the rich live,' Roshni said in a disgusted voice, looking about my study.

'Please, take a seat,' I said.

She sat down warily on an armchair. 'I take it you didn't ask me here to discuss the weather.'

'It seems we may be able to work together after all,' I said, watching her carefully.

Distaste crossed her features. 'Unfortunately, it seems that way. Who is the girl? Is she part of the court? A servant?'

'I'm sure you can understand why I can't reveal her identity to you. Nice story, by the way,' I added.

Roshni shrugged. 'An old friend in the market asked me to tell a tale. I so rarely come into these parts of Dakaria.'

'So, what do you want with the girl?' I asked.

'That's my business. How old is she?' Roshni asked.

'Seventeen. Why?' I countered.

Roshni looked thoughtful. 'If you want my family to

protect the Silver Port, you must protect the girl until she is eighteen. Which is when?'

'In about two months' time,' I replied slowly. Two months of the mages working at the port would help me bolster the army before the Fallowmere arrived.

'You keep her safe and I'll hold up my end of the bargain. Deal?'

I looked into Roshni's fierce grey eyes for a moment. Layla would be safe in Sawan for the next two months. 'Deal.'

'I expect to be compensated for my time, as well,' she added.

I nodded. 'I will ensure you and your family are paid properly during your service.'

'I also want unfettered access to the silver.'

'For what?' I asked evenly.

Roshni looked at my desk and smirked. She took a silver goblet full of water from my table and waved a withered hand over it. The cup began to overflow with liquid that shot up to the ceiling and gushed onto the floor. The room would flood if she didn't stop!

'What are you doing?' I demanded, jerking to my feet.

Roshni waved her hand again and, just like that, all the water disappeared from the room, retreating into the goblet. 'Silver is a powerful channel for our magic. We could do more than just protect the port if we had the right tools. We can rain down hell on anyone who dares to cross us.'

'I will give you as much access as you need to make your tools,' I said diplomatically. 'Do we have an agreement?'

Roshni measured me up. 'And you swear to protect the girl?'

'Yes, you have my word.'

'Very well. We will begin tomorrow,' Roshni said.

Relief swept through me. 'Thank you.'

'If you even think about going back on your word – if anything happens to the girl – I will make sure you pay for it.'

'I will keep my word,' I repeated steadily.

Noor came in as Roshni left me with a parting glare.

'Is everything OK, Your Highness?'

'You might want to sit down for this,' I said.

20

Layla

The sun's warm rays fell against my skin, a welcome relief after constant parasols. Yunus and I trotted around on two beautiful horses, his a chestnut brown and mine a silky black. The rustling fields stretched out towards the palm trees that circled the palace, bright green under the spring sun.

'I can't remember the last time I rode by myself,' I said, holding the reins tight.

'Are you allowed to have fun in Sawan?' Yunus asked with a cheeky smile.

I rolled my eyes. 'Not if my mother can help it.'

'That must be exhausting, Your Highness.'

'Please, just call me Layla.' I smiled back, not wanting to get into another discussion about my mother. I didn't want to think about her. Or the fact that when we returned home soon, my own wedding preparations would begin. There was no way for me to run away from Dakaria without bringing danger to the royal family here.

'Thank you for keeping me company while I have been here,' I said as the horses trotted on.

Yunus met my gaze with an almost sad smile. 'I should

thank you, Layla. You've given me an excuse to be useful for once. Otherwise, I'm just rattling around the palace while my parents and Zayd play politics.'

My heart sank a little at his words. 'I take it you sit on the sidelines like me?'

Yunus shrugged, looking back out to the horizon. 'I suppose it's just my place as second born. Zayd does all the hard work, and I lounge around and look pretty.'

'Not sure about the pretty part,' I joked.

Yunus laughed, a joyous sound that made my heart warm. He was so easy to be around, unlike his confusing brother.

We ambled through the grounds in companionable silence as the sun rose higher in the sky, passing the greenhouse and the glistening green stream that stretched out towards the woods. As we rode by another field and veered back to the palace, a number of figures loomed in the distance.

'Fancy a game of gillidanda?' Yunus asked, nodding at the group.

'Who are they?' I asked.

'Other children from the court. Come!' He led the way, bringing us towards a trio of young women – Noshin I recognized, along with some of the boys Yunus had introduced me to at the ball.

I dismounted as gracefully as I could and handed the reins to one of the palace servants.

'Your Highness,' Noshin gushed, rushing forward to greet me. She and her friends curtseyed.

'Ready to play, Prince Yunus?' one of the boys said.

'Princess, how are your reflexes?' Yunus asked, chucking a leather ball at me.

I caught it - just about. 'I prefer weapons,' I said, throwing it back at him.

Yunus laughed. 'Come on, let's have a game!'

I hadn't played gillidanda since I was a child but joined the others as they assembled by a makeshift stump to begin batting. I watched the others go first: Yunus threw the ball and they tried to bat it as far as it could go. A servant out in the distance brought it back if Yunus didn't manage to catch it.

Noshin took her strike and managed to bat the ball rather far. She handed the bat to me next.

I took my spot, ready to lift the bat, when the sound of footsteps approaching made me turn.

Zayd walked towards us with his guard in tow. The sun turned the tips of his dark hair chestnut, his strong jaw set in a hard line as he looked around. He caught my eye. My heart stuttered in my chest.

I looked away quickly and nodded at Yunus, ready to strike.

Yunus threw the ball towards me at lightning speed. I just managed to bat it, and sent it flying past his head.

'Not bad, Princess,' Zayd's low voice came from behind me.

I turned and saw him standing a few paces away. Noshin and her friends hurried over to him, fluttering their ever-present fans and eyelashes. Something about the sight irritated me.

'Taking a break from your busy schedule, Prince?' I asked him, my voice colder than I had intended.

I saw a small furrow in his brow, which he smoothed out. 'All work and no play makes for a dull life, wouldn't you say, Noshin?' he said, turning to her.

She simpered and giggled.

Ugh.

I handed the bat to one of the boys and stood back, trying not to listen to Noshin gush at Zayd droning on about housing plans in the south. I cast a discreet glance back and saw him smiling down at her, his face attentive as he listened to what she said in response.

I refocused on the game.

Zayd's arm brushed mine as he stepped past me to take his turn next. His strong, sweet scent wafted over me, taking me back to last night in his room when his lips had just been a moment away. Last night in the city with Zayd had felt like a precious secret. And that moment in his bedroom had been too ... until he had pulled away.

As he took his shot, the court girls swarmed him, laughing loudly.

'Refreshments!' a servant called, bringing a tray with a selection of fresh juices.

Everybody milled around the table where the drinks were set out.

I took my glass and watched Zayd hand out glasses to the other girls. Was he doing that to goad me? Or had he always been a flirt?

'Shall we have another round?' Yunus asked the group. 'Brother, do you want to throw?'

'I think he's too weak of a shot to throw, no?' I found myself saying, looking at Zayd pointedly.

There was a chorus of low laughter.

'Is that a challenge, Princess?' Zayd said, looking right back at me. 'I'd love to see you try first. If you can manage it.'

'By all means show me how it's done, Prince,' I said courteously.

'Ladies first?' he countered. 'Unless you're too afraid to show everyone that you can't throw a ball.'

I scoffed. 'You talk a loud game - are you too scared to start things off?'

'Can someone just throw the ball?' one of the boys grumbled behind us.

Zayd walked up to me. 'I'll go. Good luck to your future husband, Princess - it seems you love to argue,' he said with a gracious smile as he went to take his spot by the stump.

Sniggers filled the air.

'Ignore him,' Yunus said consolingly, bumping my shoulder with his. 'He's just trying to put you off beating him.'

'It's no bother,' I said, feigning a smile. 'I'm sure *his* future wife will enjoy teaching him some manners. If she doesn't run away screaming at the sight of him first.'

I saw Zayd bristle at my words. More sniggers in the air.

Ha. Good.

Zayd wasn't a bad shot - much to my dismay.

When it was my turn, one of the other boys offered to help me fix my stance.

'You're standing too narrow, Your Highness,' the boy said, all wide brown eyes and an easy smile. He was knocked out of the way by Zayd.

'Sorry, Rashid, didn't see where I was going,' Zayd said coolly.

Rashid nodded and pulled back. 'Not to worry, Your Highness.'

'What was that about?' I grumbled.

Zayd looked down at me with an icy gaze. 'You're a trained fighter; I hardly think you need some boy to teach you how to stand.'

'And what if I wanted him to?' I countered.

Zayd's expression was unreadable.

I turned away to take my shot, the anger of our interaction causing a familiar current to hum through my veins. I forced myself to blow out slow breaths. I couldn't let Zayd get under my skin - not when I was in front of a crowd of people.

I threw the ball with more force than I intended, the small sphere of leather whistling through the air with speed and disappearing into the woods. The boy with the bat looked at me helplessly. Hoots of appreciation chorused behind me.

'Wow, that was incredible!' Yunus said.

'Do we have another ball?' Noshin asked, cosying up to Zayd again.

But his eyes were on me.

The buzz in my veins was making it hard to think clearly. 'I'm just going inside to rest. I think I overexerted myself,' I said to Yunus.

'Let me walk you back, Princess?' Zayd offered from across the field.

'No, I don't need an escort.'

The others bowed hastily as I rushed past them, back towards the palace.

Moments later I heard footsteps behind me.

'Princess.'

Zayd.

I ignored him. I could still see the others playing gillidanda; I just needed to get far away from them.

'Layla, wait.'

Why wasn't he leaving me alone?

I stopped when he put himself in front of me, forcing

me to look at him. I couldn't talk to him now; I had to get away.

'Is there something wrong?' he asked, his brow furrowed.

'There is nothing wrong,' I snapped. 'Faisal, can you please tell the prince that I do not need an escort.'

Faisal cleared his throat, springing forward. 'Is there something I can help you with, Your Highness?' he said to Zayd.

I stalked off, leaving Zayd to murmur his excuses. The next set of footsteps I heard behind me were definitely Faisal's. Finally, I was away from the damn prince.

21

Zayd

It seemed I'd lost Layla's good favour again. I supposed I should have been grateful it was after I'd gotten the deal with the water mages, at least. But I felt unsettled, like I'd done something wrong.

She had seemed on edge. Like she was trying to get away. *Why, though*? I wondered.

I thought back on Roshni's interest in her, how much more softly she had spoken with Layla ... even though she had an evident disdain for royals. So why didn't that extend to Layla?

Could she have sensed something within Layla that nobody else knew of – perhaps not even the princess herself? Or was I clutching at straws, imagining that the crown princess of Sawan might be a mage?

I blew out a sigh, shaking my thoughts away as I headed back to the others still playing. I watched Yunus strike a shot.

'Your Highness,' Noor called. 'It is time to meet with the Sultana.'

'Yunus, why don't you join us?' I suggested.

My brother looked at me in surprise but nodded readily.

'What was that with you and Layla, then?' Yunus asked as we made our way towards the emerald room.

'Nothing, just some friendly game talk,' I said, absently rubbing my aching arm. Throwing a ball had done it no favours.

'That definitely wasn't friendly, Brother. It seems like she really hates you,' he said with a laugh. 'What the hell did you do to her?'

'I may have held her at knifepoint the first time we met – she was in my room, thinking it was hers,' I explained hastily.

Yunus looked aghast. 'What is wrong with you?' he hissed. 'Like her mother needs more excuses to invade us! No wonder Layla hates you.'

'Yes, thank you for your observation,' I grumbled.

Mother met us outside with her entourage. 'Ready, sons? Time to face the lioness.'

We made our way inside the parlour, taking our seats on the plush armchairs by the grand fireplace. Minutes later, the Sultana of Sawan waltzed in. Once pleasantries had been exchanged and tea had been poured, the meeting began.

The Sultana smiled. 'As you know, Sawan is a wealthy nation with plentiful natural resources. However, an abundance of silver would benefit our state greatly. I know that you have given Valthar a twenty per cent reduction in fees, so I am sure you will have no qualms in giving Sawan fifty per cent.'

I almost choked on my tea. 'Fifty per cent?' I repeated, incredulous. My hand felt weak, the cup in it unsteady. I put it down.

My mother placed her hand on mine for a moment,

quieting me. 'Valthar has been given twenty per cent in exchange for military support. Will Sawan be pledging the same?'

The Sultana laughed. 'Military support? I'm afraid that's not possible.'

'Really? Didn't you say the Fallowmere would be boosting your military numbers?' my mother asked innocently.

The Sultana's glowing mask faltered for a moment. 'We have other uses for our soldiers.'

'Unfortunately, our silver has attracted the attention of many pirates and pathetic states who use scoundrels to try and loot from us,' Mother said cuttingly. 'We cannot give you such a steep discount on prices for nothing in return.'

The Sultana of Sawan regarded my mother. 'What a shame. And here I thought we were becoming friends.'

Yunus coughed – though it sounded suspiciously like a snort.

'Is your friendship contingent on receiving only?' I asked, looking the Sultana in the eye. 'I thought Sawanis prided themselves on their generosity. Or at least the late Sultan used to.'

I had the satisfaction of seeing the Sultana blanch. She smiled thinly. 'While I am dedicated to charity, I cannot focus all my efforts on helping Dakaria, though I can see you are in desperate need of it. Perhaps I can write to some of our neighbouring lands – see if any of them might offer you some aid.'

I could feel my mother's rage radiating off her.

'How kind of you. But we are not in need of charity the same way you seem to be – clearly our silver is beyond your means,' I said, smiling pleasantly.

The Sultana's eyes darkened.

'Perhaps it is best we keep our relations as they are,' Mother said tightly. 'After all, now that everybody has found out you are bringing the Fallowmere back, the word "traitor" will be associated with Sawan for a long time to come. At least, that is what the papers are saying.'

The Sultana's mask fell. She glowered at us. 'Very well. There isn't much else Dakaria has to offer Sawan anyway. I'm sure I will find better rates elsewhere.'

'I think we can continue this meeting later,' my mother said pointedly. 'We shall see you at dinner, Your Majesty—'

There was an urgent knock at the door.

'Come in,' Mother called.

A Sawani guard rushed inside. He bowed before hurrying towards the Sultana, whispering something in her ear.

The Sultana's eyes flew wide open.

'I will be leaving earlier than planned. It seems there is urgent business to attend to at home,' she said with a fake smile, rising from her seat. 'Jumna, have the rest of our things packed immediately. We will leave tomorrow morning.'

'Surely you can stay a few days more?' Mother asked in a monotone.

'No, I must leave as soon as possible. Do visit Sawan if you have time: Layla's wedding will be the party of the century!' she said airily before she hurried away with her guards.

'What is going on there?' Yunus asked as the door shut behind the Sultana.

'I am sure we'll soon find out,' Mother replied with a frown.

22

Layla

I paced my room, the stress in my body fizzing, ready to explode. I had the urge to spin until I soared into the sky, to singe away everything in sight – there was just so *much* pulsing through my blood.

Hurrying to the bathroom sink, I splashed cold water onto my face, willing myself to calm down. Why was this happening to me? *How* was this happening?

A knock on the door interrupted my thoughts.

'Not now!' I called.

'It's urgent, Your Highness,' Mira's voice called back.

I cursed, splashing more cool water on my face before drying myself. 'All right, come in!'

'Sorry to disturb you, Your Highness,' Mira said in a rush. 'But Her Majesty has announced we are leaving tomorrow morning.'

My stomach dropped. 'What? Why?'

'I think it may have something to do with this,' she said tentatively, pointing to the papers left for me on the parlour table.

I walked over and took one of the newssheets.

DISSENTERS STORM SAWAN PALACE GATES

Riots have taken full hold as the people of Sawan
protest the looming marriage of Princess Layla and
Prince Edmund of Fallowmere . . .

'They're trying to storm the palace?' I gasped.

'It's a good thing we are not there,' Mira said worriedly.

'Why would they be so foolish? She'll have them all executed.'

This couldn't go on. My mother had to accept my engagement was the worst idea she could have come up with.

Mira stayed silent, but her dark eyes locked with mine in sympathy.

'I can't take this any more,' I fumed, storming out of my room.

I hurried along the hallway and down a flight of stairs as Faisal's footsteps echoed behind me.

Not bothering to knock, I walked into Mother's chambers. She was sitting in the parlour with newssheets spread out before her.

She looked up at me. 'What are you doing here?'

'Mother, these protests—'

'Are being dealt with,' she said tersely.

'This marriage isn't good for Sawan. Why can't you just call it off? Strike a trade deal with Fallowmere instead – I don't need to marry their prince!' I said desperately.

Mother glowered at me. 'Now is not the time for this. Once you are married, they will have no choice but to accept my decision. Marriage is the strongest alliance there is.' Her words were firm, her eyes resolute.

Hatred for my mother bubbled up inside me. 'If Father were here, he would never have let this happen. He hated the Fallowmere.'

Mother flinched. 'Yes, well he isn't here any more, is he? The old man died, leaving me a young widow with an obstinate brat for a daughter.'

'He was the Sultan, not an old man,' I growled.

'Yes, may his grave be filled with light,' she snapped back hastily, hearing Jumna cough from the other room. 'But he is dead. I am Sultana. I make the decisions here, and I will do so until you can prove you are capable of thinking rationally.'

'Even if it's tearing our country apart?' I demanded. 'Please, Mother, *please* call it off. Then this will all stop!'

'And who do you think will marry you if we renege on this engagement?'

'Then I won't get married!' I said exasperatedly. I knew it was dangerous talking to my mother like this, but at least while we were in Dakaria there was only so much she could do to me.

Mother scoffed, her face contorting with anger. 'A likely thought. You will marry Edmund and make heirs and secure my reign. We will head home tomorrow and put a stop to this nonsense. Now get out before I lose my temper with you.'

Heat began to grow in my palms again. I clenched my fists quickly and fled from the room, rushing back upstairs.

I flew past Mira packing away my things and rushed into the bathroom, plunging my steaming hands into cold water. My body was shaking.

I had to do something. She would never listen to me.

Once we were back on Sawani soil, I would make my move.

*

192

I moped around in my chambers for the rest of the day. Mother had secluded herself in her quarters, so I went to dinner alone. Sultana Aysha and Yunus carried most of the conversation as we ate, while Zayd sat quietly on the other side, barely looking at me.

It left a pit in my stomach that he wouldn't make eye contact with me, but perhaps it was for the best. I was leaving tomorrow morning and Dakaria would soon be a distant memory.

'It has been so wonderful having you here, Layla,' Sultana Aysha said warmly. 'I always wished to have a daughter of my own. You must come and visit whenever you want; there will always be a room here for you.'

I looked at the Sultana in surprise. I couldn't understand why she spoke so kindly to me. 'Thank you, Sultana. That means a lot.'

She smiled back at me, her olive eyes twinkling in the candlelight. The exact same shade as Zayd's.

I looked back at my plate and tore another piece of naan.

After our dishes had been cleared, Zayd got up to leave.

'Have a good evening,' he said to no one in particular.

'What's up with him?' Yunus said after he had left.

'He's just been under a lot of pressure,' Sultana Aysha said sadly. 'Your father's health and the wedding – it's a lot of change. You boys are still so young.'

Yunus scoffed. 'I am no boy – I'm turning eighteen next year. I also expect a very lavish party to celebrate.'

Sultana Aysha patted his arm affectionately. 'Yes, dear, whatever you wish.'

We moved to a smaller, more intimate parlour and drank tea together until the candle wax had disappeared down to the wick. Half of me didn't want to leave; this family was more loving than anything I had in Sawan.

I eventually left as well and headed back to my chambers. I hesitated outside, looking at the golden double doors that led to Zayd's room. It felt strange, this ice between us, like after our first meeting. But it was my doing. I had no right to expect any more from him. He'd made it clear he wasn't interested beyond being future allies.

The significance of all those looks, the fleeting touches, had just been my mind playing tricks on me.

My trunks were sealed and ready by the door. Mira helped me undress and I got into my nightgown.

'See you in the morning,' I said to Mira.

'Sleep well, Your Highness.' Mira departed.

23

Layla

D arkness engulfed me but I lay in bed, tossing and turning. Tomorrow, I either ran from my future or was dragged into it.

I gave up tossing and sat upright, grabbing a shawl before I traipsed across the marble floors to the balcony. The cool night air greeted me as I pushed open the latticed doors. I walked towards the edge, looking out to the darkness. It was hard to discern anything in the distance - a few stars glimmered in the sky, but it seemed the moon was in seclusion tonight. There was no sign of her pearly shine.

I followed the large balcony as it wrapped around the entire floor and took a seat against the colourful cushions scattered across the corner sofa at its far end.

An unlit lantern sat on the wooden table. A reckless urge came over me and I drew my fingers slowly into the lamp, urging the flames from my hand. I lit the lantern and warm light glowed, bathing the seating area in gold.

There was no pain, no burning sensation. I drew my hand back - my fingers were entirely unscathed.

A sigh in the night made me jump up. Behind me a dark

figure was slumped on the twin balcony, looking out to the dark horizon.

'Zayd?' I said hesitantly.

The figure stood straight. Golden light streaming out of his windows illuminated one side of his face. His eyes were devastating in the half-light.

'Layla? What are you doing out here?' Zayd asked, his brows creasing.

I drifted closer to the edge of the balcony, a few feet between the railings separating us. 'I just thought I'd enjoy the scenery before we head home tomorrow.'

'It's dark out,' he said pointedly.

I sighed. 'Fine. I couldn't sleep. Why are you out here?'

He looked at me intently, his eyes drifting momentarily to my nightgown. His jaw tightened.

I felt a blush creep up my cheeks, suddenly aware of how thin my gown was. My shawl had slipped off one shoulder. I drew it tighter around me.

'I couldn't sleep either,' he said eventually. 'It's a shame you're heading home so soon.'

'Is it?' I replied. 'I thought you'd be glad to see the back of us.'

He looked at me, curiosity in his eyes. 'What gave you that impression?'

'I'm guessing the meeting about the silver didn't go too well,' I hedged.

He almost smiled. 'As well as we were expecting.'

A gust of wind blew around us, sending a shiver down my spine.

'You should go back inside. You'll get cold,' he said, his voice low. There was that look in his eyes again.

'What if I don't want to?' I replied.

Now he smiled. 'You love to have the last word, don't you?'

I shrugged. 'Maybe. Fancy sneaking out of the palace again? One last night of freedom?'

He raised a brow. 'You've been cold with me all day, and now you want to hang out? Sounds like you're using me, Princess.'

'I'm surprised you noticed – you seemed rather busy with the court girls,' I retorted.

His lips twitched. 'Bothered you, did it?'

I bristled. 'You wish.'

'You're the one who mentioned it,' he replied with an infuriating smirk.

The retort I wanted to hurl died on my tongue. *Damn it.* 'Whatever. I should probably go to bed.'

'Layla, wait,' Zayd called as I turned to leave.

'What?' I said coolly over my shoulder.

'Why don't you join me for a nightcap?' he suggested, all humour gone from his expression.

I searched his face, hesitating.

'Come on. You can't sleep, I can't sleep – we might as well pass the time together.'

'Only because I have nothing better to do,' I said grudgingly.

He fought a smile. 'As you say, Princess. Wait – what are you doing?' Zayd's voice rose with alarm as I climbed onto the railing. He rushed forward. 'Layla, stop!'

I stood up on the stone balcony and jumped over the small gap, landing lithely before Zayd. He grabbed my waist, steadying me – as if I needed it.

'Are you all right?' he demanded. 'You could have fallen!'

'The gap was barely there, calm down.' I laughed.

'Do you have a death wish?' he continued, his fingers tightening on my waist. 'You're not just anyone – you can't just risk your life when you feel like it.'

'Zayd, calm down, I was hardly endangering myself,' I said defiantly. But the panic in his eyes made me unsure for a moment.

'Why are you so stubborn?' he said, his voice dangerously low.

'Why do you care?' I countered, my own a murmur.

'I don't know,' he confessed in a whisper. One of his hands drifted up, his knuckles brushing the side of my face. He tucked a strand of hair behind my ear, his fingers trailing back along my jaw.

The urge to lean in and touch him was desperate. I carefully lifted a hand and placed it on his cheek, the fine stubble of his beard grazing my skin. Zayd's eyes closed as he leant into my hand with a sigh.

I traced my thumb over his soft lips.

His eyes flew open and the depth of dark hunger in them took my breath away.

'Layla,' he said, his voice strained.

'Sorry,' I mumbled, pulling away. What was I thinking?

His hand tightened on my hips. 'Wait. You don't have to leave.'

Desire coursed through my veins.

The air between us was heavy. I felt frozen under his touch, afraid to move in case I broke the spell.

It would be so easy to close the distance between our lips. One turn of my head, one moment, one mistake.

The sound of a door slamming made us jump apart.

'Your Highness, I have your tea!' a woman's voice called from inside Zayd's chambers.

'Leave it in the parlour, Iris!' Zayd called back, running a hand through his hair. 'I'll be in shortly!'

'OK, Your Highness!' she replied.

The door closed again.

Zayd watched me warily. 'Tea?'

'Maybe I should go,' I said, though my limbs wanted to do anything but move from here.

Disappointment flickered across his eyes. 'Yes. Maybe you should.'

'Thank you for everything,' I said finally.

Zayd stepped forward slowly, as if trying not to startle me. His hand drifted back up towards my cheek as he leant in, pressing a soft kiss to my forehead. My eyes fluttered shut as I revelled in his warmth.

'You never have to thank me,' he whispered, cupping my face. 'Whatever happens next ... with the Fallowmere ... know that you always have a friend in Dakaria.'

A friend. Right. I nodded, lips pressed together, afraid of what I might say in response.

'Look after yourself, Princess. Be safe.' The devastating look in his eyes nearly stopped my breath. I nodded again and pulled myself away, Zayd's hand falling back to his side.

I jumped over the balcony and hurried towards my room before I did something I couldn't come back from.

24

Zayd

I watched Layla disappear, my heart beating unevenly in my chest. I had half a mind to leap over the damn balcony myself, beg her to stay a little while longer so that we could ... so that I could ...

The desire to be near her was all-consuming, some kind of magnetic pull I couldn't shake off. The smell of her jasmine and rose scent still hung in the air. The memory of her warm body against mine left me with an ache.

Her warmth. It was almost unbearable, like she was an open flame.

I blew out a sigh and headed back into my room. This was foolish. This was chaos.

She was beautiful. Bright. Funny. Infuriating.

And possibly a mage.

That night in Dukhha, I had been so distracted by what had nearly happened afterwards that I hadn't even stopped to consider whether the story Roshni had told might be true. Could Layla be their supposed saviour?

But whether Layla truly *was* didn't concern me - so long as Roshni believed it and worked with us.

I shook my head to get rid of the confusion brewing

inside and withdrew into my room. Layla was going home tomorrow. The riots in Sawan were worrying – people saw Layla as part of the betrayal too. But the princess was heavily guarded. And if you could trust the ruthless Sultana Zahra for anything, it was to ensure that nobody would get within arm's reach of the heir that legitimized her position on the throne.

All I needed was for Layla to stay safe until I was married. If the mages could help stave off attacks on the Silver Port in the meantime, I could work on strengthening the army while Valthar sent their soldiers to aid ours.

I woke with the dawn, pushing myself out of bed. Remnants of last night threatened to plague me, but I squashed all thoughts of Layla as I headed over to Father's quarters.

Father was still asleep when I reached him, but the servants had begun to prepare his breakfast.

Eventually, he rose, a smile spreading across his face when he saw me. 'Son, you are early.'

'A true Sultan rises with the dawn, as you said,' I replied with a faint smile.

Father wheezed. 'Come, eat with me.'

We ate in companionable silence. Coughs continued to wrack his body all through breakfast. Eventually I stood to hold him up, rubbing his back as he shook. 'Hakim, can you bring Father's medicine,' I called.

'I'm fine,' Father grumbled. He coughed harder, putting a napkin to his mouth. Specks of blood flecked the cloth. My stomach lurched. Father put the napkin hastily away.

'Of course you are,' I said firmly. 'You are the Sultan. You will make it out of this.'

Once Father had taken his medicine, he leant back and breathed heavily. 'You'll have to face reality soon, my son.'

His eyes watered a little as he looked at me, the intent in his words clear.

I stilled.

'Zayd,' Father continued, his voice a sigh.

I shook my head. I couldn't bear to have this conversation again.

'Let's talk about something else,' Father said lightly. 'Did you make contact with the water mages?'

I sat back down. 'Yes, I did.'

'And?'

'They have agreed.'

Father's eyes widened. 'Really? They agreed? What did they want in return?'

'Access to the silver,' I said. I wasn't lying, really. 'It's a tool for them to channel magic.'

'Is that all?' Father asked, his brow creasing.

'Should there be more?' I countered.

'No, I just – well, I never thought I'd see the day,' he said with awe. 'Zayd, I am proud of you. You did the impossible. Now we can breathe until the Valthar soldiers arrive.'

The smile on his face only made me feel guilty. If he really knew what I had bargained with Roshni for . . .

'We should tell your mother,' he said, just as the door opened.

Mother glided in, her emerald sari flowing behind her. 'Tell me what?'

I shared a look with Father.

'Well?' she pressed, taking a seat beside Father. 'Don't keep me in suspense.'

'The water mages have agreed to help at the port in return for access to the silver,' I said.

Mother's mouth fell open. 'What?'

'This is good news,' Father said keenly. 'Our soldiers will have a reprieve.'

Mother looked at me in confusion. 'When did they agree?'

'I met with the chief yesterday.'

'Well, it's of great benefit to us, I suppose,' Mother said, eyeing me warily. 'Just be careful, Zayd. If the mages sense any ill behaviour towards them, their powers can be unforgiving.'

Guilt continued to fester in me. 'Yes, Mother. All is well, though. It's a simple trade.'

A knock sounded on the door. Noor came in. 'Your Majesties, Your Highness – the royals of Sawan are leaving now.'

Father patted my hand. 'I'll see you both later.'

I nodded and followed Mother out. My feet began to feel like lead against the gravel paths.

'Mother, I just need to get something from my room, I'll meet you there,' I said.

'All right, dear,' she said without stopping.

I turned towards my quarters.

I dropped into a chair in my parlour as Noor unwrapped my arm and reapplied the salve. It was better if I didn't say goodbye.

Once Noor had finished fixing my arm, I traipsed out to my balcony and looked over to the main courtyard. The royal carriages of Sawan were trundling away. My throat felt tight as I watched Layla disappear.

25

Layla

I took steadying breaths as we rode away from the palace of Dakaria and the small slice of freedom I had experienced. Mira was already dozing off, her faint snores filling the carriage. I blew out a sigh.

Why hadn't Zayd come? I had hoped to see him one last time. What business did he have that couldn't wait for a moment to say goodbye? Was this the kind of 'friendship' he was offering?

My heart twisted. Perhaps it was better this way.

I could still feel the warmth of his embrace, the press of his lips against my skin.

I sank back into my seat, willing myself to think of anything but Zayd. I had bigger things to worry about – like how I was going to run away.

Once I was in my cabin on the ship back to Sawan, I opened my trunk and stashed as much gold as I could in my pockets. The silver daggers Zayd had gifted me could probably be sold, so I stowed them inside my cape, plus a couple of my own for extra security. I needed to travel light – clothes and food could be bought along the way.

Would Mother know I had run away, or would she suspect something else? At least once we were back in Sawan, she couldn't blame the Dakaria royals for any foul play. I could give them that much after all the kindness they had shown me.

The heat that danced beneath my skin reaffirmed my decision. I had to escape before Mother found out about me. Before I was married. This was my only chance.

'Tea, Your Highness?' Mira asked, entering my quarters, with a tray laden with pastries and tea.

'Sure, thank you.' I watched Mira make her way across the wooden floor, placing the tray carefully on the table as the room continued to sway from the ocean.

Would I ever see Mira again?

My heart lurched in my chest. She was my only real friend: the one person left in my life who felt like family. I knew I could persuade her to leave with me, but what if it all went wrong?

It was better if she didn't come. She would be safer that way.

'Are you all right?' Mira looked at me in concern. 'You look sad.'

'Just tired. Thank you for always taking care of me.' I crossed the room and grabbed her in a hug.

Mira hugged me back, laughing. 'Are you feeling seasick already?'

I shook my head, holding her for a moment longer.

Once we were back on Sawan soil, I would make my move.

As the hours bled by on sea then back on land again, fatigue began to claim me. I forced myself to stay alert as we rode under the afternoon sun. We finally came to a stop outside an inn that sat alone in an expanse of field, encircled by woods.

'I need to use the bathroom,' I said to Faisal, hurrying away from him and Mira and into the inn.

Mother was complaining loudly about the uneven roads as she stretched her legs.

My heartbeat raced as the innkeeper led me towards the bathroom as Faisal trailed behind. I gave the innkeeper my thanks and slid inside, waiting several beats as her footsteps faded away.

I scaled the bathroom wall to reach a medium-sized window. I pushed it open, the pane creaking under a layer of dust. I hoisted myself up and over the lintel, landing quietly on the soft grass outside. The back fields were entirely empty.

I wouldn't have long until Faisal realized something was up. My heart thundered in my chest as I cut a fast line into the forest. Coins clinked within the folds of my dress. I just needed to find a town where I could purchase a horse and then get as far away from my mother as possible.

The woods beckoned me with gnarled arms, the canopy of leaves above welcoming me into their dark shade. My feet crunched against the debris on the ground just as the shouts cried out. Faisal must have sounded the alarm.

I rushed on, my shins burning with exertion as my cape flapped behind me. My breath was heavy in the air as the din grew louder.

A twig snapping ahead stopped me dead in my tracks.

I waited, listening.

Snap.

I whirled in the direction of footsteps. Something darted behind a thicket of trees.

Snap.

I spun again, only for a loud *crack* to fill the air as something bludgeoned into the back of my head.

A cry of pain ripped from my throat.

'Princess!' Faisal shouted, his voice nearby.

'Faisal!' I cried out, trying to sit up.

I lifted my heavy head and saw Faisal running towards me, brandishing his sword.

I heard the whistling of an arrow cutting through the air, and saw the fatal shock in Faisal's eyes as an arrow pierced through his back and protruded out of the space where his heart was.

'Faisal!' I screamed, as the guard who had watched over me since I was a child lost his life and fell to the ground.

Another sharp *whack* hit the back of my head.

Everything went dark.

26

Zayd

I spent the next couple of days in my study, ignoring the persistent throbbing in my arm as I wrote up a story for the newssheets about how we were mending ties with the water mages. It wouldn't be long before word started to spread of strange occurrences by the Silver Port. But Roshni's word was true; we'd had no successful attacks since her family had erected a towering wave in the ocean. Anyone who managed to push through found themselves in a whirlpool that spat them back out, away from the port.

'What is my beloved brother up to today?' Yunus sang, bursting into my study.

'Do you ever knock?'

'Why would I do that?' he asked, dropping onto a chair.

I rolled my eyes. 'What are you doing today? I thought you were sitting in on the hearings.' Normally I sat in on the hearings, a weekly affair where all our subjects were invited to come and bring their urgent problems to our attention - land disputes, social issues and so on. But I had passed the responsibility onto Yunus today. I had to start preparing him, just in case.

'They finished; we didn't have that many people today,' Yunus said. 'What have you been holed up in here doing?'

I looked at him for a moment before handing him the statement I had written.

Yunus's eyes widened as he read through it. 'Water mages?' he said shocked.

'Yes, they've agreed to work with us for a fee. There's nothing to worry about,' I added as concern crossed his features.

'This is magic you're dealing with, Brother. What if they turn against you?'

'Like I said, we have an agreement,' I repeated. *If only he knew the half of it.* 'We've already had a reduction in attacks because pirates can't get through the mages' ocean barrier.'

'Well, I guess that's good,' Yunus said, sounding uncertain. 'I still remember the scary stories about mages.'

'Fiction sells more than fact sometimes, Brother,' I said, almost smiling at the fanciful tales Mother would tell us as children before bed.

'How did you even find the water mages?' Yunus asked.

'One of the healers here is related to the chief of the water mages,' I said.

'Oh – is it that Sayyidah Shafiya? So *that*'s why you've been seeing her,' Yunus said. 'Is ... your arm healed?'

'It's getting there,' I said shortly.

Guilt flashed in his eyes, but before he could reply, the door burst open on the heels of a hasty knock. Usman strode in, brandishing a newssheet.

'Your Highness, terrible news from Sawan,' he said breathlessly.

I snatched the paper from his hand.

PRINCESS LAYLA OF SAWAN –
KIDNAPPED BY RESISTANCE MOVEMENT

'What? How?' I spluttered.

'They all say the same thing,' Yunus said in an ashen voice, scouring another newssheet from Usman.

Last night, upon their return from a diplomatic visit to Dakaria, the Sultana and the Princess of Sawan were ambushed.

The princess was abducted from an inn close to the Black Forest south of the palace – a forest known for its shadowy depths and endless predatory creatures. The royal guards were slain by a rain of arrows, and the princess was heard screaming before she was taken away.

Riots have been erupting all over Sawan since the news broke that Princess Layla has been betrothed to a Fallowmere prince, including outside the Palace of Asad itself, where dissenters lit fires beside the palace walls.

Now a group calling themselves The Resistance are claiming responsibility for the violent kidnapping of the heir to the throne. The Sultana is devastated, and has announced handsome rewards for anyone who has information that can help return the princess. Over a hundred members of the Resistance have so far been arrested and sentenced to death.

Palace sources say the Sultana is determined to find her only heir and ensure the royal wedding still goes ahead . . .

'Brother,' Yunus was saying. 'Brother?'

I looked up at him blankly.

The door to my study burst open and Mother rushed in. 'Have you heard?' she asked.

'Yes,' Yunus answered. 'How did this happen?'

'It seems the Sawanis really don't want this wedding to go ahead,' Mother said worriedly. 'I tried to counsel that woman, but she wouldn't listen. Why take the princess? She's just a young girl!'

'They seek to bargain with the Sultana - as if she gives a damn about a hair on Layla's head,' I growled. Dread pooled in my gut.

'Surely the Sultana will be able to get her back soon?' Yunus said.

I looked over the papers again. 'If the newsheets only got hold of this for the evening print, she's already been missing for a day. They could have taken her anywhere by now - across the borders, even.' My hands shook. I threw the newssheet down.

'We must send assistance, to show good will,' Mother said urgently. 'Zayd, can you free up any soldiers around our border?'

'Maybe a dozen or so - I will go with them,' I said.

Mother gasped. 'You are to marry in a matter of weeks; you cannot go out on any field missions!'

'I won't sit idly by while the princess is out there - abducted after she left *our* home!' My voice was rising. 'We'll be lucky if her mother doesn't accuse us of orchestrating this.'

'Send me, then,' Yunus said.

'Don't be ridiculous,' Mother snapped.

'Absolutely not,' I said, glowering at him.

Yunus glared back at me. 'Fine. Then let me come with you.'

'I will not have both of you out there risking your lives!' Mother thundered.

'This is not up for discussion,' I snapped. 'I am going, and I am going alone. I'll leave at dawn.'

'You cannot be serious, Zayd!' Mother raged. 'I insist you remain here. We can send our best soldiers, especially now that we can relieve some from the Silver Port.'

I looked at her evenly. 'I am the incoming Sultan – I will go, and my word is final.' I didn't relish the thought of throwing my title around, but I couldn't stand by, not if Layla had been abducted – or worse.

Mother glared at me. 'You had better come back in one piece or there will be hell to pay!' She turned and strode out of the room.

Yunus threw me a sullen look before he stalked out too.

I kicked at my chair. 'Damn it!'

What if Layla was … ?

No, I couldn't believe that. I wouldn't.

If this resistance group had taken her, they would keep her alive, so the Sultana would bargain with them.

Roshni's demand was seared into my mind – I had to keep Layla safe until she came of age.

Mercifully, Roshni didn't know who Layla really was. But if she managed to figure it out, if Layla's portrait started circulating – everything could fall apart.

I had to find her.

PART II

27

Layla

My eyelids began to flutter. I felt like I was blinking against sludge, trying to force my eyes to open.

A groan escaped my lips. My senses came back to life, one by one. My hands were tied achingly behind me with rope, my throat was raw and dry, my head pounding with pain.

My eyes finally focused. I was in a dark room, wisps of light sneaking through wooden shutters over the tiny window.

I looked around. It was a small room. The door was wooden too, a small hole carved out of the middle of the frame. An eye looked back at me.

A chill ran down my spine.

Muffled voices – Sawani. Footsteps.

The door opened. A young boy entered, perhaps no more than eleven or twelve. His face was wary as he held out a glass of water to my cracked lips.

I gulped the water down. 'Who are you?' I rasped after I was finished.

The boy didn't reply, his eyes wide with fear. He scurried out.

'What do you want?' I shouted.

We had been riding home, back in Sawan … the inn …

This was all my fault.

If I hadn't tried to run away, if I hadn't …

Faisal.

A sob ripped out of me.

Eons later, more footsteps sounded, and the door creaked open once more.

A surly-looking woman stood in the doorway, her blue eyes appraising me with contempt. Her dark hair was pulled back into a bun, accentuating her sharp face.

'Who are you?' I demanded.

'My name is not important,' she said dismissively.

'Why am I here?' I asked through gritted teeth. If they wanted me dead, they would have killed me by now. Clearly, they needed a bargaining chip.

'Our demand is simple,' she said in a cold voice. 'We will release you once the Sultana ends your engagement and breaks off all ties with the Fallowmere.'

I shook my head, a tired laugh escaping my lips. 'You are delusional. My mother cannot be threatened into action.'

'Is her own daughter's life so worthless?' she said, a sneer on her face.

'You have no idea who you're dealing with,' I said, laughing again. I was hysterical. This was ridiculous. And I was so tired. 'If you wanted to force the Sultana's hand, you should have picked someone she actually loves. Your heads will roll before she cedes to your demands.'

The woman blanched, her sneer faltering. She quickly rearranged her features in a blank mask. 'It doesn't matter. You are the heir to the throne. She will agree. Once our demands are met, we will release you.'

'Good luck with that,' I huffed, grimacing as a spasm of pain ran through my arms.

The woman left abruptly, the door slamming behind her.

Nobody had ever gone up against my mother and won, least of all me.

A gust of wind rattled the window shutters. The simple dress I had put on to travel back home was soiled, ripped around the skirts. Cold had crept into my bones, making it harder to move.

My wrists felt raw against the rope. I tried to move, but my body was stiff. How long had I been in this position?

Would Mother even bother sending soldiers out? She had to, I reasoned. I was an integral piece in her great plan to bring the Fallowmere here.

But a small part of me doubted it. She'd sooner leave me for dead than let anybody tell her what to do.

Faisal. His empty brown eyes.

I leant back against the stone wall, breathing out a watery sigh. I just wanted to get my hands free, so I could rest without the ache pulling at my arms. My cloak was gone and with it my daggers and my money.

It felt like moments ago that I had been in Dakaria, enjoying the company of the royal family ... Zayd.

My eyes watered. I wished I could rewind time and go back to the balcony, stay under the stars with him.

Some time later, the door opened again. The young boy was back with a small plate of food: potatoes and a cut of chicken with a stone cup of water. A guard, armed with a sword, stood in the doorway.

'I need my hands to eat,' I said loudly.

'Leave the food on the floor,' the guard barked.

The boy obliged, running back out.

The guard drew his sword. My heart almost stopped.

'Stand up,' he said gruffly, eyeing me with distaste.

I struggled to get my body moving. Once I was on my feet, he turned me around roughly. I heard the slicing of thick rope and my binding fell away.

Before I could turn around, the guard had retreated and shut the door with a loud slam.

I shook my arms out, tears stinging my eyes.

I picked up the plate and inhaled the food – I couldn't remember the last time I had eaten. The water tasted murky down my parched throat.

My stomach felt hollow. I slumped against the wall. Was this how my life concluded? Withering away in a room by myself? Perhaps it was right. I was insignificant, my only value the fact I had been born to a royal household.

I hugged my knees to my chest and buried my face in the folds of my dress as my vision began to blur. I should fight. I should get up.

But I couldn't move. The darkness claimed me again.

28

Zayd

The wind whipped around me as my horse galloped towards the northern port, racing through endless fields as the sun awoke across the sky. A large number of guards rode around me in a tight formation, carrying big trunks - some packed with clothes, most rammed with weapons and supplies to last a few weeks.

I had said my goodbyes to my parents last night, but I couldn't shake the disappointed look in their eyes as I rode away. I knew they thought me reckless, but there was too much at stake.

We finally arrived at the palace of Sawan. Grand spires reached into the dusky sky - smooth sandstone dotted with iridescent arched windows. Parts of the lawn had been scorched, and some areas of the iron gates circling the palace were broken. Guards stood around every inch of the perimeter, the tension in the air thick.

My party came to a stop in the palace courtyard. I dismounted, grateful to stretch my legs as I was greeted by a number of ministers. I was quickly escorted through to the Sultana's court. The palace was rushing with people – servants, ministers hurrying with papers, guards striding around with their hands firmly on the hilts of their swords.

Golden double doors were thrown open to reveal a large domed room filled with desks and people poring over maps.

The Sultana stood in the centre in deep discussion with a high commanding officer whose many medals gleamed upon his chest.

My arrival was made known.

'Prince Zayd,' Sultana Zahra said by way of greeting. She strode over to me. 'Very good of you to come here.'

'Put me to use, Your Majesty. Where shall I start searching?'

'We are interrogating a number of criminals, but they all claim to know nothing,' the Sultana said angrily.

'The attack was planned, but rushed,' I posited. 'They must be sticking close to home. Do you have any more information on their leaders?'

'Over here,' she said, leading the way to a large board plastered with sketches of faces, maps and land deeds.

I spent hours with various officers compiling a list of areas to search. I opted to join the party heading west at dawn, where most of the resistance leaders appeared to hold land.

Perhaps I had misjudged the Sultana's affections towards her daughter. This was an extensive effort to recover Layla. I was glad to see she was leaving no stone unturned.

Sometime after midnight, I was taken to a room to retire. Noor joined me to reapply the salve and wrap fresh bandages on my wound. I did my best not to look at the poisonous black veins spreading down my skin. The balm was a welcome relief, dulling the sting that gripped my arm.

'You don't have to go out with the search party, Your

Highness,' Noor said in a quiet voice. 'The wound is getting worse. You should be resting.'

I shook my head. 'I can't just rest while she's out there.'

'The Sultana's entire army is looking for the princess, Your Highness,' Noor said, frustration colouring his tone. 'You are one person amongst thousands; you do not need to be on the field.'

'I won't sit here idly while she's missing in who knows what condition,' I snapped. 'Besides, if our new partners find out ...'

'All the more reason why you should have stayed home and not roused suspicion,' Noor said quietly. 'It won't be long before they hear about it. A missing princess will be global news.'

'I am doing this for Dakaria. Perhaps it will keep the Sultana from invading if I can help find Layla,' I said.

Noor looked at me warily. 'That wound on your arm is a ticking timer for how long we don't even know. You need rest and you need—'

'That will be all, thank you, Noor,' I said pointedly. I was in no mood for a lecture.

Noor sighed but nodded, withdrawing from my chambers.

I felt a restless energy take hold of me. I slammed my hand down on the bed and stormed over to the balcony, taking in the cold night air. The palace sat on a high vantage point, offering an unrivalled view of the capital city that glimmered below.

I looked past the city lights to the darkness that spread out to the horizon. I could only pray that Layla was OK, and that we found her in time.

29

Layla

Sleep came and went, mocking me. The skin around my wrists was sore from their being bound again while I was asleep. My head felt foggy. My mouth tasted tangy.

I kept taking myself back to Dakaria. I wanted to disappear into the palace again, lose myself in the lush green hills and waterways that spread like veins through the country. I kept remembering how I'd first been accosted by Zayd, the intensity of his olive eyes. The panic on his face when he realized who I was. How he'd offered me tea. The way he looked at me. Laughing with Yunus as we rode through the palace grounds.

Flames growing at my touch.

Was I dreaming?

The floor around me was rough, cold tiles. I tried to touch the walls, but my vision blurred. They gave me water again, the little boy with the scared face. Some bread and cheese. My stomach wouldn't stop rumbling.

I tried to ask for my release. I promised I wouldn't reveal their identities or seek revenge, if they would just let me go. I would walk all the way home if I had to. Silence was my only answer.

The window shutters wouldn't open. I tried to move them, banging my head against them to no avail. I tried to summon power in my hands, hoping to burn the ropes off, but the energy that lived deep inside me felt muffled now, as if it was locked up somewhere I couldn't reach. My head wouldn't stop hurting.

'What's happened to her?' A voice, still my foe.

'Didn't you realize her head was bleeding, you fool? What use is a dead princess?'

Someone was carrying me. Another room. It smelled like dust and old wood.

Gentle hands pressed something cool to my head. Put something cold to my lips. Poured something warm down my throat.

'You need to eat,' somebody said.

I was so tired. I just wanted to sleep for ever. Perhaps I could see my baba now.

30

Zayd

The horses thundered as we headed west. The battalions had been split up, spreading out in four directions. We would comb through every town, every village, until we found the princess.

The first town we stopped at lay beyond a river that separated it from the capital. I scanned the surrounding dwellings – mainly small farmhouses with grazing livestock and stables scattered through the fields. The Sawani soldiers were rough as they searched each home, turning over almost every item of furniture. I stood back with the captain, a severe looking man called Sayed, surveying every possible shelter, feeling around for loose floorboards or hidden ceilings.

It was nightfall by the time we finally stopped, having searched through a dozen villages. Camp was set up in a safehouse that belonged to the Sultana, set in a quiet field with a stable for our horses to rest.

My nerves felt like they were on fire. I tried to get some sleep, but all I could think about was that the odds of finding Layla alive were narrowing. Were we heading in the wrong direction?

I tossed and turned in the creaky old bed, my arm throbbing with pain.

'Respectfully, Your Highness, can you be quiet?' Noor grumbled from the other side of the room.

'The bed is uncomfortable.'

'Perhaps if His Highness tries lying still it might help.'

I snorted. 'Have you had any word from Dakaria?'

'There should be a messenger arriving tomorrow,' he replied sleepily. 'All will be well.'

Guilt gnawed at me as I thought about Father in his weakened state. Hopefully I wouldn't be away for much longer.

The days blurred into one another as we raided endless towns and villages, making our way through each and every home. Terrified people looked back at us, but I had to keep reminding myself what we were doing this for.

At the end of the night in another safehouse a messenger from the royal guard arrived with news.

'Her Majesty received a ransom note this afternoon.'

I snatched the note out of his hand, Sayed reading over my shoulder.

> The princess will be returned alive once the
> Sultana calls off the marriage to Prince Edmund
> of Fallowmere. Failure to do so will result in the
> princess's death. We will allow you three days to call
> off the wedding.

My stomach sank. The note was dated today. 'What will Her Majesty do?'

The messenger looked back at me worriedly.

'Her Majesty will not call off the wedding, Your Highness,' the captain replied gravely. 'Prince Edmund and his family are already on a ship on their way here.'

My stomach sank. 'Then we only have three days to recover the princess?'

The captain nodded grimly.

31

Layla

The next time I blinked awake, I was lying on something soft. There was a small window in the wall, just big enough to show sunlight streaming through a fan of leaves. *Trees.* I was surrounded by palm trees. I tried to listen out, but all I could hear was the chirping of birds.

My hands were bound in front of me now, causing less strain. I looked around; the room was bigger, but just as empty. I was lying on an old sofa - faded blue, worn with holes. I righted myself with a struggle, breathing heavily.

My insides ached; my outside ached; fatigue threatened to pull me under again. I swayed.

'You're awake, at last.' The woman was in front of me again. 'Eat,' she said, putting bread to my lips.

I took a bite with difficulty.

'Now drink,' she said.

My throat hurt as I glugged down the odd-tasting water. I slumped back against the sofa. 'Did you take lessons in hospitality for prisoners while I was asleep?' I huffed out.

The woman narrowed her eyes at me. 'We are not the bad ones here.'

'Really? Is somebody else abducting young women?'

The woman blanched. 'Our people suffered greatly under the Fallowmere. We will not allow them to darken our shores again.'

'Take it up with my mother,' I spat out.

'The Sultana does not listen. We have written letters, tried to meet with ministers. We have been ignored at every turn, imprisoned for expressing our opinions. We have been left with no choice,' the woman insisted angrily. 'Our people are destitute. And our fates will only get worse when the Fallowmere come back to subjugate us once more. Our labourers are already forced to work for cheap – how much more labour will they enforce? Will they pack us onto their ships again and take us as slaves back to their lands?'

I felt a pang of guilt. 'I am the last person who wants this wedding to go ahead.' I almost regretted my words, but what did I have to lose?

The woman's eyes widened with shock.

'But my mother cannot be backed into a corner,' I said.

'How do you propose we reason with her?' the woman pressed.

'If you find the answer, let me know,' I said.

The woman looked away, stress written across her sharp features. Clearly their plan was not going well.

'Has she refused your demands already?' I remarked with a hollow laugh.

The woman scowled. 'The Sultana is bluffing. If you die, so does her reign. She has soldiers raiding towns every day. That doesn't sound like someone who doesn't want you back.'

I felt a flicker of hope.

'But perhaps she needs some ... encouragement,' the woman said coldly, staring at me.

My body flooded with dread.

It happened in a flash. The woman lunged, a glint of silver – my arm seared with pain. She wiped a cloth against my wound as I screamed out, the blood stark red against the white, and before I could thrash my way out of her hold, she grabbed me by my hair. I shrieked and felt the rough slicing of the knife again as she took a lock. She shoved me away and stalked out of the room.

I looked down at the gash on my arm. Blood was pooling out of the wound. Using my good arm, I covered it as much as I could, willing the bleeding to stop.

I needed to get out of here. There was no way Mother would give in to their demands. I was as good as dead.

Clamping my eyes shut, I tried to reach for my powers again. But nothing called back to me – no spark or twitch of magic. It felt like they were behind a door somewhere, my mind too hazy to unlock it. Damn them. Whatever they were putting in the water had weakened me in every sense of the word.

Some time later, hours or minutes, the young boy entered. He carried supplies in his hands. I watched with bleary eyes as he quietly cleaned up my arm and bandaged my wound.

'Can you help me out of here?' I whispered, barely breathing.

The boy looked at me, regret in his face. He shook his head minutely. His eyes gestured over his shoulder.

A guard stood by the door.

I sank back against the sofa, succumbing to sleep.

32

Zayd

We ventured deeper west, into the countryside. We overturned a home that belonged to one of the men who had been arrested in the riots, but Layla was nowhere to be found.

Time was running out.

The next house we searched was a few miles away from the last village, an isolated wooden building where a middle-aged man resided. He eyed us distrustfully as the soldiers searched every inch of the house.

'Captain, we've got something,' one of the soldiers called.

My head whipped over toward the soldier, but he was merely brandishing an old leather book.

'Arrest him,' the captain said.

'What? I haven't done anything!' the man protested as the soldiers sprang to action and bound his hands behind his back.

'You're a fire mage, aren't you?' the captain said as he inspected the book.

The man paled. 'N-no, it's just for research—'

'Seems like a book of instructions on how to wield fire.' The captain looked at the man severely. 'Suhail, Rizwan, take him back to the palace for questioning.'

I watched in horror as the man was dragged away, pleading for his life.

'Why is he being taken to the palace?' I asked the captain as we headed out of the house.

'Sultana's orders,' he replied gruffly. 'Any mages found must be brought to her for questioning.'

'What happens to them?' I asked.

He shrugged, his face impassive. 'They don't come back out.'

The nonchalance of his words stunned me. The Sultana was capturing mages? To what end? Was this to do with the Fallowmere?

Endless questions circled my head, but I didn't question Sayed again. My focus needed to be on Layla.

That night, another messenger came with news from the palace. A cloth covered in blood and a lock of Layla's hair had been sent as a warning.

'We're going in the wrong direction,' I fumed, looking at the map of Sawan.

'We are meant to cover west—' Sayed began.

'The abductors sent another message within a day. That means they can only be a day's travel away from the palace. How far away are we?'

Sayed looked at me in surprise. 'We are two to three days away, Your Highness.'

'Draw a perimeter around the palace. I want to see everything within a day's travel,' I instructed.

Sayed got up to oblige, taking several minutes to

calculate measurements. He began to draw a steady circle around the palace.

'Now, where have the other battalions searched?'

Sayed began crossing off areas one by one.

'There's a gap here unaccounted for, why?' I asked, zeroing in on an expanse of northwestern ground.

'It's mainly mountains and swamps. We are raiding through every registered village and town. There aren't any in this area.'

'Seems like the perfect hiding spot to me,' I said.

Sayed gave me an approving look. 'Not bad for a child prince. And here I thought you were just a pretty face.'

I snorted. 'Send word to the Sultana; we're going to double back. There's no way they could have sent the warning that fast.'

'Unless their messengers were already on their way by the time the first note arrived?' Sayed suggested.

'Then we split up,' I said. 'Send half the troops to keep going west. I'll take another regiment and head to this area.'

'Very well,' he said with a tired sigh, rubbing his eyes.

'We leave at dawn.' I strode out of the room and retired to my bed. Noor was already snoring loudly.

I sat down, my arm throbbing and my head pounding. They had harmed Layla. These people were good to their word.

If we found her too late … My insides twisted at the thought. Was Layla terrified? Was she aware soldiers were looking for her? I hated the thought of her suffering alone. She was strong. But there was no telling what more her captors might do to her. The Sultana had pushed her people too far.

Another thought crept into my mind, unwanted. It

wouldn't be long before the water mages discovered who Layla really was. Then what would become of the Silver Port?

Dawn couldn't come fast enough. The journey back through the towns was met with frosty silence from the subjects of Sawan. People eyed us frightenedly, doors and windows slamming as we rode through what felt like ghost towns. Nobody wanted a repeat of the overhauls they had been subjected to. Not that I blamed them. But it seemed the Sawani soldiers were under strict instructions to use brute force, breaking through fences and barging people out of the way with their horses.

It wasn't hard to understand why the Sultana was so hated and feared here. There was only so much oppression people could take before they finally fought back.

I hated that Layla was caught up in the middle of her mother's mistakes. She didn't deserve this.

We passed through endless fields and forests, out of clay cities, until the afternoon sun began to wane and we found ourselves in the empty lands of the northwest. An expanse of swampy terrain stretched out to the horizon, drooping palm trees scattered about. We stopped to rest our horses briefly, the sounds of whinnying and murmuring of troops the only noise, before we set off again.

We passed down a sloping hill that opened towards another stretch of land. The sun continued to set, blue fading into muted violets and reds as night slowly encroached.

It felt like we were searching for hours. My arm continued to blaze with pain, but I ignored it as much as I could – I had no time for my own issues. Time was of the essence. I had been so sure this was where they were keeping Layla.

Dismay began to wash over me.

'Halt!' Noor hissed. Silence descended around us.

'What is it?' I murmured, forcing my horse to a stop.

In the quiet of the sunset, I scanned the horizon. The silhouette of palm trees lined the distance, but there, just between two of them, was the peak of a roof.

'Everybody dismount,' I ordered. 'Tie the horses here; we go the rest of the way on foot. If this is where the resistance are keeping the princess, they may kill her if they hear us coming.'

The soldiers murmured in agreement, and we all dismounted, tying our horses to the nearest trees.

Anticipation made my nerves prickle. 'Fan out – we close in by a circle formation. I want every inch of that house surrounded.'

33

Layla

I was dozing in and out of sleep again. In my more lucid moments, I tried thinking of ways to escape but how? I was so tired.

I looked up as the burly man keeping watch brought me food on a steel plate. My hands were untied and I was treated to more bread and cold chicken. Once I was bound again, the sour-faced woman appeared and tried to force the odd-tasting water in my mouth. The cup was made of ceramic. I spat the water in her face.

She slapped me in return.

I headbutted her – she dropped the cup and it shattered when it hit the floor.

She backhanded me, and I made a dramatic fall to the floor, covering the broken pieces.

'Get up!' she shouted, grabbing me violently.

I closed my eyes, clutching my tied hands to my chest, as she and her minions fluttered around to sweep up the broken crockery.

When they were finally gone, I sat up slowly, my back to the door. I looked at the piece of broken ceramic I had managed to swipe and hid it within my sleeve, settling myself down again. My heartbeat was loud in my ears.

I had tried to map their comings and goings: I was given two meals a day. Once in the morning, once at night, they took me to a dingy bathroom with a chamber pot in the ground. I tried to keep my intake of the spiked fluids to a minimum. It seemed to help. I was starting to feel sharper again.

The minutes dragged by. I longed to go home, to never leave. And to think I had been dreaming of running away. If I hadn't been so foolish, so selfish, so childish in the first place, Faisal would still be alive.

There was no place for me in this world. The people of Sawan saw me as part of the problem, not someone who also suffered under the rule of the Sultana. If only they knew. If only *I* had known how they really saw me.

My eyes were drooping shut again after another depressing lump of bread for dinner. Suddenly, the guard burst into the room.

I reached for my makeshift weapon and held it tightly in my palm.

'Get up,' he said roughly, grabbing me by the arm.

'What are you doing?' I protested as he pulled me out of the room.

'Time for a new house, Princess,' he snapped.

'Unhand me!' I shouted. Why were they moving me? Were my mother's soldiers close? Faint hope flickered in my heart.

'Shut it!' he snarled. I tried to fight him off. He grabbed me by the hair and yanked me along with him.

'Let me go!' I screamed, thrashing against him.

'Quiet!' he growled back, clamping a clammy hand against my mouth.

I gagged and tried to kick out at him.

His grip was too strong.

I was pulled along dank corridors dimly lit by lanterns, the smell of must pervading the space.

A wooden door loomed ahead. The guard grabbed an assortment of keys from his pocket and hurriedly put one through the lock, keeping one hand on my arm. He kicked the door open with a heavy creak and pulled me roughly through.

Fresh air. I gulped it in. I breathed with relief as the cool evening wrapped itself around my body. The sky was losing its light, but there was still enough to let me see that we were coming out into a field in the middle of nowhere. In the distance, I could hear shouts, and I prayed with every fibre of my being it was my mother's soldiers.

I needed to act now, before they took me somewhere. I grabbed the shard of ceramic and jabbed it into the guard's arm.

'Agghhh!' he screamed, letting me go.

I turned and fled, heading for the thicket of palm trees. I could hear the guard's heavy footfalls as he pursued me.

My body ached, stiff from the lack of movement. I stumbled but forced myself up. I couldn't stop. I had to run. I dove into the cover of the trees, my heart racing against my chest.

'Not so fast,' the dreadful woman's voice snarled. She grabbed me and rammed me into a tree, pinning me there with her arm against my throat.

She pulled a blade from her side. *My silver dagger.* Her eyes were feverish with panic and rage. 'Even if I fall, there are hundreds waiting to take my place. Maybe we can't stop the Sultana, but perhaps the Fallowmere prince will think twice before marrying an ugly bride.' She dragged the blade across my face.

Pain seared down my cheek and a blood-curdling scream ripped out of me.

The sound of running footsteps made both our heads turn.

My heart almost stopped.

Zayd stood there in his steel armour, flanked by two soldiers with their swords raised. His dark hair was dishevelled; he had grazes on his face. His olive eyes were cold. Was I hallucinating?

'Drop your weapon. Step away from the princess,' he commanded, and lifted his bow and arrow.

The woman hissed. Pulling my body to cover hers, she placed the knife at my throat. I could feel blood dripping down my stinging face, splattering onto my torn dress.

'You have three seconds,' Zayd said, stepping closer. I could feel the woman assessing him, and I used the distraction to slam my head backwards as hard as I could, connecting with the woman's nose violently.

My head roared with pain. The woman cried out, silver flashing before me as my dagger fell from her hand. I dropped to the ground and heard the unmistakable sound of an arrow cutting through the air – piercing flesh, the strangled scream of my captor – before I lost consciousness.

34

Zayd

I woke at dawn. I had slept like a log last night, on a proper bed at the Sawan palace at last. Noor sat up in the chair beside me and immediately handed me a vial of medicine, setting about changing my bandages.

I almost didn't want to look, but I forced myself to see the wound.

The black poison had spread down my veins all the way to my elbow. I sucked in a sharp breath.

'I must insist we return home immediately, Your Highness,' Noor said, tersely. 'You have barely slept or eaten – this is the exact opposite of what Sayyidah Shafiya ordered.'

'I'll be fine; stop fussing.'

'With all due respect, Your Highness,' Noor said through gritted teeth as he applied the balm, 'you are not fine. You are the crown prince and you have been poisoned. All you have done these past few days is make yourself worse.'

'I couldn't stand by and do nothing,' I snapped back, rubbing my temple. My head was pounding.

'Her Highness is safe now. We must return to Dakaria immediately.'

'I must speak to the Sultana first. She needs to understand who recovered the princess.'

The disapproval rolled off Noor in waves, but he said nothing. I had put him in a difficult position; he had been livid this entire mission. Not that I blamed him. He was bound to serve the royal family, to keep me alive, and here we were, doing the exact opposite.

Was Layla awake? Was she well now? It was all I could think about as I chewed hastily through a platter of roti and bhazi with chai that a servant had delivered. I wolfed the lot, famished after last night.

I bathed vigorously, scrubbing off the dirt and grime of the past few days. My reflection was haggard in the mirror – dark circles beneath my eyes, my skin sallow, so unlike its usual brown tone. I threw on a long black thobe and waistcoat. From a drawer, I took out the silver daggers that I'd recovered from Layla's captors and slipped them into my pockets.

'I shall see the Sultana now,' I announced, leaving the room.

'The Sultana is in a meeting with her ministers,' Noor advised me, 'but the princess is awake if you wish to see her. Our carriage will be ready to leave in a couple of hours.'

I nodded.

Led by one of the Sawan guards, we walked quietly through the vast sandstone corridors until we reached Layla's wing of the palace.

The walls were darker in her chambers, painted a deep shade of indigo. The door to her bedroom stood ajar, a murmuring of voices coming from within.

'Her Highness is just waking up,' Mira said. 'Please, take a seat.' She beckoned me into the parlour.

'Could you give us a few minutes?' I asked Mira quietly.

She hesitated, then nodded. 'I will go and prepare some tea, Your Highness.'

I stepped through to Layla's room, closing the door behind me. The curtains were pulled wide to let in the morning sun, and endless rows of books took up one wall. A desk was positioned opposite her bed, covered in disorganized papers and quills that made the corner of my mouth turn up. Another nook held a display of weapons – daggers and arrows with a dartboard hanging in the centre. This room felt like Layla.

She was standing by the edge of her bed, holding on to a golden post for support. Tenderness swelled in my heart at the sight of her.

Her normally warm golden skin was pale and there were dark shadows beneath her eyes. A long piece of gauze covered the gash down the side of her face.

She looked at me in surprise. I crossed the room in three strides and wrapped her in my arms, my body sighing with relief. She was alive. She was safe.

Layla's arms came up around me and she held me tight, her breaths shaky. I didn't dare hold her too close in case I hurt her; one look at her yesterday in that torn dress, cuts and bruises plastering her skin, had told me she would be recovering from her injuries for weeks to come.

I drew back. 'How are you feeling?'

Her soft brown eyes looked up at me. 'Relieved, mainly. I owe you a life debt, Zayd. Thank you.'

'I told you: you don't ever have to thank me, and you don't owe me anything,' I replied. 'I'm just glad you're safe.' I traced the side of her face, careful not to touch the bandage covering the gash on her cheek.

She looked at me strangely. 'Why did you come?'

'I had to,' I said.

'You had to?' she repeated, still looking unsure.

I hesitated. I wanted to tell her that I had come, sailed across an ocean, thundered over foreign soil, with the single purpose of finding her safe and whole because the opposite would have finished me. I wanted to tell her that killing one assailant hadn't been enough; I wanted to annihilate every single wretch that had so much as looked in her direction. I wanted to tell her that since the day we'd met, she'd crept under my skin, seeped into my bloodstream and found her way into my heart.

I wanted to tell her. But I didn't.

'The thought of you being out there, alone, abducted … I couldn't live with myself if I didn't do something to help.'

Layla looked back at me, her eyes slowly filling with tears. She blinked them away rapidly, sinking down onto the edge of her bed. 'My body feels like it was run over by a carriage.'

My stomach fell. 'What did they do to you?'

'Nothing more than what you can see,' she said, shuddering a little.

I knelt down before her, taking hold of her hands. They were cold, and a ring of sore red skin circled her wrists. 'They tied you up?' Anger clouded over my vision.

'Don't,' Layla mumbled, taking her hands out of mine.

'Don't what?' I asked, confused.

'I don't need your pity,' she said irately.

My stomach sank. 'Do you think I pity you?'

The ferocity in Layla's gaze dissipated, leaving her looking unbearably sad. 'I don't know,' she confessed, covering her face with her hands.

'Layla, I don't pity you,' I said gently. 'I care for you.'

'I don't deserve your kindness,' she said quietly.

I tugged carefully on her hands. 'Why would you think that?'

She looked up at the ceiling, tears pooling in her eyes. 'It's all my fault - I tried to run away.' Her words were a breathless rush. 'If I hadn't escaped out of the bathroom at the inn, they wouldn't have got me in the woods, and my guard, Faisal ... he'd still be alive.' Her face crumpled as she wiped hastily at her eyes.

Damn. She had actually tried to run away? 'Layla, none of this was your fault,' I said firmly. 'You didn't plan for them to take you, to do these things. Do you hear me? This is *not* your fault.'

She shook her head, tears streaming down her face. 'I was powerless. Bound like an animal, drugged and fed scraps of food with no way to defend myself. I really thought I could run away from my problems like a selfish child.'

'Layla, listen to me,' I said, taking her hands in mine once again. 'You have more power than you know. You are the heir to the throne. Do you really think your future husband is coming here just to sit as prince consort? Your mother will be dethroned in no time, and you will be coronated as Sultana.'

Layla shook her head, holding on. 'My mother will rule, even if I am titled Sultana.'

'When you are Sultana, you can put her in her place,' I said. 'You can rule differently. You aren't meant to live your life in the shadows; you will be the light your people need.'

'My people hate me. I am no Sultana.'

'Your people hate your mother; there's a big difference,' I said, brushing her jaw with my fingers. 'No one could ever hate you, Layla. You're too good for this world.'

It was reckless of me to say these things, to be here with her, but the ache in my arm made me want to make the most of whatever time I had left. I pressed my forehead to hers, possessed by a need to be as close to her as possible. Her sweet breath fanned out onto my face. I traced her lips with my thumb, dismayed at the thought that this might be the only time I could hold her like this. Her eyes were like firelight as she gazed back at me, a look I could never forget as long as I lived.

It was maddening, being this close to her. Just one tilt of my chin and I could taste her, find out if those lips were as soft as they looked.

'I have tea, Your Highness,' Mira called loudly from the parlour.

I jerked back.

'When do you leave?' Layla asked quietly.

'In a couple of hours,' I replied, straightening up. 'Here, these are yours.' I took her daggers out of my pockets. Layla looked surprised but took the daggers from me. I caught her fingers for a moment.

'I was going to sell these,' she said with a faint smile.

I almost laughed.

'Why don't you stay longer?' she asked, turning away to place the daggers on her bedside table. 'You must be exhausted.'

'I have to get back. I've been away long enough,' I said, guilt twisting my gut.

She smiled sadly. 'Duty calls.'

I hesitated before I stepped forward, closing the space between us.

Her eyes widened slightly, her mouth parting temptingly.

'Goodbye, Princess. Look after yourself,' I murmured, leaning in to press a kiss to her forehead.

I felt her sigh against me, her hand gripping on to my arm for a moment before we both stepped back.

35

Zayd

Noor greeted me as I emerged from Layla's chambers. 'The carriage is packed and ready to go, Your Highness. Her Majesty will see you in the foyer.'

I nodded, my feet feeling unusually heavy as we left the princess's wing.

'Prince Zayd,' Sultana Zahra called when we entered the central hall. She stood in the centre in a regal golden sari, flanked by her ministers.

'Sultana Zahra, thank you for accommodating me,' I said, inclining my head.

'Our thanks is owed to you, Your Highness,' she replied. 'My captain told me how invaluable you were - that it was your idea to turn back and cover the barren lands.' She eyed me with an impressed look. 'Once you are wed, I would welcome you sending one of your commanding officers to offer their training tactics to my special corps. We are grateful for your service.'

'Of course. Dakaria will always be happy to assist our neighbours in any way we can,' I replied. 'As you can see, Your Majesty, working together can be very beneficial for both of our nations. I dread to think what would have happened if I hadn't been there.' I was laying it on thick, but it had to be done.

The Sultana nodded, a thin smile on her face. 'I would like to revise my earlier offer for the silver. I'll take twenty-five per cent.'

I felt a flicker of triumph for a moment. 'I shall finalize the offer when I return home.'

'I look forward to receiving your letter.'

I bade the Sultana farewell and retreated into my carriage, sinking gratefully against the seat. My chest felt heavy as we journeyed home, my arm raging with pain, my head pounding. There would be hell to pay, and the currency was my health.

It was nightfall by the time we reached home, no trace of light in the sky as I dismounted from the carriage. I yawned, stretching out my sore limbs, hiding a grunt as my arm spasmed with pain. Noor had been casting me sideway glares the entire way home.

When I entered the candlelit foyer, Mother and Yunus were already there.

'Zayd, are you all right?' Mother demanded, enveloping me in a hug.

I held on to her. 'Yes, I'm fine,' I said, drawing back and stifling another yawn. 'The princess was recovered safely.'

'Our messenger said you found her and led the rescue effort?' Mother asked.

I nodded. 'I led a team towards one of the suspected sites. I'm just grateful the princess is safely home. She suffered a few injuries while in captivity.'

Mother nodded grimly. 'I trust the captors have been dealt with?'

'Yes, Your Majesty – most executed, and a couple of them are being tortured by the Sultana's soldiers, for information,' Noor replied. 'They suspect there is a larger resistance network afoot.'

'Goodness,' Mother gasped.

'Some good news …' I put in. 'I no longer think Sawan will invade once their princess marries.' I tried not to sound annoyed. 'The Sultana agreed to twenty-five per cent.'

Mother's eyes flew open. Even Yunus looked shocked.

'You got her to agree?' Yunus repeated, confounded.

'I told you both – helping rescue the princess would be beneficial for us,' I said firmly. 'And I was right. It needed to be me: the Sultana would not have agreed otherwise. Perhaps from now on you will trust my judgement.'

Mother sighed with relief. 'Excellent. Good work, Zayd. I'll draw up the letter tomorrow. I am sorry we doubted you, Son.'

I nodded. If only they knew my true intentions. 'How is Father?'

'The same, dear. He is asleep now, but you can see him in the morning,' Mother replied, rubbing my arm.

I held back a scream of pain.

'Brother, how are you?' Yunus asked warily, his eyes flickering to my arm.

I nodded at him. 'I'm fine. I expect a report on my desk tomorrow to catch me up on all I've missed.'

'It's already there,' Yunus said, holding his chin a fraction higher.

Noor coughed behind me.

'Good,' I said, clapping him on the back. 'I'm in need of my bed. I'll speak with you both tomorrow.'

Sayyidah Shafiya was waiting for me in my parlour, a deeply disappointed look on her face.

'Your Highness, you are doing yourself no favours,' she said irately, undoing my bandages.

'I hope you have a stronger salve,' I tried for bravado, but the reality of my situation was beginning to weigh on me.

I looked at the wound on my arm. The black vines had grown thicker as they snaked down past my elbow. I wanted to retch.

'How long do I have left?' I asked tiredly.

Sayyidah Shafiya sighed through her teeth. 'I need you to promise me you will stay within the palace until we find a cure. Otherwise, I fear you won't even make it to your honeymoon.'

My stomach dropped. 'How long if I stay inside?'

'A month, maybe two at a push?' she hedged, twisting my arm this way and that. 'I will increase your dosage. You'll need a stronger salve if we are to ward off the poison's effects. But the true cure will only come when we can mix in the tears of an earth mage.' She handed me three vials. 'Drink.'

I didn't need to be told twice. The bitter taste of the medicine in three shots almost made me gag. I kept my revulsion to myself as the healer ground ingredients with her pestle and mortar, creating a newly blended salve that was darker in colour, closer to ash than bottle green.

It stung deeply. I knew I only had myself to blame. But I didn't regret my decision. Layla was safe now; she was home.

Sayyidah Shafiya was wrapping my arm in fresh bandages when the doors to my room were thrown open and Yunus flounced in.

'Brother, I know you're tired, but I was hoping to talk to—'

I jerked my arm away, hastily pulling my sleeve down,

but Yunus's mouth falling open told me he had already seen too much.

'Your Highness, if I may escort you back outside,' Noor said quickly, rushing over to him.

Yunus shoved Noor away. My brother gaped at me, his dark eyes wide with shock. 'What the *hell* is going on here?' he demanded.

36

Layla

I watched the sun set slowly from my bed, strokes of violet and pink slowly fading into darker blues as the sky wound down for the night. When I'd planned to run away, I thought I was solving my problems - the wedding, my mother - but all I'd done was create several more.

Mira had brought me the newssheets from the last few days. Riots and protests were still erupting all over Sawan. Sometimes they came to the palace gates, and I heard explosions as Mother's soldiers set off cannons to disperse the crowds. Mother was having dissenters arrested, but it wasn't deterring anybody.

The thought of leaving the palace terrified me. Faisal's lifeless eyes haunted me in my sleep. I kept expecting to see his head poke through the door, to hear his voice in the corridor.

A new guard had taken his place, a brawny man called Mustafa who seldom smiled and spoke even less than Faisal had.

My eyes flickered to where Zayd had sat only hours ago. The touch of his smooth hands. The warmth of his embrace. I missed someone I had no right to miss.

'Good evening, Princess Layla,' Mira said cheerily. She was doing her best to lift my spirits. 'The cook made your favourite snack: naan chanay.' She placed the gold tray beside my bed.

'Give him my thanks,' I murmured. I tore a piece of the naan and dipped it into the chanay. The flavours were warm and aromatic, but nothing tasted the same since I'd returned home.

After I ate, Mira helped me out of bed. My body ached in several places as I moved towards the dressing table. I sighed with relief as I sat down again, and Mira began to brush my hair.

My reflection was ghastly. The strip of bandage that ran down my face was damning. I was glad I hadn't been awake for the stitching. My fire powers still felt far away, trapped beneath sludge. Bruises patterned my skin, but the red rings around my wrists were what really stung, proof I had been bound.

Tears welled in my eyes. 'Please stop,' I said, pushing Mira's hands away. 'Leave me alone.'

'Your Highness, it might help to get dressed,' Mira said faintly, worry in her soft brown eyes.

'Later. Just leave me, please.' Tears began to stream down my face.

Mira squeezed my shoulder and left the room.

Guttural sobs broke from my chest. Faisal. He was gone. They'd drugged me. Carved me. I thought they were going to kill me.

I tore the bandage from my face and looked through my streaming eyes into the mirror. The angry red gash on my cheek would forever be a reminder that I had been too weak to stop those people from hurting me. I felt so violated.

Perhaps the Fallowmere prince will think twice before marrying an ugly bride.

I wiped hastily at my eyes, willing myself to stop crying, but it was minutes before I could control my tears. I curled inwards, sobbing into my knees until I started to lose the air in my lungs.

I forced myself to breathe in and out, trying to calm my frantic heart. I was home now. I was safe again.

But I didn't feel safe. I felt small. I felt terrified. I felt damaged.

I forced myself to look in the mirror. I took steadying breaths and wiped at my face, drying my tears—

My hand stopped on my cheek.

The cut was gone.

I stared at my reflection. Pressed my face up against it. Pulled at my cheek to see where the hell the wound had gone – but it was smooth as a newborn's skin, nothing but a faint pale line where the woman had sliced me.

My breathing turned shaky.

I had healed myself. My tears had healed my scar.

A cold feeling snaked through me. How was this even possible?

No matter how long I stared at my reflection, the gash didn't reappear. Some buried knowledge from folklore crept into my mind about earth mages with the power to heal people. All this time, I'd thought perhaps it was a fluke how nature responded to me. But this was impossible to deny.

I splashed my face with water and wiped it dry. I found the medicine box Mira used and placed a new strip of gauze carefully over the skin that had been cut. I couldn't let anyone find out, lest I end up in the dungeons.

*

The morning light roused me from my sleep. I sat up slowly, my limbs still aching. I had half a mind to fall back into bed, but I needed to ready myself before Mira came in and tried to change my bandage.

I peeled the bandage off my face. The thin silvery scar taunted me in the mirror. It was real – my tears had healed the wound.

Fear pulsed through my body. Who was I?

Mira arrived soon after I was finished in the bathroom, readying me for the day in a simple kameez I pulled out from my wardrobe.

'How are you feeling, Princess?' Mira asked as I sat down to breakfast in my parlour.

'More or less the same as yesterday,' I said, taking a spicy omelette.

'Her Majesty wishes to see you in the court chambers this morning,' Mira said gently.

I grimaced. Mother had flitted in and out of my room once or twice over the past couple of days, checking I was recovering OK, but her motherly concern only went so far. This would be about business, no doubt.

I walked alongside my new guards; their expressions were solemn as they looked ahead. Tensions were running high in the palace as the riots continued. When it was especially quiet, sometimes you could hear the din of voices roaring outside. I didn't look too far out of the windows any more.

When I arrived at the court chambers, Mother was sitting at the head of the table, her ministers surrounding her. They all stood as I entered, murmuring their greetings. I could feel their eyes roaming over me, inspecting the bandage on my cheek.

'Good morning, child,' Mother said absently.

'Good morning, Mother,' I said, sitting down opposite her.

'How are your injuries?' she asked, looking at me over her papers.

'Painful,' I replied.

'You will recover soon, no doubt,' she said with a dismissive smile. 'I wanted to go over what you learned while you were held captive. Did they say anything about their numbers, their leaders, any other bases?'

Everybody's eyes were on me, intent.

I felt my insides shrink. 'No, Mother. They didn't divulge any information. They just kept reiterating their demands: for you to call my wedding off and end ties with Fallowmere.'

Mother let out a short laugh. 'As if I would. Idiots. I suspect a larger resistance network exists, with bases all over Sawan. I may have to lower the taxes some more, quell the dissenters. Perhaps set up a new mill in the north to create more jobs ...' She sighed.

'Your Majesty, if I may,' Hussam said, clearing his throat from his position to Mother's right.

'Yes?' I could see the effort it took Mother to not roll her eyes.

'We are nearing civil unrest. The people have not been dissuaded by some among their number being arrested – even killed,' he said severely. 'Perhaps we ought to listen to their legitimate concerns about the princess being married to a Fallowmere prince.'

'Layla's marriage has been arranged and her betrothed is on his way – the Fallowmere will be here in a few more weeks. There is no room for discussion,' Mother snapped.

'The princess can marry anyone she wishes – perhaps somebody the entire country does not detest,' Hussam replied evenly, his face darkening.

'You dare to defy your Sultana?' Mother growled, sitting up straighter.

'With all due respect, Your Majesty, you are the Sultana Regent until the princess comes of age, whereafter she must be coronated as Sultana immediately. It was what the Sultan wanted – I was witness to it myself.'

I froze, along with the eleven other advisors.

Mother's eyes narrowed into slits. 'Layla will be coronated when she is ready to take on the responsibility of running a kingdom.'

'Princess Layla *is* the heir to the throne,' Emran broke in. 'There is no stipulation about her needing to be ready in any of the laws – she should take the throne immediately once she turns eighteen.'

I think I stopped breathing.

'Are you trying to dethrone your Sultana?' Mother raged.

'No, we are merely stating facts,' Hussam replied. 'We are advisors to the crown for a reason. We are here to help steer the ship, to ensure the best for Sawan. Never before in the history of our great nation has a member of the royal family been *abducted*, and on our own soil! This is our country's greatest embarrassment.'

'Hear, hear!' a few quiet voices muttered.

'It would be wise to cancel the wedding, Your Majesty, lest the country breaks out into civil war,' Emran agreed gravely. 'We have to do what is right for our nation. Nobody wants the Fallowmere back here – the princess nearly lost her life because of this.'

'She was recovered!' Mother shouted, slamming her fist down on the oak table.

'And if she hadn't been?' Hussam challenged. 'We could have been thrown into more chaos. With no heir to the

255

throne, the late Sultan's nieces, Princess Mariya or Princess Aroosa would have had to take the crown. We must do something to calm the people, and there is only *one thing* to do. Call off the wedding.'

I watched Mother stare back evenly at Hussam.

For a moment, I thought I saw a flicker of hesitation cross her features. Perhaps I could get out of this marriage after all.

'This meeting is over,' Mother said in a cold voice, rising from her seat.

I sat, frozen, as Mother departed with her guards. The ministers began to rise one by one, throwing me pitying glances as they left, until only Hussam remained.

'Thank you,' I said quietly.

'Your father would have never forgiven me if I hadn't spoken up,' Hussam said, looking at me across the table. 'He wanted you to become Sultana – he left assurances. I know that. Your mother knows that too. I am sorry I cannot do more for you, Princess.'

I looked at him curiously. 'What do you mean *assurances*?'

Hussam looked at the door pointedly.

I nodded with understanding. 'Perhaps we can find a time to talk later.'

He nodded, rising from his chair.

As Mustafa walked me back towards my rooms, I replayed what had happened in my head.

With all due respect, Your Majesty, you are the Sultana Regent until the princess comes of age, whereafter she must be coronated as Sultana immediately.

Mother had always spoken about my coronation as if it were some distant dream. But even if I were to take the throne in a couple of months, how long would I *remain* Sultana if anyone found out about my powers? Would the people accept a mage over my ruthless mother? I highly doubted it.

Could I keep this part of me hidden for the rest of my life? Would Edmund and I live separate lives in the palace like Mother and Father had?

As I sank down on a chair in my parlour, I felt the surge of energy in my body begin to return. Instead of panic swelling through my veins, I felt the thrum of power, running in tandem with the magic that was beginning to wake up again. All that time I had spent in captivity, unable to reach my powers, it had felt like a part of me was missing.

I took a few deep breaths. My body temperature returned to normal, and yet I could still sense the power there, humming under the surface, waiting for my command. Never had it felt quite so easy to control. Is this what it could be like when I came of age?

There were just a few weeks to go. A few weeks until I turned eighteen. Until I was married off to Edmund. Until my mage affinities came to full fruition.

The urge to run away had been overwhelming before, but now ... ? There was no way out for me - not from Edmund, and certainly not from my mother.

Zayd had sounded so confident about my prospects as Sultana. It had reminded me of how my father used to speak to me, the wisdom he would impart to ensure I would be a good ruler one day. Hussam said Father had left assurances for me to take the throne. What could that mean?

It had been a while since I'd visited my father's office.

I instructed Mustafa to wait outside as I opened the

curtains. Flecks of dust danced in the sunlight, freshly woken from slumber.

I stood in the middle of the room. It still smelled of Father's pine scent and the bukhoor that he had loved to burn. I half-expected him to come marching in through the door, papers in one hand, chai in the other. I had to commend the servants who took care of this wing of the palace; everything was clean and tidy, just as it always had been.

I trailed through his bookshelves, unsure of what I was looking for. The leather covers were cold to the touch.

I began to take out books. Some were magnificent tales from around the world; others were about politics and geography. There were some dark boxes along the bottom shelves. I knelt down and pulled a few out, finding stacks of letters from Father's correspondences over the years.

I leafed through them, noting letters from Zayd's parents, from my cousin's in-laws from Nevarim, the royals of Asvakar, Torkmen …

I opened a letter from Valthar.

Your Majesty,

I appreciate your discretion in this matter. You have my word, on my life, that I will never disclose this information to another soul for as long as I live.

Please consider this a humble thank you for your understanding. I forfeit all my rights and give them to you in the matter we have discussed.

Regards,
Sultan Arun of Valthar

I checked for more correspondence, but the boxes were empty. *Forfeited all his rights?* To what? For what?

We had minimal relations with Valthar – was this letter why?

I tucked the letter into the pocket of my dress and put the boxes back.

I retreated to Father's desk after a while, noting how it looked the same; his ink and quill bathed in sunlight, a stack of empty papers for writing, a bottle of his favourite ittar.

Curiosity had me pulling open some of his drawers, wondering what else was inside. I found some more correspondence from other rulers, an old stuffed doll of mine, more ink and feathers ... The last drawer wouldn't open. I tried pulling on it a few times until I realized there was a small brass keyhole in the corner.

I felt no shame rooting around the entire study to find the key.

I tried the other drawers, the bookshelves, the boxes. I even felt around the oak floors for loose boards, in case Father had got really creative. He couldn't have kept it far from this room – this place had been his sanctuary.

Where else could it be? There were some plants dotted around, leafy palms and a small olive tree by the windows. I found myself lifting up the olive tree, the roots and soil housed in a beautiful blue pot decorated with mosaic tiles. There, covered in soil, was a small brass key.

I snatched it up before I could consider whether I was invading his privacy and fitted it into the lock. The drawer clicked open.

There were only a few items inside: a couple of envelopes and a leatherbound journal.

I picked up the first envelope.

Your Majesty,
I hope you and your family are in good health. This is all I could find on the subject of mages with more than one power. Please find enclosed. Let me know if you need anything else.
Your good friend,
Sultan Anwar Hussayn

I unfolded the pages the Sultan had enclosed. A gasp escaped me. They were the pages missing from the book I had been reading in Dakaria.

Mages with more than one affinity are extremely rare. While there is limited evidence to suggest they exist at all, a prophecy persists.

THE TALE OF THE SAVIOUR

Long ago, it was foretold, a mage would come to rise from the ashes of destruction wrought upon their kind. This mage would come to be known as the saviour, destined to bring the mages out of misery and fear and restore them to their rightful position in the world.

The saviour would rise out of darkness, and all would come to know them by their mark:

Born from fire and earth, bestowed with water and wind, the saviour will lead an army to the gates of darkness. Only when the fire has fallen can light prevail.

All will be as it once was.

I stared at the tale in confusion. *Born from fire and earth? Bestowed with water and wind? Lead an army to the gates of darkness?* I looked through the rest of the pages, trying to see if there was anything about a mage with just two affinities, but the pages only spoke about what kind of unprecedented power that would be, and the dangers of such a being.

I had those two affinities, I realized with cold dread. Fire and earth.

What if ... It couldn't be ... *me*, could it? No, surely not. But ...

I recalled the story of the saviour from that night in Dukhha. The fortune teller had looked right at me when she spoke about it.

Had Father known? Was he a mage?

If this was about me, born from fire and earth meant both my parents had the mage gene. But neither of them had ever shown such affinities for fire or earth.

I tried to sift through my memories, recall Mother or Father doing something unexplainable. If Mother had been a mage, she would have used her powers for her own gain, this much I knew. And she hated mages – persecuted them in fact.

Folk tales were rife with stories of earth mages who could carve out the land with their hands and sink entire cities, water mages who could drown anybody of their choosing, fire mages who walked out of burning houses unscathed, wind mages who could send storms that ripped homes apart. But I'd never seen either of my parents do even a fraction of such things. Unless it came from their parents?

My father's parents had passed away before I was born. Mother rarely spoke of her family. She was too embarrassed that her father had been a groundskeeper, that she had been assimilated into the court out of pity and favour. Her mother she spoke of even less; they'd never seen eye to eye. I could not recall her weeping for either of them when they died many years ago.

Was it Grandfather? Was that why he loved to tend to the palace gardens? Perhaps …

A clattering of footsteps in the hallway made me shove the pages back into the drawer hastily.

Mira entered, breaking my train of thought. Her face was ashen.

'What's happened?' I demanded.

She looked at me in shock, lost for words.

'Mira? Is everything all right?' I sprang up from the chair, reaching for her hands.

Outside, panicked voices could be heard. Unease began to creep through me – had the rioters broken in?

'It's Hussam, Your Highness,' Mira said shakily. 'They found him in his study. He's dead.'

37

Layla

An aura of fear settled over the palace as news of Hussam's murder spread. His body was returned to his family for burial. Mother was secluded in her office most days, leaving me free of her wretched company at least.

I knew it was her. One minute he was standing up to her, the next … he was gone.

But the official line was that Hussam had choked on his food and asphyxiated.

Guilt racked my body. His family were heartbroken. Father had respected him so much. This was all my fault.

All because of this stupid alliance, this stupid marriage. Why couldn't my mother see that this engagement was ruining our country?

Because I was too weak to stand up to my mother, she was wreaking havoc.

I knew running away wasn't the answer any more. I had to face my responsibilities, accept them, even. But how?

I wandered about my room, noticing that the golden plate upon which the day's itinerary was usually delivered had a letter on it instead. I rarely received correspondence.

Curious, I picked up the envelope and recognized the coat of arms on the seal. It had come from Dakaria.

I looked at the letter, nerves fluttering in my stomach, and carefully unfolded it.

Dearest Layla,

How are you? I returned to Dakaria earlier this week after a pleasant sail.

I wanted to extend my well wishes again for your recovery. I myself am a bit ill from my travels so I will be recuperating at the palace before I resume my duties.

It would cheer me up if you could write back to me soon and tell me if you are feeling any better, as well as what book you're reading at the moment, as I am in need of some recommendations.

I eagerly await your correspondence.

Yours,

Prince Zayd

My heart flickered with warmth. Zayd had written to me. I thought when he left that would be the last I heard from him. He was going to marry soon. So was I. But friends could write to each other, couldn't they? And aside from Mira, I didn't have any other friends to talk to. Zayd's letter felt like a beam of light on a dark night.

Dear Zayd,

Thank you for writing. It was nice to receive your letter. I, too, am stuck in the palace, though I find myself unwilling to leave anyway. The world doesn't seem so friendly a place now.

My recovery is progressing; each day the pain seems to lessen, and my wounds are healing. Perhaps by the time this letter reaches you I will have stopped resembling a purple grape and will have morphed into a raspberry.

How are you? How is His Majesty? You mentioned you were ill — I'm sorry you were troubled to come all the way here.

If you are looking for something to read, I have enclosed a book. Critics remarked that this is the author's worst work yet, a terrible satire on the state of Sawan, but I found it hilarious. My mother has banned any more copies from being printed, so keep it safe.

Warm wishes,
Princess Layla

Dearest Layla,

If this book is what you deem hilarious, I hope you never make a mockery of me. I'm not sure whether I was offended or appalled, but I can see why the book has limited accolades.

How are your injuries now? Are you a raspberry yet or have you morphed into another fruit?

I'm much better now. Unfortunately, my father seems to be taking a turn for the worse, so I'm trying to make the most of my time with him.

I never used to think about death much before. But now it is here, right before me, and I find myself questioning everything. What use is being amongst the most powerful people in the kingdom when we cannot even stay the hand of death so that we might hold on to our loved ones a little longer?

I'm sorry that you are finding it hard to leave the palace. I can only imagine the trauma you faced. What you went through was terribly cruel.

But if you ever want to venture outside, send me word and I will gladly traverse the ocean to take you wherever you wish to go.

Yours,

Zayd

P.S. Send me another book — I am in the mood for something devastating.

Dear Zayd,

My heart breaks to hear about your father. Nothing can prepare you for the loss of a parent, and no kind word can save you from the grief. I can only pray that he is at ease and that you and your family are comforted during this difficult time.

I am so surprised you didn't enjoy the comedic masterpiece I sent you. I have enclosed another book, <u>Layla and Majnun</u> – heralded as the greatest love story ever told. I shall let you judge if it deserves the title.

I'm resembling a type of melon at the moment – but my injuries are lessening. I think the ache in my body is finally subsiding, so that is wonderful progress. I hope you are now fully recovered?

Thank you for your kind offer. When I am feeling brave enough to go outside again, I look forward to walking together.

Yours,
Layla

Dearest Layla,

I think Majnun was rather foolish to just mope around and wait for his Layla. If they really wanted each other, they would have found a way to make it work instead of just pining for each other in silence and secret. Love should be more than just words — it should be action too. Majnun should have crossed oceans for her, instead of circling around the woods with animals for friends. Devastating perhaps — dreadful, more so.

However, I did like these lines:

'Though parted, our two loving souls combine,

For mine is all your own and yours is mine.'

Yours always,

Zayd

I stared at the lines of poetry longer than I should have.

'Well, what does this one say, then?' Mira asked, pretending not to look over my shoulder as she brushed my hair.

I rolled my eyes. 'Nothing that you need to worry about.'

She made a face. 'When somebody starts writing *me* love letters, see if I share them with you.'

I held back a laugh as I folded the letter away and hid it in my drawer with the others.

Some commotion sounded outside my chambers.

'I'll go see,' Mira said, putting the brush down and hurrying out.

I turned, wondering what was happening as Mira's voice exclaimed with surprise with the guards outside. Moments later, she came rushing back into the room.

'Your Highness! He's coming!' Mira said breathlessly.

'Who?' I demanded, hoping for one ridiculous moment that the words in Zayd's letter *had* been meant for me. That he was taking action, coming back here – coming back to me.

'Prince Edmund! They've arrived early! They'll be here any moment!'

38

Zayd

I stood by the water's edge, the faint morning sun slowly rising over the palace. A note from Roshni hung limply in my hand as I waited patiently, an ache in my head and burning pain in my arm. Water lapped lazily along the banks of the green river until a strange whooshing sound filled the air.

My eyes narrowed as something began to swim at pace through the water, like a large fish powered by a thousand fins. I cast a glance behind me, but Noor stood several steps back, and the rest of the fields were empty.

Roshni emerged from the river, shaking off water as she climbed up onto the bank. Water dripped from her clothes and grey hair as she came to a stop before me.

'Boy,' she said by way of greeting.

I looked back at her steadily. 'You wanted to meet?'

Her cold grey eyes assessed me. 'Indeed. It seems you forgot to mention something rather important when we struck our deal.'

I kept my expression blank. 'Really? What was that?'

The hint of a snarl pulled at her thin lips. 'Do not play the fool with me, child. You know very well what I'm talking about. Her portrait was all over the country when she was abducted. Princess Layla of Sawan is the girl, and you didn't think to tell me?'

'I thought you didn't care for titles,' I remarked.

Roshni glowered at me. 'Don't get smart, boy. I told you to keep her safe.'

'Well, as you know, I helped recover the princess, and she is perfectly safe at home now. So, what is the issue?'

'She will come of age soon, no?' Roshni challenged. 'I need to meet with her.'

'Why?' I pushed. 'What's so urgent that you need to speak to the princess about it?'

'None of your concern,' she hissed. 'You're lucky I don't let that barrier fall in the sea right now, after your deceit.'

'I haven't broken any terms of our agreement – the princess is safe, heavily guarded. What do you want with her?' I countered.

'You will get me another meeting with the princess,' Roshni demanded, ignoring my question. 'Or my family and I will stop protecting the Silver Port.'

Damn it. I stared back at Roshni, measuring her up. 'And how do you propose I demand the princess of another nation to come here on a whim?'

'Well, you are getting married soon, aren't you?' Roshni replied sardonically. 'Send her an invitation to the wedding.'

'And if she doesn't come?' There was no way Layla would be coming to my wedding, not after what she'd been through.

'Then you and I are taking a trip to Sawan, boy.'

I sighed tightly. 'Fine. I will invite her to the wedding if you give me your word you will carry on protecting the port.'

'Done,' Roshni said, a flicker of something like triumph crossing her face. 'You don't look well, boy.'

'I don't suppose you've heard word of an earth mage yet?' I asked her.

'No,' she replied thinly. 'Take rest while you still can.'

Her words were chilling. I watched as Roshni dove back into the water and disappeared beneath the rippling green waves.

'How did it go?' Noor asked as we traipsed back to the palace.

'It's fine. I just need to send a letter,' I said with a huff of breath.

'Brother! What are you doing?' Yunus called from the palace doors.

It seemed I had acquired a new shadow. Since Yunus had discovered my poisonous predicament, he lingered around me unnecessarily, guilt and worry always on his face. The poison was making me weaker, spreading further down my arm and now creeping up towards my heart, despite Sayyidah Shafiya's various elixirs and salves. Without the tears of an earth mage, the salves were just a temporary relief for the pain. My only solace was that my parents were still unaware.

'I am not going to explode, you know,' I grumbled as Yunus followed me to my study.

'I wanted to discuss something with you,' he said quietly.

I hated this side of him: calm, serious, apologetic. I preferred it when he was animated, annoying – carefree.

We entered my study. I gestured for Yunus to take a seat while I downed another vial of medicine.

'What is it?' I asked as I sat opposite him.

Guilt washed over him as our eyes met. The shadows beneath his eyes were growing darker day by day.

'Haven't you slept? You've been in the library non-stop.' I said.

Yunus shrugged. 'I'll sleep later. You'll never believe what I found,' he said, handing me an old book bound in faded green leather.

'What is it?' I said, eyeing the tome curiously. It seemed to be a book of records, the pages thick and yellowed.

'This book holds birth records from the time of the Great Revolt,' Yunus said, his olive eyes bright. 'Look here,' he said urgently, pointing at one.

Name	Date of birth	Residence	Mage	Gift
Sumon Akash	03/09/1099	Dilli	Yes	Earth
Afiya Begum	17/05/1100	Raalpind	No	No
Mina Waleel	23/08/1105	Dukhha	No	No

'Sumon Akash has probably been dead a long time,' I said. 'This was over a hundred years ago.'

He pulled out a scroll of parchment and handed it to me eagerly – an old newssheet from decades ago. 'Sumon Akash married and had children. Those children are still alive. He was involved in the liberation of our lands from colonial rule.'

I looked at him in confusion. 'So who are his descendants?'

'Do you even know the girl you are marrying?' Yunus said impatiently.

'What do you mean?'

'What is your future father-in-law's full name?' Yunus pressed.

'Arun Bakshi,' I answered.

'His *full* name. Arun Bakshi Junam Sumon. His father was named after *his* grandfather.'

'Wait, so that means—'

'Your in-laws could have the earth gene,' Yunus said excitedly. 'It can skip a generation, or skip siblings, but chances are the Sultan or one of his children could be an earth mage!' Yunus was triumphant.

I looked at him in shock. 'How did you figure this out?'

Yunus snorted, a flicker of humour returning to his eyes. 'Whilst you're off prancing around as heir to the throne, I have to stay at home and study. It's called having a brain – something you know little about.'

'So, you really think Munira's family could be earth mages?'

'It's not *could be*, Zayd. Their great-great-grandfather was an earth mage. The gene is in their family,' he insisted.

'How can we even broach that subject with them?' I asked. 'I doubt a royal family would admit to being mages. It's still taboo.'

'Maybe on the wedding day, if they're all crying, we could bottle the tears somehow,' Yunus speculated, running an agitated hand through his curly mop. 'We could make up a pretend ritual, say it brings good luck to collect tears in Dakaria, or something. Or we could just ask them.'

'We can't just ask them; that will be too suspicious,' I said. 'And how do you know for sure this is the same Sumon Akash? There're thousands of people across our lands with that name.'

'We have to try,' Yunus insisted. 'What other chance do we have to find a cure?'

I handed the book back to him. 'Thank you, Brother. Find Sayyidah Shafiya later and share your theory. Perhaps we can gather their tears without arousing any suspicion. She may have an idea. But for now, you need to sleep.'

Yunus nodded, stifling a yawn, and left.

If Yunus was right, perhaps I could be cured after all. But I couldn't bring myself to hope.

After I had eaten breakfast, Noor came in with the morning newssheets and a letter, a knowing look on his face. It was foolish how much joy I got from seeing the princess's seal on the envelope.

'Something on your mind, Noor?' I asked as he handed it over.

He smirked. 'Not at all, Your Highness.'

I shook my head and tore the letter open as the door shut behind him.

Dearest Zayd,

If you think Layla and Majnun is a terrible story, I wonder if there is a stone in your chest where your heart should be. They can't do anything but pine for each other, sworn away from ever marrying by their families. And here is another quote, just because I know how much you enjoyed it:

'My longing for you is the consolation of my heart, its wound and its healing salve.'

What could be more honourable than refusing to give up on the love in your heart, even if you are forbidden from acting on it?

Anyway, my sincerest wishes for luck to your future wife, is what I'm saying.

I miss being in the library at your palace; it's such a beautiful place to lose yourself. It feels like forever ago I

was in *Dakaria, but it was probably one of the best trips
I've had.*

I hope you and your family are well?

Yours,

Layla

I stared at the line of poetry, my hand shaking the page. A strange ache spread through my chest.

I knew what I had to respond with. Roshni had made that clear. And what was I doing anyway, writing letters to Layla as though I could court her when my own wedding was imminent? A wave of guilt washed over me as I considered my future bride – Munira. I had given her little thought since our engagement had been arranged. But she would be here soon, and I would have a role to play.

I wasn't sure if Layla would actually come to the wedding. She was going to be married soon too, her betrothed would be arriving before long. Given the political climate in Sawan, it would make sense for her and her mother to stay put. But, knowing the size of the Sultana's ego, I doubted she would want to come across as cautious or scared.

A feeling of dread filled me as I considered that Layla might be in attendance to see me marry. And I would have to watch her from afar, when all I wanted was …

I blew out a sigh. I was being foolish. These thoughts needed to end.

I took out my paper and quill and wrote her back, enclosing a piece of gilded parchment that I'd rather have thrown into the fire.

PART III

PART III

39

Layla

I thought I might be sick. Each step towards the gardens was twisting my stomach. I had been forced to change into a purple floral gown – something that must have come from Fallowmere. The fabric was stiff, like it belonged on a curtain pole. My hair had been curled, my face painted. I'd finally given up the bandage on my cheek, but nobody seemed surprised that the wound was fully healed.

Mother had arranged for several marquees to be erected in the garden for afternoon tea, Fallowmere style. A long table covered in flowers stood on one side, laden with teacups and plates upon plates of dry cakes and sandwiches. Mother sat on a wicker chair with an older man, a pot of black tea and two cups on a small table in front of her. A younger man sat nearby.

'Layla, come,' Mother said in an overly sugary voice. I noted she was speaking Falmere, despite the accepted custom between royals being to speak the local language.

I went over and sat in the one available seat – next to the younger man.

'This is Prince Edmund,' Mother said with an undercurrent of glee in her voice.

I looked at my betrothed. He was different from his portrait. He looked taller, a bit older; his eyes had some lines around the edges. His irises were a friendly shade of blue, his hair the colour of bleached sand. Dare I say, he was sort of ... all right to look at.

'Princess Layla, it's such an honour to meet you at last,' he said in clear Falmere, standing up to bow.

'It's nice to meet you too,' I replied in Sawani, feeling hot around my neck.

Edmund stared at me blankly.

'What did she say?' the older man asked, his brow furrowing. 'I thought she spoke Falmere?'

'She does, she does!' Mother replied warmly. 'Layla, our guests do not speak Sawani,' she said pointedly.

'Oh, what a shame.' I switched to Falmere. 'A pleasure to meet you, Your Highness.'

'And this is Prince Frederick. He is Prince Edmund's uncle, and has escorted the prince here on behalf of the King and Queen of Fallowmere,' Mother said proudly.

'Delighted to meet you, Princess – your Falmere is surprisingly good,' Prince Frederick said, eyeing me curiously. He was an old man, with greying hair and a round, lined face that looked like it seldom smiled. The princes wore similar suits, dark in colour and studded with military medals. 'I say, you looked whiter in your portrait.'

I stared at the old man, mortified.

'Summer is coming and she tans so easily, but it disappears again in the winter,' Mother said quickly, shooting me a quick glare.

I'd only ever walk under parasols again.

'You are radiant, nonetheless, Your Highness,' Edmund said graciously.

280

'How kind of you to say so,' I said in a monotone, forcing a smile.

Thankfully, Mother was never short of things to say about herself, so she kept the conversation going as we drank our tea. While Mother entertained Prince Frederick, Edmund moved his attention to me. He met my eyes and smiled. 'I have heard about Sawan's beauty for some time now – I am most excited to see it for myself.'

I looked down at my teacup.

'Yes, it's all very exotic, isn't it?' his uncle said in a droning voice.

'Quite,' my mother simpered.

I wanted nothing more than to be swallowed into the ground.

'Are you enjoying the weather today, Princess?' Edmund asked, a warm smile on his face.

'Yes, it's nice,' I replied. 'I hear the sun doesn't reach Fallowmere much.'

'No, this is the hottest weather I've ever experienced, and it's only spring here, isn't it?' he said with a low chuckle, wiping his brow with a handkerchief.

I smiled back fleetingly. 'Yes.'

'I am going to go and introduce Prince Frederick to the council. You two carry on,' Mother said with a pointed smile.

'Of course, we shall see you later, Your Majesty,' Prince Edmund replied.

'Talk to him!' she mouthed, before she fixed a doting smile on her face and led Prince Frederick away.

Well, perhaps I could scare him off. 'Would you like to see my father's crypt?' I asked the prince, rising from my chair and leading him away from the marquee. Moments later I felt the shade of a parasol above me from one of the guards.

Edmund's ocean blue eyes widened with faint horror. 'Oh … um …'

'It's customary here. We really like spending time at graves,' I said sombrely as I directed him towards the family crypt. 'It helps you appreciate life when you reflect on death, no?'

'Quite,' he said, trying to feign a smile.

'We also offer a blood sacrifice,' I said seriously. 'As you're new, you'll have to cut your hand for the first offering.'

'I wasn't told about this …' His eyes darted around. 'But I suppose I can cut my hand. Would you recommend my left or my right?'

I narrowed my eyes at him.

Prince Edmund burst out laughing. 'Your mother said you have a peculiar sense of humour.'

Damn it. I pursed my lips and carried on walking.

The prince kept pace with me. 'I see I have a difficult task ahead of me then,' he said, laughter still in his voice.

'*Difficult task?*' I said, stopping under the veranda, which was wrapped in lilac and wisteria. 'Am I another country you plan to conquer and pillage?'

Prince Edmund looked surprised by my words. 'Forgive me, Princess. I misspoke. I only meant that I look forward to courting you.'

I held back an eye roll.

Edmund looked at me with soft eyes. 'I am just as nervous as you are, Princess Layla,' he confessed, a hesitant smile on his face. 'I am here in a new country – I have left all my family and friends behind – and I imagine that you, much like me, did not have a say in the matter. But I would like to see this as an opportunity.'

'I ... I'm sorry,' I found myself saying, surprised by his words. 'I just ...'

'I understand.' Edmund took my hand in his gently. 'You are to be my wife!' he said with something like pride. 'I would love to spend the next few weeks getting to know you so that, when our wedding day comes, you will look at me with a smile on your face and happiness in your heart. Because I know I will. You are truly a vision,' he said with a breathless shake of his head.

The feel of his eyes travelling over my body was uncomfortable. I pulled my hand carefully out of his.

'Why don't we have dinner tonight – just the two of us, without an audience?'

'That sounds like a sensible idea,' I said hesitantly.

'I promise I do not bite,' he said with another laugh. 'We're going to spend the rest of our lives together. Let's start off by becoming friends.' He held out his arm to lead me back inside.

I took it gingerly, and we walked back towards the palace. Edmund remarked on the landscaped grounds, filling the mild air with his chatter. I looked down at my hand resting in the crook of his elbow.

Part of me had imagined I'd walk with Zayd like this. But it wasn't his arm I was holding, and it never would be. When I'd opened his last letter and found his wedding invitation inside, it had felt like someone had doused my heart in ice. Whatever I thought we had shared was gone now.

Perhaps it was time I accepted the cards I had been dealt, and learned how to win.

*

Our private dinner had been approved by Mother. I entered the dining hall to find Edmund inside. Endless red roses decorated the table; hundreds of candles lit up the room. It was as romantic a setting as any.

And Edmund was the charming fiancé. When I came in, he stood and looked at me with reverence in his eyes. He was undoubtedly handsome, too, dressed in a long grey jacket and breeches, his blond hair brushed neatly to one side, his blue eyes glimmering in the candlelight.

'Wow,' he said breathlessly. He came over and took my hands, lifting one to plant a gentle kiss with his cool lips. 'You are exquisite, Princess. The picture of Eastern beauty that the explorers who first discovered your lands spoke about.'

I recoiled inwardly. However handsome he looked, the arrogance of the Fallowmere laced his every word. 'You look nice too, Your Highness,' I forced out of myself, hating that I had to do this – that I had to charm the man my people hated. But I couldn't see a way out of this marriage. I had to get Edmund on my side.

'Please, call me Edmund,' he said, leading me to my chair.

I took my usual seat and Edmund, notably, sat at the head of the table. I was surprised to see cutlery had been laid out for us – or Edmund, rather.

'*Edmund*,' I said slowly, sounding out his name. 'Does your family have a nickname for you – one I could use?'

A smile danced in his eyes. 'You can call me whatever you like – darling, sweetheart, lover ...' he said, looking at me in that way again.

I cringed, leaning back in my chair, but forced myself to continue. 'Are you flirting with me, Prince Edmund?'

'Can a man not flirt with his future wife?' he countered, a coy smile at the edge of his lips. 'Especially when she is this beautiful?'

What had I done wrong to be subjected to such torture? I looked down at my plate as one of the servants lifted the lid.

'So, tell me about yourself, Prince,' I said, hoping to change the subject.

'Well, there's not much to say,' he said. 'My father, Prince David, is brother to the King of Fallowmere. I have three brothers, two sisters. They all live on an estate not far from the main palace with my mother, and Father splits his time between there and the palace. I enjoy horse riding, hunting and conversations with beautiful women.' He levelled another smile at me.

'Women?' I repeated. 'Are you confessing yourself to be a womanizer, Your Highness?'

He laughed quickly. 'Not at all – but nice sidestepping of my compliment. So, tell me about yourself.'

'Nice save,' I scoffed. 'There's not much to say,' I repeated back to him with an even look. 'I am an only child. My father, the late Sultan, passed away a few years ago. You've met my mother.'

'Yes, she certainly is a force of nature,' he said with a chuckle.

'Mm, that's one way to describe her,' I muttered, picking at my food.

Edmund suddenly took hold of my hand, his cool fingers lacing through mine. 'I want you to open your heart to me, Princess,' he said earnestly.

'We haven't even opened the dessert yet,' I said, pulling my hand away.

He chuckled again. 'You have a wicked sense of humour. I have no doubt our marriage will be full of laughter.'

I tried to feign a smile.

Edmund mercifully picked up his fork to eat his dinner. We chewed silently, the clinking of cutlery and glasses the only noise in the room as I looked fixedly down at my plate. All thoughts of winning Edmund over as though we could be allies had fled from my head the moment he had taken my hand in his.

'Are you looking forward to doing the balcony wave tomorrow?' Edmund asked after we'd finished.

I looked at him in surprise. 'What do you mean?'

He returned my confused look. 'Didn't your mother tell you? She wants us to wave to the people tomorrow – show our marriage is secure.'

The same people who had been rioting since news of our marriage had been announced?

'No, she didn't,' I said thinly. My heart began to race. I didn't want to see anybody, let alone the people who hated me now.

'And I, for one, can't wait to show off the most beautiful woman in Sawan on my arm,' Edmund continued, oblivious to the panic beginning to simmer in my chest. 'I heard about your terrible incident. I assure you I will always keep you safe, Layla. Those dirty commoners won't dare lay a hand on you when I am your husband.' His hand came up to cup the side of my face.

I flinched away.

Edmund dropped his hand.

'It's not customary in our lands for the betrothed to touch so much before they are married.'

Edmund opened and closed his mouth. 'I'm sorry, Layla. I didn't realize.'

'It can be seen as quite scandalous,' I said.

'Right, of course,' he said, redness creeping up his neck.

Dinner concluded in painful silence. I was only too happy to retire to bed.

'Her Majesty wishes you to join her in the dungeons, Princess,' Mustafa said quietly to me as I arrived back at my room.

My stomach recoiled. To watch her hurt more mages? And be around her as if she hadn't just had Hussam murdered? She could go to hell. 'No. I am tired. Tell Mother I have been busy with my fiancé and need my beauty sleep if I am to win his heart.'

I had been sorely hoping that our balcony appearance was a misunderstanding on Edmund's part. But the next morning found Mira lacing me into a frivolous pale-yellow gown – another gift from Edmund – that made me look as sick as I felt. She tied my hair back in a bun and draped a dupatta over it, adding a string of diamonds around my neck.

My body was shaking as I walked down the corridor towards the central wing. I clenched my fists, the undercurrent of power fizzing beneath my skin. Mother stood tall in a regal red gown, her usually pinched face open as she laughed with Edmund and Prince Frederick.

'Ah, there she is,' Edmund said, catching sight of me. 'My beautiful fiancée! Let's go,' he said, leading the way out.

I hung back. 'Mother,' I began, 'I don't think—'

But before I could get another word in, she was pushing me after Edmund. 'Just a few smiles and a wave, and then you lovebirds can be off,' she said in gushing tones.

The glass doors were thrown open and we stepped out into the spring light, the warm sky bright blue. I took steadying breaths as we moved towards the edge of the grand stone balcony and looked down.

The crowd was eerily quiet. I heard the guards below bark orders, and a smattering of applause broke out. I could feel the tension in the air.

Faces that had once looked at me with warmth now stared up at us with disdain and worry.

'Wave,' Mother hissed behind me.

I forced myself to lift a hand and wave as Edmund did the same with a bright smile on his face. He clasped his hand so tightly around my limp one that I was unable to let go. Father would have been so ashamed of this union. The guards barked another order and the crowd applauded again, but the lack of enthusiasm was deafening. I saw my future laid out in front of me in that moment. Dread filled me.

40

Layla

The next few days were filled with walks and candlelit meals I couldn't get out of. But I did my best to avoid Edmund, opting to train as often as I could instead. The more time I spent with him, the less I felt that we could court - nothing about Edmund made me want to marry him.

I threw daggers with one and then *both* eyes closed, punched through dummies and battled my trainer, Junayd, with swords. At night, in the privacy of my bedroom, I sat in the middle of my floor and tried to summon flames with my palms.

It was difficult at first. Unless I was feeling a strong emotion like anger or fear, the current that hummed away beneath my skin seemed harder to call. But I didn't want to access my power only when I was panicked. I wanted to control it, so it no longer controlled me.

I used the nights to focus, trying to grow a small flame into something larger. I was sweating by the time I'd finally accomplished the feat. The energy was there, but it felt so alien - like we were both getting to know each other still. But I kept trying. I was adamant never to be powerless again.

A knock sounded on my door. I quickly closed my palms, vanquishing the flames. 'Yes?' I called.

'Your Highness,' Mira said warily, coming in. 'The Sultana wants to see you.'

I groaned. What a terrible end to the day.

Reluctantly, I made my way to my mother's office.

'How is it going with Prince Edmund?' she asked keenly, beckoning me to sit down.

I dropped into the armchair with a sigh. 'Fine. He seems nice.'

'Fine? Is that it?' she pressed. 'Don't you like him? He looks much better than his portrait suggested.'

'It's not just about how he looks, is it?' I muttered, staring out of the window.

'You should be grateful,' Mother snapped, her real tone reappearing. 'Not everybody gets a husband who dotes on them or is attractive.' Envy coloured her voice.

'What's that supposed to mean?' I replied, looking back at her evenly.

Mother scowled. 'Nothing. Just count yourself lucky that *your* husband isn't still moping over his first love. Your father's first wife might as well have been alive, the way he kept on about her.'

I couldn't think why my father had kept longing for his dead wife when he'd had such a pleasant one in front of him.

'Anyway, I can see the prince is doing his best to woo you. Make sure you are giving him the same effort.'

I inadvertently made a face.

Mother's nostrils flared. 'This is for the good of Sawan, for your people. We will be enriching our nation through this marriage. Before the year is out, we will have Dakaria and Valthar bowing to us.'

'What? But you agreed to a lower rate with Dakaria for their silver,' I said, confused.

'I was feeling charitable after the prince helped rescue you,' Mother said dismissively. 'But that doesn't change our long-term goals.'

'Why are you doing this? There is no need—'

'Silence!' Mother snapped. 'You are not Sultana yet. It's a good thing Edmund is here; he has much more of a strategic mindset. With him by your side, I can trust that when I'm gone, Sawan will not be driven to ruin. Now go and get your beauty sleep, you've been looking haggard lately. We leave for Dakaria tomorrow.'

I bristled. 'I don't think I should go.'

'Nonsense. We must show everybody that we will not be intimidated. I will have extra guards, and you can carry weapons on your person. Besides, Sultana Aysha has personally invited us. It would be rude not to go.'

'But ...' I hadn't left the palace grounds since my attack.

'But what?' Mother scoffed. 'You survived. You are fine. Get over it. You are to be Sultana one day – death threats come with the job. Do you think I have more friends or enemies?' she said. 'Now, go. Edmund will be joining us, too, so you will have company for the wedding festivities.'

I stared at her in shock. 'Edmund is coming? Have you told Sultana Aysha?'

'I'm sure they will have read about his arrival in the papers by now and expect him to join us,' Mother replied tartly.

'The Fallowmere haven't been back to Dakaria since they were forced out by the revolutionaries,' I reminded her. 'Don't you think you should give Dakaria some notice?'

'Enough with your insolence!' Mother jerked out of her

chair. 'You will not talk back to me! I am your Sultana and you will do as I say!'

I stilled.

'Your job now is to marry and make children. State affairs do *not* concern you.' She leant over the table. 'I have given you *everything* – the finest education, the best armed training a princess could hope to have, jewels and fineries others only dream of. You have always been taken care of and taken care of *well*. And you will repay me for my generosity by doing as I say and creating multiple heirs, so that if it turns out one of your children is as obstinate, unruly and ungrateful as you are, you will have other children to fall back on. Now *go!*'

There was a coldness in her glare that chilled the blood in my body.

I wanted to scream back at her. I wanted to launch myself across her desk and claw her eyes out.

Control yourself, Father's voice murmured.

I rose from my chair and exited the room.

I balled my hands into fists as tremors threatened to shake them. Instead of going back to my quarters, I went to Father's study, gratefully shutting the door on Mustafa so I could be alone.

I used the rage that was simmering in my blood to generate flames in my palms, casting them onto the fireplace to warm up the room before I fell into Father's chair.

Since Edmund had arrived, I hadn't come back here. I took out the brass key I now always kept on a long chain around my neck and unlocked Father's drawers. The pages Zayd's father had sent offered me no more insight about my powers. Perhaps he had sent more?

A leatherbound journal sat in the drawer. I picked it up and saw two envelopes underneath. They were both sealed with Father's coat of arms. A pang of longing went through me as I touched the wax. I missed him so much.

A quick flick through the journal told me this was Father's diary. I closed it, unwilling to invade his privacy.

The envelopes were unaddressed. I hesitated, wondering if it was right to poke around in Father's belongings like this but maybe there were more answers in here about my abilities.

By order of Sultan Aziz Emran Asad II

Princess Layla Afreen Asad is legally recognized as the daughter of Sultan Aziz Emran Asad II in the event of any bloodline disputes. The Sultan is aware of the princess's true lineage and has freely chosen to adopt Layla Afreen Asad, daughter of Zahra Bhatt, hereby granting her status as the Sultan's only heir.

All legal rights of parenthood over Layla Afreen Asad remain with the Sultan and Sultana Consort.

I stared at the piece of paper.

What had I just read?

It was dated around my third birthday.

I was ... he wasn't ...

But how?

The Sultan had loved me. He'd been the only real parent I had. And he wasn't even my real father?

My heart began to pound.

A knock sounded on the door. 'Your Highness, I have some tea,' Mira called.

I put everything back into the drawer with shaking hands and locked it up again, a hollow noise ringing in my ears. I was going to be sick. I was going to explode. I shoved the key back under my dress.

Gasping, I stumbled out onto the balcony. I tried to force myself to breathe. I tried to shake my head clear, but I couldn't think – couldn't function.

Without thought, I took the steps leading down from the balcony and ran out into the gardens, past the fountains and the orchards, heading straight for the hunting woods that lay beyond the palace fields.

I didn't care what danger lurked in the dark trees. Let the beasts eat me alive; let the Resistance find me and finish the job.

Everything I had known was a lie.

Pain raked my lungs as I ran as fast as I could, my shins burning. It was so hard to breathe, so hard to see in the darkness of the night.

I stumbled on a mound of roots and went tumbling onto the ground, my body rolling until I thudded to a stop before a great oak. I struggled up to my knees, my head spinning. I was so sure my heart was beating too fast to keep going any more. I couldn't … I didn't …

A feral scream full of primal rage and despair ripped out of my body, searing through the woods. Animals shrieked in return as the trees began to rustle with movement. I pounded my fists on the forest floor, screaming so loud I couldn't hear, I couldn't think, I couldn't be.

The world around me began to shake. The current that hummed through my veins felt like it was spilling out of me, seeping into the ground beneath me. My life was a lie. The one good thing I'd had in it wasn't even mine.

Alarm bells began to sound in the air. What did I care any more? Let them find me out here. Let whatever punishment my mother fancied be wrought upon me.

I was nothing. I was no one. Just some bastard child my mother had conceived before she married Father.

She always got the last laugh.

'Princess! Princess!'

The feel of gentle arms around me turned my screams into sobs.

'What are you doing out here?' Mira's voice rang out. 'Quickly, there's an earthquake! We need to get back!'

Mustafa's voice added to the din. 'Your Highness, we need to get you inside!'

'I can't go back,' I screamed. 'I can't!'

'Hush, Princess, it's OK,' Mira said, holding me tight. 'Come on, let's get you to your feet. That's it. If Her Majesty realizes you went missing, we'll all be dead.'

I let Mira and Mustafa drag me up as the world steadied around me. They pulled me through the fields as the palace lit up from within, urgent voices crying out.

'Quickly, come on,' Mustafa urged, hurrying us out of the gardens and back up the stairs to Father's study.

No. Not my father's study. The late Sultan's.

We were about to walk past the desk when I pulled away. 'Wait outside, please,' I ordered shakily.

Mira and Mustafa looked at me questioningly but obliged, closing the study door behind them.

I wiped the tears still streaming down my face and rushed back to the desk. Perhaps I had read the document wrong? Maybe I was imagining this?

But when I unlocked the drawer and pulled the document out again it was all still there, clear as day. My adoption paper.

A sob ripped from my chest. I felt like I'd been punched in the gut.

The second envelope sat there but I couldn't bear to open it and find out another shattering secret. So I took it, along with the adoption paper and Father's journal, stowing them away beneath my dress. I locked his empty drawer and left the study; I couldn't bear to be in there any longer.

I felt like a corpse as I trudged back to my room with Mira and Mustafa in tow. My entire life – it had all been a lie.

41

Zayd

Sayyidah Shafiya stared at me disapprovingly as she applied the salve to my arm and forced two vials of medicine down my throat. She was increasing my dosage with each passing day. I hated the sight of my poisoned arm – its ash-grey skin, the thick black veins that twined towards my wrists, curled up towards my heart. I tugged my sleeve down.

Trumpets blared outside. Our guests had arrived.

I sank deeper into my armchair.

A loud knock sounded on the door. 'Zayd!' Mother called. 'They're here!'

'Time to meet your bride,' Yunus said, ambling in with a smirk.

'Marvellous,' I said through gritted teeth. My only solace was the hope that one of the Valthar royals was an earth mage whose tears might be mixed with the salve to heal my arm.

Mother led the way to the grand entrance hall where we were to receive our guests. I half hoped Layla would walk through those doors instead.

We headed out onto the balcony to watch the display. A crowd had gathered outside the palace gates to watch the large procession come down the lane – four hulking great elephants decked in patterned cloths, each carrying one of the royals of Valthar. The Sultan and his sons waved from their elephants' backs. An intricately carved wooden howdah sat atop the last elephant, no doubt carrying Princess Munira.

The sound of pounding dhol drums filled the air as my future in-laws proceeded into the palace courtyard, cheers and singing audible above the fray.

'Smile,' Mother hissed in my ear.

My jaw felt tight. I had agreed to marry Munira for the sake of Dakaria – I didn't need to pretend otherwise.

'Let's go down,' Mother instructed.

We made our way back to the entrance hall. The silver palace doors had been thrown open.

The Sultan of Valthar walked in, smiling half-heartedly through his fatigue. Behind him was the crown prince of Valthar, Asim, a couple of years older than me. He looked almost like a carbon copy of his father, the same strong forehead, dark brown eyes, and short stature. His youngest brother, Azaan, came next, looking bored.

'May I present my sister, Her Royal Highness, Princess Munira,' Prince Asim said, gesturing behind him.

A number of Valthar guards parted to reveal a young woman draped in an emerald cloak, her eyes plastered to the floor.

She had dark hair that peeked out from beneath her emerald dupatta, her complexion a soft brown. Her dark eyes met mine.

'It is a pleasure to meet you all – Your Majesty, Your Highness,' Munira said in a clear voice with a curtsey.

'And you, my dear,' my mother said graciously. 'Come,

you must all be tired from your travels. Let me show you to your rooms.'

'Pleased to meet you all. Do rest up after your long journey,' I said to no one in particular, making a quick bow and an even quicker exit.

As I walked away, I could feel my mother's eyes burning into my back, and Yunus striding right behind me.

Once in the main hallway, I steered left towards the library and sank into one of the armchairs.

'You know Mother will have your backside for that,' Yunus said as he flopped into a chair beside me.

'Why? She's getting what she wanted. I don't see why I need to perform for anyone. I doubt Munira had a choice in the matter, either.'

'Perhaps that's why you should show your future wife some grace,' Yunus said sombrely.

I looked at my brother. Stubble lined his jaw. He was starting to look less like a boy these days and more of a young man. It dawned on me that I might not see my brother grow up – see him be crowned Sultan.

'What is it?' Yunus asked, looking at me strangely. 'Why do you look so sad, Zayd?'

I opened and closed my mouth.

Realization dawned on his features. 'You are going to survive this,' he said fiercely. 'Don't get soppy on me now.'

'Yunus, you have to be prepared if I don't,' I said gravely. 'You will have to take my place.'

'Stop it,' Yunus snapped. 'I'm not losing you, too. Munira and her family are here now. We just need to figure out which of them has the gene.'

My arm throbbed with pain. 'And what if it's Munira? She isn't of age yet. Whatever mage abilities she might have won't manifest for a few more months.' Time was no longer on my side. I had weeks left before this poison claimed me – if that.

The library doors burst open. Mother strode in, fury written across her face. *'Pleased to meet you? Rest up?'* She glared at me. 'Are these the only words you have to offer to your future wife? You were meant to stay, help me welcome them from their long journey!'

I looked back at Mother tiredly as Yunus shrank back in his seat. 'You seem to have everything under control, Mother.'

'Don't sass me,' Mother fumed. 'You need to make Munira feel welcome and assure her family you are going to be a good husband!'

I stared back at her, rage simmering. 'If she doesn't take a liking to me, that's not my problem. I have agreed to marry her for the sake of our country. You can't force my affections.'

Mother's nostrils flared. 'What has got into you? This is not the time for rebellion – you are the future Sultan. Start acting like it, do you hear me?'

I stared back at her evenly.

'We will be having lunch with them in an hour,' she continued. 'I expect you to be the picture of charm, understood?'

I shrugged. What use was any of this? I might be dead soon.

Mother made some sort of disgruntled noise before storming back out, the end of her sari flowing behind her.

I buried my head in my hands. When I closed my eyes, all I could see was Layla's face. All I wanted was to be near her again. Her presence alone was enough to make me forget about the pains that tormented me.

'Are you all right, Brother?' Yunus asked quietly.

I sighed. 'Everything is going wrong, Yunus. What's worse is I don't think I have the energy to try any more.'

'You can't give up,' he said firmly. 'We're going to get you this cure. Then everything will be OK.'

The earnest look on his face was too hopeful to bear. He clapped me on the back before leaving the library.

I looked out of the windows. Sunlight was beaming across the hazy sky, bright and daring. How many mornings did I have left?

'At least take her for a walk!' Mother moaned, inches away from slapping me around the head. Her hand twitched by her side. 'You barely spoke to her at lunch the other day! What must she be thinking?'

'I'm busy, Mother,' I said, pointedly looking down at the export reports on my desk.

'The mehendi ceremony is in a week. You need to court her!'

'Why do I need to court her when our marriage is fixed?' I demanded. 'There is no debate here, no discussion to be had. We are being wed. Courting implies I need to convince someone to marry me, but you have already taken care of that, Mother.'

'She is leaving her family behind to come and live here, to be your wife!' Mother shouted at me, finally snapping. 'Does she not deserve even a modicum of attention from her future husband?'

I looked into my mother's tired, enraged face. Her green eyes were narrowed at me. 'Fine, whatever. Noor, send word to Princess Munira that I would like to escort her on a walk in the gardens this afternoon.'

Noor nodded from beside the door. 'Yes, Your Highness,' he said.

'There, happy?'

Mother's eyes were filled with disappointment. '*This* is not how my son would behave. Whatever issues you have, resolve them, before you ruin that poor girl's heart.' And with that, she stalked out.

I sighed and leant back against my chair. My arm felt heavy, as though weighed down by the poison. Even simple things like holding my quill were becoming painful.

Yunus had been trying harder than I had to get to know my in-laws. I watched them at mealtimes as he made them all laugh and spoke with them at length about everything from our childhood to Munira's. *He would have been a better choice of husband for her*, I had thought more than once.

But neither of us could see anything to suggest they had any kind of mage power. It seemed the only way we were going to find out was if we asked.

After another miserable lunch, I made my way to Father's chambers. He was sleeping – this tended to be his usual state now. His body was growing frailer by the day, his cheeks hollowing, his skin sallow and pale. How could I promise him everything would be fine when I was dying too?

I sat next to his bed for a while, my head resting by his shoulder. Just months ago, my father would have been able to fix everything.

And now here we were. If we found an earth mage, perhaps Father could be cured too. But it didn't seem like either of us would survive the search. What would I do if he left before me?

I supposed I wouldn't have to wait long to find out.

Perhaps I would meet him in the next life, and we could sit together until the rest of our family joined us. There was some peace in that.

Yunus had responded well to the extra responsibilities I was giving him. He was taking the lead of more meetings with the ministers, working hard to ensure the smooth running of our new roads and houses. He would make a fine Sultan if I fell. *When.*

I knew I should tell my parents. But I couldn't let Father find out. I couldn't let him die fearing what would become of us. I could give him a peaceful goodbye; I owed him that much.

Hakim came in with tea and the day's newssheets.

PRINCESS LAYLA AND PRINCE EDMUND
SET SAIL FOR ROYAL WEDDING

Her Royal Highness Princess Layla and her betrothed, Prince Edmund of Fallowmere, set sail for Dakaria today with the Sultana of Sawan. The Fallowmere's attendance at the wedding of Dakaria's Prince Zayd and Valthar's Princess Munira is unexpected. This is the first time a Fallowmere royal has been to Dakaria since the Great Revolt . . .

I dropped the paper, my hand shaking slightly. I let out a breath. My gut twisted.

So she was really coming. And she had her betrothed in tow.

'Noor, I shall take Princess Munira for a walk now,' I called, rising from my chair. 'I'll see you later, abbu.' I squeezed his frail hand gently and left.

I went out to the gardens to meet Munira for our afternoon promenade. The fresh air did little to calm my agitation. I tried not to think of Layla – if she was enjoying her betrothed's company– or the fact that I'd have to see them both together when they arrived.

A pattering of footsteps made me look up. I saw Munira walking with her entourage. She wore a deep blue lehenga, her hair pulled back beneath her dupatta. Jewellery adorned her neck, glistening bright against her warm brown skin. For a moment, I had the strange thought that she resembled Layla. They had the same high cheekbones.

What was wrong with me? Now I was seeing Layla in my future wife? I had a sickness.

Munira smiled nervously at me as she approached.

I returned the smile briefly. 'Your Highness, I thought we might take a walk,' I said as she stopped before me.

'What a lovely idea, Prince Zayd,' she replied kindly.

I nodded and strode ahead, Munira following after. Noor coughed. I slowed my pace so we could walk beside each other.

The afternoon sun lit a warm glow about the palace grounds. We walked down the landscaped pathways, past the colourful flowers and trees, but I found little to say. After several minutes of silence, it seemed the princess didn't have much to speak about either.

'How are you finding Dakaria, Princess?' I tried as we neared a stone bench. I gestured for her to sit.

Munira sat down graciously, her blue skirt fanning around her. 'It's really lovely, Your Highness.' She looked up at me with soft dark eyes and, for a moment, I was struck with shame. She was going to be my wife. I had to do better.

'I'm sorry,' I found myself saying. 'I'm not sure how to do this whole … engaged thing.'

Munira sighed with relief. 'I'm so glad you said that! Me either! I've never felt more awkward in my life.'

I looked at her in surprise. 'What? Really?'

Munira grinned, her eyes lighting up. 'I can't get my head around the idea we are to marry in a few days, and we know nothing of each other. It's terrifying, isn't it?'

'It is, absolutely,' I agreed with relief.

'I was worried you would have no sense of humour,' Munira said thoughtfully, looking about the grounds.

I found myself smiling. 'Ah, so you thought me dull?'

'That, and you hated me,' she admitted hesitantly. 'You've looked absolutely bored at mealtimes.'

'Forgive me, I was … It's just a lot to come to terms with.' I tugged my sleeve down.

'I know, for me too,' Munira said kindly. 'Perhaps we can agree to be friends before we are made anything else?'

I looked into her earnest face and put my hand to my chest. 'Friends.'

Munira repeated the gesture, a smile on her face. 'You can call me Munira.'

'You may call me whatever you wish,' I replied. 'I believe a few choice swear words might be suitable after how I've been.'

Munira laughed. 'Zayd will do just fine. I'm not one for pet names, so let's not go about calling each other *jaanu* or *shona* – you get the gist.'

'Noted completely, Munira,' I said.

She beamed brightly. 'Excellent. This friendship is off to a good start.'

Munira was a kind person, I realized, as we continued

talking. I felt like we could be great friends. But when I looked upon her face, despite her beauty, it didn't move me. Perhaps, I thought, as today's newssheet flashed in my mind, I just needed to try.

'Did you see that the Fallowmere prince is coming to our wedding?' Munira asked. 'It's scandalous they didn't even tell us.'

I bristled. 'Nothing was said to us either. The nerve of them.'

'Perhaps it is a peace-making effort,' Munira suggested. 'My father told me the Sultana accepted your rates for the silver.'

'Perhaps, though I wouldn't hold out hope where the Sultana is concerned,' I replied. 'She can just as easily change her mind.'

'Yes, she is a dreadful woman,' Munira agreed.

'Do you know her?' I asked.

Munira shook her head. 'Not personally, but my mother used to tell me stories about when they were young. The Sultana came to visit before she was married; rumour has it she was completely obsessed with trying to win a place as a wife in the court.'

My eyes widened. 'Really?'

Munira nodded. 'Well, it looks like she finally got what she wanted when she married the Sultan of Sawan, despite her lineage.'

'That would explain why she is so power hungry,' I mused. 'She has that much more to prove.'

'We didn't have too many dealings with Sawan once Sultana Zahra married the Sultan – Father kept our relations minimal because of how difficult the Sultana is to work with.'

'Difficult is one word for it,' I said. 'I don't know how Princess Layla copes with her.'

'Me either,' Munira said.

'I look forward to the day Princess Layla reigns,' I said. Her name felt precious on my tongue. 'We could do great things with our nations more closely aligned.'

'If the Fallowmere let her,' Munira said with a scoff. 'I can't imagine they are back in our lands for any good reason. Whenever they go to a nation for trade, they end up invading weeks later.'

I grimaced. 'Hopefully it won't come to war again. We are prepared this time, at least.'

'Looks like we'll have our work cut out for us, I suppose?' she said, smiling at me.

I found myself smiling back before I looked away, across the vibrant green grounds, and found my heart beating slightly faster in my chest. My vision began to spot.

'Prince Zayd, you are needed back at the castle,' Noor said quickly, rushing to my side.

'Sorry, Munira, allow me to escort you back inside?' I offered.

'No, you go; I'd like to sit a while,' she said cheerfully.

I bade her farewell and quickly departed with Noor.

It was painful trying to keep it together until we got to my room. If the servants saw, if anyone suspected any-thing, chaos would ensue – especially now that Munira and her family were here. I just needed to make it to the wedding day.

The palace began to spin. I fell against the wall, barely registering Noor pulling me into a vestibule before I collapsed.

*

I awoke to Noor and Sayyidah Shafiya in my face, waving fans and holding out water. We were in a small, dimly lit room. I managed to take the water, eventually allowing Noor to pull me up.

'We need to get His Highness to bed; he needs rest,' Sayyidah Shafiya insisted.

'He can't be moved right now,' Noor replied worriedly.

'He is fine,' I grumbled, shrugging off Noor's hold. The walls stayed steady. 'Let's go.'

We made it back to my room without incident. The sun was low in the sky; I must have been blacked out for hours.

Noor summoned Iris who laid platters of fruit and pastries while Sayyidah Shafiya reappeared with a suspiciously green drink that was entirely hideous. Part of me wondered what was the point taking these medicines any more? My time was almost up.

Unless we found a cure. It was my only hope.

I would need to speak to Munira properly tonight, see what I could find out about her family's history. Surely one of her party would have the gene? Then I wouldn't need to tell my parents, and everything could be saved.

After some rest in bed, I woke up and found my dinner outfit had been laid out.

I sat up, groaning as my arm ached with the pain of a thousand blades. I chugged down the green concoction that had been left on my bedside table and wiped my mouth.

Slowly, I got out of bed and freshened up. I brushed my hair to one side and put kohl along my bottom eyelids to try and stop myself from looking so gaunt. I took my shirt off to pull on the outfit that had been left for me. I caught my reflection in the mirror, the dark veins were inching closer and closer to the space above my heart. I blew out a sigh.

I finished dressing and went over to my parlour. The door opened suddenly and in strolled Yunus.

'What is it?' I asked.

'Nothing. Just came to see what you were doing. I tried broaching the subject of mages with the youngest prince of Valthar, but he seemed clueless. Have you spoken to Munira?' he asked, flopping down onto one of the velvet armchairs.

'Not yet. I'm going to speak to her tonight,' I said.

'I hear you actually went for a walk with her.'

'It's about time I got to know her, isn't it?'

'Just a bit strange,' he said casually, 'given you've been moping around here for days. You were more excited when Princess Layla came to visit.'

I snorted. 'You have the imagination of a writer – maybe you should try jotting down your delusions instead.'

Yunus smirked. 'Just funny that you sailed an entire ocean for a girl who isn't yours, yet when your future wife is here, the most you can do is take her for a walk.'

I looked back at him evenly. 'Layla was in trouble. I had to help.'

'One day, Brother, you're going to need to accept you can't save everyone,' he said, his eyes flickering to my arm.

'Did you come here to lecture me?'

Yunus eyed me gleefully. 'Are you coming to dinner, then? You'll be pleased to hear Princess Layla has almost arrived. Mother sent extra guards to escort her party from the port.'

I looked up sharply. 'Layla's coming?'

'Careful, Brother, anyone would think you cared for her,' Yunus said shrewdly.

'Cease talking your nonsense,' I grumbled. 'Let's go.'

42

Layla

'Can I do anything for you, Your Highness?' Mira asked tentatively.

I shook my head, pressing my forehead against the carriage window. Mira had been trying to get me to talk for the past couple of days, but words evaded me. Shock still permeated every fibre of my being.

My body was stiff from not moving much these last two days. A thick stupor seemed to surround my senses. I felt around inside my cloak pockets for the silver daggers Zayd had gifted me, the cold press of the metal against my hands cooling my feverish skin. I'd thought I'd feel more afraid as we left the palace, but I only felt numb.

I had lost everything. I had nothing to fear any more. My father had no real heir. I had no claim to the throne. I was a fraud, parading around in a castle I didn't belong in.

And my mother, the conniving puppet master ... was this why she hated me so much? I was a reminder of whoever my real father was. I was a threat to her marriage, her reign. If anybody found out, she'd be cast aside just like me.

Perhaps that wouldn't be such a bad thing. Then I wouldn't have to marry Edmund.

310

And what would I do instead? Where would I go amongst a people who hated me?

Maybe that was a problem for another day.

My stomach sank as we pulled up to the moonstone palace of Dakaria and passed through the gilded gates. I thought I saw Zayd in the courtyard, but it was one of the guards, tall and dark-haired. I was overcome with a desperate ache to see him, to be near him again. If I could unburden myself to him, perhaps it would make the truth hurt less.

The Sultana of Dakaria met us in the reception hall. Her exchange with Mother was cordial, but her eyes lit up with warmth when she saw me.

'Layla, radiant as ever!' She pulled me into an embrace.

I hugged the Sultana back, unwilling to leave her warmth and comfort too soon.

'Are you all right, dear?' she whispered into my ear.

I nodded. 'Just tired, Your Majesty. It's a long journey.'

'I can imagine, especially after all you have been through, that you need rest,' she said firmly.

'And this is my future son-in-law, Edmund,' my mother announced loudly.

Sultana Aysha was gracious as ever as Edmund introduced himself, despite Mother not having sent word we were bringing our Fallowmere guests and letting the papers do the job instead.

'Thank you for having me at your beautiful home,' Edmund said courteously in Falmere. 'We are so delighted to be here together. I'm looking forward to observing the rituals of an Eastern wedding.'

The Sultana replied in Falmere too. 'I'm so happy to have you both here. Come, we shall take you to your rooms, and then we can all meet for dinner.'

'Thank you, Your Majesty,' Mother said, sauntering away.

I followed after her, stepping out of Edmund's hold as our entourage walked to the guest chambers. We had different rooms this time, in a new wing of the palace. There seemed to be more servants running to and fro, and beautiful decorations had been put up all around the palace. Garlands made of white roses and jasmine cascaded down from the high ceilings.

'I'll see you both at dinner,' Mother said, disappearing into her room.

'Layla, I shall see you later, darling,' Edmund said, placing an affectionate kiss on my cheek. I recoiled inwardly and hurried into my room, sighing with relief as Mira closed the door.

Mira grimaced. 'He's very touchy-feely, isn't he? Must be a Fallowmere thing.'

'Indeed,' I mumbled, falling face forward onto the soft, plush bed.

After I had bathed, I changed into a sari. It was beaded with silver and elegant thread work that covered the entire length of fabric. Mira placed matching sapphire jewels around my neck and tied my hair back into a fishtail bun that exposed the sparkling earrings hanging from my ears. She placed a silver tikka atop my head and dusted a dash of rose powder on my cheeks and lips.

I looked at my face in the mirror. My skin looked warm, the pink just disguising part of the silvery scar on my left cheek. As much as I was grateful the cut was miraculously healed, I hated the reminder of how I'd gotten it in the first place. I had half a mind to take it all off and burrow under the bedcovers.

Mira draped the end of the sari atop my head, the rest of the silk fabric cascading down my back. 'There. My future Sultana,' Mira said affectionately.

My heart sank. If only she knew. 'Come on then, let's go.'

Mira looked confused as I hurried out the door.

Entering the hall, I felt like I was walking into a candlelit garden overflowing with flowers. String musicians played in the background, while servants hurried about, laying down dishes and fixing the floral décor that hung from the walls and ceilings.

Edmund was already there with Mother and Prince Frederick, who was looking around the hall with curiosity.

When Edmund saw me, his eyes lit up. 'Princess Layla, you are an exotic vision,' he said breathlessly.

'Thanks,' I mumbled, appraising him. 'You look nice too.'

He wore a dark suit studded with his naval medals. I felt the heat of shame at the thought of walking by his side as he displayed his badges of colonialism. 'Thank you,' he replied confidently.

I caught Mother's expression and saw a layer of thin contempt on her face before she looked away.

The hall was brimming with guests, royals from all over the eastern part of the world. I followed Mother and Edmund as she introduced us to the various nobility. Some faces were new, some familiar – and my cousin Mariya was here, which made for a pleasant reunion. But an odd pit had formed in my stomach, and all I could feel was nerves. It was strange to be back in Dakaria; so much had changed since I was last here.

I felt him before I saw him. The air shifted in the room, my heart skipping a beat as I turned.

Zayd entered the hall with Yunus, and a hush fell across

the crowd. He looked every bit the handsome groom in a fitted navy sherwani that showed off his lean, muscular frame, and dangerously dark kohl that made the green in his eyes more piercing. His hair was swept to one side, his beard neat along his sharp jaw. I hated how just a look at him made my heart leap.

Zayd's eyes roamed the room until our eyes locked. His gaze held mine, and all I wanted was to push past everyone to reach him, but he looked away and the spell was broken.

'Are you all right, my dear?' Edmund asked, touching my arm gently.

I nodded, exhaling a breath. 'Shall we take our seats?'

'Yes, let's do that,' Edmund said happily.

Somehow, being in Edmund's company felt even more wrong than it had before. People were casting him and his uncle surprised looks, some curious, but most with carefully contained disgust. I hated that I was the reason the Fallowmere were being tied to our lands once more.

The servants helped us to our chairs. We had been seated near the top of the table, by the Sultana of Dakaria. Zayd took his seat opposite me, beside his mother and Yunus. Lush white flowers and candles adorned the table, setting off the gleaming silver cutlery around our clam-shaped plates. It seemed the Sultana must have had cutlery laid out to accommodate those royals who didn't normally eat with their hands. Pity; I preferred eating with my hands – the food just tasted better. At least I had several knives to drive through my skull – if Edmund didn't bore me to death first.

The music changed to a gentle tune, something that reminded me of sunset at the end of summer, the loss of innocence, of love.

My eyes flickered to Zayd. He was looking right at me, his jaw tight. I looked away. I couldn't bear it if his face bore the same look of disgust that had been following me around since I entered the hall with Edmund.

Another hush fell upon the room. I looked over and saw the royals of Valthar gracefully arrive. The Sultan was a broad man, the hair on his head greying but his beard full and dark. His sons, the princes, walked behind him, but my eyes were on the princess slowly walking in last of all.

She was beautiful, much to my dismay. Her face was soft, but she had sharp, high cheekbones and beautifully long hair that was twined with jasmine beneath her dupatta. She wore a sage lehenga that glittered with gold stones as she moved, contrasting beautifully against her warm brown skin. Her doe-like eyes were rimmed with kohl, giving her a striking look as she gazed about. A smile lit up her face as she caught sight of Zayd and my heart stuttered in my chest.

I turned hastily away, looking back at Edmund. He smiled softly at me, dropping a kiss by my cheek. 'What a beauty you are, Layla,' he murmured, his eyes travelling down my face, stopping at my lips.

My skin crawled. 'Edmund, I said we're not supposed to touch until we're married,' I replied quietly.

'How can I resist such a mysterious jewel like you?' Edmund said with a leering smile.

I pulled away, and just caught sight of Zayd, who wore a dark expression on his face as our eyes locked.

Princess Munira took her seat beside Zayd. I tried not to notice how he leant in close to talk to her, or the way she laughed at whatever he said.

I should have just jumped off the boat on the way here. This was shaping up to be one of the worst weeks of my life.

A life I didn't even deserve to have.

Dinner was excruciating. Mother was even more emboldened by all the guests and was boasting loudly about my wedding to anybody who would listen.

'How are you, Princess Layla?' Yunus asked from across the table. 'You're looking as radiant as ever. Have you been out in the sun?'

I laughed for the first time that day. 'All the better to be seeing you, Prince Yunus.'

Yunus chuckled. 'Is this your betrothed, then?'

I switched to Falmere. 'Yes, Yunus, this is Prince Edmund; Edmund, this is Prince Yunus.'

They exchanged pleasantries, but I found my eyes drifting towards Zayd and Munira, who seemed busy chatting away. I stabbed my chicken tikka a little too forcefully.

'Careful, dear,' Edmund said cheerfully, putting his hand over mine. Then in a whisper, 'You should be more gentle; it's more ladylike.'

I wanted to say something very unladylike in reply, but Mother stuck her head past him and glared at me. 'I prefer to eat with my hands,' I said pointedly.

Edmund looked pained by my response. 'It's more refined to eat with cutlery, dear.'

'I don't need tips on refinement from the land of colonizers, *dear*,' I snapped.

Edmund looked taken aback. 'Well, you know, the past is the past, my darling.' Red began to creep up to his cheeks.

'Don't worry, she's just joking,' Mother cut in quickly. '*Aren't* you, dear?'

'Of course,' I said with a fake smile. 'My whole life is a joke,' I muttered into my plate.

Sultana Aysha stood, tapping her glass with a spoon. Silence fell across the table.

'Dearest friends and family, we are so delighted to have you all here for the wedding of my beloved son and my wonderful future daughter-in-law, Princess Munira.' The table broke into applause. I zoned out as she gave her speech, looking down at my plate so I didn't have to see Zayd and Munira.

Once the Sultana sat back down, our dinner plates were swapped for dessert.

'I say, this is spicy!' Edmund said, half-choking on his gajar halwa.

'Spicy? It's sweet carrot,' I said, eyeing him with confusion. 'What's spicy about it?'

'No, it's quite spicy,' his uncle chipped in from beside Mother. Prince Frederick clicked his fingers at one of the servants. 'Take this away, now.'

I bristled. The Fallowmere hadn't even been here a moment and they were already acting like they owned the place.

'We do not click our fingers at servants, Prince Frederick,' Sultana Aysha said loudly. 'It is customary to speak to people with manners here. Much like it is customary to speak the language of the land you are in, and not to turn up announced.' She smiled pointedly.

'Forgive me, Your Majesty,' Prince Frederick said in a voice that certainly didn't sound sorry. 'I'm used to doing things in a different, proper way.'

'Our definitions of proper are *very* different, I am sure,' the Sultana replied cordially.

'Apologies, Your Majesty, we have had long journeys and much to deal with, what with my daughter's abduction, as you can imagine,' my mother said, laying her woe on thick. 'It completely slipped my mind to tell you I was bringing Layla's in-laws. You can only imagine how difficult these past few weeks have been.'

'Of course, Your Majesty,' the Sultana said in a softer voice, though her eyes still showed distrust. She turned towards the Sultan of Valthar and began conversing with him quietly.

Once the most awkward dinner in the history of dinners had concluded, I tried to hurry away before I had to watch Zayd and Munira playing the perfect couple any longer, and before Edmund could catch up to me.

But the devil found me anyway. 'Shall I walk you back to your room?' he oozed, putting his hand in mine.

'If you want,' I hedged.

A loud cough came from behind us.

I turned and my heart faltered in my chest for a moment.

'Your Highness, how are you?' Zayd asked politely, his eyes flickering towards Edmund and our entwined hands.

'I'm well, thank you,' I replied. 'Allow me to introduce you to Prince Edmund.'

Edmund leant forward to shake Zayd's hand and I quickly took the opportunity to pull my own back.

Zayd's expression darkened as they shook hands. 'Welcome to Dakaria, Prince Edward.'

'It's Ed*mund*, Your Highness. You have a beautiful home here,' Edmund said jovially.

'I hope you will enjoy your stay,' Zayd replied drily. 'Princess, are you well? Have your injuries healed fully?' His eyes were a little softer when they looked at me.

'Yes, I'm fully recovered, Your Highness.'

His eyes drifted down my face, and I hated the fact that I couldn't reach out for him. I wanted him to hold me again, so I could forget about everything that tormented me.

But we were standing in a crowded room. I was here to attend his wedding. For a moment, I thought I could see the same thoughts swirling in his sad eyes.

Edmund smiled back at Zayd, unaware. 'We must go hunting together, Your Highness. I'd love to hear more about Dakaria.'

'I will see if I can find the time,' Zayd said stiffly.

'I really love how vibrant the colours here are ...' Edmund prattled on.

We had never really acknowledged this thing that had grown between us. Our last letters to each other had ended abruptly as his wedding loomed. Part of me wondered if I'd dreamt the whole thing up – the way he'd looked at me, the way he'd come to help find me, how he'd held me in my room before he left.

But the emotion in his olive eyes told me that it wasn't all in my head.

'If you'll excuse me, Princess.' As Zayd walked past me, his fingers brushed mine ever so slightly. I clenched my hand shut to stop myself from holding on to him.

'Is something wrong, Your Highness?' Mira asked as she helped me undress. 'You look sad.'

'No, I'm fine.' I forced a smile.

'Mm, and I'm next in line for the throne,' she murmured, pulling out my plait and beginning to brush it through.

I almost smiled. 'Mira, can I ask you something?'

'Yes, Your Highness, anything.'

'Have you ever been in love?'

Mira's eyes widened. 'In love? Me? Gosh, no. No. Well, there was a – someone. I don't think it was reciprocated. But I suppose I was in love.' Her words were a garbled rush.

'But how did you know you loved them even if it wasn't reciprocated?' I asked.

Mira looked uncertain. 'I couldn't say, Your Highness. It all depends on the individual, doesn't it? Why? Are you in love with … someone?' she asked quietly.

'I don't know,' I confessed. 'What do you do when you're not sure how the other person even feels?'

Mira seemed sad as she looked away, her face pensive. 'I am afraid I have no wisdom to offer, Your Highness. Some of us aren't allowed to love the ones we want anyway.'

I wanted to ask her more, but Mira quickly left the room.

43

Zayd

Three cups of masala chai were keeping my eyes from drooping shut as the after party which consisted of more desserts and endless streams of tea wound down for the night. I'd been waiting for an opportunity to speak to Munira in private, but as she was the guest of the moment, everyone was eager to chat with her as we moved into the ruby hall to mingle. My eyes roamed the room, narrowing at the sight of Edmund and his pretentious uncle mingled with the Nevarim royals. That insufferable leech.

'You seem distracted. Is everything all right?' Yunus asked.

'Huh?' I looked back at him.

'What were you staring at?' he said, turning around.

'Nothing,' I said curtly. 'Come on, let's go and see if one of these in-laws of mine has what we need.'

Yunus gave me a strange look but nodded, leading the way towards the fireplace where Prince Asim stood nursing a cold drink.

'Prince Asim, I hope everything was to your liking at dinner,' I said, clapping him on the back.

He looked around, startled. 'Hm? Yes, everything was perfect. Your mother is an excellent host.'

'I look forward to visiting Valthar soon,' Yunus said. 'The history of your land is so fascinating. Are the national archives still open?'

Asim looked at Yunus in surprise. 'Yes, are you a history fiend?'

'You could say that,' Yunus said with a laugh. 'We've been tracing some lineages; it's fascinating stuff. Your great-grandfather was Sumon Akash, right?'

Asim nodded. 'Yes, my para dada. Why?'

'He has some interesting stuff written about him,' I hedged.

'Ah, yes, all that mage stuff? He was an interesting man. I heard you've got some water mages working for you now?' He looked at me curiously.

'With me, I'd say. But yes, they've proven to be useful allies.'

'Well, be careful,' Prince Asim said, his eyes aimed over my shoulder, no doubt towards Edmund and his uncle. 'If those snakes are returning, they might go after the mages again.'

'We all need to be careful with them back,' I said.

'Are there many mages in Valthar who would need protecting?' Yunus prodded.

Asim looked thoughtful. 'Not really. The mages who are left keep to themselves, and we don't bother them, either.'

Should I just ask him outright if he was a mage? I wondered.

'If your great-grandfather was an earth mage, did nobody else in your family inherit his power?' Yunus asked quietly.

Asim shook his head, lowering his voice. 'No, not to

my knowledge. It must have skipped our family. Shame, though. Perhaps if one of us had, we could have done something more for Valthar,' he added bitterly, looking over my shoulder again.

'What do you mean, done more?' I asked carefully.

Asim shook his head. 'Nothing. Just make sure you treat my sister well, Prince Zayd. I should get to bed.'

Asim sloped off, leaving Yunus and me to the crackling fire.

'Well, *his* tears would be worthless,' Yunus said.

'This whole thing might be worthless,' I said with a sigh.

'Let's hope your future wife is the answer to our problems,' Yunus said, nodding his head towards Munira.

I walked over to the centre of the room, where Munira stood chatting with some of the other princesses.

'Princess, how are you? Did you enjoy dinner?' I asked as she broke away from the group.

'I'm well, thank you,' she said, smiling up at me. 'Dinner was wonderful. Did you …'

'Yes, Dakaria still seems it has a long way to go—' Edmund said as he walked past us with Sultana Zahra and his uncle in tow. My blood began to boil.

'Zayd?' Munira said uncertainly.

'Sorry, what was that?'

'I suppose you're quite the daydreamer,' she said with a gentle smile. 'I was just asking if you think you'll dance at the mehendi?'

My eyes widened. 'Dancing? Me?'

'Go on, Brother, you must show everyone your moves,' Yunus chimed in, sliding in beside me.

'I'll leave that to you,' I said.

'Can you dance?' Munira asked Yunus.

'Who do you think taught Zayd all he knows, Princess?' Yunus said with his cheeky grin.

My eyes drifted away as Yunus and Munira spoke. The Sultana of Sawan was in deep conversation with the uncle from Fallowmere. Edmund had sauntered off somewhere.

I pulled at my collar. It was getting incredibly warm in here.

Noor coughed behind me. 'Your Highness, we have an update from the mines.'

'I'll be back later,' I said to Munira and Yunus.

I followed Noor out of the hall, trying to eavesdrop on the Sultana of Sawan as I went.

'I trust Edmund knows what he's doing—'

'Don't worry, that boy hasn't met a girl who wasn't putty in his hands,' the uncle replied.

What the hell?

'Your Highness, the mines were attacked by land and sea today,' Noor told me quietly, diverting my attention as we left the hall.

'Are you being serious?'

'Yes. Usman is in his study.'

I walked quickly through the hallways, weaving through guests and servants. I'd thought the water mages protecting the port would give us an advantage over our attackers. Perhaps I'd been foolish to think it would make us invincible.

'What's happened?' I demanded as the chamber door slammed behind me.

Usman was standing by a large map, his eyes shadowed.

'Your Highness,' he said. 'The pirates used the River Ujad to get onto land and mount a surprise attack from behind. The mages managed to recover, but one was injured.'

'But there were no fatalities?' I pressed.

'No, our forces and the mages were able to take the pirates down. It seems they are using the wedding as a distraction.'

'And the mages will still work with us?' I demanded. As long as the mages held firm, we still had a chance.

'Yes, Your Highness.'

'Did they capture anyone?'

'All dead, Your Highness.'

'Next time there's an attack, I want prisoners. I need to find out who these pirates are led by, and how the hell we get them to give up. We can't keep doing this. And find out how they got past our border controls around the River at Ujad – they shouldn't have made it into land.'

'It's our endless waterways, Your Highness – it looks like they swam in undetected and proceeded on foot,' Usman replied.

I let out a curse. 'Get some sleep. You look worse than me.'

'My mother would disagree, Your Highness,' Usman replied dryly.

I snorted, leaving his office. My arm was throbbing with pain. I traipsed back to my quarters and sank into the first chair I laid eyes on, letting out a shallow breath.

Tugging back my sleeve, I watched the black ink in my veins pulse.

What kind of crown prince was I? I had been rendered useless by a poisoned arrow. I couldn't even wield a sword to defend my country.

How was I going to marry Munira like this? How long did I even have left?

I eased my sleeve back down before pulling out my

drawer and chugging down another vial of medicine. The burning sensation subsided a little.

I needed a cure. But if Asim thought no one in his family had the gene, then I was royally screwed.

44

Layla

I walked beneath a canopy of green trees towards a beautiful glimmering lake. The water was turquoise blue, and pink lilies floated serenely atop the surface. The trees curled towards me as I walked, the wind brushing over my skin like an embrace. I inhaled fresh, warm air, the summer sun hanging low in the orange sky.

A hand on my shoulder made me turn.

'Baba?' I gasped.

His soft dark eyes lit up. His greying hair and beard seemed pearly white in the light, his smooth brown skin glowing. 'Hello, my child.'

Cold washed over me. 'But I'm not. You lied to me.'

Father sighed. 'It's not like that, meri jaan. You know a piece of paper doesn't change anything. You're my whole heart; you always have been.'

'I'm not - I'm nothing—'

Father took my hands in his. They felt so warm and solid. But I knew I was dreaming. And yet it felt so real. 'Listen to me. I will always be your baba, and you will always be my little girl.' His eyes were fierce. 'Don't you ever stop calling me baba, OK?'

I nodded, hope crashing in my chest.

'Don't let your mother's nonsense become your inner voice. You are incredible. You are destined for great things. And you are the rightful Sultana. I made sure of it. Do you think I would have left you without protection? So, you will fight for your throne, you will fight for your crown, and you will win. Do you hear me?'

'No, I can't,' I said, shaking my head. Tears pooled in my eyes.

'Yes, you can!' he said urgently. 'Do you hear me? You can! Do you hear me?'

'Can you hear me? Princess, can you hear me?'

I startled awake.

Mira looked back at me guiltily. 'Sorry to wake you, but it's almost noon. You slept through breakfast and Her Majesty, your mother, demands your presence at lunch.'

I blinked blearily into the bright light and rubbed my eyes. 'OK. I'll be along. Give me a few minutes.'

Mira nodded and withdrew.

I looked around, dazed, half-expecting to see my father again. Had it really been a dream? It felt so real.

I shook my head as if I could dispel the remnants of my dream. But even as I got ready and arrived at the dining hall, Father's words were all I could think about. I saw Edmund and his uncle already seated, but I diverted and went to sit with my cousin Mariya and her husband.

'How are you, cousin dearest?' Mariya said, squeezing my hand.

'Better for seeing you.'

'I have to say, I was very surprised by your choice of groom,' her husband, Samer, said quietly.

Mariya snorted. 'I wasn't. It's just like her mother to do that. My uncle would be turning in his grave.'

My heart sank.

328

'It's not your fault, dear,' Mariya said quickly, patting my arm. 'Everyone knows how power hungry she is. I can only hope you'll be coronated soon so you can put things right.'

'If she lets me,' I said half-heartedly.

Father's voice rang in my mind. *You can.*

'Don't let her ruin everything our family built,' Mariya whispered fiercely, her dark eyes intent. 'Soon you will be of age – you can put an end to her foolish reign.'

'And if you need help, we are here too, cousin,' Samer offered.

I nodded gratefully.

Much to my dismay, Mother appeared by my side and pulled me away to sit with my betrothed.

'You need to show a united front,' she hissed in my ear.

'How did you sleep, my darling?' Edmund asked as I sat down next to him. 'You must have been so tired after last night to miss breakfast.'

'Mm, I think I'm still sick,' I said, feigning a cough and hoping it might keep him away from me.

Mother sat beside Prince Frederick and launched into a discussion about the price of Valthar silk and her plans to build more garment houses in Sawan.

Yunus walked into the room, followed by Sultana Aysha. I waited a beat, but Zayd didn't follow.

Munira and her family came in soon after. The Sultan of Valthar looked our way briefly before they went to find their seats. Mercifully, they weren't anywhere near ours. I couldn't take sitting close to Munira now. Guilt and envy gnawed at my insides.

Sultana Aysha made her way over to us, dropping a kiss on the top of my head. 'How was your rest, Princess?'

Mother cut in before I could reply. 'Very good. I had no idea you had larger rooms,' she said in an overly sweet voice. 'I almost didn't know what to do with all the space!'

'I am glad you were comfortable,' the Sultana replied with a pleasant smile. 'Prince Frederick, Prince Edmund, I hope you were comfortable too?'

'Hm? Yes, yes, excellent, all good here,' Prince Frederick said absently, reading a newssheet. 'You know, Dakaria seems to be doing really well for itself, given the state it was in when my ancestors came here. It's come a long way,' he said admiringly.

I saw the Sultana stiffen. 'Yes, we were able to turn our fate around after your ancestors left, having stolen all our resources.'

Prince Frederick laughed. 'I wouldn't say stolen. That's just how things were back then. Empires rose and fell, kings ruled and conquered—'

'Perhaps we can save this conversation for after the wedding,' my mother interjected with a sweet smile. 'I'm sure the Sultana has many other guests to speak with.'

'Quite,' Sultana Aysha said thinly. 'If you'll excuse me.'

I looked at Prince Frederick, who was chuckling to himself as he told my mother how sensitive women were.

Mother rolled her eyes in an amused way. *Traitor.* If anybody else had made such a hideous statement, she would have been the first to draw her dagger.

'Are you all right, my darling?' Edmund asked, leaning in.

'I'm fine,' I said, leaning away. 'Shall we eat?'

He nodded with a smile, putting his hand on my knee. I brushed him away and started eating my paratha.

As Edmund started droning in my ear, I looked around and saw Munira sitting at the head table with her family and the Sultana. Zayd still hadn't come to lunch, but she was in conversation with Yunus beside her, laughing away. She would slide perfectly into this family, I realized, with a pang of jealousy that took me by surprise.

I looked down sharply at my plate and tried to eat some jackfruit. It tasted sour in my mouth.

Lunch was painfully long, but eventually it came to an end. Edmund and his uncle were planning a hunt with some of the other royals, so I bade them farewell and asked the guards to take me to the greenhouse.

They led me out to the bright, green grounds. I took in a deep breath, tension rolling off my shoulders as the warm sun hit my face. But just a moment later I was being shaded by a large parasol held by Mustafa. I rolled my eyes and carried on down the sandstone pathways, the warm, musky smell of jasmine filling the air as we walked past a row of bushes.

Where was Zayd? It was strange for him not to be at lunch. It was his wedding week, after all. And soon it would be mine. Would I have to play the role of happy couple with Edmund while Zayd stood in attendance with Munira? I still didn't know what to do with my life now that I had found out I was adopted.

Had Father really appeared to me? What protection had he left for me? Or was it just my subconscious trying to comfort me in the wake of this news?

I tortured myself as I walked, barely taking in the endless flowers that decorated the large grounds of the palace. When we arrived at the greenhouse, I told my guards to join the Dakaria guards already stationed along the perimeter.

I stepped inside, the humid, hot air greeting me immediately. I let out another deep breath. Solitude, at last.

My hands brushed over various trailing plants as I walked, their leaves trembling, reaching towards me. I let the vines wrap around my palm for a moment, breathing in the earthy air.

I wished I could speak to Father again. That dream had felt so precious. I couldn't remember the last time I'd dreamt of him. It had been frequent after he passed away – always him consoling me, hugging me, until eventually he faded away. It couldn't have been a coincidence that he'd appeared to me last night.

But I didn't know if I had the strength to do what he wanted – to go up against the Sultana. For all my hatred towards her … she was still my mother. There had been glimpses of her care when I was younger: a soft smile, a parting kiss, a moment when I felt like she might have loved me.

But now she had morphed into someone I didn't recognise. Was this what these powers of mine were meant to be used for? To best her somehow?

I shuddered at the thought. If it came to it, if I really challenged her for the crown, I knew she wouldn't hesitate to fight me.

'If you keep thinking so hard, the glass will break,' a deep voice murmured.

I whirled to find Zayd standing close behind me. Too close. His olive eyes were sombre.

'Layla,' he sighed my name, looking into my eyes.

'Prince Zayd,' I said, taking a step back.

His eyes flickered with something – hurt? – before his jaw tightened. 'How are you enjoying your stay?'

'It's fine, thanks,' I said, deliberately giving my attention to a nearby flower still in bud. 'You must be so excited for the wedding. Munira will be a wonderful Sultana.'

'Do you really think that?' I could feel his eyes boring into me, but I couldn't bear the thought of looking at him, of drowning in the intensity of his gaze.

I shrugged. 'It's not really my business, is it? I'm just a guest at your wedding. Someone to keep relations between Sawan and Dakaria sweet.'

'And I suppose I'll be a guest at yours,' he countered. 'I take it I don't need an invitation for Munira - I can just turn up with her unannounced?'

I looked up, angry. 'It wasn't my idea to bring him.'

Zayd shrugged, his face a cool mask. 'But you seem to be having a grand time together - you clearly don't have a problem marrying the coloniser.'

The cruel words felt like a stab. 'Why do you care? You seem preoccupied with your future wife anyway,' I bit back.

'Bothers you, does it?'

My blood boiled. Here was the prince who held me at knifepoint. All his charm gone. 'Why would it bother me? It's not like there's anything between us.'

'Do you really believe that?' he said with a snort.

'In three days, you will be wed. And what then?'

'I have a duty to fulfil,' he replied tersely. 'But that doesn't mean ...' His words trailed off, his eyes softening as he looked at me.

'Whatever. I'm not doing this.' I turned to leave, making it two steps before he spoke again.

'Do you think I want this marriage?' he said angrily. 'I'm doing what I have to do.'

I froze.

He crossed the distance between us, his warm hand curling around mine, pulling me back to bring us nose to nose.

'Is there nothing between us, Layla?' he murmured, leaning down towards me. His thumb circled the inside of my wrist.

'Don't put this on me,' I said as he came dangerously closer, his mouth a breath away from mine.

'Put what on you?' he whispered.

'Zayd,' I warned, gripping his arm to push him away, but instead I found myself holding on.

'Yes?' he replied. 'Do you want me to stop?' He drew back slightly, bringing his eyes level to mine.

I couldn't speak. My mind was in chaos. I could smell his heady scent, the warm, golden oud that invited me closer.

'Tell me to stop,' Zayd murmured, his hands tracing up my waist.

I couldn't. My limbs were liquid.

Zayd's eyes burned with glorious desire as he pulled me closer. The feel of his hard body pressed against mine was dizzying. His lips were so close I could almost taste them.

'Layla,' he sighed.

I brought my hand to his face. He closed his eyes, leaning in. It would take just one moment to close the space between us—

The sound of a door slamming made us jump apart.

Zayd's guard came down the pathway, running. 'Your Highness, are you all right – oh.'

'I'm fine, Noor,' Zayd said shortly.

'My apologies. I didn't realize – a thousand apologies.' He looked between us for a moment. 'I have business to discuss with you. Urgent matters, I am afraid.'

'I will be along,' Zayd said tightly.

His guard nodded and scurried away.

'If you'll excuse me, Princess.' Zayd said curtly, leaving.

How could he ask if there was nothing between us? Couldn't he hear the way my heart stuttered in his presence? Couldn't he feel the way my body melted under his touch? Had he no clue what he did to me?

Perhaps I had been too proud to realize it at first. But from the moment we'd met, his soul had captured mine. I had tried to resist it, but it was pointless.

I was hopelessly in love with him. It was devastating. But not loving him would have been the end of me too.

I watched him walk away, each nerve in my body on fire. Every flower on the bush in front of me had burst into full bloom.

45

Zayd

I forced myself to walk out of the greenhouse. I wanted to turn back to Layla, to pick up where we had been so rudely interrupted. The feel of her hands on my chest - her lips so close to mine—

This was ridiculous of me. I was playing a dangerous game. But a large part of me simply didn't care. I was a dead man walking away - so what if I stole a bit of life before I went?

How was I to convince myself that I didn't want every single part of her? What cruel twist of fate was it that we had met before I was to be married? Why could I not have been betrothed to her instead? My parents would rage if I walked away from Munira now. Layla's mother would never allow it.

I blew out a sigh and looked back at the greenhouse. Vines and leaves blocked out the glass; I was sure nobody had seen us. But if they had? What if Munira's family found out? *Would that be so bad*? I reasoned. A cancelled wedding? Perhaps there was another way to form alliances with Valthar, one that didn't involve tying myself to Munira for the rest of my short life.

My parents' expectations - the Sultana of Sawan's

threats – my poisoned arm – filled my head. Layla was the enemy's daughter. What was I doing, playing with fire like this?

I rubbed my face with my hands, trying to dispel my foggy thoughts. It was no use. I was done for.

'Was there actually news, Noor?' I asked him.

'Her Highness, Princess Munira, wishes to take a walk with you.'

I laughed bitterly. I couldn't help it. Talk about perfect timing. 'She does, does she?'

'Well, Her Majesty suggested it,' he added hastily.

I shook my head. 'Very well.'

I was probably going to hell. Mooning over Layla while my mother forced me to court Munira. Neither of them deserved this.

Munira was waiting for me in the eastern courtyard, sitting by a stone fountain that poured water from an elephant's trunk I watched Munira dip her hand in the water, a smile on her face.

I cleared my throat.

'Zayd,' Munira said, turning her smile on me. 'Have you got time for a walk?'

'Of course,' I said.

Munira stood and followed as I led the way out towards the gardens, far away from the greenhouse.

'You weren't at lunch,' she commented.

'I just had some business to sort out,' I replied.

'I suppose that is the life of a Sultan,' she said lightly.

'How was it? Did you have good company?' I asked.

'Your brother, Yunus, is very welcoming and funny,' she said affectionately. 'Luckily we were not seated near the

Sultana of Sawan, so I didn't have to hear her gloating about the wedding she'll be throwing soon.'

'I take it you don't want to go?'

'I wouldn't mind,' she said casually. 'It would be interesting to visit Sawan. Would you like to go?'

'I don't think I'll have the time,' I said tightly. 'We've got a lot to sort out here.'

'How are things by the Silver Port? Father said more of our soldiers will be on the way soon,' she said with a smile.

'It's getting better,' I hedged. 'We have a new ally.'

'The water mages, right? I heard about that. I didn't think our lands had any mages left.'

Now was my chance to see what she knew. 'Aren't there any in your land?'

'I think they mostly live in hiding. Nobody really speaks of them in Valthar,' she said indifferently.

'That's a shame,' I said carefully, 'I was hoping that as future rulers, that it was time we allowed them to live freely amongst us again.'

Munira hesitated, as if battling with herself. 'Well. My grandfather used to tell me stories about them. He thought his father was an earth mage. But Father hated it; he called them fanciful fairytales and forbade us from talking about it much.'

Interesting. Did the Sultan have something to hide?

I spied a rose on the bush coming up and plucked it, handing it to Munira. If she was an earth mage, whether she knew it or not, the books I'd been reading said the elements would respond to her touch. I watched closely, curious to see if the flower reacted in any way, but it was still.

Munira beamed. 'Thank you,' she said delightedly.

Guilt washed over me.

*

'Here comes the groom,' Father said with a teasing smile as I came into his room.

'Isn't he a beauty?' Yunus drawled from the armchair.

'How are you feeling, Father?' I asked.

'I am fine, beta. It seems like just yesterday you were crawling through these halls, and now here you are, getting married.' His eyes glistened.

I looked down at my hands. 'Time flies,' I muttered tiredly.

'You are doing the right thing for your country, Zayd, remember that,' Father said gently.

I looked up at his sincere face and nodded. 'You seem more vibrant today.'

'My son is getting married. Death can wait.'

'You must be looking forward to getting out of this bed, Father?' Yunus asked. 'I see the carpenter has built you the chair to bring you to the wedding.'

Yunus gestured towards the new oak chair in the corner. It had wheels instead of legs.

'Indeed, Son,' Father said. 'It will be nice to see something other than these four walls. I only wish I was able to ride again. How are my horses doing?'

We entertained Father a while, filling him in on the status of the palace and its various gardens and animals, but his eyes kept drooping. Eventually, sleep overtook him.

When the clock struck eleven, I beckoned Yunus to leave so that I could update him on our search for an earth mage.

'I think Munira's father might be a mage – she said he forbade her grandfather from telling them stories about mages. Sounds like he has something to hide.'

'How the hell do we get *him* to cry?' Yunus said, perplexed.

339

'We'll have to find a way without telling him the truth. He'll call off the wedding if he finds out about me.'

Yunus nodded grimly.

I rose despairing the next morning, as my arm continued to blister with pain. As the wedding drew closer, I couldn't help but feel like a failure. I had been raised as the next Sultan, but here I was, closer to my deathbed than my coronation. I needed to speak with Sultan Arun today. If I could just get those tears, half my problems would be solved.

'Your Highness, you will be dining in the ruby hall,' Noor said as I emerged from my room.

I narrowed my eyes at him. 'Why?'

'Her Majesty has set up a private breakfast for you and Princess Munira,' he replied.

Of course she had. 'Very well,' I said with a sigh. 'Also, can you send word to the Sultan of Valthar that I'd like to have a drink with him later?'

It was time to get to know my future father-in-law.

46

Layla

The last time I had been in the training room, I'd ended up under Zayd. I shook the memory off as I stood with a bow and arrow, practising my strikes from the centre of the room. It was quiet today: I was the only one in here besides Mira, who sat to the side with water and towels. I needed to distract myself from what had happened with Zayd yesterday.

I tried to close one eye, but the weight of a bow and arrow was very different from that of daggers. Still, it helped to imagine my mother's face in the centre of the board.

There wasn't long left now until the wedding. The festivities would begin soon – the haldi, the mehendi, the marriage ceremony. For all of Zayd's reluctance, it was still going ahead. Not that I had a leg to stand on, attending his events with Edmund. Bound by duty, expectations, the weight of our titles. Perhaps Zayd and I were more alike than I thought.

Eventually, when my muscles had grown weary, I traipsed out of the room, following the path back towards my quarters. As we made our way to the grand staircase,

I caught sight of Zayd and the Sultan of Valthar below, heading into one of the lavish parlour rooms. They appeared to be in deep discussion.

Well, the man was to be Zayd's father-in-law. I supposed it was expected that they'd be off having private conversations together. But something about it looked too intense for wedding planning.

I had to stop caring about what Zayd was doing. Was it normal to feel this way, to feel like one person was the centre of your universe? I was driving myself insane. But it was either that or think about my father, the truth of my birth and my mother's deceit. I hadn't even begun to wonder who my real biological father might be. It was all too much to bear.

Was this why Mother had constantly complained that I looked like Father, to try and sell the lie? Of course it was. She was ever the performer.

I hated her. I wished it were the other way round – that Father was my biological parent and she had adopted me. The thought of her blood running through me made me feel sick.

'Princess, what's going on? You seem so upset lately,' Mira commented as she helped me dress after my bath.

'Life isn't the same any more,' I replied.

'You will heal, Your Highness,' Mira said comfortingly, patting my arm.

I wasn't sure I would, not from all of this.

'I don't mean to pry, but what happened that night, when the earthquake struck?' Mira asked carefully. 'You were so upset – at first I thought it was shock. But you haven't been the same since.'

I looked down at my hands, away from her concerned gaze. 'It was nothing. I just have a lot on my mind.'

Mira thankfully didn't push for more information. For a moment, I wondered how she'd respond if I told her about the powers I'd been experiencing. But I couldn't take that risk right now.

Tonight was the gaye holud. Happily, the men were not a part of this ceremony, so I was spared Edmund's company and the judgemental stares that came with it. I opted to sit right at the back, avoiding eye contact with my mother as she waltzed in and made her presence known.

I watched Munira walk in with her ladies-in-waiting, dressed in a bright yellow sari and with marigolds in her long hair. She beamed as she took her seat on the cushions by the stage.

Music started up, a lively tune on the sittar, as Munira was covered in turmeric paste to cleanse and brighten her skin for the big day. The Sultana of Dakaria came and helped apply some too, the pair of them laughing together like mother and daughter would.

A stab of longing coursed through me. I looked at my own mother, in conversation with the Sultana from Nevarim, and wondered how things had gone so wrong.

As the party got into full swing, I decided to make my exit while Mother was occupied.

A gentle hand on my arm stopped me.

I turned and almost jumped. Munira stood before me, her skin glowing from the haldi that had been scrubbed off her, a warm smile on her face.

'Layla, I've been meaning to introduce myself. I'm Munira,' she said, leaning in to kiss my cheeks.

'Pleasure to meet you,' I forced myself to say.

'How are you finding your stay?' she asked as though she were Sultana of Dakaria. She would be soon.

'It's lovely. Sultana Aysha always takes such good care of me,' I said truthfully. 'How are you?'

Her smile fell a little. 'Nervous, to be honest. It's so strange getting married to someone you barely know, isn't it?'

That we could agree on. 'Definitely. They are a lovely family, though. I know they'll treat you well.'

She smiled, seemingly assured by my words. 'I'd love to get to know each other more. Do write to me, and come for a visit after the wedding. Yunus says you were so much fun to have around.'

'That's kind of him; he's far too generous.' I smiled despite myself.

'Were you heading off now? Why don't you stay for the mitai?' she implored.

'I am feeling a bit unwell,' I lied. 'Enjoy the rest of your evening, Princess.'

Munira gave me a parting smile that made me feel more ashamed than when my father caught me breaking his chandelier with a badly thrown ball when I was a child. A lump swelled in my throat.

I skirted the crowd and slipped out onto the balcony, hoping I might be able to get a few moments to myself without being tailed constantly by guards. I took the steps down into a courtyard.

I followed a winding path that led me back to the palace and tried to walk with the air of someone who knew where they were going. The few guards dotted around paid me no mind, hopefully thinking I was just another wedding guest.

The palace in the evening was serene, the moonlit corridors bathed in a golden glow from the lanterns along the walls. I found myself in another courtyard, beautiful blue and green mosaics colouring the floor. In the centre was a large fountain, pouring from a collection of stone water lilies.

An elderly man sat to one side, leaning back heavily in a wheeled wooden chair. The guard behind him stood to attention at my arrival.

'Apologies, I was just walking,' I said.

The elderly man looked up. A smile fell across his tired features. 'Princess Layla, is that you?'

'Yes,' I said, realizing with a lurch that it was His Majesty – Zayd's father.

'Come, my dear! I haven't seen you since you were a small child!' he said fondly, ushering me forward with a slow hand.

I walked over to him, curtseying. 'Your Majesty, it's a pleasure to meet you again.'

He looked at me with a warm familiarity that reminded me painfully of my own father. 'Your father would have been so delighted to see the beautiful young woman you have become.'

His words might have comforted me once. But now they only made me feel hollow.

'Oh dear, sorry – have I upset you? Ignore me, I rarely get to speak to people these days. The carpenter made me this fantastic chair, so I'm trying to enjoy the gardens while I can.'

'No, you haven't; it's fine,' I said quickly. 'It's just been a long day.'

'Yes, weddings can be brutal, especially with as many

events as ours,' he replied with a chuckle that turned into a hacking cough.

Alarmed, I hovered, unsure what to do as the guard began to rub the Sultan's back.

'I'm fine, it's OK,' the Sultan wheezed, his coughing coming to a stop. 'Oh dear, sorry! As you can see, my health isn't what it used to be.'

'Forgive me, Your Majesty. I will let you get your rest.'

'No, please stay; no need to go on my account,' the Sultan said cheerily. 'Come, why don't you sit?' He gestured to the bench beside him.

I took a seat and the Sultan motioned for the guard to retreat.

'Your father was a good man, Princess Layla,' the Sultan said sadly, looking deeply at the fountain. 'Few rulers were as honourable as him.'

'I miss him terribly,' I confessed quietly. 'But …'

'But?' the Sultan prompted.

'Sometimes I feel like he just left me,' I said, fighting back the lump that was swelling in my throat.

The Sultan's face fell. 'No, dear, don't think that. Your father loved you more than life itself. After he lost his first wife, he was broken. But then you came along, and he doted on you, more than you can ever know.'

'I didn't realize you knew him that well,' I said, looking at the Sultan curiously.

'We were always in touch, more so before we became rulers,' the Sultan replied, his eyes drifting away to another time. 'We travelled a lot together as young boys with our parents, trying to learn how to be rulers on these foreign visits. Trying to see if we could restore these lands to what they once were.'

My nerves prickled with anticipation. Perhaps the Sultan knew my father better than I had. 'Like, bringing back the mages?'

The Sultan's eyes snapped back to me. He looked around us before speaking. 'How do you know about that?'

'I found the letter and the pages you sent him,' I clarified.

He hesitated. 'Your father was an inquisitive man. He was gathering information about mages from our extensive libraries, though he never said why.'

The hairs on the back of my neck rose. Could Father have known about my affinities or my parentage – was my birth father a mage?

'It seems my father had a lot of secrets,' I mumbled.

'Perhaps, but everything he did was for your future, dear,' the Sultan said comfortingly. 'Which is why I never understood why your father changed his mind and left your mother in charge.'

'What do you mean?' I asked, confused.

The Sultan looked back at me uncertainly. 'Your father told me it was always his intention should anything happen to him that you would take over the crown. Your mother was only ever to be an advisor to you at most, never Sultana Regent.'

Before I could fully process what he was saying, approaching footsteps sounded in the air and Zayd and Yunus appeared at the entrance of the courtyard.

'Father, what are you doing out here?' Yunus called, walking over. 'Princess! You're here too!'

'Yes, we were just enjoying some fresh air,' the Sultan replied happily.

I saw Zayd's eyes zero in on me. The way he looked at me felt like an arrow to the heart.

'You'll get cold, Father, let's get you inside,' Zayd said as he neared, concern furrowing his brow.

'Very well. But why don't we have some tea to finish the night?' the Sultan said as Yunus came to steer his chair. 'You're more than welcome to join us, Princess.'

'That's kind of you. I should head back, though.' I rose from my seat.

'I'll walk you back to your room,' Zayd said. 'It seems you've given your guard the slip.'

'That's not necessary,' I said hastily.

'Nonsense. Yunus can take me back, and Zayd can accompany you,' the Sultan said warmly. 'Good evening, Princess.'

Zayd squeezed his father's arm gently as he passed.

I set off towards the guest wing, hoping to lose Zayd before something else ridiculous happened between us.

'In a hurry?' Zayd called quietly, catching up to me.

'I need my beauty sleep for all your wedding events,' I replied dryly.

'Layla, wait, please,' Zayd said, catching my hand.

I hated how much I wanted to hold him. I hated how much I loved the feel of his rough hand against mine.

I turned, snatching my hand back. 'Stop it. You can't keep doing this – *we* can't keep doing this.'

Zayd looked pained. 'I know I shouldn't. But I can't stay away from you. It's killing me, watching you with him.'

'Oh, and I'm just having the time of my life here, at *your* wedding?' I snapped back, anger fuelling my words. 'Enough is enough, Zayd. You have your duties, and so do I. Just stay away from me.'

The devastation in his eyes threatened to undo me. So I did the only thing I could – I left.

348

I rushed back to my rooms, heart hammering away in my chest. I sank against the bed, taking deep breaths until my racing heart steadied.

I hated the effect Zayd had on me, like I was a helpless addict, desperate for just a moment with him. I shook my head as if I could dispel my feelings for him so easily. I had other things to worry about.

What had the Sultan said? *Your father told me it was always his intention should anything happen to him that you would take over the crown. Your mother was only ever to be an advisor to you at most, never Sultana Regent.* As far as I knew, my mother was always supposed to be in charge until I came of age – though now she kept saying I had to prove I was ready before I could assume the throne.

Had she lied about this too? I wouldn't put it past her. Look what she'd done to Hussam!

My thoughts swirled around my head as I paced the room until I found myself wandering to my wardrobe where I had stashed a satchel from my trunk.

With shaky breaths, I opened the bag and took out the items I'd stolen from Father's study.

I wasn't sure I was ready to read his journal yet, so I took out the second envelope I had yet to open. What horrors lay inside this one, I wondered as I gingerly broke the seal and pulled out the parchment inside.

By order of Sultan Aziz Emran Asad II

Princess Layla Afreen Asad is legally recognized as the heir to Sultan Aziz Emran Asad II and will be crowned Sultana in the event of the Sultan passing.

Should the Sultan pass before the princess comes of age, it is His Majesty's wish that the princess is supported by the court advisors to rule. Her Highness, Layla Afreen Asad, is to be coronated immediately upon the Sultan's death.

The Sultana Consort, Zahra Bhatt, shall be given the title of Valide Sultana. Her Highness, Layla Afreen Asad, may decide whether she wishes her mother as Valide Sultana to have a place as an advisor in her court or not.

Witness signatures:
Sultan Aziz Emran Asad II
Sultana Consort Zahra Bhatt
Minister of State Affairs Hussam Rabat

The letter shook in my hands. Father had put it in writing. He really wanted me to continue his reign even though I wasn't his real daughter?

I wiped the tears from my face, feeling something like relief spread through me. If Father had sought to make sure I became Sultana, he really did see me as his child. Just like he'd told me in my dream.

I looked at the paper again, zeroing in on my mother's signature as a witness.

She had known all along. I could only imagine how she had engineered her way into becoming Sultana Regent. It couldn't have been hard to convince the court she was better off ruling in the meantime – I had barely been fourteen when Father died.

She had stolen my crown. And I knew she had no intention of ever giving it back.

A part of me wasn't surprised, but I felt hollow. Father knew what Mother was like. He'd tried to secure our country in case he passed away. And once again, Mother got her way instead. And now she had made it so that I would be an irrelevant part of my own kingdom – a womb to carry her heirs while she controlled my life.

47

Zayd

I didn't want to spend my last days like this, parading around playing groom to be. I wanted to spend them with this impossible girl whose smiles felt like they could put the sun to shame. But this was no fairytale. This story only ended in tragedy. It was time I accepted that.

In the morning, I found Yunus at the desk in his rooms poring over books, Sayyidah Shafiya beside him.

'What's going on here?' I asked.

'Your Highness, good morning.' Sayyidah Shafiya stifled a yawn.

'Brother,' Yunus greeted me briefly. 'Did you have any luck with Munira's father?'

I sat down on an armchair. 'No, but he's hiding something. He didn't even want to talk about the mages in Valthar, let alone admit his great-grandfather was one.'

'Could it be him?' Sayyidah Shafiya said.

'Possibly. Maybe he's worried it would threaten his reign if anyone were to find out,' I mused. 'Especially with Sultana Zahra next door rounding up mages.'

'I can't fathom the evil that runs through the world sometimes,' Sayyidah Shafiya said gravely.

'Can we get his tears somehow?' Yunus asked.

'The only way I could do that is if I tell him about my injury, and if I do, there's every chance the wedding will be off.'

Yunus grimaced. 'There has to be another cure – another ingredient that can strengthen this salve, one that doesn't rely on an earth mage. We're running out of time.'

'I'm yet to find anything else, Your Highness. I am sorry,' Sayyidah Shafiya said.

'I'll stay close to Sultan Arun at the mehendi tonight, see if he starts crying,' Yunus added.

'Is that tonight?' I asked, confused.

Yunus rolled his eyes. 'Surely you know when your own wedding events are happening?'

Apparently I did not.

In the evening, I was entrapped by Mother and forced into the hands of the groomer, who trimmed my hair and my beard, and sprayed a ridiculous amount of ittar over me.

'How is my handsome son looking?' Mother asked excitedly. She waltzed into my room in an orange sari decorated with gold florals.

'He looks ridiculous,' I muttered, eyeing my reflection unhappily. I had been dressed in a deep emerald sherwani with my sword strapped to my side. I felt like a prize goat.

'Nonsense, you are the most gorgeous prince in the world!'

'Once again, Mother, you have another son,' Yunus said dryly, appearing by the door.

'And when you get married, you will be the most handsome prince in the world too,' Mother said dismissively, taking me by the shoulders. I tried not to wince as I shrugged out of her hold. Hurt flickered across her face.

'Your father is so excited to come to the mehendi,' Mother said, attempting to sound cheery. 'Would you like to come to his room now? We can all arrive together.'

Father was in joyful spirits as Hakim and Noor helped him into his chair. The next battle was the grand spiral steps.

'We should have had a ramp made,' Yunus huffed beside me as we helped carry Father down in his chair.

'Good idea, beta,' Father said cheerily.

Hakim pushed Father's chair once we had descended, while I trudged behind my family, heart pounding. My family were in jovial spirits as we walked towards the grand hall for the mehendi, even Yunus.

I had half a mind to turn and flee towards the horses. But I kept putting one foot in front of the other until we arrived. The string band was in one corner, playing soft music that receded as we entered. The guests applauded at the sight of us. Father hadn't been seen in months. People rushed forward to greet him.

Discreetly, I scanned the hall and found Layla.

I nearly lost my breath. She was a vision in emerald and gold, white flowers trailing down her hair. Her eyes were outlined with kohl, her lips painted a soft red. Her golden cheeks were rosier than before, almost the same shade as her lips. She raised a nervous hand to tuck a stray strand of hair behind her ear as she looked around warily, golden bangles falling down her arm. Then that weasel Edmund came over to her and gave her a drink. My stomach almost heaved.

Sultana Zahra, arriving beside them, caught my gaze and raised her glass to nod at me.

I nodded back. That smug smile she always wore should have been a crime.

'Zayd, Munira is making her entrance soon. You need to sit down,' Mother said, appearing from nowhere and taking me by the arm.

I followed Mother towards the front of the hall, where a number of thrones had been set up. Father was sitting in one, his eyes already looking slightly droopy with fatigue. But the pure smile on his face was unmistakable.

I sat down beside him and watched with everyone as drums sounded and Munira entered, wearing a bright orange sari and gold jewellery. She walked gracefully, followed by her family. I looked at my hands, pretending to inspect something. When I glanced up, I saw Layla looking back at me with a sadness I felt in my bones.

'Smile, Son,' Mother murmured from behind me.

I plastered on a smile and looked at Munira. Her father and brothers came and hugged me as she sat down on the throne beside me. I mumbled a polite greeting to her as everybody applauded and goggled at us.

'I love that people are clapping for us despite our doing nothing,' Munira whispered.

I smiled briefly. She was a good person, kind-hearted. I would get used to her, in time. Grow to love her, even.

If I live for much longer, a small voice inside my head whispered.

The evening passed by in a blur of laughter, cake feeding between our families and conversations I didn't care to absorb. A dancing procession came in and performed a number of lively songs. The crowd applauded and cheered, delighting in their display. Munira was swept away after a while to have her hands decorated with henna, leaving me to my family's company. I felt like I was having an out of body experience. How long until everyone discovered my secret?

Father had almost fallen asleep a few times, so we bade him goodnight as Hakim and his guards took him back to his quarters. Mother worked the room, graciously playing host, while Yunus demolished most of the food from the tables around the edges of the hall.

I only wanted to speak to one person, but Layla stayed far back, a downcast look on her face. She was never particularly happy in her mother's presence, but something else seemed to be weighing her down lately. Perhaps it was the trauma of her abduction, or the leech she was being made to marry. She would be turning eighteen in a matter of days. Idly, I wondered … if she was a mage, was she experiencing the change? Was she scared? I wished I could know what she was thinking, know if she was OK.

'Try to look excited, Brother,' Yunus said, flopping into the throne beside mine. 'You look like you're at a funeral.'

'Maybe it's not long until you're at mine,' I said quietly.

Yunus looked at me angrily. 'Don't you dare,' he hissed. 'We aren't giving up.'

'You need to start preparing, Yunus,' I said heavily. 'This crown might be yours sooner than you think.'

'Shut up,' he growled, averting his gaze.

Sadness flooded my bones. 'I'm tired. I'm going to get going,' I said, stifling a yawn.

I quietly slipped out of the grand ballroom before Mother could notice and took a heavy breath. I was walking back down the corridor, Noor behind me, when I heard voices around the corner. I stopped so abruptly that Noor almost collided with me.

He was about to speak, but I clamped a hand over his mouth and gestured ahead.

'What have you been saying, Zahra?' The Sultan of

Valthar's voice trailed around the corner. 'I will not have you ruin my daughter's marriage with your vicious lies!'

'What lies would those be, Arun?' came Sultana Zahra's silky voice.

'Just stay away from my family and keep your mouth shut.'

'Don't flatter yourself, Arun,' Sultana Zahra scoffed. 'You aren't anything special. Then or now.'

'Really?' he said, his tone turning to mockery. 'You seemed to think I was something special when you were begging me to make you my mistress.' The vitriol in his voice was poisonous.

Sultana Zahra laughed darkly. 'You had your way with me in your wife's bed,' she hissed. 'And then you tossed me aside like I was nothing! You ruined my life!'

'Well, you got married to a Sultan barely months later so your life was hardly ruined, was it?' he snarled back.

I looked at Noor, his eyes widening with horror like mine. 'Back, back!' I mouthed, grabbing him and heading swiftly the other way.

Noor and I rounded another corner just as I heard Sultan Arun's footsteps begin to follow. We raced back to my quarters, neither of us breathing a word until we were inside my room.

'Can you believe it?' I said, aghast as I sank into my armchair.

'I guess that explains the frosty relations between Valthar and Sawan all these years,' Noor replied, shocked, as he sat down on the other chair.

'Munira told me that Sultana Zahra had once tried to find a place in the Valthar court ...'

I couldn't believe it. Sultana Zahra had married the

Sultan of Sawan soon after her tryst with Sultan Arun. And given birth to Layla.

'Noor, I need to go to the library. I need to check something.' I sprang up from my chair. I had to be sure about this before I could speak to Layla. If I was going to tear her world apart, there could be no doubt.

48

Layla

I couldn't wait to leave the mehendi party. Watching Zayd play husband on stage had been crushing; watching him get married in two days would destroy me. I sloped off before Edmund could regale me with another story about his dogs in Fallowmere.

When I stepped into my rooms, I shrieked with fright. Mother was sitting in the parlour, a cup of tea in her pale hands.

'Daughter! Where have you been?' she asked sweetly.

'I just left the mehendi,' I said slowly, shutting the door behind me.

'Fun, wasn't it?' she continued, all sugary. 'I think Prince Zayd and Princess Munira make a beautiful couple, don't you?'

I nodded automatically.

'It's funny … He doesn't seem that interested in his bride,' Mother said speculatively, taking another sip of tea.

I stayed silent.

'Almost as funny as the fact that he seemed more interested in looking at you all night.' She narrowed her eyes at me.

'That's ridiculous,' I managed to grit out.

'Yes, I thought that. How could someone like you catch the affections of a prince without it being arranged? But it seems you two have been spending quite a bit of time together alone, no? The other day, after breakfast, I hear you went to the greenhouses ... where Prince Zayd also just happened to be. Is that not strange?'

Panic began to swell within me. 'A happy coincidence, no doubt, Mother.' I feigned a smile.

'Really very strange,' she said thoughtfully, looking around the room. 'Almost as strange as his travelling all the way to Sawan just to rescue you.'

'He did that to try and improve relations between our lands,' I said indifferently.

'That's what I thought, at first. But now I hear that, just last night, you snuck away from the gaye holud without your guard. Rumour has it you were spotted in one of the courtyards with the prince.' Her voice had lost all its sweetness, her tone darkening.

'I went for a walk alone and bumped into him,' I said. 'And I'm tired of being followed all the time. I should be able to walk about a guarded palace without someone breathing down my neck.'

'Really? Is that the best you can do?' she said with a sneer. 'It would be awfully scandalous if word got out that the prince had been seen with you, unchaperoned on multiple occasions.'

'I don't know what you're trying to insinuate,' I said.

Mother rose gracefully from her chair and strode over to me. Before I could back away, she raised her hand and struck me across the face.

I cried out, lights flashing in my eyes. I clutched my sore

cheek and righted myself, but Mother grabbed me by the throat and shoved me into the stone wall.

'Do not play games with me, you little wench,' she snarled in my face, her dark eyes seething with rage. 'What have you got going on with the prince?'

'Nothing, I swear!' I gasped.

Mother slammed my head back against the wall. Pain spread through my skull and tears involuntarily dripped down my cheeks. 'Try again. And do not lie to me – my guards have been watching your every move. I know exactly where you go and who you are with. What were you doing last night with the prince? And in the greenhouse?'

'We – just – talked!' I gasped as Mother's slender fingers tightened around my throat. 'I – can't – breathe!'

Mother rammed me back again. My head raged with pain. 'What were you two doing? Is he in love with you?'

I was choking for air. Stars danced in my vision. She was going to kill me. I couldn't breathe. My mother was going to kill me.

She made a disgusted noise and let go.

I collapsed against the wall, but before I could feel relief at the reprieve, she grabbed me by the hair and pulled my face towards hers. 'Is he in love with you?'

I shrieked in pain. 'No! He isn't in love with me!'

'Liar!' she growled. 'Tell me the truth, or Mira is going to lose a limb for your insolence!'

My heart sank.

'You ungrateful brat!' Mother snarled. 'I have given you an excellent husband in Edmund, but here you are, getting up to no good with another boy!'

'I'm not – I didn't—'

'Shall I start with Mira's hands?' she sneered. 'Chop off any chance of a livelihood?'

'No! Please!' Panic swelled in my chest. 'We just – we just talked! He's marrying Munira; there is nothing between us! It was just – a fleeting moment.'

'Here's what you are going to do,' Mother said in a triumphant voice. 'Convince Zayd to call off this wedding. Tell him you want to marry him – promise yourself to him, whatever it takes.' She paused to look me up and down, as if assessing a prize horse. 'Once the wedding is off, Valthar will be too angry to give Dakaria any kind of military aid. Then you will marry Edmund, and with the might of Fallowmere on my side I can take control of Dakaria, and soon enough Valthar.'

I couldn't believe what I was hearing. My head and throat hurt so much; my vision was spotty.

Mother snarled into my face, 'Agree, or I'll make sure Mira doesn't make it back to Sawan.'

Fear chilled my blood. 'OK,' I whispered, my voice hoarse.

'And when we get back, I will deal with you and your lies,' she said, dropping me at last.

'I hate you,' I ground out, clutching my throat.

'The feeling is mutual, child,' she retorted with disdain. 'If you'd never come along, I could have done better for myself than marrying that ancient man you called Father.'

Anger coursed through my veins. That lying, scheming witch. I clenched my fists as my hands began to tremble. 'No wonder he never loved you,' I said coldly. 'You were as good a wife as you were a mother.'

Mother flinched.

I wanted to confront her. I wanted to tell her I knew

everything but before I could form more thoughts, she grabbed me again, her nails digging into my arms.

'I am ten times the Sultan that man ever was,' Mother growled, her face contorting with rage. 'Everybody thought I was just a simple girl with a poor father who was given titles and pity by the Sultan – destined to skulk in royal shadows. But when I conquer Dakaria and Valthar, everyone will remember *my* name, *my* legacy.'

She gave me a last contemptuous glare before storming out of my room.

I fell to the floor, wiping hastily at my face. I willed myself to stop crying, to stop shaking, but I feared I was unravelling at the seams, that there would be nothing left of me.

I wished I'd never been born. I wished I'd never come here. I wished the criminals who had taken me had finished the job.

My hands were heating up. I crushed them to my chest, forcing the current beneath my skin to recede. I couldn't lose it now.

Mira came into my chambers. I heard her gasp as she rushed down to my side.

'Princess! What happened?' she demanded, trying to help me up.

I shook my head, unable to form words.

She grabbed a pitcher of water from the table beside my bed. 'Here, have this.' She held a glass to my lips.

I drank sloppily, my breathing ragged.

'Deep breaths, Your Highness,' Mira instructed, her brown eyes wide with worry. She smoothed my hair down. 'What happened, Princess?'

I couldn't speak for a while. Instead, I fell into Mira's arms and tried to calm my breathing, but my heart continued to hammer away, as though it were going to burst through my chest. The pain was excruciating. It was so hard to breathe.

Mira was my only constant in this world, my only real friend. If anything happened to her, I could never live with myself. How many tears had I cried on her chest? How many times had she picked me up when Mother struck me down?

Zayd was the Sultan of another kingdom. He would survive. He would move on.

But Mira was all I had. She had no other protection. I couldn't condemn her.

49

Zayd

I found it hard to sleep. My arm throbbed with pain despite the extra medicine I'd taken.

I replayed the conversation between Sultana Zahra and Sultan Arun over and over. They'd as good as confessed to having an illicit encounter. According to the archives, Layla had been born a couple of months early, but was in perfectly good health.

From what she'd told me about her father, he'd doted on her. I wasn't sure I had it in me to take away the one parent who had actually cared for her.

She could be Munira's sister, I realized grimly. What a cruel twist of fate. The poets would have a field day with this one.

But if Layla was Sultan Arun's daughter ... could she be an earth mage?

I stilled in bed. Had I seen Layla do anything out of the ordinary? I couldn't recall anything significant. I'd given her a flower outside the greenhouse, but I didn't remember it reacting to her in any way.

Unless she was good at hiding it. Her mother was rounding up mages in Sawan. What if Layla was hiding her powers? Roshni had agreed to work with me purely because of her.

This had to be it. What if Layla was the answer to everything? If she could heal my arm, perhaps she could heal my father, too – and with the Fallowmere coming we could negotiate some other agreement with the Valthar army, something that didn't involve me getting married.

I didn't dare let myself hope. But I had to speak to her in the morning.

The grand hall was full of guests as I trudged towards the head table with Mother for breakfast. The Sultan of Valthar greeted me.

'How are you, beta?' he asked as I sat beside him. His smile seemed genuine. It appeared he was unaware of my presence last night, thankfully.

Before I could reply, the Sultan gulped. 'Oh, take cover. The snake from Sawan has arrived.'

I looked over and saw Sultana Zahra enter with Layla, who looked exhausted. She must have realized, and tried to feign a smile as they passed.

'I have somewhere to be,' Sultan Arun muttered, getting up and leaving.

I tried not to watch as Edmund entered and oozed up behind Layla, constantly chattering in her ear and putting his hands on her.

'Can I sit here?'

I looked up to find Munira with a tentative smile on her face. 'Yes, of course, Princess.'

She took her seat beside me.

'How was your evening last night? Your mehendi looks nice,' I said, gesturing to the dark red patterns adorning her hands.

'I came to show you, but you'd already left,' she said

hesitantly, concern in her eyes. 'Are you all right, Zayd? If I didn't know any better, I'd think you were avoiding me.'

'No, I'm sorry,' I said hastily. 'There's just a lot going on with our borders. It's hard to find a moment to relax.'

'I would have thought they'd give you some time off during the week of our wedding, at least,' she said.

'No rest for the wicked, I am afraid,' I replied with a brief smile.

We ate our breakfast in painful silence, words failing me.

'Would you like to go for a walk?' Munira asked.

'I'm afraid I have to get back to my study, but I can accompany you out?' I offered pathetically.

Munira nodded, a tight smile on her face.

'Thank you for having breakfast with me,' I said as we exited the hall. 'I shall see you later.'

'Zayd, wait,' she called as I turned.

I looked back.

Munira looked upset. 'I know this is not what either of us has chosen, but I am going to be entirely alone here when my family leaves. I have given up my gods, I have left my friends, my family, my life as I knew it, to come here and marry you. And you won't even look at me for longer than a few moments.'

Shame flooded me. 'Munira ... I'm sorry,' I said. 'So much is happening right now – with the silver mines, with Father. I'm not quite myself.' I knew I should take her hands in mine, promise her that things would get better. But instead I stood, hands by my side, rooted to the spot.

Munira looked disappointed. 'Well, when you are yourself again, I look forward to meeting you.'

I watched her leave. I turned away and retreated to my study.

No sooner had I sat down than Usman came knocking.

His hair was dishevelled as he swept in, his dark cheeks flushed red. 'We've captured a pirate. He is in the dungeons.'

I rose again. 'Only one?'

'The rest slit their own throats when they realized they were surrounded,' Usman said grimly.

I followed Usman quickly through the labyrinthine halls until we descended into the dungeons. The dark corridors reeked of damp as we headed through the empty cells.

Usman stopped halfway down the corridor, and unlocked a cell door.

A tall reed of a boy, perhaps fifteen, stood back against a corner, looking at us fearfully as we entered. His light eyes were big; and he had a scraggly beard attached to his small jaw. A mop of damp hair fell around his sharp face.

'Please, let me go,' the boy said desperately, his voice cracking. 'I don't even like being a pirate!'

'Then what were you doing attacking my land?' I asked coldly.

The boy's lips trembled. 'I had no choice! Captain Derra took me from the streets! I thought I could work and make a better life for myself, but they just lied! Please don't hurt me!' The boy began to cry, sinking to the floor.

'Is this Captain Derra still alive?' I asked.

The boy nodded, wiping his streaming face.

'What land do you hail from originally?' Usman asked.

'From Valthar,' he replied through sobs. 'The coastal city of Jagnur. I haven't got any parents. Please let me go – I promise I won't make trouble.'

'What else do you know about this Captain Derra?' I asked. 'Answer well and you might find yourself in better quarters than this cell for the rest of your life.'

The boy forced himself to stop crying. 'I don't know much. He just runs the ship. He reports to someone else; she's the real boss.'

'Who is that?' Usman demanded.

The boy seemed to shrink from fear. 'Nobody knows who she is – her name, or what she looks like. But they say she's a powerful dark mage and the captain does her bidding.' He shuddered.

A powerful dark mage. Fantastic news.

'What does she want?' I pressed.

'We don't know. But ...'

'Spit it out,' Usman snapped.

The boy looked between us, terror on his face. 'We were all given orders: if any of us saw a member of the royal family, we had to shoot a poisoned arrow to kill. Please don't tell them I told you!' He burst into tears.

My blood turned cold.

Usman tried to get more answers out of the boy, but he was hysterical, wailing and blubbering. I almost felt sorry for him.

'Give him some food,' I ordered Usman. 'Then see what more you can get out of him.'

'What's happened?' Noor asked as I emerged from the dungeons.

'Another complication,' I replied grimly.

50

Layla

Once breakfast concluded, Mother grabbed my hand, pulling me towards her. 'Make sure you do what needs to be done today, or Mira will pay,' she whispered coldly in my ear.

I looked into her empty brown eyes and nodded stiffly.

Once I was in the sanctuary of my room, I sank onto one of the sofas.

How could I convince Zayd to call off his wedding? His father was dying. He would be crowned Sultan soon. He needed this alliance with Valthar. He had made it very clear that his duty was more important than anything.

But I had to fight for Mira. I needed to find a way to get her to safety.

I mustered the energy to leave my room to seek out Zayd. I wasn't sure what I was going to say to him yet. All I knew was that I needed to see him, to feel his reassuring presence. Mustafa fell into step behind me.

We passed by Mother's room, down the corridor, where loud laughing could be heard. I recoiled inwardly, the hairs on the back of my neck rising. A deep voice joined her.

I paused, hesitating.

'Who is in there with my mother?' I asked Aslam, the guard outside Mother's door, genuinely curious.

'It is Prince Edmund, Your Highness,' Aslam replied hesitantly, not looking me in the eye.

'What? And Prince Frederick?' I asked, confused.

'No, just Prince Edmund, I believe,' he said nervously.

More laughter echoed inside. Mother never laughed like that, as though Edmund was the funniest man in the world ... not unless she was flirting.

I moved past Aslam and pressed my ear to the door.

'Your Highness!' Aslam began to protest.

'Keep back, or you will be going back to Sawan jobless,' I hissed.

I pressed my ear even more firmly against the door. I heard muffled sounds, two voices laughing and mingling together.

And then. Oh, and then.

Mother started moaning. And so did Edmund. Their voices gathered pace. A faint thumping could be heard.

My hand flew to my mouth. *No, they couldn't be.*

'Your Highness, please,' her guard appealed, his brown face turning ashen.

'Stay back!' I growled.

With bravery I didn't know I possessed, I cracked the door open ever so slightly. I had to be sure.

'Zahra!' It was undoubtedly Edmund's voice.

Through the crack in the door, I could see the green jacket he'd been wearing today, littered on the floor. I poked my head through.

I would be scarred for life. They hadn't even made it to the bedroom. They were on the sofa - undoubtedly

371

Edmund's sandy blond hair, undoubtedly his broad shoulders, undoubtedly my mother's hand clawing into his back, undoubtedly their voices as they cried out in passion.

I closed the door as quietly as I could. 'I was never here, understood?' I told both of the guards. 'Breathe any word of this and I will make sure you never work again.'

Mustafa's face turned pale. Aslam looked abashed. 'Yes, Your Highness,' they chorused quietly.

'Swear to me,' I demanded.

'I swear I will not say anything,' Mustafa said. 'Please, I need this job. My wife just gave birth.'

Shame filled me, but I couldn't falter. 'As long as you stay quiet, I will not act.'

Aslam looked back at me worriedly. 'I won't say anything, Your Highness. You have my word.'

'Good.'

That damn bitch.

My blood was boiling as I raced away, not heeding where I was going. Mustafa trailed behind me, afraid to get too close.

I arrived at the library. 'Stay outside,' I called back.

I let the doors close behind me, my legs finally caving in. I sank onto the floor.

My mother was having sex with my betrothed?

I wanted to be sick. I wanted to drive a knife through them both.

How could they?

Edmund had been so keen – sometimes too keen. He'd been all over me.

He'd been playing a part, I realized with horror.

Of course. It had all been an act. How long had it been

going on for? Was that why Mother was so jealous? Did she covet him for herself or because she couldn't stand to see me have anything of my own?

My chest ached as the tears welled in my eyes. I didn't want to cry – not over them. But it couldn't be helped. She'd made a fool out of me, yet again.

It shouldn't surprise me how low my mother would stoop. She'd spent my whole life insulting me, degrading me, ensuring I always knew my place: beneath her.

I was sick of her games. I was sick of playing along.

I would make sure Zayd married Munira if it was the last thing I did.

It was not hard to track down the Sultana of Dakaria. She was in the large banquet hall, orchestrating the decorators as they prepared the final flourishes for the wedding tomorrow.

'Sultana,' I called. 'Could I have a moment of your time? I have something to tell you.'

Sultana Aysha looked at me with a warm smile. 'Of course. Is everything OK?' She took my hand in hers.

'I have to confide some things to you, and I hope you will not hate me for it,' I began, steering her to a far corner of the room where nobody could hear us.

'I would never hate you,' the Sultana said kindly, patting my hand. 'But you are worrying me. What's wrong, dear?'

I took a deep breath, hesitating. But then images of Mother clawing Edmund's back rose unbidden in my mind, and I carried on.

'My mother intends to invade Dakaria, and thereafter Valthar, once I am wed to Edmund, with the support of Fallowmere,' I said quietly. 'She wants me to stop the wedding tomorrow.'

The Sultana kept her expression blank, but a flicker of panic crossed her eyes. 'And how would you do that?'

'Zayd and I ... we ... care for each other,' I confessed quietly.

Realization dawned across her face. 'How long?' she whispered, eyes darting around us nervously, but the servants were paying us no mind.

'It doesn't matter,' I said in a rush. 'I am willing to betray my mother if you will help me and Mira disappear. If I don't do as my mother wishes, she will kill Mira and make me suffer for the rest of my life. But if I do as she wishes, I will be responsible for bloodshed, and I refuse to be a part of her games any more. Please help me.'

'This is a lot to take in,' the Sultana said quietly. 'What do you need?'

'I need safe passage out of the palace tomorrow morning. I need to send Mira to safety, somewhere my mother cannot hurt her. And I need a carriage and enough money for safe passage on a ship.'

'And you would do all of this, defy your own mother, to help my son and our kingdom?' The Sultana eyed me uncertainly.

'I will,' I said, steel in my voice. 'She has taken everything I have. It's time I returned the favour.'

'Very well, dear. I will definitely give you my tailor's details, and ensure she gives you the best service,' the Sultana said cheerfully with an almost imperceptible nod as a servant came by.

'Your Majesty, would you like the silver bows or the red?' he asked.

'Do both please and alternate,' she instructed with a false smile.

374

'Come to my room in the south wing discreetly at dawn,' Sultana Aysha whispered once he had retreated, embracing me. 'My guards will escort you and Mira out of the palace to somewhere safe.'

'Please don't tell Zayd,' I whispered back. 'I don't want him to look for me. It's better if he doesn't know.'

We drew apart.

She nodded, understanding in her eyes. 'Thank you. I don't take lightly what you are doing.' She patted my arm and walked away.

I let out a sigh and left the hall, fighting the tears welling in my eyes. I got back to my room and scribbled a note out to Zayd, then ordered Mustafa to take it to him. He nodded, a new worry in his eyes when he looked at me. Guilt gnawed at my insides.

All I wanted to do was curl into a ball and disappear. But I had to keep up appearances, at least for one more evening. From tomorrow, I would never have to play a role again.

But first, dinner.

Mother glared at me to sit beside Edmund. I wanted to walk straight past them, but I couldn't let her realize I knew. It could blow up my plan before it even came to be.

'Are you all right, dear?' Edmund asked me. 'You seem upset.'

'I'm fine,' I replied in a clipped voice. 'There are so many beautiful people here, aren't there? I think Prince Dana from Kursahan is quite handsome. What do you think?'

Edmund frowned. 'I do not think it becoming of you to comment on another prince, my dear.'

'Would you rather look at parents? Which Mother here is most beautiful, do you think?'

Edmund's eyes widened, but he quickly recovered. 'I

cannot say, dear. You are the only woman I want to gaze upon.'

I looked at him impassively. 'I don't feel well tonight. I shall be eating my dinner in silence.'

Edmund smiled uncertainly and looked away.

The slimeball.

My blood was boiling as Mother's voice boomed around me, cracking jokes with Edmund's uncle, going on about her many talents. I ate my dinner quietly, trying not to look at the head of the table where Munira and Yunus sat laughing, while Zayd looked about as miserable as I felt. I supposed if you looked hard enough, you could see that he hadn't been doing a good job hiding his lack of enthusiasm for the wedding. And it would take every drop of artifice I had to convince him to go through with it.

I left dinner without another word and sought refuge in the library. Sinking down on the window seat, I pressed my forehead against the glass, blowing out shaky breaths.

I knew my mother to be a cruel woman, but this was beyond the pale. If she was so desperate for Edmund, why didn't she marry him instead? Soon she would no longer pull the strings in my life. I almost wished I was staying, just to see the look on her face when she realised I had defied her.

As moonlight began to fill the darkened library, I waited anxiously for Zayd to arrive. Finally, the silver doors swung open.

Zayd's eyes fell on me. He began to walk towards me, and I got up hastily, quickening my pace until I was in his arms, crushed to his chest. I held onto him tightly, willing this moment to last for ever.

'Layla, I need to tell you something.' Zayd was trying to draw back.

'Not now, please,' I whispered, cupping his face with my hands. I blinked rapidly as tears threatened to form in my eyes. I touched the rough edge of his jaw, his hollow cheeks, touched the skin beneath his beautiful green eyes. My fingers trailed along his lips.

Zayd kissed my hand, closing his eyes for a moment. 'You make it so hard to think straight.'

'Then stop thinking.'

'As you wish, Princess.'

Zayd pulled me tighter against him, his hands roaming up my back, tangling in my hair. I held him close. My body felt like it was molten.

He tilted my chin up slowly, his gaze drifting down to my mouth. The way his eyes darkened with hunger made my bones feel weak.

I could see the conflict in his eyes. I pushed away all the expectations and rules we'd been trying to live by and leant closer until my lips touched his and his mouth parted for mine.

I didn't just want him. I needed him. Even if it was just for one night, one moment, one second.

Zayd's warm lips were soft and hard against mine, drawing me in so deeply I felt like I was drowning. My lips seemed to move of their own accord, responding to the pull of his like they were magnetized. We were devouring each other, and I never wanted to stop.

But it would. This would be the last I ever saw of him.

Unbidden tears began to fall down my face.

Zayd pulled back. 'What's wrong?' he asked, wiping a stray tear away with the pad of his thumb.

I shook my head and pulled his lips back to mine, my tears mingling with our kiss. Zayd drew me closer still, the hard lines of his body pressing against me as we stumbled backwards until I felt the cold press of a wall against my back.

My hands drifted into his hair, as if it were possible to pull his face any closer to mine. I needed him. I needed all of him.

'You are so beautiful,' Zayd whispered breathlessly, moving his warm lips down to my throat.

I was melting or combusting – I wasn't sure which.

His mouth drifted back up and he kissed me deeply, his soft lips undoing my senses. Time stopped. It was just us in our own world.

At some point, we resurfaced, gasping for air. Zayd leant his cool forehead against mine. 'Layla, I ...'

I brought my finger to his lips, quieting him. 'Don't, please. I hope you have a happy marriage with Munira,' I whispered.

Zayd's eyes widened. He drew back. 'You say this after we just kissed?'

'You have to marry her. For the good of Dakaria. ' I said, then forced myself to say the ugly words 'What, did you think that I would run away with you?'

Hurt flashed across Zayd's face. 'What?'

'Zayd, you were a ... distraction. A way to escape my sheltered, boring life.' I made myself look Zayd in the eye as I spoke, hating every part of myself for the pain that was wrought across his features.

'You were just bored?' he repeated in a hollow voice.

I pushed through, my heart aching, my voice cool. 'Maybe there was a spark between us. But my duty to Sawan

378

is more important than this act of rebellion. It's pointless to risk our futures for a bit of fun.'

'Well, it's good to know where we stand at last,' Zayd remarked with a bitter laugh. His eyes were full of anger but he stood straight, ever the composed prince. 'Perhaps you're more like your mother than I thought.'

I flinched. 'Goodbye, Zayd,' I said, holding back tears as I fled from the room.

Mustafa sprang into action, hurrying to keep up with me.

I wiped at my face, willing myself to calm down. *Don't come after me. Please come after me.* It was lies. All lies. Surely he knew that?

The hurt on his face had been clear as day. Whatever we had, I'd destroyed it.

With a painful ache in my chest, I felt the treacherous muscle inside begin to splinter apart.

When I got back to my room, I knew I only had moments before Mother came. I washed my face hurriedly, patting it dry. I needed to look composed. I couldn't let her get even a whiff of my betrayal.

I heard the door to my chambers swing open. I hurried out.

'Is it done?' Mother asked, looking at me suspiciously.

'Yes,' I said, mustering bravery from the pit of my soul. 'I told him we would run away to Sawan in the morning. He told me to meet him in the south wing at dawn, before everyone wakes up.'

Mother smiled, triumphant. 'Excellent. Pack a bag – make it look believable. After he fails to show up for the wedding, I will meet you back at home.'

'What about the guards?' I asked. 'How will I meet Zayd with them trailing me? We need to disappear together.'

'Yes, you need to slip away quietly,' Mother said thoughtfully. 'If anyone suspects a thing, they could capture Zayd and still force him to marry. I'll tell your guards to stand down tonight, say that mine will cover the hall until morning. Can you make your way by yourself?'

'I know the way.'

Mother nodded. 'Get this done. Perhaps I will show you mercy when we return to Sawan.' She smirked and left.

I let out a shaky breath. So I didn't have to think about what I'd done, I began pulling clothes out of my trunks, searching for something plain and unassuming amongst the silk and chiffon.

'What's going on?' Mira asked when she arrived to ready me for bed, staring at the mess I had made in my room.

'Mira!' I grabbed her hand. 'I need to tell you something.'

I hated this – being forced by my mother to upend the lives of people I cared about. But Mira didn't deserve to be punished for my actions. This was it, then in the morning I'd finally be free of that evil woman.

51

Zayd

I wasn't sure how long I stood in the library after Layla left. The sting of her words caused a pain I hadn't known was possible to feel. One moment I had been in utter bliss and the next ...

I could still feel her treacherous, sweet lips on mine. The rush when I'd finally felt her kiss, the soft curves of her body against me, how perfect she'd felt in my arms. I could still taste the salt from her tears on my tongue.

Perhaps I should have known better. My entire universe had shifted the moment I met her.

But she'd merely been *bored*.

Eventually, I forced myself to move and made my way back to my room in a daze. I sat on my bed, staring at the wall, as if that could solve anything for me.

A raging ache in my arm began to overpower the stupor in my mind. I tried to ignore it, but before I knew it, a fire unlike any other began to course through my body.

I groaned in agony, trying to hold it together. I pulled up my sleeve and nearly retched as the black veins in my arms writhed like snakes. My ears began to ring, my vision blurring.

I needed to call for help. But I felt paralysed, falling to my knees as my body began to shake with pain. My teeth rattled in my head.

Was it time already?

Everything went dark.

52

Zayd

I was lying in a golden lake fed by waterfalls, surrounded by glimmering silver trees, and by mountains coated in snow. The fire that had raged through my body had been extinguished, purged from my flesh by the purity of the waters.

It would be so peaceful just to stay here. I could bathe in this pool for eternity, watch those emerald skies dance with a myriad of colours I'd never seen before.

But there was something I needed to do. Something that nagged at the back of my mind as I tried to give myself up to bliss.

It was her. It would always be her.

53

Zayd

When I opened my eyes, I was greeted by cries of relief and panic. I looked into the worried faces of my brother, my guard and my healer.

'What's happened?' I asked, sitting up slowly. A chill brushed my bare chest. 'Where's my khamis?'

I looked down at my torso and stopped.

The black veins that had been plaguing my body were gone.

I tore off the bandage that had hidden the worst of the ugly wound I'd sported for weeks, but my skin was healed, a faint silvery scar the only proof of its existence. I twisted my arm this way and that: no more ash grey, no more tinges of green or spidery black veins in sight.

'How?' I said aloud, looking up at all of them.

'Did you find an earth mage?' Sayyidah Shafiya asked in shocked tones.

'No! I didn't—' I stopped.

'Was it Munira?' Yunus asked. 'Did she cry on you or something?'

'But the tears needed to be combined with the elixir,' Sayyidah Shafiya said confusedly.

'Munira wasn't the one crying,' I said slowly.

'Then who was?' Yunus pressed.

Layla. When we'd kissed last night, she'd been crying.

'Is that possible, to be cured by tears alone?' I asked Sayyidah Shafiya.

She looked back at me. 'It's unheard of, Your Highness. Unless the mage is exceptionally powerful, but even then, this is unprecedented.'

'Send for Roshni, *now*,' I barked at Noor, getting up and rooting through my wardrobe for a shirt.

'What's going on?' Yunus demanded. 'Zayd, just stop for a second.'

Roshni knew something I didn't about Layla. I was done playing her games.

'I shall take my leave too, Your Highness,' Sayyidah Shafiya said, hastily following after Noor.

Yunus yanked me by the shoulder, turning me to face him. 'What's going on?'

I looked at the closed door. 'It wasn't Munira. It was Layla.'

'Layla? How?'

'This stays between us, do you hear?' I demanded.

Yunus nodded, confusion colouring his face.

'I think Sultan Arun has another child he never told anybody about,' I said.

Yunus's mouth fell open. 'What?'

I pulled a black shirt over my head, relieved to find the movement no longer hurt. 'Long story short, he had an affair with Sultana Zahra before she was married to the Sultan of Sawan.'

Yunus swore. 'But then that means – Layla is Sultan Arun's daughter?'

'I need to find Layla, now,' I said. 'Keep this to yourself, do you swear?'

'I swear, Brother. But what was she doing crying on you?'

My jaw set.

Yunus's eyes widened. 'I damn well knew there was something between you two!'

'Now isn't the time for this,' I said shortly. 'Besides, it was nothing.' As Layla had made abundantly clear.

Yunus looked at me, anger brewing on his face. 'What about Munira, then? Are you going to wed her when you've been playing away all this time?'

'I'm not marrying her.' I realized it was the truth. My life had been saved. I couldn't spend the rest of it living a lie.

Yunus looked at me like I'd grown another head. 'And you were planning on sharing this information when? At the ceremony?'

'I don't know; I just can't go through with it,' I said tersely. 'She deserves better.'

'That we can agree on.'

'Look, judge me later, but I need to speak to Layla first,' I said, heading for the doors.

Seeing Layla again was the last thing I wanted but if she was as strong as Sayyidah Shafiya said, perhaps she could help Father, too.

I raced towards the wing where Layla and her mother were staying. The Sultana's guard stood outside the door, looking surprised at my arrival.

'Where is the princess?' I demanded.

'Sleeping, I think, Your Highness,' he said hesitantly.

'Open the door,' I ordered.

The guard knocked. No reply came.

'Where is her maid, Mira?'

'I haven't seen her since last night. I don't think she's awake yet, either, Your Highness,' the guard replied. He knocked again, but still no reply.

I pushed the door open as the guard began to protest, and walked into an empty parlour. The bedroom was empty too, but it looked like a storm had passed through with clothes, jewellery, shoes thrown haphazardly around the space. Layla hated her mother. She'd always dreamt about running away. Perhaps she'd finally gone through with it.

'Where is she?' I demanded.

'I don't know, Your Highness,' the guard replied, panicked.

'How has she left without you knowing?' I circled back to the balcony doors but they were locked. She had to have left through the main door.

'I was off duty all night; the Sultana's guard kept watch,' he replied nervously.

I turned on my heel and rushed out but the Sultana's guard was nowhere to be seen, and her room was empty too. Maybe they were all at breakfast. I rushed towards the central wing. Footsteps raced to keep up behind me.

Shouting thundered in the central foyer.

I cursed and went to see what the commotion was. The Sultana of Sawan was there, berating my mother. Prince Frederick and Edmund stood behind her.

'This is unheard of! How could my daughter just go missing?' Sultana Zahra was shrieking. 'The royals of Dakaria have abducted my child!'

A sense of dread crept over me. Something hadn't made sense about last night. We had been kissing and she had been crying – and then she pushed me away. Would it be foolish to think that there could be another reason she said those words to me?

'We would never do such a thing, and I would caution you from uttering such baseless accusations!' my mother angrily replied.

'Lies! There is no other explanation for it! Your son is in love with my daughter and has shut her away somewhere to keep her as a mistress!' the Sultana bellowed.

I bristled as the onlookers gasped. Heads swivelled my way.

'Slander!' my mother snarled.

Shock passed over Sultana Zahra's features as she registered my presence, but she quickly recovered. 'You!' she stormed towards me. 'What have you done with my daughter?'

I descended the stairs into the fray. 'I have done nothing,' I fumed. 'The better question is what have *you* done?'

Something flickered behind her eyes as I approached. 'Lies! Layla told me you're in love and planned to run away together this morning. She was supposed to meet you in the south wing! I tried to talk her out of it, but she said *you* were insistent!'

The crowd around us gasped.

I wanted to laugh. 'Is that so? Then who are you conversing with if I have eloped with Layla?'

Sultana Zahra's nostrils flared. 'You are just trying to cover up your misdeeds so this sham of a marriage can go ahead today! What have you done with my daughter?'

Layla's words from last night rang in my mind. *You have to marry her. For the good of Dakaria.*

'You wanted me to call off this wedding,' I said with realization. 'This is nothing but your own failed plot to destabilize our nations, so you can bring back colonial rule with Sawan at the helm. Admit it.'

Her mother must have found out about us somehow, used it to threaten her. Why else would she have disappeared and told me to go through with the wedding?

Gasps ran through the crowd.

If my accusation had wrong-footed her, Sultana Zahra covered it well. 'Nonsense! I wish stability and prosperity for all our countries, and my alliance with the Fallowmere will only enhance—'

'Don't insult us with your deception,' I snapped. 'You treat your daughter like she's scum. Nobody needs to help her escape – she was clearly desperate enough to leave a life of luxury behind just to get away from you.'

'How dare you speak to me like this, boy!' the Sultana snarled.

'Watch your tone, *Zahra*.' I was seething. 'You are no better than the Fallowmere leeches come to suck our lands dry once more.'

'Hear, hear!' a few voices echoed.

The Sultana flinched.

'Well, that is rather rude, Your Highness,' Prince Frederick said indignantly, translating for his nephew in whispers.

'Who invited you here?' I spat back.

He and Edmund had the decency to look embarrassed.

'Perhaps we can have a private conversation?' my mother said in a steely voice.

'There is nothing private to discuss!' Sultana Zahra replied angrily. 'Return my daughter at once, or else!'

'Or else what?' my mother replied. 'Will you be marrying Edmund instead?'

Scandalized gasps ran through the crowd.

Zahra froze.

'My servants have heard rather uncouth sounds coming from your bedchamber, Your Majesty. It seems Prince Edmund comes to visit you a lot – day and night – entirely alone.'

'Come now, this is becoming rather nasty!' Prince Frederick said.

'What are they saying?' Edmund asked. His face turned red as his uncle translated.

The colour drained from Sultana Zahra's face. 'You dare accuse me of such a thing? I would never – that is preposterous – he is my daughter's betrothed!'

'We all know that, but clearly you don't,' Mother replied thinly.

The Sultana rounded on her. 'I will not stay here and be defamed in such a horrific way! If war is what you want, war is what Dakaria and Valthar shall get!' She turned and stormed out of the entrance doors. Edmund and Frederick hurried after her.

A tense silence fell over the crowd: the Sultana of Sawan had finally made good on her threat. War was coming to Dakaria.

I looked around and saw groups of stunned faces looking back at me.

'Let's go somewhere private, *now*,' my mother demanded in a voice of thunder, walking away to one of the side rooms.

I followed after her, Yunus right behind me. Noor closed the door.

'How could you, Zayd?' Mother began. 'All these lies—'

'Lies?' I scoffed. 'If you hadn't given Layla passage out of here—'

'I did no such thing!' Mother said indignantly.

'Stop lying!' I said. 'Her mother said she was to meet me in the south wing – *your* wing. So where is she?'

'Zayd, you need to get a hold of yourself,' Mother said sternly. 'It will take work to smooth over what just happened here, but you are to marry Munira *today*.'

'Forget marrying Munira!' I exclaimed. 'We need to reach Layla – she could be in danger. You have no idea what her mother is capable of!'

'I am *well aware* of what that woman is capable of,' Mother said in a voice made of ice. 'She threatened Mira's life – Layla has left with her to escape her mother's wrath. Which is why it is imperative that you marry Munira, seeing as Sawan has just declared war on us after your foolish actions!'

So that's why she left. To save Mira. 'I don't care about some stupid wedding—'

'Brother, calm down,' said Yunus, putting a firm hand on my shoulder.

'Yunus, listen to me,' I implored. 'Layla can heal Father, and he can forge another sort of alliance with Valthar – this can all be fixed!'

'She could heal Father?' Yunus repeated, confounded. 'But the tears – they can't stop death.'

'She's not an ordinary mage, evidently – there's no telling what she can do. We have to try!'

'What are you talking about?' Mother demanded.

I turned to face her. 'We have found a cure for Father.'

'Impossible.'

I took a deep breath. 'It's true – Layla can heal Father ... because she healed me.'

Confusion coloured Mother's face. 'Will someone tell me what on Earth is going on here!' she shouted.

'That day Yunus went missing, months ago, before the Sawan royals arrived, I was struck by that arrow at the Silver Port. But it was no ordinary arrow – it was laced with dark magic, poisoned to kill.'

'Dark magic?' Mother spluttered. 'You've been walking around all this time with a poisoned arm – dying – and you didn't think to tell us?'

'I didn't want to worry you,' I said tensely. 'And now it's all OK. Layla healed me, and she can heal Father too.'

'What do you mean she *healed* you? You're telling me she's an earth mage?' Mother looked like she was losing her mind. 'I need to sit down.'

Yunus rushed forward and helped her into a chair.

'I cannot believe you kept this from me,' she said in a hollow voice, looking at me with sad eyes. 'Poisoned? Running around with another girl while you were betrothed? When did my son change into someone I don't know?' The disappointment in her eyes was almost too much to bear.

I looked away. 'Just tell me where she went, and I can bring her back. We can cure Father. We can establish a different alliance with Valthar and present a united front against Sawan.'

Mother's anger faltered, but she was far from convinced. 'Even if all you are saying were possible, Layla is likely no longer on Dakarian soil. She left at dawn. I gave her a carriage, money and safe passage on a ship.'

My stomach dropped. 'Where is she going?'

'I couldn't ask; her safety will depend on her ignorance,' Mother said. 'But she made a choice, to leave and give you the chance to save Dakaria and go through with this wedding. Are you really going to abandon your people, your country – your kingdom – to go after her now?'

The question hung heavy in the air. My whole life had been for Dakaria. It always would be. But if there was a way to save Father, I couldn't let it pass.

And Layla, whether she had feelings for me or not, had just risked everything to help save our lands from her mother's plans. She would be in grave danger now. I couldn't just leave her to deal with her mother's wrath.

Suddenly, Hakim burst into the room, urgency in his eyes, his chest heaving – evidently he had run all the way here from my father's chambers.

'Your Majesty,' he gasped. 'The Sultan is dead.'

Epilogue

Layla

I sat on the top deck of the ship, watching Dakaria disappear behind me. My heartbeat was loud in my ears as the high sun seared across the sky. Everybody would know by now what I had done.

There would be no more petty comments or aggressive lessons to take by my mother's hand. No, I had changed the stakes for ever.

This would be war.

I tried not to let the ache in my chest spread, thinking of what was probably happening back at the Dakaria palace. Zayd would be wed to Munira. Our moments together would stay a piece of the past, fleeting, forgotten soon enough. I hope one day he would understand why I had told him all those ugly lies.

The wind blew my hair around my face. I splayed my hands out on the ship's railing, feeling the current of power more potently than I ever had before.

The elements had never felt closer to me than they did now. It was like freedom had released something inside me. My affinities wrapped around my senses, just waiting to be called on, power surging through my veins. I summoned a ball of flames in my palm, marvelling at the golden-orange colours that danced freely before me.

I'd spent so long being afraid – of my mother, of myself, of the future. But with Mira hidden away somewhere safe in Dakaria, Zayd wed, and the alliance with Valthar secured, I had nothing to fear any more. I closed my palm, vanquishing the flames.

It was time for me to be brave, to stand up for myself, for my people. I was finally going to put my mother in her place.

This was my path, my path alone, and there was nothing anybody could do to stop me from taking what was rightfully mine: the throne.

A Letter from the Author

Dear reader,

I've always wanted to write an epic love story. Having grown up watching Bollywood films and reading *Romeo and Juliet, Wuthering Heights* and *Pride and Prejudice*, to say that I love a dramatic love story is an understatement. *The Silver Kingdom* is inspired by the various empires and dynasties that rose and fell over historic India. But I didn't find the right framing for it until a few years ago.

I was talking with my parents one day about their experiences of the Bangladesh Liberation War. Following the end of British colonial rule, India was partitioned into two countries in 1947; India and Pakistan. The region of Bengal was split into West Bengal under India, and East Bengal became East Pakistan. A Bengali nationalist movement in East Pakistan for self-determination eventually led to the creation of Bangladesh in 1971 after a war with Pakistan.

My dad had been a small boy when war broke out. He told me of his family's experience going into hiding to escape the Pakistani army; the war planes circling and bombs falling on his city, shops set on fire, families and communities destroyed. As my dad spoke, I knew that I wanted to commemorate this part of our family history through the best way I knew how: by writing a story.

I drew on images of the Mughal reign of India and ancient architecture to build out the grand palaces in *The Silver Kingdom;* memories of my own trips to Bangladesh colour the lush scenery we see in the book. I wanted to use fantasy to explore the impact of politics and war, set against a love story that has the power to destroy everything. While this story explores difficult themes, it's also a celebration of the culture I grew up with.

And ultimately, this is a human story about love, loss and life. Zayd and Layla have the world on their shoulders and want to do what's right for their people. But when duty and desire clash, their choices could threaten everything they know.

I really hope you enjoy stepping into this world – but don't forget to take your shoes off before you come in.

Best wishes,
Radiya Hafiza

Acknowledgements

My hugest thanks to my agent, Alice Sutherland-Hawes, for her guidance and support throughout the creation of this story, before and beyond.

To my editor Arub, thank you for your editorial expertise and passion for Zayd and Layla's story. It's been so wonderful to work on this story with you.

Thank you to my copyeditor Hannah Shepherd and proofreader Sarah Dutton.

Thank you to Elizabeth Irwin in publicity and Beth Robertson in marketing for your support in getting this book out into the world.

My thanks also to Lucy Pearse, Lauren Atherton, S&S Design Team, Laura Haugh and Danielle Wilson in Sales, Maud Sepult and Tanya Hill in Rights, and Sophie Storr in Production.

Thank you to my parents, brothers and bhabi for supporting me and my career. Thank you to my cousins/ big sisters, Yasmina and Farhana, for always cheering for me and supporting my bookish dreams.

My special thanks to the cornbread queen of my heart, Zainab, for being my sounding board to bounce ideas off. I'm so grateful for our late-night transatlantic calls where you let me talk through endless ideas. It's a joy to know you.

To my incredible friends who are always there for me, guide me and keep me sane, my endless thanks: Naznin, Naomisha, Mariam, Sara NA, Sumi, Nadine, Nida, Shahla, Halima and Sara A.

To my husband, thank you for everything.

And thank you, dear reader, for picking up this story and stepping into Zayd and Layla's world.

During the editing of this book, I lost a very special person in my life. I dedicated this book to Bushra, my childhood friend who has seen every version of me and loved me regardless. Who always championed my stories and supported my dream of being an author from when we were kids, reading my terrible drafts and attempts at writing novels. She was one of the few people I felt truly safe with.

Bushra, I'm so glad I got to tell you about this book before you left. You always listened intently to my ideas, as though these were real people I was telling you about. Thank you for a lifetime of laughter, friendship and love. Words aren't enough to describe the weight of your absence. I miss you every day.